THE HOUSE OF STYX

First published in electronic book format
in 2020 by Solaris

This first print edition published 2021 by Solaris
an imprint of Rebellion Publishing Ltd,
Riverside House, Osney Mead,
Oxford, OX2 0ES, UK

www.solarisbooks.com

ISBN: 978-1-78108-805-0

This book is a work of fiction. Names. characters, places and
incidents are products of the author's imagination or are used
fictitiously.

10 9 8 7 6 5 4 3 2 1

A CIP catalogue record for this book is available from the
British Library.

Designed & typeset by Rebellion Publishing

Printed in the UK

THE
HOUSE
OF
STYX

DEREK KÜNSKEN

SOLARIS

I dedicate this book to my Québécois uncles
and aunts and grandparents and great uncles
and great aunts and first and second and third cousins.
I am rooted in river and field and forest and village with you.

ONE

MARCH 1ST, 2255 C.E., 45km above the surface of Venus:

"We might still be able to patch it," Pascal's father said in French over the radio.

Distant lightning squawked in the radio band. Drops of sulfuric acid fell on the faceplate of his helmet. Yellow mist surrounded them. Few storms began this deep under the clouds, but a big storm could punch all the way down here.

"I give us five minutes," Pascal said, "maybe ten."

"Give me one minute!"

A shiver of fear began in Pascal's stomach. They were cutting it close, despite his estimates.

Pascal stood on the head of one of the big cloud-living Venusian plants, what they called a trawler. A bulbous head about five meters wide and shaped like a garlic clove contained all the buoyancy of the plant. Beneath it hung a long tail of carbon fiber, ending forty meters below in a woody weight. The trawlers bobbed through the clouds of Venus and even the hot haze beneath, attracting lightning or collecting static charge with their long carbon cables.

George-Étienne and his children had a dozen trawlers, gathered in a wide herd by adjustable sails they mounted on the heads. They'd grafted additional equipment onto each one, turning each one into a minuscule factory. This one carried tanks and hydrolytic equipment to crack the water out of sulfuric acid. It shouldn't have sunk this deep, but its woody pumps were failing. Even though Pascal could walk across its whole top in five stretched steps, it was an island, invaluable to surviving in the clouds. And it would soon vanish.

"*Minute!*" Pascal said.

"*Câlisse!*" George-Étienne swore.

"Let's salvage what we can," Pascal said.

The haze was inscrutable. Sunlight glowed spongy orange here, with line of sight faltering after a thousand meters. A storm could be right beside them and they'd never see it. Lightning squawked in the radio band again and, shortly, they heard the rumble.

"*Tabarnak!*" George-Étienne swore again. "Okay. Pass me a rope."

Pascal didn't feel any better than his father about this. They sold oxygen, water, and the heavy metals they collected from the volcanic ash in the lower cloud decks, but they wouldn't have money to buy another trawler, and wild trawlers were hard to domesticate. The loss of this one would just make them that much poorer.

Pascal anchored the middle of the rope around the

mast at the top of the trawler and lowered one end to George-Étienne as he began tying the other end to an inflatable bag. The lower end of the rope soon tugged tight, squashing some of the straggly black weeds that colonized the outside of trawlers.

Pascal pulled up the rope, lifting a steel tank, slick with a water-repellent, high-pH slime to protect it from the sulfuric acid rain. A flexible pipe came out of his pouch. He fitted one end to the tank and the other to the bag, to start inflating it with oxygen. While this went on, he began taking down the sail and untying all the ropes before turning back to pulling up three more tanks and a woody container they'd woven themselves out of the walls and resins of old trawlers. They wouldn't have the time to turn the remains of this trawler into anything useful.

"Pa," Pascal said. "You think we got maybe six minutes?"

The radio squawking of lightning became more persistent.

"*Oui.*"

"What do you think about cutting off the cable?"

"We'd never cut it in time," George-Étienne said, "or hold its weight."

"I have two extra float bags," Pascal said. "I've got a saw. Let me try."

In his father's silence, static burst three more times. Lightning crackled somewhere ahead, at their altitude. Was his father doing the same math as Pascal? The time to the storm hitting, versus the time needed to cut through the tough carbon fiber cabling, versus the loss this trawler represented?

His father grunted, his helmet appearing over the edge of the trawler, slick with sulfuric acid. He climbed up and Pascal gave him a hand. Many acid burns over the years had browned and blackened Pa's survival suit, and patches held it together in dozens of places.

"Give me the tools," George-Étienne said. "I'll do it. If the storm looks close, you run for the habitat."

"I'm stronger, Pa," Pascal said, "and faster. Trust me. You fill the float bags and salvage everything else."

His father hefted the dark float bags.

"Be careful," George-Étienne said. "And when I say we run, we run."

"*Oui*, pa," Pascal said, giving his father one end of a new rope.

Pascal scrambled down the side of the trawler, slipping on the slime and mushy plants, until he hung from the edge. He had to catch the next footholds by swinging his feet, gripping tight and inching his way down. Brown hanging grasses, dripping with sulfuric acid, colonized the underside of the trawler. He had to find the ropes among them. At the base of the head, he wrapped his legs around the long cable and shimmied down about a meter.

He locked his legs and pulled free his saw. He had to be careful with anything sharp. Even a pinprick in his suit could let in a drop of acid. Venus had never been interested in *colonistes*, and took every opportunity to shake them from her skirts. Pascal sawed into the sides of the carbon cabling, making notches around which he tied the rope he'd brought down with him. It was still slack.

"You can fill the float bags, Pa," he said.

"Okay."

A gentle tug started, then a hard pull.

"I'm going to cut fast."

"Go ahead."

Pascal set the teeth of the saw against the edge of the cable and began cutting.

The tree-like trawlers began their lives as sprouts barely a meter long, dangling from the undersides of their parent plants. Once on their own in the winds, they took electricity from the clouds and carbon dioxide from the atmosphere. Enzymes organized the carbon into nanofilaments and kept the buoyant oxygen in the bulbs. When the weight of the trawlers pulled them too deeply into the atmosphere, the cables stopped growing, while the heads grew bigger and bloated with oxygen. When the buoyancy of the trawlers floated them to colder altitudes, their metabolism slowed and the inevitable leaking of oxygen eventually sank them back into the middle and lower cloud decks. The trawlers lived slow, elegant lives in bodies that were never quite the same from one day to the next.

"Almost done?" George-Étienne asked.

"Almost halfway," Pascal grunted, sawing harder.

"I inflated another float bag. I hope it holds all the weight."

The clouds ahead of them were backlit blindingly for a moment before thunder shook their bones. The cable creaked, thousands of its filaments cut and curling. The sawing went faster. The weight on the remaining cables strained to tear them. Between his legs the cable shuddered and he almost slipped.

"Are you ready?" Pascal asked.

"Are you ready to jump?" his father said.

"Itching to."

Pascal lay the saw into the cut again. His breath steamed the inside of his faceplate and the drizzle of sulfuric acid rain stopped. A bad sign. Wind pressed against him. He drew the saw along the strands and the world suddenly snapped. The head section shot upwards as the cable and bob plunged downward. The cable holding Pascal snapped and he hung weirdly motionless as bulb and cable vanished from sight.

The blow wrenched his shoulder painfully, but he still held the saw. His inner thighs stung and he was tumbling in the brown-yellow mist, past the cable, already out of sight of where they'd been. His father's voice came through the radio, but only a grunt, prodding him. Pascal pressed the release on his wings and the spring extended them and started the little jet motor.

He suddenly had weight again, and swooped up in a wide arc, following the swirl in the gloom where the float sacs and the cable had sunk.

"Pa! Are you okay?" he shouted.

"*Oui*!" came the response through the static. "I'm towing the supplies. Where are you?"

Pascal grunted unintentionally.

"Are you hurt?" his father asked.

Pascal pulled his legs up awkwardly as he flew to look at where his legs stung. His survival suit was ripped over his inner thighs, as if someone had dragged claws across them. His blood welled—not much in this pressure, but acid rain slicked the opening.

"Patching my suit," Pascal said, pulling first aid pads from his suit pockets.

The pain got worse. He could tell the pain of a cut from the burn of acid. He felt both. He cracked the seals and pulled out carbon fiber gauzes embedded with a paste of sodium carbonate to neutralize the acid. Not big enough, but they would have to do. He pressed one against the inner-thigh of his right leg, unrolled an acid-resistant plastic wrap several times around his leg, then annealed the edges together with a sealant. He did the same for the other leg.

"*Ça va?*" George-Étienne called on the radio. "Let me come to get you!"

"I'm patched," Pascal said, but then lightning flashed closer. "I'm not far from the cable."

He'd lost a lot of height and had drifted with the wind while patching his suit, but he saw the bottoms of three dark float-sacs above him, slick in the yellow light. His father had measured the buoyancy of the bags against the weight of the cable pretty well; they slowly inched upward. Pascal flew close to the base of the cable, climbed until he was about to stall, then cut the power and grabbed tight with both arms and legs. The cable pressed painfully against his wounds, but the weight at the base of the cable formed a partial seat, taking some of the weight off. He wouldn't be here long; his little island had started sinking again.

"Where are you?" George-Étienne demanded.

"Get the salvage back to the *Causapscal*!" Pascal said. "I'm tying a rope to the cable so I can pull it back. I'm going to need your help when I get there."

"Soon?"

"Soon!" Pascal said, tying a non-conductive rope just above the bob.

He tied the other end to his belt, started the motor in his jet wings, and dropped into the rain again. Lightning cracked near enough that the haze around him lit bright yellow. The lightning was more dangerous now. The severed cable would attract it, and so would the rope attached to Pascal, non-conductive or not. Enough rain coated it to carry a charge.

He flew upward, and every time he came to the end of the rope and the tension pulled the cable closer to the habitat, he let himself swoop down, gain more speed and then throttle forward and up again. This was the job of a float-drone. They had some, but not enough to do all the jobs they needed. Up above the clouds, *la colonie* had more necessities. In the depths, they made do.

Bit by bit, his salvage came higher and closer, even though he couldn't see his home through the clouds. Weak radio signals guided him. Five hundred meters to go. Four hundred. Three hundred.

Then high rumbling sounded outside his helmet and, from ahead of him, lights.

His father flew past him on thick wings, around the salvage, and then to the rope. George-Étienne grabbed the rope close to the floating cable and tugged hard as he flew, adding to the thrust. Every time he was about to stall, he loosened his grip, letting the rope play through his fingers and, once he got enough speed, tightened his grip and pulled again. They moved faster.

The big shadow of the *Causapscal-des-Profondeurs* loomed before them; a great trawler three times the size of the one they'd just lost, with a long cable hanging into the haze. A black gantry hung beneath their habitat all around the central cable. His father darted ahead and landed on that open platform, took the end of a rope and jumped back into the clouds, towards Pascal.

"Untie!" his father said.

Lightning flashed ominously close and the thunder rolled over them, the two atmospheres of pressure giving the sound speed and power. Pascal fumbled the rope off his belt and swooped back the way he had come.

George-Étienne tied a knot between the two ropes, standing nearly straight up as his jet wings keened. The jet wasn't made to hold a man up, so he was sinking. His father dropped to gain airspeed and then climbed in tight circles. Pascal got his hand around one of the three sacs and cut the rope. With only two float sacs, the salvaged cable plummeted, yanking hard on the rope George-Étienne had tied, and then bumped softly against the big vertical tail of their home. Sparks and licking blue arcs crackled along it, shorting between the two cables. Their home would generate less electricity for now, but electricity had never been their problem. They needed real building materials and they'd managed to save some. Pascal angled down, pulling the float sac nearer and nearer. The oxygen was too buoyant.

His father landed on top of the float sac, hands grabbing the material, his jet wing motor whining at full throttle, and they got the sac out of the rain, under their habitat. They tied it to the gantry and then George-Étienne was hustling Pascal into the storm shelter.

The shelter was just a cage made of conductive trawler cable, with the floor of the gantry beneath and the curving shell of the trawler above them, with its dripping black epiphytic growth drooping over them. It didn't shelter them against acid, heat, pressure and wind, but it was grounded to the cable beneath the habitat by heavy wires and would survive lightning strikes.

Lightning boomed beside them, blinding, searing the clouds yellow and white. Then another bolt cracked on the other side. The world outside the cage incandesced. Water and sulfuric acid vaporized off the surface of the habitat. Pascal and George-Étienne gripped each other with a strength born of primal fear. Lightning struck again and again, before the bolts finally began cracking farther off. The booming receded, but its power vibrated in their bones for long minutes.

The gantry under their feet was just a grille of pressed carbon nanotube filaments. A haze of acidic vapor roiled beneath it. The grille was the only thing beneaththeir feet for forty-five kilometers. The emptiness after the lightning strike evoked a haunting beauty. Pascal's hands shook, but he felt alive, electrical himself, part of the shapeless clouds, and despite the pain in his legs, immune to their violence. He belonged to these clouds and they to him.

"*Ostie d'tabarnak,*" his father swore. "That was close."

Pascal's breath fogged the inside of his faceplate. His heart thumped. "We saved the cable."

His father nodded wanly inside his helmet. "Yeah, we did," he said, his tone meaning *we still lost the trawler.*

"Let's get inside. My suit may not be patched well."

They waited a moment more, listening for the patterns of thunder, before slipping the latch and hurrying to the airlock. They opened it and began rubbing themselves with neutralizing pads. The insides of Pascal's thighs stung more and more with the characteristic pain of acid burns. It took eight minutes to neutralize right. No one wanted to ever do it wrong. A drop of sulfuric acid where someone could inadvertently touch it was nothing to wish on anyone.

Hot carbon dioxide blew them dry; they cycled through the airlock and climbed up into the outer layer of the habitat. This ring, more like the inside of a torus, was dark, woody-walled, veined with thick webs of vasculature and spotted on the floor with quietly flexing pumps. This outer ring held one and a half atmospheres of pressure, sixty degrees cooler than the atmosphere outside.

They moved to the next airlock and cycled through to the wide living area. Alexis, blond and ten years old, stood two meters from them, almost hopping with excitement, but he didn't cross the line his grandfather had made on the floor. Pascal and his father were still hot to the touch, and they might have missed some acid.

"Lightning hit the *Causapscal!* Lightning hit us!" Alexis said.

Jean-Eudes stood beside Alexis, almost as excited, but also anxious. Jean-Eudes was shorter than his father, and the first flecks of gray spotted his beard at twenty-seven. He worked as an assistant to George-Étienne. He could be fastidiously good at reading dials, cleaning equipment and changing filters, as well as keeping Alexis occupied. Jean-Eudes was Venus's only Down Syndrome child.

"Did you see the lightning?" Alexis said. "Did you see it?"

"It was so loud!" Jean-Eudes said.

Pascal and George-Étienne hissed open the seals of their helmets and took them off. The air was clean, twenty-six degrees, pressurized to just one atmosphere.

"You ripped your suit!" Alexis exclaimed, pointing at Pascal's legs. Jean-Eudes moaned in worry, but didn't cross the line on the floor.

"I patched it," Pascal said.

His father put down their helmets, shucked his gloves and sat Pascal down right there.

"Bring me the medical kit, Alexis," George-Étienne said. "Jean-Eudes, get him some water. Or something stronger if he wants it."

Jean-Eudes ran after his bolting nephew, but then turned back uncertainly.

"You want something stronger, Pascal?"

"Water is good."

The stinging got worse now. George-Étienne unfolded a knife and sliced through the patches and wrapping that

18

Pascal had made around his legs.

"Any pain under the suit?" he asked.

Alexis ran up with the medical bag and dropped it beside his grandfather, who pushed him back beyond the line on the floor.

"A little."

George-Étienne looked at the angry red burns on his son's legs and started dabbing sodium bicarbonate all over them with a soft brush. He gingerly lifted the edges of the shredded pant legs and brushed the paste underneath. He brushed his own fingers similarly, then moved to the next edge.

"You burn yourself?" Pascal asked through gritted teeth.

"Not the first time," his father said, brushing Pascal's legs more quickly. "You'll burn your fingers when you have your own children. I lost count of the fingertip burns I got from cleaning up Marthe and Émile and Chloé." He became quiet. They didn't usually mention Chloé in front of Alexis.

"*Maman* got her legs burnt too?" Alexis asked quietly.

"Not so much," George-Étienne said. "Your *maman* was always too smart to damage her suit. Not like your uncles. Or Marthe. *Calvaire*, don't get me started on Marthe. That girl could get an acid burn in her hammock."

Despite the tension, that got Alexis giggling. Jean-Eudes knelt beside Pascal with a closed cup of water.

"How come Jean-Eudes gets to cross the line?" Alexis complained.

"He doesn't ask too many questions," George-Étienne said.

George-Étienne unsealed Pascal's suit on the front and began directing Jean-Eudes on taking it off.

"I can take off my own suit," Pascal said.

"I'll help," Jean-Eudes said.

When his suit was peeled down to his waist, they stood him up again and George-Étienne directed Jean-Eudes to hold Pascal from behind, around the chest, in case he fainted. His brother hugged him hard.

Pascal looked away as his father worked down the suit, took out the tubes and wiped him. The pain was constant, and wouldn't get worse or better. He didn't want to look.

"*Ouach!*" George-Étienne said in disgust. "You're going to have some pretty scars. But no one's going to doubt you're a man."

A queasiness turned over in Pascal's stomach.

"As long as I can still use my legs."

"Oh, you've still got legs," his father said. "Jean-Eudes, hold him while I take off the rest."

His big brother grunted, and lifted him, not so gently, while his father worked off his boots. Alexis stared wide-eyed at the process. He was scared, and George-Étienne sensed it.

"Can you imagine how many times they had to do this for Marthe?" George-Étienne asked the boy.

Alexis grinned nervously. "I won't get burned," he said.

"Everyone gets burned a little," Pascal said. "The trick is practicing so that when it happens, you're fast and you know what to do."

"I know what to do," his nephew insisted.

"Sit him back down, Jean-Eudes," his father said.

A bit awkwardly, Jean-Eudes lowered him. Pascal pulled his suit to cover his crotch before looking at his legs.

"No need for modesty," George-Étienne said.

Angry red welts had risen under a layer of neutralizing paste on the inside of each thigh. Some spots had burnt black. It stung more now that the adrenaline had ebbed. His toes wiggled. He wasn't losing blood. The acid had been stopped. His father popped a couple of pills into his hand.

"These are good ones," he said. "Can you walk to bed?"

Pascal took the pills with the water. "I think so."

"Good. Jean-Eudes, help him to bed."

And his big brother helped him walk slowly to their room.

TWO

MARTHE ROSE QUIETLY from the hammock and shivered in the cold. Émile had said he'd fixed the heat circulation system, but it was obviously buggered up again. She pulled the curtain aside to peek at the brightness. The *Causapscal-des-Vents* floated five kilometers above marbled ocher clouds extending in every direction, out to a horizon that revealed the planetary curve. The bulk of the dirigible's buoyancy tank blocked the direct sunlight that would have made the three-room habitat too hot. The clouds were deceptively calm, frozen in the moment of a roiling turn, a reaching finger, a changing color. Their deliberateness suggested lethargy, but Venus was anything but slothful. She hid her tantrums with the highest hazes and clouds.

"*Câlisse,* I thought you said we would sleep in," Noëlle said, grumbling from the hammock.

"Sorry," Marthe said. "I couldn't sleep."

"Now I can't sleep."

Marthe shivered and padded back to the hammock and slipped under the covers.

"Don't be like that," she said. "I'm sorry."

Noëlle huffed and turned her naked back to her. Marthe spooned close, but Noëlle shrugged away the contact, leaving Marthe to stare in frustration.

"Why do you care?" Marthe said. "You don't even want to go."

"It doesn't matter whether I want to go or not," Noëlle grumbled. "You should go with me."

"You hate those people. So do I."

"Do you want us to stay in all the time?"

"What would Délia say if she saw us there?" Marthe asked. "You just want to make her jealous."

"Fuck you."

"Gossip gets to my ears just like anyone else's."

"You should know what they say about you, then," Noëlle said.

"I know what they say about me, and I know what they invent about me when they get bored."

"'The ice bitch', they say..." Noëlle said, sneering.

Marthe laughed. "*That's* what you think I care about?"

Noëlle threw the covers off, onto Marthe, and hopped from the hammock. Marthe enjoyed the view. Where her own skin was cloud-pale, Noëlle came by hers from Haitian Québécois ancestors. Marthe's liaisons with Noëlle were shallow and brief, whenever Noëlle and Délia were on the outs, but Marthe hoped that something more might be possible. Until one of them blew up about something, like now. Noëlle finished pissing loudly in the head, took a paste-pack from the cooler, and then started putting on her survival suit. Marthe came off the hammock.

"Let me help you."

Noëlle swatted her hands away. "I'll cycle myself out."

"Fine! Do that!" Marthe said.

She flopped back into the hammock and covered herself against the cold. Noëlle left in a huff, making sure to kick and slam things on the way to the airlock. After a time, the *Causapscal-des-Vents* quieted, but for the creaking of age and the snaps of pressure changes as the slow leaks all over the habitat triggered compressed air to replenish the atmosphere.

Her brother hadn't been here when she'd arrived, drunk, with Noëlle, and she didn't hear anything now. It was just the two of them up here, sixty-five kilometers above the surface of Venus, living in a piece-of-crap habitat she was embarrassed to show Noëlle.

Causapscal-des-Vents was in some ways better than *Causapscal-des-Profondeurs,* where her father lived with two of her brothers and her sister's son. Marthe floated in the speeding winds of the high atmosphere, flying over the outspread fields of heaven. The bitterly cold, sunlit heights had only thin, ghostly turbulences, and the acidic spite of Venus had to struggle to reach them here. She sometimes succeeded, but not like down home. The spots and ridges of red acid scars on her hands and arms and neck attested to that.

Still, she missed the depths: her family, the sweltering

heat of their habitat, the struggle to pit her cunning against Venus to stay alive and scrape some subsistence from the deep clouds. And if she had been with her family in *Causapscal-des-Profondeurs,* she wouldn't be fighting with her words, making enemies and no friends.

But she wouldn't have Noëlle either, not even for a night. She would be lonely in different ways.

Pascal might be lonely. He was sixteen now, and stuck with a cranky old man, a child nephew and an adoring brother. Pascal was smart, funny, and good-looking. He needed company his own age. And given how poorly Émile had been doing here, maybe they ought to switch. Her father and Émile could try to make up, though that was a long shot. And she could look after Pascal. Introduce him to some girls. Or boys. Whatever.

She had other people to take care of too. She had two messages on her pad from families in the depths. Réal Chartier's family needed their insulin supply increased. The med computer said Réal's insulin dose was too low, but central supply didn't want to increase it without a doctor saying so, and the doctors were all waitlisted. The Chartiers had given Marthe their proxy vote in *l'Assemblée* because she could often persuade the ration managers.

The Cousin family at fifty-fourth *rang* had gotten their oxygen ration late last time, and only a half-ration this time. They borrowed from other deep families for now, but Marthe knew what was happening. Oxygen supplies were low for everyone. The systems that cracked carbon dioxide into carbon and oxygen were broken on one habitat; on another, the solar cells weren't working. Repair crews were getting ready to switch the solar cells from one habitat to another next week. Marthe would see if Pa could spare some oxygen. He would grumble about it, though. He could get more for his oxygen on the black market. And the D'Aquillons needed any boost they could get.

A loud hiss sounded. She rolled out of the hammock and ran toward the source. Near the back of the gondola, at the airlock to the engines, a seal hissed.

Câlisse!

Émile was supposed to maintain the *Causapscal-des-Vents*. That was his job. Either he hadn't done it, or he hadn't done it right. The lazy jackass wasn't even here.

She lit a cigarette, took a drag and watched where and how fast the smoke moved. Sound could mask multiple leaks. This turned out to be a solitary leak, but it couldn't wait. Still naked, she pulled out a small slow welder and a patch kit.

Goddamn Émile.

Apply epoxy and putty over the hole. Press in. Don't trust the seal. Use the heat gun to soften the putty. Paint the area with adhesive. Place the plastic laminate. Take a piece of metal. Weld.

Her cigarette had burned down to her lips by the time she finished, and she'd burned her finger with the welder.

Goddamn Émile.

THREE

THE HABITAT BUCKED on the edge of an eddy, then resumed its creaking sway. In the other hammock, Jean-Eudes snored softly. Remnants of sunlight, attenuated by kilometers of clouds, still pushed through the woody chambers, outlining shadowy veins flowing with acidic sap. Scratchy eyes open, staring blankly ahead, Pascal couldn't summon the energy to move.

If he didn't move, he could feel like part of the habitat— serviceable, elegantly functional, if ugly and meaningless. His body felt as if it were at a remove, strange and alien. Tough stubble caught on his pillow, and the feeling worsened. He didn't want to get up. But he couldn't leave anything on his face. He couldn't think about it.

He swung out of his hammock. The woody floor was warm. He opened a flap and pissed into a tiny urinal made of the same tough plant fiber as the rest of *Causapscal-des-Profondeurs*. Water was valuable, and so was nitrogen; the filtration system would reclaim it.

He moved to the sink without turning on a light. A tiny mirror hung above it, but he'd learned not to look into it. He mixed a bit of water with paste to make a lather and steeled himself to rub it onto his face. Touching his... the stubble... was strange, disorienting. He did it quickly. Every day, the hair seemed to be so thick he couldn't stand it, even though it was still only a fuzz compared to Jean-Eudes's beard.

Pascal closed his eyes, guiding the straight razor by touch, taking his mind elsewhere, as if touching someone else's face. The scraping tugs made him queasy, but he'd gotten faster every day since his father had taught him to shave. He rinsed the razor in the bit of water in the sink, flushed it and dried himself.

A child's voice sounded outside, followed by a squeal. Pascal quietly pulled aside the curtain, woven of old plant fiber. The main room of the habitat, a toroidal space about twelve meters across, centered on the trunk of the great Venusian plant they lived in. The woody walls sloped, worn smooth by feet and bumps and the living of day-to-day. Light chairs and uneven brown tables gave shape to an eating and living space. Near the thick trunk, big batteries, compressed air, and radio and radar equipment rested on platforms over tangles of wires. In the floor, the main pumps, a small field of muscular valves, slowly pushed carbon dioxide out of the habitat into the two atmospheres of pressure outside.

His father crept around the big room with exaggerated steps. Alexis hid under the table, staring at Pascal with wide, excited eyes. Then George-Étienne swept down and tickled him. The ten-year old squealed.

"Careful, Alexis," Pascal said, "you'll use up all the oxygen."

The boy paid him no mind and rolled on the floor, listening to his voice change as his chest and back thumped on the wood. George-Étienne hugged Pascal and then continued his game with Alexis, which turned into a wrestling struggle on the floor. Alexis always wanted to roughhouse and Pascal never did. He sometimes felt like a bad uncle, but tried squashing those feelings as much as he could. Everyone felt out of place sometimes.

A picture of his mother hung on the wall over the table. Pascal barely remembered her. He'd been very young when she'd been injured. They'd been too deep to get her to the doctors twenty kilometers up. And even if they hadn't been, *la colonie* had been on the other side of the planet at the time. Her absence outlined a weird gap in his life, a shape whose contours he could neither understand nor ignore. An itch.

He knew that she'd loved him, all of them, and that she'd loved Venus as much as he did. A rust-spotted mirror hung beside her picture, so that any of the children could look at themselves and at her at the same time, to see her in themselves.

He saw bits of her in Jean-Eudes, and bits of his father. His precise memories of Marthe and Émile were fading. Marthe hadn't been down in a year, and Émile had left five years ago. But they too looked like both their parents. Pascal only looked at his reflection beside his mother's picture. He'd been growing out his hair for some time.

Sometimes, when he pulled it the way she wore hers in the picture, he could see her in him, and the gap faded.

"She was beautiful, eh?" George-Étienne said from under a struggling Alexis.

Pascal nodded. "*Oui*."

"No sleep?"

Pascal shook his head.

"Me neither," George-Étienne said. "I was always jealous of your mother. She could sleep through anything, anywhere, anytime. You should have taken after her."

The *Causapscal-des-Profondeurs* rocked, and the thrum of propellers vibrated low in his feet.

"Close to full speed?" Pascal said curiously.

"The volcanoes of Atla Regio are rumbling."

Pascal felt the slow rock of the habitat like a sailor on Earth might have known his ship and the ocean around it. The deep clouds of Venus felt natural. He'd lived his whole life wrapped in them. The thrum of the props wasn't the only vibration; thunder shook the atmosphere, a long way off, maybe a couple of days.

Venus's rages could be astonishing. Some of her volcanoes blew metal-rich ash dozens of kilometers into the atmosphere, where storms might swirl the dust even higher, to where filmy plant membranes could catch it. And they could collect those plants and that dust in the depths. It was still impractical to mine the surface for metals on an industrial scale, so *la colonie* was desperate for metal and had to import it from asteroidal colonies. In good months, the D'Aquillon family could trade a dozen kilos of iron, lead and silicates on the black market, or to the government.

But that wasn't why his father had them heading south, past Atla Regio.

Pascal padded to the navigational screen. Their course had changed sharply overnight, tracing a southerly path over the volcanically inactive plains of Rusalka Planitia to intersect, eventually, with the Diana Chasma, the deepest place on the surface of Venus. Pascal knew where that would take them.

"You really want to do this?" he asked.

"I finished fixing the old probe," George-Étienne said.

"The bathyscaphe? I thought it didn't work."

"*Non,* the old probe with the bad Stirling engines. I dropped it about an hour ago."

When Pascal was ten years old, George-Étienne had made a really, really good trade with another *coureur* who happened to be the son of Marie-Claude Duvieusart, the first *coureur des vents* and the first person ever to reach the surface of Venus. The bathyscaphe she'd used was six hundred kilos of steel and, even then, overengineered and antique. The government had never found out that the D'Aquillon family owned it, and didn't even know it still existed. It was so secret that Pa had never shown Émile, Jean-Eudes, or Alexis, although Marthe knew about it. George-Étienne had resisted all occasions to scrap and sell it, and he'd even gone to the surface twice himself.

But sending down the probe made more sense. Despite the odds of losing a hundred kilos of metal in a probe, they sometimes sent them all the way down to the surface to salvage easy-to-reach metal, or even to drop off mining equipment whose components could survive a few days at those depths.

"How long?"

"We'll be there this afternoon," George-Étienne said.

They breakfasted on vat-grown algae and on a desulfurized stew of Venusian plants before Pascal went to the daily work of maintaining the *Causapscal-des-Profondeurs*. Very little automation was possible in the clouds of Venus. *La colonie* already had few metals, and the acid of the clouds attacked them relentlessly.

For forty years, *la colonie* had been bioengineering the Venusian cloud-living plants, exploiting their buoyancy, their ability to harness electricity from the clouds, and the parasitic plants that clung to them. But even the toughest plant habitats occasionally burst from pressure or temperature differences, or succumbed to acids or parasites. So every day, the woody valves and seals and pumps had to be checked, neutralized, the batteries changed, the new water flushed into long-term storage tanks, and so on. The inner mechanical parts, like the computers and communications equipment, needed to be inspected and re-protected from acid, and the ones on the outside likewise.

Pascal loved Venus, felt safe in the layered, pressure-resistant habitats in the middle and lower cloud decks. A few times, he and his father had taken trawlers deeper into the atmosphere, all the way to the base of the sub-cloud haze, breaking through into the clear air that began at about thirty-three kilometers.

He'd seen the face of majestic Venus herself: vast plains of corrugated basalt, low mountains, flat, circular plateaus, high mountains and volcanoes. Before him, George-Étienne had taken Pascal's older sister Chloé, his brother Émile, and his next sister Marthe. Only a handful of the Venusian *colonistes* had ever seen naked Venus. It was an experience of awe for George-Étienne, a rite of passage he needed to share with his children.

Only Jean-Eudes had not been able to go. It was too dangerous for anyone who couldn't handle all the equipment themselves. Pascal, the youngest, had gone down several times now that most of his brothers and sisters lived elsewhere. It had been a year since the last time, and Venus called him again. With Chloé gone, George-Étienne and Pascal were raising Alexis, so they'd hesitated to go again in person, but sending a probe was the next best thing. Pascal found himself itching by the controls at the trunk, waiting for the probe to break through the clouds.

Jean-Eudes came up behind his chair and put a warm hand on his shoulder. "Is it scary?"

The monitor showed the yellow mist of the lower cloud deck whipping past the cameras of the descending probe. Thirty-one kilometers. Two hundred degrees Celsius. Nine atmospheres of pressure.

"Not for the probe," Pascal said. "It's been built to survive all the way down to the surface."

"And the acid!" Alexis said helpfully.

His nephew had grown bored of the images of the descent. He'd seen recordings of other probes and even some of the ones George-Étienne had made on his own journeys. He lay on his back, rolling a ball up the rounding floor, seeing how high he could get it before it rolled back. Alexis's body was new-born perfect, unblemished; Venus had never touched him.

Jean-Eudes turned his palms up, then down. The same lines and spots of red wrinkled scar tissue that every Venusian eventually carried marked his hands too. Acid frightened Jean-Eudes. Pascal took his brother's hands in his fingers. His own bore their generous share of ropey scars.

"The metal is coated with carbon. Soon, it will be so hot outside the probe that it can't even rain. No rain means no acid."

"Were you scared when you went?" Jean-Eudes asked. Thirty kilometers.

"A little bit," he said. "Pa took care of me. Do you want to go someday? With me?"

Jean-Eudes looked unconvinced. "Look!" he said, pointing at the monitor.

"What? What?" Alexis shrieked, coming close.

The mist had cleared and the yawning darkness of Venus's surface loomed below, lit a diffuse yellow. In a few spots, ember-like orange glowed at the base of towers of black smoke. That wasn't so normal. The volcanoes were busy. The sub-cloud haze still surrounded the probe, but in patches, none of which obstructed the view. He pulled Alexis onto his lap and pointed at the screen.

"Look. See that's Atahensik Corona, and—"

"That means crown!" Alexis said.

"—and on one side is the Dali Chasma, a long trench. And there's Ceres Corona—"

"Like the Bank!" Alexis interrupted again.

"And right there, that long line is Diana Chasma, the deepest place in all of Venus."

"The deepest?" Alexis asked.

"That's where *papa* keeps his storm," Jean-Eudes said.

FOUR

ÉMILE D'AQUILLON CYCLED into the airlock in the base of the *Baie-Comeau,* the largest floating habitat in the entire *colonie.* Twelve floors of shiny metal and plastic housed the government, some key manufacturing efforts, meetings of *l'Assemblée,* and apartments for some two hundred people. It was the future. They'd learned enough about Venus that someday, dirigibles of this size would house whole villages of people, and even bigger ones would be possible.

Thérèse leaned against him, survival suit to survival suit, distant intimacy. He stroked her arm through their suits nonetheless. Her hand pressed against his crotch, through layers of padding and insulation and acid-resistant films. He wanted to respond. The airlock finished cycling, and the door opened into the lower engineering areas of the *Baie-Comeau.* Thérèse sometimes worked down here. It was quiet and empty, if a little chilly. A good place to get romantic. He hissed open the seal on his helmet and took it off. Émile reached for the seals on the front of his suit, but she stilled his hand as she pulled off her helmet.

"Patience, Roméo," she said.

She pulled a flask from a suit pocket and took a swallow before passing it to him. He groaned. He'd been aching for a drink. He tipped it back and coughed before swallowing. She laughed at him as it scoured on the way down.

"Whose *bagosse* is it?" he wheezed.

"Ninety-six proof," she said.

He coughed again, sniffed at the neck of the flask and took another swallow. The burning down his throat settled in his stomach like a weight. He'd needed this badly. His own stock had run dry a day ago.

"It kicks harder than anything I've ever made," he said.

She took back the flask and took three swallows.

Everyone made *bagosse*, although it was lightly illegal. Using corn and grain rations to make alcohol wasted needed calories. Even diverting compostable food waste to ferment bitter *chasse-cousin* was against the law. He'd gone hungry himself a few times as a child during food shortages in *la colonie*. Not that the rations for the D'Aquillon family were ever of the highest quality, or on time.

Thérèse spun the wheel on a big steel door. It was beautiful: clean, uncorroded, almost shiny. She stepped into a larger bay where nine people in survival suits already milled around, flasks in hand. On the front was a wall-to-floor-to-ceiling door, so that larger objects like small planes and drones could be winched into the *Baie-Comeau.*

Thérèse was greeted with hugs and kisses, some kisses more deep and long-lasting than Émile liked. He knew most of them. Some of these artists and sculptors and poets were good. Some still sought their voices, like him. They toasted each other. Émile started to feel a slight buzz. Thérèse took his hand and leaned against him.

"Do you trust me?" she whispered.

Émile nodded, emptying her flask. "What is this?" he asked playfully. "A performance? A reading? An orgy?"

"Worship," she said, "of Venus."

She planted a kiss on his cheek, then spun away, moving to the bay door, trailed by gloved clapping and last-minute swills from flasks. She bowed theatrically with her hand on the bay door controls, then held up her helmet in one hand as her eyes narrowed. Her ennui was knowing, like the weight of ennui had stamped her with secret, exhausting truth. Her smile, beneath that exhaustion, was courageous, a stab at the darkness. She was so powerful, so real, a human truth.

"*On n'est pas chez nous,*" Thérèse said. "We are not home. We live in boxes of metal and plastic. We never touch the wind. We never touch the rain. We see the stars and sun only through glass."

Her eyes became dreamy, staring into a distance that could not be contained by the bay.

"We can't find our souls like this," she said, "hidden away in houses in the skies, cut off from one another and from nature. We wither. We drink."

A woman beside Émile hooted. A deep-voiced man said solemnly, "We drink."

"We cut," Thérèse said, stroking her raised forearm, buried beneath layers of survival suit. "We acid," she said, touching the tiny scars on her face with glove tips. "We fuck."

"We fuck," someone behind Émile repeated.

"All this just to feel not-dead, because we have no souls," Thérèse said. "We create poetry, murals, sculptures—striving, reaching ephemera, trying to show we exist—but we can't mean anything. The rat in a lab has no soul."

"No soul," Émile whispered.

"I'm the rat in the lab," Thérèse said, with a crack in her voice. "The Earth is dead to me, a fantasy, a vision. I've never seen it. And I've never taken Venus into my heart. I don't belong here because Venus hasn't embraced me. I've never courted her as she deserves, never worshipped her sunrise with authenticity in my heart."

Émile's thoughts followed her languidly. The *bagosse* was hitting him harder.

"Venus is a lover who takes us only with pain," she said, "not because she's cruel. She's alien, unknowable, unfathomable, but her price is the same price as any goddess: she wants to be embraced."

"Embrace her," the man beside Émile whispered.

"I'm going to embrace her," Thérèse said. "I will touch her with my lungs. I will look upon her with my naked eyes. We seek to make ourselves whole."

"Whole," Émile whispered. He felt it, deeply. He

DEREK KÜNSKEN

wanted to mean something.

"No one need come with me," Thérèse said. "This is my quest."

Thérèse put her helmet back on and Émile's heart thumped to bursting with wanting her, to be important to her, to be part of her life. The others were putting on their helmets. Émile snapped his on and sealed it with automatic movements. He looked at the world through glass again, felt the world through gloves, heard the world through speakers. He was alone, cut off from everyone, from the world itself.

A red light flashed on the wall. A hiss sounded briefly, then quieted, as if noise itself were being bleached of meaning. When the pumps had removed enough of the air, vents opened on the bay door and the last breath puffed away in a gasp.

The flashing became more insistent, and the bay door lifted, hinged along the top, revealing at first a flat beam of sunlight reflected off yellow clouds. The light widened into a blade that cut across the ceiling, lowering and expanding until the cloudshine of Venus kissed their foreheads. Émile squinted at the brightness.

The bay door finished opening, leaving before them a square of blinding light. They stood still in shadows, hidden from direct sun and from Venus, while puffy fields of sulfuric acid stretched away into infinity. They could sail these airy seas forever and never come to shore. Venus had no shore. That was a truth of Venus the human heart couldn't grasp. She told them stories they couldn't understand.

43

Émile swayed on his feet, the *bagosse* making his hearing and movements indistinct, blurry. He swayed around the people, to Thérèse.

Her gloved hand went to the neck of her helmet. Her faceplate fogged with her rapid breathing and then her heroic exhalation. She popped the seals and her eyes widened. She took off her helmet and blinked in the bitter cold. Her face and eyes reddened in an atmosphere only a tenth of what she'd just been breathing. And she stared out onto the clouds with her naked eyes, struggling to take the raw carbon dioxide into her lungs.

Of its own volition, Émile's hand rose and snapped open the seals at his neck. Even drunk, he knew his training. He exhaled and exhaled and exhaled until his chest ached and black spots peppered his vision. He took off his helmet.

Venus touched him with the coldest and most ghostly of fingers. He couldn't take a breath, not a real one, but he could taste Venus, smacking his lips around the gasping atmosphere she offered. Her parched clouds tasted of bitter sulfur, biting salt, and a stale sterility, drier than anything he'd ever felt.

No one had worshipped her before. The trawlers and rosettes and blastulae and all the microscopic organisms in the clouds could not. No one had loved the love goddess, and Venus had no soul because no one loved her. And *les colonistes* had no souls because they had no world.

He stepped closer to the edge as his vision narrowed.

Venus didn't want blood. How many *colonistes* had

she killed? Dozens? Hundreds? His mother. His sister. His brother-in-law. Venus drank blood aplenty. Venus wanted a breath of life. Venus wanted to be loved, as they did. This was their sacrifice. His helmet slipped from his fingers and rolled backward. Émile stretched out his arms. Thérèse, as naked to Venus as he, took his hand.

He collapsed to his knees, his joints on fire with pain. Thérèse collapsed beside him, soundlessly. Heavy footfalls vibrated and someone must have pressed the emergency close panel. The big door, the eyelid for this miraculous vision, began to close.

FIVE

"WHERE DOES *GRAND-PÈRE* keep his storm?" Alexis demanded. He squinted at the small monitor.

"*Grand-père* is chasing it," Pascal said.

Alexis screwed up his face. "You *chase* a storm? I thought we stayed away from them."

"We do," George-Étienne said. "This one is on the surface. I want to see it."

"Why?" Alexis said in exaggerated bafflement.

"Because I don't understand it! *Grand-mère* and I didn't come to Venus just to get away from the cities and from an empty life. We wanted to explore, to see things no one had ever seen."

Alexis was getting bored.

"There's a storm on the surface that shouldn't be there," George-Étienne explained. "No one knows it exists and no one's seen it up close, before today. We're going to look today."

George-Étienne had discovered it years ago, sending a

probe down to salvage lost equipment, and had found it in the same spot over the years. Pascal had inherited his father's curiosity. Whatever strangeness lay at the deepest depths of Diana Chasma, he wanted to know it too. The chasma cut almost three kilometers into the surface, a winding trench system a thousand kilometers long, where the pressure passed ninety atmospheres. They were both captivated by the anomalous weather in those depths.

Pascal expanded the view, but the image could only go so far before pixelating. They'd built the probe from scrap, with only the equipment it needed. Until now, it hadn't needed a good telescope.

"It's a funny storm," Pascal said gently. "There are no clouds and the air is transparent, and it's too hot for rain, so it's like an invisible storm, even up close. Sometimes it blows dust around, but most times it's quiet."

"I don't see it," Alexis said, hopping off Pascal's lap. "It's stupid."

"Don't say that about *papa's* storm!" Jean-Eudes said hotly.

"*Ça va*, Jean-Eudes," George-Étienne said placatingly, wiping oils off his hands with an old towel. He peeked at the screen. "Hours yet."

The image in the screen grew more fine-grained every minute. Thickening atmosphere slowed the probe more and more.

Pascal sent an instruction to the probe. Its camera eye swiveled, from straight down to a horizon view. Hundreds of kilometers away, Maat Mons towered five kilometers off the surrounding plain, its volcanic peak and shoulders shiny with frosts of bismuth and lead sulfides. He swiveled the camera down again, to the Aphrodite highlands beneath the probe and the great fields of jagged wrinkles of Nuahine Tessera, shadowless and untouchably distant. That feeling of dispossession made sense to Pascal, lived in his bones each day, woke with him each morning. They floated in the clouds, bobbing along, surviving, unable to touch, as if waiting for something unknown.

Pascal wasn't interested in the highlands, where windspeed never topped a few meters per second. His father's "storm" was deeper. Despite centuries of exploration by satellite, and decades of high-altitude dirigibles and even robotic ground rovers, scientists still couldn't decide what geological processes had formed the especially-deep Diana Chasma—so near mountains that, in some places, the terrain dropped down a straight slope for almost seven kilometers.

The altitude of the probe reached twelve kilometers. The temperature outside had risen to three hundred and sixty degrees Celsius and the pressure to forty atmospheres.

"*Voyons*, Pascal," George-Étienne said. "You should eat something."

Jean-Eudes brought Pascal a thick soup and he ate it in front of the display. Pascal put his dish away when even he finally got impatient at the four-kilometer mark. The temperature outside the probe had reached four hundred and thirty degrees Celsius, and the pressure was now seventy atmospheres. Very soon, the pressure would be so great that the carbon dioxide in the atmosphere would take on the properties of a fluid, capable of dissolving organics, making Venus even more hostile. That was alien, even to the *colonistes* who lived in the clouds. George-Étienne leaned in close with Jean-Eudes.

"You take it, Pa," Pascal said.

"Watch the descent speed," George-Étienne said. "Slow it near the surface. And watch for cross-winds."

Pascal wanted to keep piloting the probe—which was mostly autopiloted anyway—but he didn't want to mess this up. They were risking a lot of metal. But he knew machines. He liked machines. They were beautiful. Elegant. They were what they appeared to be. They were all surface.

The probe's descent speed slowed as the atmosphere thickened. He swiveled a second camera to the northeast. The closer view of the peaks and shoulders of the Nuahine Tessara was vertiginous. He was used to clouds in every direction, to a line of sight that extended no more than a few kilometers. Nuahine looked close enough to touch, even though her jagged lines lay dozens of kilometers distant. False perspective.

The view slowed even more. The wait was no longer interminable. Even Alexis had come close to stare at the screen, draping his arms over Pascal's shoulder. The ground closed in, all sharp lines and pebbles, as if the rock had been recently broken. Venus's lack of rain, plate tectonics and even meaningful wind meant that the surfaces were either sharp and fragmented or rounded in whatever bulbous shape the magma had possessed when it had frozen into rock.

Just above the base of the uneven, pebbled floor of the Diana Chasma, Pascal gave a little power to the propeller. The air was so thick at ninety-three atmospheres of pressure that the probe rose slightly before resuming its lethargic descent through an invisible bath of supercritical carbon dioxide to touch Venus. The monitor showed its big carbon-wire frame wheels bowing and steadying. The thermometer reported four hundred and sixty-five degrees.

"I don't see your storm, *papa*," Jean-Eudes said.

"It's always near the northern wall of the chasma," George-Étienne said.

They'd landed near the target coordinates, within a trench cut three kilometers into the rock of the Rusulka Planitia south of the Ceres Corona. The floor of Diana Chasma was uneven, strewn with stones of all sizes, from sharp gravel and fines to jagged landslide debris fallen from steep walls. Pascal directed the rover forward. Although colonists on the moon and Mars and the asteroids had highly autonomous robots, none of the handy materials needed to make the processors would survive the heat of the surface, or the acid of the clouds. Anything made to work on the surface had to be designed with a minimum of moving or smart parts and made entirely of metals and ceramics that didn't expand or deform with heat, and all of which had to be imported. So Pascal was the brain inhabiting the rover, peeking through the probe's constricting cameras, as if through a curtain at a magical place.

The black face of the northern wall rose up out of the

line of sight. Pascal would have liked to have looked up, but it wasn't safe to tilt the cameras too high while driving. Millennia of crumbling had deposited uneven gravel that could catch the wire wheels. As the rover neared the chasma wall, the patterns on the ground changed. The southern face of every bump and ridge was clear of dust and stones, while gravel chips and powder had gathered on the northern side, as if in the lee of a wind.

"There shouldn't be any wind here," Pascal said, showing his father the video captures.

"My storm." George-Étienne's subdued tone covered a youthful excitement.

Pascal magnified one of the pictures. In the lee of heavier rocks, wind tails had formed. Fine lines of whites, grays and blacks marked the tiny piles of grit.

"A storm wouldn't have left all the wind tails pointing in one direction," Pascal said, "and it wouldn't have had time to sort grains by size." It was a mystery, and Pascal felt his excitement growing.

"At this pressure, even a little wind would be powerful. Keep going. We have only an hour or two before we have to bring the probe back."

Pascal resumed the drive, bouncing over ridges and following skirts of rockfalls fanning from the escarpment. The amount of stone and pebbles and sand continued to shrink as if the area had been partly blown clean, revealing the unevenness of the surface and immense, multi-ton boulders.

George-Étienne pointed at the monitor. A wind blew in the direction of their travel at six kilometers an hour, slightly faster than on the surface of the highlands. It might have been just a bit of wind-tunneling, except that the wind wasn't following the chasma; it headed northward, towards the escarpment wall. It shouldn't have done that.

The probe didn't have a microphone *per se,* but the thick atmosphere transmitted sound very well, setting vibrations in the probe's hard armor. When Pascal subtracted the normal vibrations of the motor and the jarring of the uneven ground, a low moaning remained.

"That sounds like a storm!" Alexis exclaimed.

"It might be what a storm looks like," George-Étienne said, "on the surface."

A windspeed of six kilometers per hour seemed leisurely, but ninety-three atmospheres of pressure would turn that into an irresistible deep ocean current. It was strong enough to tip the probe if Pascal wasn't careful.

He began to get nervous. "Should we get it out of there, Pa?"

"Why?" Alexis asked. "What's wrong?"

"Jean-Eudes, could you take your nephew to check all the valves?" George-Étienne asked.

Jean-Eudes's eyebrows rose. "*Oui.*"

"But what's wrong?" Alexis whined.

"The *valves!*" Jean-Eudes said emphatically. "We have to check *all* of them. That's a two-man job."

Alexis did not look convinced and scuffed his feet on the floor as he followed Jean-Eudes to get little lamps for the task.

On the surface, the wind had picked up to eight

kilometers per hour and the sluggish response to the controls made Pascal nervous. The probe's interior was pressurized to just two atmospheres, so on the somber surface, it was almost neutrally buoyant, with little traction. The wind rocked it dangerously.

"It's too fast," Pascal said.

George-Étienne expanded the view and then tagged a broken boulder almost four meters tall. "Shelter."

"What if the wind shifts?" Pascal asked, steering the probe across the dark rock field.

"The wind never shifts in this storm," George-Étienne said.

"That's not possible," Pascal said. He couldn't say more. He carefully turned the probe, hoping not to tip it.

"Storms are different here," Pa said. "They're not caused by convection currents and Hadley cells. We're the first to see this, ever, and we're going to find out what makes it tick."

The probe drove across the current, its wheels dragging and hopping. For a few minutes, Pascal doubted it would reach the lee of the boulder, and a sheen of sweat formed on his face. But he got it there just before the faster wind tipped it. In a kind of terrified relief, Pascal examined the display with Pa. Other boulders blocked the view of a low rise where the wind carried swirling sand and rock chips in its flow.

"We can't see anything from here," George-Étienne said with irritation.

A mystery lived down there, and this screen was their only window into that mystery. It was a kind of telescope that they couldn't move, and they'd reached their maximum resolution, with the seven-kilometer-tall rock face still a hundred and fifty meters away. Whatever pulled this wind hid beyond their angle of view. So close.

"*Calvaire*!" George-Étienne swore.

"What is it?" Alexis called from the other end of the *Causapscal-des-Profondeurs*.

"Somebody's going to regret it if they don't get those valves inspected," George-Étienne said.

Alexis peeked around at them and then ducked his head back around the bend. That was their problem. Seeing around a bend with a probe forty-five kilometers below them.

"*Pa,* how's the spare camera on the probe?"

"Should be in its case in the outer hatch."

"Are you willing to risk breaking it?"

"What are you thinking?"

Pascal explained nervously. George-Étienne was reluctant. He thought it risky and unlikely to work. But he had no better idea, unless they wanted to return the probe to the lower cloud decks without having seen where the wind was going. The mystery had Pascal in its claws, and had sunk them even deeper into his father.

Pascal gave the commands for one of the manipulator arms to open an outer storage panel containing small wrenches, cable, spare manipulator arm, spare wheel, and spare cameras. Pascal attached the end of a three-hundred-meter carbon nanotube cable to the inside of the storage panel, and then got the arm to pay out meters and meters and meters of cable, until only the two ends remained affixed to the probe. The current of supercritical carbon dioxide caught loops of it and rolled them over, pulling more and more out past the boulders.

The next part was harder. The little camera was old, just a spare, bought on the black market with hard-earned water and rare metals. The lens of industrial diamond resisted acid, but would still crack if hit the wrong way. The backup battery would last an hour, and it also had an emergency transmitter. Most important equipment on Venus did. The *colonistes* never trusted just wiring; acid had a way of sneaking in eventually and chewing at it. They called the phenomenon *bébittes*, after the bugs of Québec on Earth.

Pascal needed both manipulator arms to attach the camera to the axle of the spare wheel and then to tie the axle to one end of the long woven carbon nanotube cable. All told, it took nearly a half hour to finish all the preparations.

"Do you think it will work?" Pascal asked, eyeing the second screen now available to them, through the transmitter from the spare camera. The color had greened slightly, an artefact of the high-temperature circuitry nearing its tolerances.

"Go ahead," his father said.

Pascal directed a manipulator arm to throw the camera and axle out of the lee of the boulder. It didn't go far. The low-strength arm was throwing an object through a medium as dense as water. The view from the spare camera spun crazily, until it sank with slow deliberateness to strike the hard basalt. It bounced once, then rolled lethargically. Black rock filled two-thirds of the screen, but then the view rotated in a dizzying spin.

The surface wind rolled the wheel and camera along drunkenly until the drag of the long cable angled the camera forward. Then the weight of the wind scraped the spare wheel forward, like a drogue chute. The view bumped and jumped along the rock, most often with the camera facing forward. It staggered around boulders, swept by eddies, and picked up speed. When it hit the base of the slope, the slow-moving weight of the ninety-three atmospheres of carbon dioxide began pushing it upwards inexorably.

"*Sapristi*!" George-Étienne said. "You did it!"

"What did he do?" Alexis called plaintively from the galley.

"Come see."

Alexis ran and Jean-Eudes followed, and while they both made noises of astonishment, after a time, they found the view less remarkable than they'd expected. The hopping, dizzying view of the camera slowly followed the wind up the slope. Alexis slipped away to his room. Jean-Eudes returned to checking the valves. The camera view topped the rise, and a heavily-eroded cave mouth came into view. The image stopped advancing, but the wind buffeted the camera left and right.

"We'll figure out how to process these to get some good stills," George-Étienne said.

Pascal paid out more cable and the view from the spare camera swayed more wildly in the wind. At fifteen kilometers per hour, the density and weight of the air gave it more force than even a category seven hurricane on Earth. And the wind was blowing *into* the cave.

"Where the hell is all that air going?" George-Étienne asked in astonishment. "Maybe it comes out of a hole at a different altitude? Like a gopher hole."

Pascal didn't comment. His father occasionally made references to the Earth of his boyhood that meant nothing to his children. But the atmosphere of Venus at this depth distributed pressure evenly, so wind being sucked into this hole couldn't be explained by the pressure difference with the other end of the tunnel, even if it somehow emerged at the top of the escarpment seven kilometers above them.

"We can't see in the dark," Pascal said, with disappointment. He hadn't prepared for any of this.

The spare camera didn't have a lot of extra features. It had a grainy IR camera, more for taking the temperature of its environment than for resolving images. He flipped the view to IR and the world became blotchy and indistinct. Useless. Except that the cave was cooler ahead of them: four hundred and twenty degrees, compared to the four hundred and eighty around the probe. He pointed at the reading.

"Venturi effect?" George-Étienne said, shaking his head. "The air is moving so fast through the tunnel that the pressure and temperature are dropping. I've never seen anything like this."

Pascal switched the camera back to visual band. The image became scratchy.

"What's wrong?" George-Étienne asked. "The shaking getting too bad?"

"I don't know. The transmission isn't great. Maybe the transmitter's already giving out? It's just an old camera. The transmitter's not made for this range."

"Can you turn on the light?"

"It's not very bright, and it'll use up the battery even faster," Pascal said.

"We're already having transmitter trouble and we can't see into the cave," his father said. "Let's have a quick look. I don't know when we'll have a chance to come back. It's far windier than I ever thought, too much to risk a probe again."

Pascal switched on the light, which, in the outside gloom, didn't help much. But he slowly had the cable unspool and the camera, still ducking erratically in the wind, began to enter the cave. Twice, the spare wheel protecting the camera hit the sides of the cave, but the diamond lens didn't crack.

The little light swung dizzyingly, showing near-random partial views of the cave. The walls were unlike anything they'd seen before. The basaltic rock, old and volcanic, was polished smooth, every outcropping and bump rounded.

Erosion. They were seeing erosion, and not just a bit. The smooth walls reflected light. These surfaces had been scoured by wind for years, maybe centuries. Only the rare wind blew faster than five kilometers per hour in the deep ocean of supercritical carbon dioxide on the rest of the surface of Venus, except for this one spot, where wind had been cutting for ages. How?

The image filled with static, even though the camera had only reached ten meters into the cave.

"We may lose the signal soon," Pascal said, paying out another five meters of cable.

"Is it recording?" his father asked.

"The camera's memory buffer is tiny. I've got it snapping pictures and storing environmental measurements every ten seconds."

"Let's go as far as our cable will take us," George-Étienne said.

The spare wheel containing the camera began slamming into the wall of the cave.

"*Crisse!*" Pascal said. "The cave is turning and we're caught in turbulence."

He unspooled cable quickly. The image became grainier, but the camera hung steady now, maybe caught in the lee of an outcropping on the bend in the cave. It swung lazily, slowing and unwinding its tension until it looked quietly at a depression in the wall, where sand and grit had collected. The grit occasionally made small, furtive movements, like silt caught in the wind, but the current of the eddy kept bringing it back to its little drift.

"I've got about fifteen more meters of cable," Pascal said. "Want to risk it?"

"*Vas-y,*" George-Étienne said quietly.

Pascal signalled the probe to unspool the last fifteen meters of cable. The image spun disorientingly again, dropping deeper and deeper into the cave with the current. Side channels fed wind current into the main channel. The image became so grainy and static-filled that they couldn't make much out at all. He toggled to infrared.

The temperature had by now dropped to three hundred and ninety degrees and the pressure to fifty atmospheres, conditions that they shouldn't have found below nine kilometers of altitude. That was a measure of how fast the wind was blowing through the tunnel.

"Go back to visual!" George-Étienne said.

"We can't see anything," Pascal said, switching back to the grainy, swaying view.

As he unspooled the last of the cable, the camera threw itself about crazily as it passed another bend, and then settled in a slow eddy in the lee of the bend.

"What the hell is that?" George-Étienne demanded.

The swaying had stopped, but the snowy static almost filled the screen. A triangular shape showed in outline under the silt. Then static swallowed their view.

SIX

EVEN WHEN PASCAL began rewinding the cable, he couldn't get a signal back from the camera. He worried he'd lost both the camera and the spare wheel in the terrible wind, that maybe he hadn't tied the cable properly. No one could work very precisely through manipulator arms. But when, through the probe's main camera, the spare wheel and camera appeared from the gullet of the cave, relief soaked into him.

Pascal untied the wheel with the manipulator arms and repacked everything into the tool panel. The wind hadn't let up. It had, in fact, strengthened to eleven kilometers per hour around the shelter of their boulder. They had to get the probe out of there. The winds forty-five kilometers higher would carry the *Causapscal-des-Profondeurs* inexorably west, and soon they would be out of recovery distance.

Pascal launched the probe into the air, riding on a hard burst of propellers. In ninety-three atmospheres of pressure, every churn of the props lifted the probe, but the view on their screen lurched wildly as the wind sucked it towards the cave. The rock-face approached fast; when only a meter separated it from dashing into stone, the probe's buoyancy and lift finally got it above the current. It swayed drunkenly above Diana Chasma and then ascended more certainly.

An hour later, George-Étienne went outside to tie it to the *Causapscal-des-Profondeurs*. Then they turned the habitat propellers on a course to catch up with their flock, floating fourteen hours downwind of them.

George-Étienne came back in from stowing the probe, holding the spare wheel. Pascal took it with a small sense of awe. He was holding something that had traveled beneath the surface of Venus. Although it had been scratched and dented, the wind had scoured its black carbon down to the metal beneath and polished it mirror-bright. Experimentally, he held the tread face of the wheel in front of himself. In its curved surface, his face stretched, distorting so much that, for once, he could stand to see his own reflection. His inflated green eyes stared back. His distended nose overwhelmed his face. His long brown hair framed his face from a great distance.

Pascal detached the beaten camera. Remarkably, for all the blows it had taken, the diamond lens had survived. He downloaded the images.

"They're clear," his father said in wonder.

They were, as much as they could be. The still images taken every ten seconds, where not ruined by poor light or quick movement, weren't bad. None of the snowy static they'd been seeing in the live feed showed in the pictures.

"I wonder if the transmitter burnt out," Pascal said.

He began a diagnostic of the transmitter while they looked at the pictures. They had good ones of the clean walls, sometimes blurred at the edges. They had three worth keeping of the first eddy and the silt build-up. These photos would be worth a lot to geologists. What might they ask for in trade?

Then they came to two pictures at the end, in the last eddy. The graininess in them was entirely due to the fading light from the failing battery. Not static like they'd seen in their feed. The black and white pictures showed a flat triangular shape buried under silt, about four meters long. At its apex something shiny and smooth and not at all basaltic reflected the light.

"What is it?" George-Étienne asked.

Pascal couldn't even guess. He knew of no geological process that would create a perfect isosceles triangle. It wasn't made of the same materials as the rock. It had to be artificial.

"Do you think the Russians or Chinese or Americans sent down some secret probes?" Pascal hazarded.

"You mean maybe we aren't the first to find this cave?"

Pascal shrugged. He couldn't think of anything else. Maybe one of the big powers had sent something down to look at the geology of Venus up close.

"None of them have done anything on Venus for over a hundred years," Pascal said. The exploration of Venus by bigger nations had never amounted to much more than seeing Venus as a dead end on the road to colonizing the solar system. No one had contested the claim to the clouds of Venus by a new sovereign Québec sixty years ago. Why would they?

"But what if one of the Banks sent down an automated probe," Pascal said, "looking for whatever Banks look for—minerals, or rare metals, something that would make their investment worth it? The triangular shape looks a little like a wing. What if they didn't know the wind was there? While their automated probe was gliding, maybe it got caught in the wind and sucked into the cave?"

George-Étienne brushed at his beard.

"Maybe," he said. "The bloodsuckers in the Bank stick their noses into *la colonie's* business, looking to take over. Never seemed to me to be worth their while; we're too poor for them to make any real money off us. Maybe they knew something was down here."

"That still doesn't explain where the wind is coming from," Pascal said, "or where it's going."

"Whatever that probe is," George-Étienne said, staring at the frozen image, "it'll be good salvage. Three meters long minimum. In metals alone, it'll be more than we harvest."

"How are we going to get it out?" Pascal asked. "Against the wind?"

"It got in there somehow," his father said. "We'll make a salvage plan and we'll get it out."

George-Étienne wandered away cheerfully to resume chores that hadn't been done for a day, especially now that Pascal couldn't put on his suit for a few days. Pascal turned his attention back to the pictures. He flipped through them more slowly, examining each one minutely.

All the static came from the bad transmitter. They'd need a new transmitter for the next try, or he'd need to disassemble and rebuild this one. At least he could do that while his legs were healing. He ran a diagnostic program on the transmitter to see what parts he'd need.

But the diagnostic failed. Nothing was wrong with the transmitter. It passed all the tests and should have transmitted all the way back to the probe, even through the cave. He wasn't an expert on supercritical carbon dioxide, but he didn't think Venus's atmosphere could have interfered with radio waves.

He dug deeper into the camera's simple operating system. In the admin levels, he found the logs for the last ten minutes of operation, a kind of transmitter black box for diagnostics if the device stopped working. It wasn't coded for easy user interface, but he made his way through the code and memory buffers and found a lot more radio signal than there should have been.

A very defined radio wave curve showed, increasing in strength as the camera descended into the cave. Even with only ten minutes of sample, it was unmistakable. What would produce radio waves under the surface of Venus? He didn't think it was the triangular probe, if it really was a probe. It had been the same temperature as the rest of its environment, which meant its circuitry was probably inactive.

The radio signals repeated with the regularity of some

kind of machinery. But what machinery would have survived in the crushing pressure and melting depths of Venus? And why? The basaltic rock had nothing of value. Except the wind?

He ran all his calculations again, then called Pa.

SEVEN

ÉMILE PULLED THÉRÈSE close, playfully pulled the joint from her lips, took a drag and then replaced it. They lay naked under a blanket in one of the cargo bays. Music played, too low for the kind of angry yelling in the song. It was a hard-bitten album of rock rage, heavy percussion, but playing quietly, making of the music an echo of anger.

Other couples who had communed with Venus snuggled there too, under their own blankets, or stretched out on boxes, speaking in hushed voices. All mellow. No one had refused to remove their helmet. Every one of them had looked upon Venus with naked eyes, breathing her breath, as they would on Earth. It was empowering, overwhelming and humbling. Émile didn't know quite what to do with the feelings he couldn't name.

He was high. And drunk. And sore, like he had been punched over and over. He'd gotten off easier than Thérèse. The low pressure had given her two black eyes, and the white of one of them had filled with blood. His joints ached. His bones ached. But he felt like he'd done something enormous.

Across the storeroom, someone gasped in pain and stamped their foot over and over, swearing.

"Mmm," Thérèse said. "Hélène is aciding."

Émile didn't try to see. He'd heard of aciding. Hélène and her friends used acid-resistant stencils to paint new, artful scars onto their bodies. They baptized themselves with sulfuric acid, consenting to be marked by their new home, and making of the baptism works of art. Émile had seen dozens of such marks, but the idea of intentionally burning his skin with acid was still alien to him. He had too much of the *coureur des vents* in him. He'd been painfully touched by Venus many times. Before now, he'd never understood their meaning. A naked, brown-haired man about his age came across the room.

"You guys want to acid too?" he asked, crouching. A spray of five tear-shaped acid scars marked each cheek symmetrically. Old acid.

Émile shook his head. He wanted to consecrate this moment, but maybe not with acid, and not yet. He ached too much already.

"I don't want to mess with the buzz, Réjean," Thérèse said.

"You don't need it, *n'est-ce pas?*" Réjean said to Émile. "Your hands are covered. Were you in an accident?"

Émile lifted his arms out of the blanket and considered them. His muscles ran deep. Raised red spots speckled them. Snaking, wormy lines of raised scar flesh made inscrutable patterns. Deep divots showed where acid had melted his muscle before he could stop it.

"Just years in the lower decks," Émile said.

"The lower cloud decks?" Réjean said. "No shit! Just the hands?"

"All over," Thérèse said with a satisfied grin as she snuggled close to Émile.

Réjean's face twitched, then he smiled.

"What's your name?"

"Émile."

"D'Aquillon," Thérèse added.

"D'Aquillon. Aren't you the one with the retarded brother?" Réjean laughed.

Émile shrugged off Thérèse and stood. Réjean was of a size with Émile, which made him pretty big, but Émile punched him so hard that he fell back over a protesting couple, spraying blood from his lips and nose. Émile stomped over to him and grabbed his hair, his fist cocked back for another go.

"Don't ever call my brother retarded!" Émile said, shaking the man's head.

Réjean flinched, waiting for another blow. Blood painted his chin. Émile's heart thumped. He was within an ace of clocking the *colon* again. Who the *crisse* was he to call Jean-Eudes anything?

Thérèse tugged softly on his arm. She stood pale and naked beside him.

"He got it," she said. "Come on, fighter-boy. Bring your scars back under the covers." She pulled more insistently. "Come on. Less fighting, more loving. This is Venus."

Émile released Réjean's hair and stood straight, then let himself be led back by the hand to their little nest. Réjean swore in the gloom, and the others watched him slink back to the far end where he'd been aciding Hélène. Under their inadequate blanket, on their sides, nose to nose, he and Thérèse radiated warmth. Thérèse smiled.

"How drunk are you?" she whispered.

"Half?"

"How high are you?"

"The other half."

"Are you always this violent when you're drunk?" she said softly.

He shook his head.

"What's your brother like?"

He examined her face, her one blue eye, her one eye filled with bright blood, her raised brows, the thin nose and parted lips. She wasn't making fun of him. She wasn't playing for anything. She was present. She was always present. The only thing that ever shifted was the target of her attention.

"Jean-Eudes is older than me by two years," Émile said slowly. "The doctors found out he had Down Syndrome and told Pa and *maman* to abort. Pa told them to fuck off. They told Pa that *la colonie* couldn't afford to support people like Jean-Eudes and that he'd never get rations or medicine."

"That's terrible," she said.

"Maybe. Pa told them to fuck off again and got a deep trawler habitat. The rest of us were born at fiftieth *rang*."

She traced the lines of his face with slow fingers.

"Tell me."

"I'm not angry."

Her expression was not wise or sympathetic. It was predatory, on the scent of a secret.

"You hate the government?"

He worried at the rough weave of their blanket. Pinched at it. Brushed at dirt and lint.

"No," he said finally. "I agree with what they did."

"They took away rations and medicine from your family!"

He shook his head fractionally.

"The government didn't take away rations and medicine from all of us. Just Jean-Eudes. But my Pa said that if Jean-Eudes couldn't get rations and medicine, none of the D'Aquillons would."

"What did your mother say?"

"She never said. I guess she loved her son as much as Pa does."

"I'm sorry," she said after some thought.

"There's only so much medicine," he said, working at the fabric again, conscious of the heat of her eyes on his face. "There's only so much food. *La colonie* needs every pair of hands to produce something, to earn their keep, to strap up their own suits. That wasn't a secret to anyone, least of all my father when he emigrated here. If he'd been a man, he would have done the right thing."

"Abort your brother?"

"Yup," he said with a quiver in his voice. He cleared his throat. "Because of Pa's choice, we had to move into the parts of Venus that are like Hell. My father wasn't

73

man enough to bear his own pain, so he spread it over his children. My mother died down there, too far away from medicine. My sister and her husband died down there, trying to make a living in the depths, and now my nephew Alexis is an orphan."

"I'm sorry."

"It's my father."

"You just punched Réjean."

He traced the deep bruising around her eyes with his rough fingertips. She was fragile. He was fragile. And they huddled under a blanket, seeking animal warmth in high cold clouds.

"I don't hate Jean-Eudes," Émile said. "My big brother is the most innocent, gentle person I've ever known. I love him, but I hate myself for knowing my father picked the wrong path for all of us. He didn't have the right to put a curse on our family."

She stroked his chest. Her face had become pensive. The hunter of secrets had found something she didn't know what to do with, and contemplated playing with her food.

"What would you choose now, for your brother?" she asked softly.

"I'd do anything to protect Jean-Eudes. I'd fight a hundred Réjeans. Pa exiled us, but taught us one thing that's true: family always comes first."

"That's noble," she said. "You don't need to hate your own nobility."

He chuckled and his joints hurt again. "That's not nobility. Gangsters have the same values."

She laughed delightedly and stroked his cheek. "I'm

imagining you as a gangster," she said, "standing on corners, getting protection money." She smiled at her fairy tale. "How often do you see your father?"

"I saw him five years ago."

Her eyes widened. "What happened?"

He flattened her hands between his. Both of them traced the ropey red lines of acid scars on his hands with their eyes. These scars weren't artistic, just the terrible and inevitable injuries of living in the lower cloud decks. He'd survived his accidents by luck.

"I couldn't respect a man for making children pay for his choice and he couldn't see how he'd hurt his family. And he didn't like my drinking or my getting high. He called me an alcoholic."

She laughed delightedly. "*Tabarnak*, if there's one place we need a drink, it's Venus," she said.

He grinned.

"Fifty kilometers down," she said wonderingly. "You've lived wrapped in Venus. Literally. In Venusian life."

He gave a short laugh. She took his hands and kissed all the raised acid scars, one by one.

"It's beautiful," she said. "You're beautiful."

Her lips pressed against his, wet and hot.

"But you came up," she said. "You came to the sun."

"Yeah."

"Why? If you could live deep."

"Deep is shitty," he said. "It's not easy to stay alive down there, including your habitat. To keep someone alive, you have to hold up a seventy-degree temperature gradient across the inside and outside, and a half an atmosphere of pressure. For the trawler, you've got to keep parasites from latching on. You've got to graft in extra capacitors to take off the electrical strain, polish all the valves daily because they're not evolved to work across a temperature gradient, and it goes on and on. And every few years, no matter what you do, something fails."

"Could you maybe take me down?" she asked. "To visit?"

"If we can find a habitat to visit that isn't my home. Pa also doesn't approve of poets or artists."

She laughed. "You've found the right crowd. We approve of poets and artists and fighter-boys with scarred hands. I want to see the depths."

He traced the hard line of her collarbone with his fingertip. "I'll show you any part of Venus you want."

She laughed again. "You can't show me the surface."

"I've seen it."

She rolled over him, putting her elbows on his chest so that her hair fell around them.

"What?"

"Pa brought me below all the clouds and hazes when I was fifteen. Thirty-first *rang*."

"*Ostie,*" she whispered. Her eyes narrowed. "You saw it from thirty-one kilometers? I can't even imagine."

If he'd known any of this interested Thérèse, he would have brought it up a lot sooner. Most of his time in the flotilla at sixty-fifth *rang*, he felt like a country hick, disconnected from people who'd gone to school together, seen each other regularly, gone to the same festivals and parties. He'd run with a drinking, pot-smoking crowd for a while until he'd worked up the courage to call himself a poet and meet other artists. They didn't exactly give him any better sense of belonging. He stopped taking it personally when he found out that no one felt like they belonged.

"What was it like?" she asked.

"A lot like the pictures. Hadean. Stygian. Blackened. Endless. Broken. Sterile. Nothing can survive beneath thirty-second *rang,* not even Venusian life. It's the bottom of a living ocean and the top of a dead one."

"But you've really seen her."

He'd never thought about it in those terms. He'd seen Venus, but he hadn't *seen* Venus in the momentous, experiential sense she meant. Could he see Venus again, in her way?

"I can show you other things," he said. "The transparent layers at *Les Plaines* and *Grande Allée*. Between the cloud decks, you feel like you're flying and you can see for kilometers, but all the world is sandwiched between two sheets of clouds. I can show you the storms where the thunder feels like it will break your bones and lightning feels like it will blind you."

He wanted her to say yes. He could show her. And he could imagine some habitat for them at an easier depth, like fifty-second *rang*, where the two of them could herd trawlers and grow food and make art. Artists could visit and stay and create, in the clouds. The image in his mind grew clearer.

She pouted. "I made such a big deal of knowing Venus,

and I hardly know it at all. I haven't really touched it."

"I would never have looked at it with my naked eyes if not for you," Émile said.

"It was a high," she said, squirming her naked body a little higher so that her nose was above his, and her voice quieted. "But I feel like I'll never be close enough, no matter what I do, like I'll never belong to Venus no matter how much I try. What did you feel?"

Her red, Venus-marked eye stared at him.

"I felt that you touched Venus," he said, "that you belonged, and that through you, I belonged too."

She softened, looked away shyly and then kissed him. The world narrowed in the same awe-inspiring, swept-up-on-the-winds feeling he'd had when he'd stared upon Venus's clouds with naked eyes. Everything was more alive. A constant high.

Then someone kicked him in the back.

"*Champion des épais!*" a woman's voice said behind him.

His heart sank.

Thérèse looked up, looking like it was her turn to punch someone. Émile held her hands.

"Who are you, *conne*?" Thérèse demanded.

Émile rolled her beside him, wrapping her tighter in the blanket.

"This is Marthe," he said. "My little sister."

"The *Causapscal-des-Vents* started venting today, *colon*," Marthe said. She was red-faced angry, still in her survival suit, *sans* helmet, hands on her hips in tight fists.

"What?" he asked, sitting up.

"You've only got a couple of jobs, *ostie d'con*," Marthe said. "Keep the habitat floating! Harvest the crops! You're drunk or high most of the time, and I had to fix what you ought to have noticed weeks ago!"

"*Ostie*, who invited the buzzkill?" someone asked, rolling deeper under their blanket.

Marthe surveyed the storage room with the hard judgment he hated.

"*Gang de caves!* Why don't you get to work?" she said, her voice echoing off the hard walls. "Thousands of people are working their asses off trying to keep us all alive and you're just getting high and diddling around with acid."

"Get started," Réjean said sarcastically. "We'll be along shortly."

A few people snickered. It didn't matter to Marthe. He could see it in her glare. Lazy people deserved only her contempt.

"Get your fucking ass to the *Causapscal*," she said to Émile, "and go bow to stern and find every other wear spot, abrasion and piece that needs fixing, primping, or replacing and fix them."

She glared at him for a few seconds, daring him to answer back. He felt his face going hot down to his chest, heat throbbing in his ears as everyone watched him.

"He's not your slave, bitch," someone said. "If there's that much work, why don't you do half?"

Marthe wasn't tall, but she had a head of steam going and she was looking at these people the way Pa would have. She flipped them the bird. No one else said anything.

Marthe spun, marched to the door and slammed it closed after herself.

Émile couldn't read Thérèse's expression. He didn't know her well enough. His face was hot and his body felt cold. Wordlessly, he stood, grabbed his survival suit and helmet, and padded out naked.

EIGHT

IT WAS TEN o'clock and Alexis and Jean-Eudes were asleep. The walls of the *Causapscal-des-Profondeurs* still glowed with some light from the clouds, but wouldn't for long. Venus rotated so slowly that each day lasted eighty-eight Earth days, but that wasn't how *les colonistes* measured things. Those who lived in the habitats above the clouds at sixty-fifth *rang* circled Venus every ninety-six hours. They had forty-eight hours of bright daylight and forty-eight hours of auroras and misty starscapes. The winds at forty-eighth *rang* circled Venus at a more stately pace, every eight days, half in somber light, half in a dark gloom.

Pascal liked sunsets and sunrises. He'd suited up and watched many of them from the gantry, sometimes with Pa, sometimes by himself. Venus had layers and secrets and ways of being that existed beyond what he could label, that only she understood. As her clouds reddened at sunset, that wavelength of light triggered hibernation responses and buoyancy surges in the photosynthesizers, like the ball-shaped blastulae, the onion-shaped rosettes, and even the aerial bacteria of the clouds. Only the trawlers carried their wakefulness into the dark, because they fed on the atmospheric static and storm lightning, indifferent to time.

Venus never tolerated true darkness, though. On still nights when lightning didn't backlight the clouds, wind eddies triggered directionless glows from bioluminescent aerial bacteria. The clouds became embers throbbing with fairy glows of pink, turquoise and pale lime. Some *coureurs* took them as Venus's welcome message to humanity; others saw in these spectral glows will-o'-the-wisps to draw the unwary.

George-Étienne followed Pascal's look, then scanned the arc of the ceiling appraisingly, assessing the texture of the light. "About four more hours," he said. Then he turned back to the three datapads they'd placed side-by-side on the table to show Pascal's analysis. Pascal had found two or three small channels blowing into the main cave they'd entered with the camera.

"A pressure *sink*," his father said wonderingly, "is incredibly valuable if we can find out how to use it."

"It doesn't belong to us," Pascal said.

"It sure as hell does!"

"It belongs to *la colonie*, Pa. That's the law."

"Most of the laws are bullshit," George-Étienne said. "The law creates an artificial supply problem to keep metal and mineral prices high."

"Those are the laws we've got."

"Which means our pressure sink belongs to the Bank that holds the colonial debt," George-Étienne said, stabbing a finger at the still image on the pad in front of Pascal.

"It's not like *la colonie* can exploit or even explore it, Pa."

"*Non.* We'll explore it," George-Étienne said. "And we're not sharing it with a corrupt government or the extortionists at the Bank!"

"The probe nearly didn't survive," Pascal said. "Working remotely is too slow for the time we're in radio range."

His father smiled meaningfully. "We don't take the probe."

Pascal looked at him incredulously. "The bathyscaphe? Does it still even work?"

"Of course it works!" George-Étienne said. "It just needed a bit of love. We can explore the cave from just outside. With the right equipment. And we can pull out that probe."

"We?"

"It'd be cramped, but we'll need both our brains on this one."

His father's grin was infectious. A tiny, fearful thrill built in Pascal. He might see the real surface of Venus.

"What about the *Causapscal-des-Profondeurs?*"

"It runs mostly by itself," George-Étienne said, "and can for a dozen hours. And Alexis is here."

"Pa..."

"Alexis is ten years old," George-Etienne said. "At

ten, Chloé, Émile and Marthe were already maintaining the habitat and even worked outside. At ten, I was programming tractors to plow hundreds of acres of fields."

Pascal didn't roll his eyes. If half the stories his father told of his childhood were true, it was a wonder they'd been born. Twelve hours felt like a lot, but the *Causapscal-des-Profondeurs* did just mostly float with the wind. And they could control some of its propulsion remotely if needed. The larger worry was losing some of their herd of trawlers.

"We'll need to fit the bathyscaphe with cables, and a remote set of manipulator arms, and a camera," his father said. "And we should make a frame we can put around the probe or whatever it is. As we pull it out, it's going to hit the walls as hard as our camera did. I don't want to risk it coming loose or getting too dented."

"The cable has to be really long, and the camera needs a stronger transmitter, or even a repeater," Pascal said, warming to the topic. "And real radio recording equipment to listen for that signal."

George-Étienne laughed and clapped Pascal on the shoulder.

NINE

THE NEXT DAY passed quickly. Pascal had a lot of thinking to do. He had a natural aptitude for math and machines. George-Étienne had gotten him all the electronic texts and virtual professors to study engineering. And not just any engineering. To survive in the clouds of Venus, they needed people as comfortable with electrical engineering as they were with aeronautical and aerospace engineering. And, counter-intuitively, the new Venusians even needed to understand the principles of marine engineering for anything they wanted to send all the way to the surface. He needed all of what he'd learned and more for what they were planning.

The day bled out again, and Jean-Eudes and Alexis had gone to bed. George-Étienne was too excited to sleep, and he'd gone back out to modify the bathyscaphe to Pascal's specifications.

Pascal was restless, though. He looked at *maman's* picture for a long time. She was beautiful, in the effortless way some people carried beauty. Her brown eyes looked out from the picture, one fractionally narrower than the other, under a clear forehead marred by a spattering of acid scars. Her lips were thin, smiling lopsidedly under a nose bent just so. She owned her gifts and flaws with the self-knowledge and self-acceptance that created beauty out of nothing. He wanted her confidence, the *sui generis* certainty of herself.

He padded slowly to his father's empty room. There were few limits in their home and nothing was secret about his father's room. Alexis romped in there as much as anywhere else in the habitat. Still, Pascal was grown up and felt strange about stepping in. But hanging on the curved wall in old discolored plastic was a dress: *maman's*. George-Étienne had preserved as much as he could of his wife from recycling and reuse, for himself and for his children.

Jeanne-Manse's dress was both historical artifact and proof of life. Jeanne-Manse had lived. *Maman* had lived. Pascal brushed his fingertips across the crinkly plastic. The tightly-woven hemp dress was dyed green, with pink- and blue-petaled flowers painted on the material with her own hands. This was her wedding dress—vivid, fertile, alive. Venus didn't have a lot of green, so it was a special color, something many *colonistes* felt they themselves had brought to Venus. Human eyes expected to see green everywhere because they came from a green world. The absence of green from their new world made it fit strangely.

Pascal carefully lifted the plastic. The vivid colors had

faded, but still balmed the primitive, unthinking parts of his brain. His fingers found the tiny, inevitable melt-marks and then the buttons, which came undone only stiffly. The old fabric protested, but soon he held the dress before him. It didn't smell of *maman*. It smelled faintly of sulfur, like everything else in the habitat.

He hugged it tightly, and then, without thinking it through, put it over his head and slipped his arms into the sleeves. His heart beat faster and his fingers started to shake, faltering at the buttons. He took deep breaths and did one button slowly, then another. At sixteen, he wasn't much bigger than *maman* had been fully grown. The fabric creaked, but didn't break.

His father's room had a sink and head with a mirror over it. He approached hesitantly. He brushed his hair with his fingers, imitating what he could of the way *maman's* hair had hung. Then, shyly, he looked in the mirror. He flushed deep red from neck to hairline.

The dress looked good. A tiny elation grew in his chest, spreading through his body. His green eyes stared from beneath thin eyebrows. He had his mother's slightly-bent nose, her light brown hair, her thin lips. He tried smiling like her, with one side of her mouth more than the other, and found it not so hard. He belonged.

Loud laughing burst in the doorway and Pascal's heart stopped.

Jean-Eudes stood in his underwear, eyes wide, laughing louder than Pascal had ever heard him laugh, big, joyful, surprised, ridiculous guffaws, so hard that he collapsed against the door frame, sitting, holding his shaking belly.

Pascal's mouth was dust. He was so embarrassed he thought he was going to pass out.

"Jean-Eudes..." he said helplessly.

But Jean-Eudes rolled sideways onto the floor, still laughing.

Pascal wanted to be angry. At being interrupted. At being seen. He felt like he should be angry. But his shoulders slumped. Jean-Eudes's laugh was infectious. It *was* a little funny. Despite himself, Pascal began to laugh, softly at first, with a strange relief, and then harder until he was sitting beside his brother, laughing until the laughing came in after-fits, like the smaller flashes of lightning that followed a storm.

Jean-Eudes panted like he'd been running. "You wore *maman*'s dress," he said, trying to make his laughing fit come back.

"*Oui.*"

"That was so funny." Jean-Eudes giggled a bit more.

Pascal rose and looked at himself once more in the mirror. He looked like his mother, but it wasn't Jeanne-Manse staring back. Someone new and real and beautiful stared back at him.

"That was so funny," Jean-Eudes said.

Pascal unbuttoned the dress.

"Put it on for *papa*!" Jean-Eudes said, sitting up. "Put it on for Alexis!"

Pascal shook his head and then gently lifted the dress over his head.

"I might want to keep this a secret," he said.

"Awww," Jean-Eudes said. "*Papa* won't be mad! He'll

laugh. It's soooo funny." He laid back onto the floor and his voice trailed off wistfully. "So funny."

"Do you remember *maman* much?" Pascal asked.

"I remember everything," Jean-Eudes insisted, as he always did.

"You're lucky," Pascal said, putting the dress back on its hanger. "I was too little to remember much about her. I've got the pictures. And this dress."

His brother came close. "I can tell you everything about her," Jean-Eudes said. "She liked finger-painting! She made spicy food. We wrestled. She danced with me and Émile and Chloé. I can teach you." His face saddened. "I miss *maman*."

Pascal pulled the plastic back over the dress. "Me too."

"Is that why you put on *maman*'s dress?" Jean-Eudes asked. "I can tell you everything about her, okay?"

"*Oui.*"

Jean-Eudes hugged Pascal impulsively. His older brother still outweighed him and sometimes gave breath-crushing hugs out of sheer enthusiasm.

"*Papa's* gonna laugh about the dress," Jean-Eudes said.

"Yes, he will," Pascal said with a sinking feeling.

TEN

MARTHE TOOK A seat and rolled herself a cigarette while she waited for the other members of *l'Assemblée* to arrive. She took a long drag and blew smoke upward, trying to dissipate the tightness between her shoulders. Émile hadn't changed. Pa hadn't changed. Only she had changed. She'd become Pa, and now she was yelling at Émile.

Her exhaled smoke curled and dispersed into a gray fog. Smoke wasn't like the clouds. Cloud droplets were too big to stay suspended. Smoke particles were too small to see and seemed to defy gravity, like the particulate haze below forty-eighth *rang* where she'd spent a lot of her childhood. The end of her cigarette glowed bright red again and she inhaled deeply before exhaling slowly. Pa's rages, and Émile's, and hers, all defied gravity too. It took them time to come down.

Nine years ago, she'd been fifteen years old, crowded into the new *Causapscal-des-Profondeurs* with Pa, Émile,

Chloé, Mathurin, baby Alexis, Jean-Eudes and Pascal, impatiently learning all the things she was clumsy at, like patching suits. Alexis had been sleeping, rocked very deliberately by Jean-Eudes, who watched Marthe getting frustrated with *maman's* survival suit. *Maman* had died about the time Alexis came into the world, and Marthe had just grown big enough to fit into *maman's* suit—if she could cut and seal a few parts.

"*Crisse!*" she said as the tiny blade slipped through the material and sliced her finger.

"Are you okay?" Jean-Eudes whispered.

She sucked her finger, then watched the blood well.

"Are you okay?" Jean-Eudes asked again.

"Quiet," she said impatiently.

She kicked the suit away and squeezed her damn finger. Jean-Eudes held his anxious silence.

Chloé and Mathurin were out doing range work on the family's trawlers. Pascal sat across the habitat in the center of cable-shavings as he whittled a set of wings for a survival-suited figure he'd made.

"Have you been in here?" Pa's voice suddenly carried across the room.

"What?" Émile asked evasively.

Pa waved a small box in front of him. "You took my pot and tobacco?"

"I didn't take it," Émile said plaintively.

"Who did? Chloé? Mathurin? Marthe?"

Émile cast her a nervous glance. *Ciboire*. Not again. What an idiot.

"I told you not to touch my goddamn stuff," Pa said.

"You're not old enough and you haven't earned it."

"I'm sixteen! Chloé was pregnant at sixteen! I work hard!"

"Chloé has always worked hard," Pa said, stepping closer to him. Émile was already a lot taller than Pa and heavily muscled, but he shrank back. "You just about lost us a trawler last night."

"No, I didn't!"

"The transmitter was off on one-one-five. If the wind had taken it a kilometer farther, it would have blown away with thirty kilos of metal and electronics."

"*Bébittes!*" Émile said.

Marthe snorted. Émile cast her a quick, angry look.

"*Ciarge!*" Pa said. "It wasn't *bébittes!* I fixed it. You know how? I turned the transmitter on! I told you a hundred times! Double-check. That's how we stay alive!"

"Shh!" Jean-Eudes whispered to them, gesturing frantically. "You'll wake the baby!"

"You never forgot anything?" Émile said.

"I double-check everything. That's why you're still alive!"

The fight didn't stop, so Alexis did wake up in the end, upsetting Jean-Eudes. Émile was never smart enough to admit he was wrong.

She didn't have to put up with their fighting much longer. The following year Marthe came to the upper atmosphere.

She had now been running everything up here for the D'Aquillon family for the last eight years, trading one set of fights for another. Her father couldn't even stand to look at *la présidente,* and had nothing but contempt for most of the people living in the upper flotillas, indebted to the Bank of Pallas. She missed her family, but she liked running the *Causapscal-des-Vents.* Most of the deal-cutting on the black market came naturally to her, and she enjoyed the politics.

The decision of *la colonie* to separate from Québec had come a bit suddenly for everyone, including the *séparatistes.* A scorned Québec had been happy to cut its losses on the expensive *colonie.* The Bank of Pallas, smelling a banana republic, swooped in to offer loans that the new Venusians would never be able to repay.

The entire population of Venus was only about four thousand, split between a dozen big habitats, about two hundred mid-sized ones, and many dozens of small ones that could only house a few people each. All the constructed habitats floated in the upper atmosphere, between the altitudes of sixty-two to sixty-six kilometers, above most of the clouds and most of the acid. The idealistic *colonistes* on their quickly-rusting habitats had created *l'Assemblée coloniale,* a mixture of legislature and executive, composed of all the heads of families or heads of habitats.

A few hundred people lived as her father did, in the clouds and haze between forty-two and fifty-five kilometers above the surface. They survived in bio-engineered trawlers among herds of naturally-occurring trawlers from which they harvested electricity, high-energy chemicals, organics, water, and even some metal-rich volcanic ash. They were the *coureurs des vents,* the wind runners, a clever play on words from the *coureurs des bois,* the forest runners of Québec's early New France history.

Every habitat could send a delegate to the *l'Assemblée,* but this was impractical for many, so they gave their votes to other delegates. Marthe was the political delegate for her family's habitat, the *Causapscal-des-Vents,* and she held a dozen proxy votes for other deep-dwelling *coureur* families. Not that votes helped much. The delegates from the big habitats tended to carry the day; voting against them created bad blood that played out in *la colonie's* black market of food, medicine and parts. Her father's history and his criticism of the *l'Assemblée* never helped her. And her own occasionally-voiced view that *la colonie* was being incompetently managed didn't help either.

Some gray-haired delegates filed in, chatting amiably, or sending each other messages on pads. She got a few hellos, some genuine, some less so. Many delegates within radio range signed in to join the session remotely. On the other side of the hall, Angéline Gaschel entered, followed by aides. Nearby delegates immediately pressed her with requests and questions.

Gaschel had systematized the politics of *la colonie.* As a representative of one of the biggest habitats, she had resources to barter, largesse to share, and choke-points to close, and she got on very well with the Bank of Pallas.

Marthe took the last draw on her cigarette and crushed it out.

Eight years ago, Gaschel had negotiated new loan terms with the Bank of Pallas for the purchase of ten new, expensive habitats like the *Baie-Comeau*. With this demonstration of her ability to deliver the goods to *la colonie*, the vote to change the title of the chief executive from *maire* to *présidente* had passed with an overwhelming majority. *La colonie* liked having a *présidente*. It made them feel like a real nation in a way that a mayoralty never had.

The D'Aquillons knew Gaschel more viscerally. Twenty-eight years ago, Gaschel, as *la colonie's* Chief Medical Officer, had been the authority deciding the distribution of scarce medical resources. She'd been the one to tell Pa and *maman* to abort Jean-Eudes, and when faced with refusal, had decided that *la colonie* would not offer Jean-Eudes any medical resources, ever. Gaschel was the reason Marthe had been born in the clouds instead of above them.

Marthe didn't mind that she'd been raised as a *coureur*. And she didn't mind that other families facing similar choices had decided differently. But she never forgot Gaschel's choices, either. Like cigarette smoke and atmospheric hazes, some rages took a long time to come down.

Gaschel called the session to order. *L'Assemblée* voted through a series of tedious measures to correct by-laws, clarify legislation, and name new habitats to be delivered next year. Marthe voted electronically on each of these with her dozen votes, watching the *oui/non* votes shift in real time on a screen as delegates changed their minds or saw which way the winds blew. Marthe dispensed with her votes quickly on these, waiting for the economic statements.

This might be the time when *l'Assemblée* finally said no to more loans from the Bank of Pallas. Gaschel rose as graphs of debt repayment schedules flashed on screens and on their datapads. The projections showed a balanced budget in six years, with final repayment of *la colonie's* loans in 2285, thirty years from now. The numbers looked far too optimistic, and Marthe dug into the footnotes, losing track of Gaschel's argument for a few minutes.

"...propose that we accept another loan from the Bank of Pallas," the *présidente* said, "to bridge us over this last period of capital growth while we finish retooling our economy. The loan is conditional upon *la colonie* implementing austerity measures, tied to education and health, so that our full resources can be turned to industrial development, something we've never had a chance to commit to. We have political independence, but we have yet to achieve economic sovereignty. This is a map to turn Venus from a dependent state into an independent one."

The applause ranged from polite to enthusiastic. Marthe offered reserved claps. Too many missing pieces. A sizable payment to the Bank was due shortly. And the maintenance costs were too optimistic.

"Austerity doesn't mean not investing in what is important," Gaschel continued. "It means being frugal with what we have, setting reasonable standards of living, and cooperation, as any new *colonie* and state must do during its youth. We need to increase industrial capacity in the production of indigenous Venusian building materials, taken from the atmosphere and harvested from the Venusian flora, to supplement scarce metals. In the meantime, we seek the authority of *l'Assemblée* to negotiate a new loan from the Bank of Pallas for the purchase of automated mining equipment for the exploitation of asteroid 3554 Amun, so that Venus will have a stable, affordable long-term source of metals."

The applause became loud, although a few like Marthe looked dubious. 3554 Amun, as well as other iron-nickel asteroids, had been discussed a number of times. They couldn't afford it. Despite international treaties, made a hundred years before Québécois *colonistes* had reached the clouds of Venus, the Bank of Pallas, the Bank of Ceres and other Banks had bootstrapped their own mining operations to set up mining bases on most of the inner system asteroids. The asteroids that hadn't been claimed by the Banks were not worth mining. Thousands of asteroids were already being mined robotically, and often refined, so that basic, ready-to-use materials were sitting there, waiting for customers, sometimes for decades. Venus certainly couldn't afford one of those. Other Bank asteroids sat ready with dormant mining equipment. The time from activation to delivery might be ten to twenty years, even if Venus could afford it. 3554 Amun was even more expensive: an in-between asteroid, with some refined metals, ready for shipping and delivery within two to three years, and more as mining machinery worked. It would put them further into debt with the Bank.

"To buy into 3554 Amun, we need one more loan, one that we project paying off by 2285," Gaschel said. "The asteroid and its metals will make our children independent. And working together, being frugal, will free them from debt."

More applause. Marthe tried to dig into Gaschel's numbers more quickly. At times like this, she wished Venus could afford neural implants. The numbers didn't add up. Gaschel was either assuming nothing would ever break down in the entire future of *la colonie* or that everything would work on the first try. *La colonie* had plenty of experience with first tries and break-downs.

"We have some immediate needs for parts and metals," Gaschel continued, "and we would be wise to consolidate some of our resources and expand using ones that don't require us to import new metals. Notably, I propose that *l'Assemblée* acquire two or more new trawler habitats, to increase living space and industrial capacity. We would respectfully request that the Hudon family provide one at a very reasonable price, and another closer to cost— perhaps even as a gift during this time of everyone working hard to get us into prosperity."

Marthe felt her eyebrows rise. Across the hall, Marie-Pier Hudon, her long blond hair streaked with strands of white, flushed. Marie-Pier was about forty, reasonable and hard-working, with a small family. She grew bioengineered trawler habitats and traded them for all sorts of supplies, food, water and medicine. The problem was, that all happened in black-market trading with the families of *coureurs*. As far as the law went, private property was still a vague concept in a communally-rationed *colonie*. It would be hard to say no or to negotiate a good deal, now that Gaschel had stirred up *l'Assemblée*. The *présidente* rarely put Marthe on any committee or study of consequence, but Marthe would try to get on the committee squeezing two new trawlers out of Hudon.

'*This doesn't sound above board,*' she direct-messaged Hudon.

Hudon didn't make a sign that she'd read it.

"And we have to start being more aggressive about recovering salvageable materials from aging dirigible habitats," Gaschel said. "This is a necessary cost-saving measure. For now, it will only be necessary for *l'Assemblée* to nationalize one habitat, the *Causapscal-des-Vents*."

Marthe bolted straight and almost dropped her pad.

"The *Causapscal-des-Vents* has only two inhabitants, produces food for only four, and requires replacement parts regularly. Yet it contains forty-one tons of iron, nickel, aluminum, copper, solar cells, plastics, and many other materials that can be used to maintain several dozen larger, more efficient habitats. The two members of the D'Aquillon family will be offered new accommodations within *la colonie*."

Marthe's heartbeat thumped in her throat. Gaschel had landed some powerful rhetorical blows, all slightly twisted. The food production of the *Causapscal-des-Vents* was low because they lacked materials to insulate the outer envelope on four big segments. And Émile had not been carrying his weight.

The replacement parts demand was true, in part because the administration had for so long starved the D'Aquillon family of parts. What they got on the black market wasn't enough. And it was true that only two people lived in a habitat that could probably fit three times as many. The rest of the D'Aquillon family lived in the lower cloud decks as a form of protest.

There was a larger danger in this than even losing her home. Without the *Causapscal-des-Vents*, it was unlikely that Marthe would remain a delegate to *l'Assemblée*. The *Causapscal-des-Profondeurs* had no delegate, also out of her father's protest against the government. If Marthe was moved to another habitat, that habitat would already have its delegate. She could then no longer hold the votes of other families.

Gaschel had figured out how to crush Marthe and the D'Aquillons politically.

ELEVEN

GEORGE-ÉTIENNE DID NOT comment on the dress the next day when Jean-Eudes carped about it, dropping Alexis into a fit of astonished giggles. All he said was, "You should have seen the silly things Marthe did," which steered the conversation into other directions. Marthe was the wisest of them, but most of George-Étienne's "stupid children" parables featured young Marthe, to everyone's delight. But George-Étienne wasn't in much of a story-telling mood. Shortly, he clapped the breakfast finished to get Alexis moving.

Pascal and Jean-Eudes cleaned up the galley. Then Jean-Eudes brought out Pascal's repaired survival suit, while Pascal reviewed the mission profile he'd developed. Jean-Eudes was a small wonder with patches and seals. He was deliberate about checking the strength and impermeability of every stitch and seam. He'd already checked Pascal's suit twice after patching the tears on the thighs, but insisted on doing it once more. Pascal said he didn't have to.

THE HOUSE OF STYX

"Keep you safe," Jean-Eudes grumbled.

Pascal leaned his head closer. "What's wrong, buddy?" he said in a low voice.

Jean-Eudes was pouting.

"Come on," Pascal said.

Jean-Eudes cast a look at George-Étienne, slightly red-faced, as he drilled his grandson on habitat navigation procedures again. Alexis was looking flustered.

"Are you mad that we're going on a mission?" Pascal asked gently.

"When am I going to be in charge?" Jean-Eudes said, not so quietly. "I'm twenty-seven. Alexis is only ten. I'm *his* uncle."

"I know, Jean-Eudes," Pascal said. "He's not exactly in charge. You have a smart nephew, and he's good at math. This is a big test for him. Keeping a whole habitat and herd in place against the wind is a big job. He's going to have to measure wind angles, calculate course corrections and fix any equipment that breaks."

"I can fix the valves," Jean-Eudes said in a low voice. "And the computer says where to go. I could steer if the computer tells me where."

Pascal put his hand on Jean-Eudes's arm.

"Did you feel this way when I started running things?"

"*Non,*" Jean-Eudes said. "You're my brother."

"Baby brother."

"He's my *nephew!* He's not *Chloé.* He's not *Émile.* He's not *you.* I don't want *him* bossing me around. I'm his *uncle.*"

"Are you proud of how smart he is?"

"*Oui*," Jean-Eudes said sullenly.

"You helped raise him, Jean-Eudes. You changed his diapers. You washed him. You played with him. You taught him how to check valves and fix suits and clean up. But he's growing up."

Jean-Eudes scratched at his beard and brooded at the patched and repatched survival suit on the table.

"How do you think Pa felt before he put Marthe in charge of the *Causapscal-des-Vents,* to represent us all in *l'Assemblée?*" Pascal asked.

Jean-Eudes stared blankly.

"It was probably hard for him to realize that his daughter was better than him at dealing with people," Pascal said. "Pa just makes people angry."

Jean-Eudes gave a tiny snort and smiled.

"But Pa is happy she's up there," Pascal said. "And he's proud of her. And he's proud of what he did to make her who she is."

"I don't want to be bossed around by my nephew."

"Look at them," Pascal said.

Jean-Eudes followed his look, to where the talk between Alexis and his grandfather had become heated again. Alexis's eyes were downcast and his face pinkened. George-Étienne's words didn't carry, but their tone was insistent.

"Alexis is probably going to be pretty frazzled the first time it's all on him," Pascal said. "He's going to be worried and nervous and scared of making a mistake. It's a tough job."

Jean-Eudes grunted.

"Knowing his uncle believes in him will make it less scary."

Jean-Eudes sighed loudly. Twice. "You're a good brother."

"So are you."

Their father strode over. Still on the other side of the habitat, Alexis was rereading charts on his pad.

"You ready?" George-Étienne said.

"*Oui*, Pa," Pascal said.

"Suit up, then."

As Pascal suited up, Jean-Eudes walked over to hug a protesting Alexis.

TWELVE

THE INSIDE OF the bathyscaphe was claustrophobic, a tight cylinder of acid-resistant steel so thick that even a hundred atmospheres of pressure wouldn't crush it. A single long couch lay inside, with the head facing a single piece of fishbowl-shaped diamond, built over years by hard-working nano-machinery in the depths of the atmosphere, where the heat and pressure helped.

The back of the little craft was devoted to rows of small Stirling engines. They couldn't do more than keep the inside of the bathyscaphe around the boiling point of water, so their survival suits, rated to a hundred and fifty degrees for short periods of time, had to keep them alive. Short wings on the sides of the bathyscaphe made it a small aircraft with a propeller to the aft, like a torpedo. George-Étienne pointed the nose down and they began a stomach-lurching drop.

They were surrounded by most of the metal wealth their family owned, their last resort if they ever needed to trade away metal for medicine, but also their secret tool for going deep below the clouds to recover things on the surface. It was the most exciting, frightening thing Pascal had ever seen or done. They plummeted through the last fifteen kilometers of the sub-cloud haze, streams of vapor whipping past the front glass in the steadily heating wind. The temperature outside had risen from ninety to two hundred degrees Celsius by the time they finally broke through to the clear air below thirty kilometers. Gloomy red light showed gray mountains, old lava channels, and wrinkled volcanic plateaus beneath them.

It was difficult to hold the *Causapscal-des-Profondeurs* in one place against fast winds in the lower decks, so George-Étienne had decided to turn their fall speed into flight speed and race ahead of the habitat. They would reach Diana Chasma an hour before the habitat did. Alexis would slow the *Causapscal-des-Profondeurs* as soon as they were away.

"You sure they'll be okay?" Pascal asked.

"They're both good boys. I left you alone for the first time at that age."

George-Étienne pulled up on the stick. Ailerons moved and the bathyscaphe switched from free fall to a gliding descent, racing along at three hundred kilometers an hour. They shook in the straps as they crossed columns of hot volcanic gas.

The basaltic highlands of Atla Regio passed serenely beneath them, silvery frosts accenting the black and brown of the highest peaks. Small dark clouds of vaporized lead sulfide shone near the surface. George-Étienne spoiled the airflow over the wings, dropping their speed and altitude as Diana Chasma came into view. He pointed at something too small to see.

"There," he said. Pascal couldn't see the cave any better than his father, but they knew it was there.

George-Étienne extended the spoilers further. The bathyscaphe shuddered and the wind moaned louder. They banked, slipping to lose altitude and speed. The surface of Venus rose to meet them, until he could look horizontally ahead to see the highland peaks of the wrinkled gray coronae. A frisson of unease crept along Pascal's spine. He'd never been close to any solid surface, and had never had mountains and rock around him. Even from five thousand meters above the bed of Diana Chasma, a weird claustrophobia crept upon him. His breath came quickly.

"*Ça va?*" George-Étienne asked.

"*Oui,*" Pascal said breathlessly. "Is this what it felt like on Earth?"

His father grunted a low laugh. "Not at all."

Their turns tightened and the movement of the vast stone edifice beneath gave him vertigo. The clouds weren't like this. They moved constantly, shifting from one vague shape to another, but in a way, every cloud was the same cloud. This Venus was disorientingly hard and sharp-edged. The world darkened as the mountains, and finally the walls of Diana Chasma itself, occluded horizon-light.

It took some time to notice the quiet outside the bathyscaphe as it slowed. The wind became so soft that the creaking complaints of joints and seams sounded louder and louder. The centimeter of diamond they peered through made tiny crinkling noises. The centimeter-thick steel of the craft resounded as it heated up, magnified as if their craft were a drum head.

At two hundred meters above the surface, they'd stopped flying. The propeller churned behind them as if they rode a tiny submarine through an ocean. The gigantic cliff face rose before them. Slightly west of them was the mouth of the cave. Their cave.

If they cut their forward speed, they would slowly sink. George-Étienne brought the bathyscaphe nearer and nearer, and they began to notice the cross-current dragging them towards the cliff face and the cave mouth. He then turned the bathyscaphe into the current and throttled forward full speed on the propeller. Their ground speed dropped to zero and they sank, holding above a single point on the ground.

Pascal was already bringing the first of their new modifications to bear. Out of a forward tool hatch, a cable shot out on the end of a micro-torpedo. The torpedo dragged the cable around a big, immovable boulder and then looped back to the bathyscaphe. The manipulator arms they'd installed under the craft recovered the micro-torpedo and attached the cable. Pascal's readings said that the two ends of the cable were firmly attached to the stern and the loop had been secured under the boulder.

"We're good, Pa," Pascal said. At least, he hoped they were. His father cut the throttle and the current carried the bathyscaphe along, turning it, until the cables jerked taut.

"*Sapristi,*" George-Étienne cursed in wonder. "That wasn't gentle, was it?"

The cave mouth stared them in the face. Silt blew past them on the wind, moving as it would on an ocean current. The mouth yawned large, twenty meters across in a canted oval.

They bobbed gently as the current washed over the creaking bathyscaphe back to front. Beyond the little window was Venus herself, naked in her gray and black basaltic glory, close enough to touch. She was beautiful and deadly, life-giving and ugly, aspects she reconciled without apparent difficulty. To each side, the bottom of Diana Chasma extended, a hundred kilometers wide, with sharp edges that rose dizzyingly beyond the angle of their diamond porthole. In the distance, on the highlands, a smudgy column of smoke arched as it rose, tilting westward. His father slapped his arm.

"Let's get moving," George-Étienne said. "It's already a hundred and ten degrees in here. The insulation isn't as good as I thought."

George-Étienne used the manipulator arms to assemble a pre-fabricated cage made of the stiff, acid- and heat-resistant cable that Pascal had managed to save from the trawler they'd lost. It was built to fit the triangular probe in their photos. A tripod of powered manipulator arms would ride with it, controlled remotely from the bathyscaphe. And they used a trick Pascal had thought up. A small plate, no larger than a hand, was affixed to the end of the cage. That little patch, in the current of supercritical carbon dioxide, would drag like a drogue chute, pulling the cage all the way down to the triangular probe and keeping it oriented.

Pascal unspooled a second cable, tied to a good high-temperature, multi-spectrum camera with a high-temperature memory wafer. In the same mounting was a radio receiver and recorder to follow the comms emissions they'd found. Between them were mounted two powerful lights, a main and a spare. They would see and record everything this time around.

It took fifteen minutes in the gentle bucking of the current to assemble and ready their payloads. While his father unspooled the cable, letting the current drag the cage in, Pascal played out the cable carrying the camera, keeping it always five meters behind. The harsh white light showed walls of erosion-polished basalt.

About twenty meters in, they found the first of the cave branch points that they'd inferred from the grainy, dark pictures of the first trip. This second current fed the main one, widening it.

"We'll call that Branch B," Pascal said.

First the cage, then the camera shuddered around the first bend, knocking against the walls of the eddy. All they could do was feed out the cables faster and hope nothing important had been damaged. They found the source of the turbulence and eddying, too.

"We'll call that Branch C," Pascal said.

"And there's your Branch D," George-Étienne said.

Pascal stopped unspooling his cable, leaving the camera in one spot in the cave as he turned its lens and light ninety degrees, and then in a complete circle, to survey the edges of the cave. The diameter of what he was going to call the Main Branch was about forty meters across now. The current flowed at about twenty-five kilometers per hour here.

It was an enormous river of super-critical carbon dioxide. Pascal briefly wondered where all of it was going, and even why it didn't noticeably deplete Venus's atmosphere. But that was absurd, a failure of human reason to fully absorb the size of Venus. She was nearly the size of the Earth, and her "ocean" covered the entire surface. This cave was big to him because his entire home would fit in here without touching the walls, but this was just a small river. And Venus blasted thousands of tons of carbon dioxide into the atmosphere from volcanoes and hot vents every day. Her immense ocean of an atmosphere could never run dry, and she was too big ever to understand.

They paid out more cable. The cage danced ahead in the camera view, shaking worse as it approached the wall, where the current pulled ferociously. The smoothness of the eroded surface prevented the carbon fiber cage from being abraded or smashed, and it went out of sight.

Pascal unspooled ten meters of cable, fast enough for the camera to be swept around the projection without even touching it, jerking to a halt in the eddy beside the cage. Stray currents tugged at them, but for the most part, the cage and camera hung in the becalmed carbon dioxide. Just beneath lay the dusted outline of one of their mysteries.

"Your show, Pa," Pascal said. "How fast can you get that scrap packed?"

"Watch me," he said. "I've been retrieving stuff in storm winds since before you were born."

"Ha!" Pascal said. "Old man."

George-Étienne got the manipulator arms to spider-walk themselves out of the bottom of the cage and searched along the wall of the big, dark eddy until he found a fissure that had not been sanded smooth by erosion. It stuck one manipulator there and reeled the whole cage down into even calmer parts of the eddy, near the silt-covered triangle. A sense of impending discovery filled Pascal. His father's breath rasped in his earpiece, around moments of breathless concentration.

The manipulators ended in three flat fingers, which could also be configured like a propeller. George-Étienne turned one of them on and the twirling finger blades pushed the hyper-thickened atmosphere of Venus like water. The new current stirred pebbles and sand and silt, clouding the eddy, obscuring their view. Gradually, though, the silt rose high enough to be drawn away by the main stream. Pascal pointed the light and camera down, zooming the view.

George-Étienne whistled in appreciation.

The clearing silt revealed a flat brown-gray isosceles triangle, four meters long and about three wide. Raised lumps studded the base segment, like the stomata on trawlers and rosettes, with a few located symmetrically on its forward edges. A large glassy lens capped its front apex.

"What the hell did the Russians or Americans send down here?" George-Étienne said.

114

"It's not a wing," Pascal said. "There's no curvature to make an airfoil. It's just flat. That doesn't make sense if they wanted it to explore Venus's atmosphere."

The bathyscaphe creaked again. "We'll think at home," George-Étienne said.

The manipulator arms opened the cage. In the meantime, Pascal turned to the radio receiver and looked quickly at the data.

"The radio source is still deeper in the cave system," Pascal said. "Something is being transmitted up, a repeating burst every point-two-two-three seconds, like a code."

George-Étienne grunted, directing one manipulator arm to gently lift the nose side of the triangular probe. More silt clouded into the eddy. He moved the edge of the cage nearer.

"Maybe it's a distress signal, or a hail looking for a confirmation," George-Étienne said.

"A distress signal wouldn't be coded."

"Depends how secret this probe was," George-Étienne said. "This thing was obviously damaged. Maybe its flight recorder or even its CPU broke and it was carried deeper by the current."

Pascal was sweating now. One hundred and thirty degrees in the bathyscaphe. The old Stirling engines were cooling poorly now, and his suit couldn't keep him at normal body temperature for long. He drank from the plastic straw in his helmet.

"The power of this signal is in the megawatt range," Pascal said, "even after reflecting off who knows how many twists and turns in here. Why would they overpower a transmitter that much? What's its power source? This probe had been collecting dust for years, maybe decades."

George-Étienne stopped slipping the edge of the cage under the probe. He had a look in his eye.

"In the early days, a lot of long-mission probes were powered by plutonium and uranium," he said. "Do you know how valuable that is?"

Pascal felt himself sharing his father's grin. This was big. An antique probe sent by one of the early space-faring powers. A coded radio signal. Radioactives they could salvage for power. It was like a lost treasure.

"As soon as you finish caging that thing and you don't need the light, I'll start sending the camera deeper," Pascal said. "I've got another four hundred meters of cable. If it's plutonium or uranium, then maybe a power plant from a bigger facility or probe is down there."

George-Étienne slipped the cage base under the triangular probe and gently lowered the top of the cage. The manipulator arms closed the clasps and latches.

"I'm going to start pulling it up," George-Étienne said. "Go ahead with the camera."

"One problem," Pascal said. "I think we've run out of time."

It was a hundred and forty degrees inside the bathyscaphe.

"Duvieusart didn't spend a lot of time on the surface, did she?"

"Forty minutes," George-Étienne said. "I've made some improvements, but forty minutes."

"We might not even have time to bring up the probe," Pascal said.

"I'm spooling as fast as I can."

"Pa, how risky do you want to play this?"

"What do you have in mind?"

Pascal did some quick calculations, showed them to his father and explained his plan to stop the rising temperature for maybe fifteen minutes.

"*Viarge!*" George-Étienne swore. "It'll hold?"

"It's a big boulder."

His father looked at the massive piece of basaltic stone perhaps four meters wide and tall that Pascal indicated ahead of them. Then he considered the numbers. His face was awash in sweat. Probably forty degrees in his suit already. Venus was slowly cooking them.

"You don't refuse to eat when you sit at Venus's table," George-Étienne said finally.

Pascal unwound the cable at the stern of the bathyscaphe, the one binding them to their boulder. The bathyscaphe approached the yawning cave mouth in slow jerks. Twenty meters. Ten.

Neither of them needed to mention that if the cables didn't hold, they'd crash somewhere on the inside of the cave.

The diamond porthole darkened as the edge of the cave yawned past them. The bathyscaphe shuddered in the current. No big changes outside yet. Pascal turned on the exterior lamp, lighting the black surfaces. They advanced another twenty meters and came to the end of their cables.

The temperature had dropped here. The current was

moving so fast that the pressure dropped too, which cooled the carbon dioxide flowing past them. The little shell around them vibrated gently, but held. The temperature inside the bathyscaphe was one hundred and forty-one degrees, but had stopped rising.

"*Calvaire,*" his father swore. "Never thought I'd be under the surface of Venus."

"Dropping the camera further in. We've probably got another ten minutes."

Pascal unspooled more cable for the camera and lamp. The image bobbed and spun as it was recaptured by the main current. The pressure and temperature around the camera kept dropping. Three hundred degrees. Two hundred and fifty. Then the rushing current started behaving like a gas again.

"Five minutes," George-Étienne said.

The view from the camera bumped and rocked and occasionally spun. At one turbulent point, the manipulator arms nearly lost their grip and dangled from one set of fingers. The other arms didn't manage to relatch until George-Étienne pulled the whole bundle through the turbulence of one of the turns. The cage and probe smashed hard.

Pascal's camera twirled in the churn, down another turn in the cave. Not all the rock was the same. Basalt, soft with heat, eroded more quickly than a second type of rock Pascal was seeing, but not recognizing. Magma had probably covered this whole area, including some older rocks. The decades and centuries of current had carved where it could cut most easily. Who knew how many bends there were?

The spinning camera emerged in the next eddy, trapped there until he paid out more cable. He didn't have much left. The pressure had dropped a lot around the camera, and the temperature too, but the current flowed at over two hundred kilometers per hour. The twisted cable took a while to slowly unspin itself and one of the bumps had jarred the camera angle ninety degrees to the side, so the unwinding produced a lighthouse view of this new space.

"What's that?" George-Étienne asked.

Pascal had been staring hard at his screen, trying to figure out just that question despite the spin. The cave walls were dark and distant, but a sixth of each arc showed a region of salt and pepper silt. Under the silt were triangular shapes, eight or ten or even twelve. The eddy was quite large and the camera angle wasn't very good. The silt was not as deep here, and some of the triangular shapes were only lightly dusted. The camera slowly ended its rotation and stared at the shapes. The closest ones looked exactly like the one George-Étienne was hauling up. They were all the same size. Some had cracked outer casings and even jagged holes.

"Why did they send so many?" Pascal asked. "Who sent them down here?"

"One probe is something," George-Étienne said, "a fluke. But what country sends down ten, all in one cave, unless they're after something?"

"We only see the wrecks of their tries," Pascal said. "They must have gotten what they wanted."

His father hrrumphed, and kept reeling in the cage.

"If they hadn't got what they wanted, they'd still be here. Any country could have claimed Venus before Québec did. The Americans, the Banks, China, and Egypt got to every good place before we got a say."

"The radio signal is farther on," Pascal said.

George-Étienne pointed meaningfully at the internal temperature of the bathyscaphe. One hundred and forty-two degrees. And Pascal eyed the time. Alexis would be able to hold the *Causapscal-des-Profondeurs* in place for a while, but no one could keep it there forever. If he and Pa stayed too long down here, making their rendezvous with the *Causapscal-des-Profondeurs* would get complicated, since neither Alexis or Jean-Eudes knew enough to take out a little flyer safely. And Pascal and George-Étienne couldn't ask for help without people finding out they had the bathyscaphe.

The weird radio distress call still bleeped, more powerful deeper in the cave.

"In a few minutes, the salvage will be up," George-Étienne said. "How long will it take to pull us out?"

"Not too long," Pascal said, paying out more cable on the camera.

The view skimmed over the graveyard of wrecked probes. The lamp showed the outlines of fifteen. Twenty.

"What were they looking for?" Pascal whispered.

He gave slack to the camera. The main current swept it along. The cave ahead widened into dark. The pressure dropped to only a few atmospheres, and the temperature dropped into the liquid water range. Then the pressure and temperature readings stopped working. They had dropped below the range of what the camera could measure. The radio signal was stronger.

"Got it!" George-Étienne said.

The probe was only eight meters ahead of the bathyscaphe.

"We have to go, Pascal," he said.

"Pa."

The feed from the camera showed stars. Thousands and thousands of stars, in the cold black of space.

THIRTEEN

ÉMILE WAS CLINGING to the outside of the *Causapscal-des-Vents* when he spotted the approaching flyer. There was no way to know who it was, but he knew the way his sister flew, and it wasn't Marthe. The movements were less elegant and economical. They never received visitors in this shitty old habitat.

It would take the flyer another ten minutes to get here, and it was a pain in the ass to get up the side of the envelope of their dirigible, so he worked faster, rubbing in an oil that contained a base to neutralize any acid that managed to get this high in the atmosphere. The job also allowed him to check for leaks or wearing in the fabric of the plastic. It was mind-numbing in the worst way.

The whole envelope of the dirigible was multilayered. The first, inner layer was gray-black carbon weave, containing oxygen and nitrogen at pressures far lower than the ambient pressure of this altitude. This inner envelope was covered with solar cells to generate electricity to run engines, life support, and small-scale industry. The solar cells rarely got damaged, so he rarely had to check them.

A second layer of transparent plastic fiber surrounded the dirigible. It was pressurized to half an atmosphere and filled with greenhouse trays, crops, algae tanks and photosynthetic bioreactors. The gardens on *Causapscal-des-Vents* had overgrown and he'd better get in there soon to harvest, replant, and refertilize. *La colonie* had people, but not a lot of metal for automation, so a lot of the crops grew on elbow grease. In the case of *Causapscal-des-Vents,* his hands and Marthe's. Whatever they grew was more than enough to feed him and Marthe, but because of his father's stand against the government, all the real food for his father, Pascal, Alexis, and Jean-Eudes was dropped down by drone from here.

The flyer was definitely headed for him. He'd covered about an eighth of the outer surface of the envelope. Whatever. He could finish it tomorrow. He climbed back up the ropes and ladders to the work area and flat landing platform on the roof. He arrived just as his visitor flared their gauzy wings and alighted unsteadily on two feet.

He reached a steadying hand and Thérèse hugged him. His heart leapt.

He helped remove her wings and tied them down. Then they cycled through the airlock and down the ladder through the envelope to the tight living area in the gondola. They removed their helmets. Her blood-filled eye had mostly cleared to pink, and the once-black eye bruising was almost unnoticeable. She slinked closer and kissed him.

"Have you been doing enough work to keep your sister off your back?" she asked.

"I haven't been high for days," he said. "Got a joint?"

She hefted a pack on her waist, smiling.

"Is your sister around?"

"Of course not. She's off with *l'Assemblée*."

"What does *l'Assemblée* even do? Talk, talk, talk. Peel me out of this thing?"

He kissed her and began unsealing her suit. She returned the favor, then pulled a small bag of weed out of her pack and rolled them a joint. He pulled her to his tiny living space and hooked his hammock into eyelets on the walls. She lit the joint and took a long draw. He watched her longingly. Then it was his turn.

He filled his lungs. It was like inhaling skunky food. Officially, drugs were verboten on Venus, but with so many distant habitats floating in a great armada, the government couldn't enforce much. Despite this, no one had gotten the recipe right. The sulfuric taste of Venus made its way into most of what they grew. The taste could be hidden with good cooking, but no such luck for weed. A light buzz crept over him. He exhaled, satisfied. Thérèse was laying carbon stencils on the hammock, beside a personal first aid kit and a small glass bottle with a tiny brush in the cap.

"What's this?"

"Aciding," she said. "It's a new stencil I want. Do you want the same one?"

She touched his forearm, where raised red welts erupted

like a bare mountain range from the dark hair.

He and Chloé and their father had been trying to tie a new gantry under the then-new habitat, what was now the *Causapscal-des-Profondeurs*. There hadn't even been an accident, just a pinhole piercing of the suit's arm from wear and tear. He'd felt the burning and thought it had been a small one. An hour later, when the pain got worse and they all went in, they found a blistered redness the size of his palm. It was stupid, not paying attention, something a fifteen-year old would do. Thérèse loved to run her fingers along his scars. After he'd shucked his self-consciousness about them, he loved letting her.

Thérèse mostly lacked those marks of Venus's touch. Her leanness bore only a few acid burns, and parallel lines of blade scars, old and fresh, along the inside of her forearm. But deliberate aciding scars coiled up her arms and legs. Artists had applied acids to her body with stencils in the shapes of vines and leaves, nature that didn't exist here. Thérèse wore these as an evocation to Venus, the kind of thinking behind sympathetic magic.

The aciding artists timed the neutralizing step to get the right burn depth. And they could texture the burns by applying faint, thin lines or hatching, or by weakening the acid with additives. The only thing they could not control was the color of the scars. The vines coiling up her arms and legs assumed the same color as every other scar he'd seen: red. Venus only inked in blood.

"Something's changing," she said, running her hands up the earthly vines. "These were meant for bringing life from another world to here. It's time for me to worship this world. Looking on Venus with unfiltered eyes was the first step. We need to take what is hers, take her beauties, and honor her with those totems on our bodies." She ran her hands over her naked hips meaningfully, although he wasn't sure of her meaning.

He picked up one of the stencils. It was flexible carbon, about twenty centimeters long, with a cut-out of a trawler's silhouette. The garlic bulb shape, bloated and distended, with a few lines left in to give it stylized depth, connected in a straight, narrow line to the outline of a bob. He knew the image well. He'd grown up in one.

She put the joint between his lips and he sucked deeply.

"I'm thinking of putting that one right here," she said, indicating her shoulder, running her fingertips down to her elbow.

"Have you ever seen a trawler?" he asked, taking the joint from his lips.

She shook her head. He handed the joint back to her.

"Trawlers are enough to make you believe in a god, or goddess," he said. "They're so elegant. They make so much sense that it's hard to believe that nature made them. The intention and belonging behind them are palpable."

She butted out the joint and put the remains carefully back in her pouch.

"They float in complete silence," he said. "Forty-eight kilometers of dark, poisonous, baking atmosphere beneath them. Thirty kilometers of bright, poisonous, cooling atmosphere above them. Nothing around them but clouds and haze. They bob up and down, triggering the release of static between clouds, feeding themselves on the electricity of embryonic storms."

"I want to see one," Thérèse said.

"But they're not always quiet," he continued with a longing pang in him. "When a storm is coming, some winds can set their cables vibrating, resonating like a guitar string, and a trawler will play a single, solid note for twenty minutes as it comes upon the storm. And every length of cable is different and so they all have slightly different notes, like a choir."

"They sing to Venus?" she said wonderingly. "Worshipping her?"

"Down there, the pressure is two or even three atmospheres, and it's all heavier carbon dioxide, and hotter, so the notes travel quick and far, a lot farther and louder than they would up here."

"Why haven't you shown me your poetry?"

There was nothing mocking in her eyes. And yet he held back, shy about what he had inside, what he tried to create.

"*C'est d'la marde.*"

"You have the soul of a poet."

"Venus doesn't need poets, I guess," he said. "It needs leak-fixers."

"Venus needs poets more," Thérèse said. "It needs painters, even if the only canvases we have are ourselves."

He picked at the other stencils. One was a sphere, what they'd always called a blastula. More beautiful yet was the stencil outlining a rosette, which was like a small trawler, but with a stumpy hanging tail and a frond rising from its peak like the leaf from an apple stem.

"Do you want to acid me?" she asked.

"I'm not that kind of artist," he said. "I wouldn't want to make a mistake."

"You won't make a mistake," she said. "Then I'll acid you."

He considered the stencil of the trawler. He'd been born in a trawler.

"Do me first," he said, handing her the stencil.

"We're doing this for Venus," she said, "so you have to tell me something true about yourself."

He shrugged to cover sudden unease. He wasn't as interesting as Thérèse. He wasn't as interesting as most of her crowd.

"*Voyons*," she said, wiping his arm with a damp cloth. "You're not a good boy. Did you get into a lot of trouble when you were little?"

"I was never little."

She laughed. "Tell me a bit."

She laid the stencil against his arm. Spatter-burns marred his right upper arm, but his left from shoulder to elbow was pristine. She stood beside him and her nose came up to his triceps. Her fingers were cool and appreciative, but her breath was warm. Her nearness felt like being surrounded in a different kind of cloud, one that had nothing to do with buzz from the joint.

"I don't know. When I was eighteen, and Marthe was already up here, Pa found out I'd traded stuff away for some hash."

Thérèse giggled. "What's the problem?"

"We didn't have much. I hid my own food and later

on traded it away with a *coureur* at fiftieth *rang* we intercepted every few months. His daughter had gotten hash from up here. Pa was angry I'd traded away my food when Pascal and Chloé and Alexis were hungry. I didn't think they were hungry. He was angry I was doing harder drugs, but he was apoplectic that I'd managed to organize it all without him knowing. I'd sent secret messages using a radio relay on one of our trawler herd. He's a paranoid bastard and was probably worried about the government knowing where we were."

"I bet he liked how sneaky you were," she said. "You could earn his love through drug drops."

"I don't want anything from him. Certainly not his love," Émile said derisively.

Thérèse pressed the stencil against him and held the little paintbrush.

"You don't care if it hurts?" she said.

He shook his head.

"Sometimes only hurting can make us feel alive," she said.

She pressed her lips to the skin not covered by the stencil on his shoulder. That skin would soon be gone, and what came after wouldn't feel anything. He didn't know if he was numb. But he understood what she meant. Sometimes pain was like a light by which to see the soul. He didn't fit anywhere, neither in the clouds, nor in the sun, not in his family, not outside of it, not sober, not high, not drunk. Except around Thérèse. They'd only met a couple of months ago, and now she was painting Venus on him.

The tiny brush tickled his skin, leaving cold and stinging heat in its wake. The sting continued to his nostrils. Sulfur and sulfur dioxide, and the smell of oxidizing flesh. He didn't flinch. He'd felt worse. She dipped the brush in the bottle, dabbed it off, and dragged it further down the stencil. His skin reddened. This was just before blistering. Leaving it on would char the skin black as the acid dissolved its way into the fascia and muscle.

From the first aid kit, Thérèse pulled out a burn pad soaked in sodium bicarbonate paste and an ice pack. She carefully dabbed at the burn, neutralizing the acid, and pressed the ice pack against dying skin. She took away the stencil and continued to dab with the base cloth and cool with the ice pack.

"It looks so good," she said.

It stung. He knew acid burns. It would sting for hours. He raised his arm to see. The line of the trawler's cable was straight, following the topography of his muscle. The mark was angry red right now, but would calm. She laid a dressing along the new mark, and then gently wound a bandage around his arm. She stroked the arm lovingly.

"You're worshipping her now. You already have, in your own way," she said, touching the ropey old scars on his hands and then kissing them, "but now it's more true, more meaningful."

He pulled her close and kissed her. "You're worshipping her too."

"I don't feel it."

He touched the still-bruised skin under her eyes.

"You gave Venus her due," he said. "You created worshippers out of nothing. She must love you."

She shook her head, stroking the low scars on his right arm. "To get souls, to belong to the Earth, our ancestors paid in pain and blood, over hundreds of millennia. We're the ancestors here, nearly the first people. We have to learn Venus's price to make this a real home."

"Everyone is giving something."

"Lots of people give nothing," she said. "They worry about seals and crops, but don't think of belonging."

Thérèse stroked the bandage on his arm. They kissed slowly, for a long time.

"Acid me now," she said.

FOURTEEN

THEY DIDN'T SPEAK more than a few words on the way up. Pascal had wound back the cable carrying the camera as fast as he could, but the temperature in the bathyscaphe edged to one hundred and forty-eight. There was only so much the Stirling engines and the insulation on the craft could do. Pascal began retracting the other cable that held them to the boulder sixty meters to stern before the camera was even up, pulling the bathyscaphe out of the cave and into the heavy wind. He pulled them back and back and back, while the cage and their salvage spun ahead of them on its line.

One hundred and fifty degrees inside the bathyscaphe.

One hundred and fifty-one.

This was beyond the tolerances of their survival suits.

Still the camera wheeled back, bumped against rocky projections, tossing in the turbulences. Much of the data had been sent to them by radio, but so much more, and of so much higher quality, remained in the memory on the camera and on the radio receiver.

Pascal and his father stared ahead, stunned. Or hallucinating.

They'd seen stars.

That was Venus's secret.

Beneath her atmospheric finery lay a wrinkled gray and black surface no one could love. But buried beneath *that* ugliness was the true Venus, a starscape, a kind of beauty Pascal had never seen. He didn't understand her, but he'd seen her inner beauty.

One hundred and fifty-two degrees. Two degrees past the tolerances of the suits. Inside their suits was probably forty-five degrees, but he didn't want to look. Looking wouldn't help.

"We have to go," George-Étienne said a bit numbly. Sweat ran in his faceplate and his eyelids drooped.

One hundred and fifty-three. The camera and radio receiver had a hundred meters of cable between themselves and the surface.

"I know," Pascal said.

George-Étienne punched the emergency system and four oxygen tanks outside the bathyscaphe emptied their contents into four silvery bags, which inflated like limp raisins. The ninety-three atmospheres of pressure compressed the bags so that they did not look inflated, but the difference in weight between the heavier carbon dioxide and the lighter oxygen, when added to the natural buoyancy of the bathyscaphe, lifted them until they dangled over the boulder that had been anchoring them, bobbing in the slow, heavy wind.

Forty meters of cable separated the camera from them.

One hundred and fifty-four degrees in the bathyscaphe.

Pascal throttled forward the propellers and released one of the ends of their anchoring rope. They lifted, the flow dragging them towards the cave mouth, but then the buoyancy and propellers boosted them out of the main current and high above the ground. The bathyscaphe shuddered and jerked, with the cage dangling beneath them and the camera rope tugging and tugging.

Suddenly, Pascal whooped.

The view from the camera showed a straight view down at the receding ground. The cable hadn't broken! There was a fogginess in the image—the lens might have cracked or even shattered—but they'd retrieved its data!

"We got it, Pa!"

George-Étienne's tired breathing gave a laugh. And then they quieted. Their water packs were empty and if they passed out from heat exhaustion they might not wake back up. Mountain peaks receded beneath them. The bathyscaphe creaked and protested the pressure changes, but the Stirling engines soon got the temperature inside down to one hundred and thirty-eight. Pascal blinked the sweat out of his eyes and was happy. Indescribably happy.

At forty kilometers above the surface, deep in the sub-cloud haze, Pascal and George-Étienne unsealed the bathyscaphe and got outside to tie their haul more securely and cover it against sulfuric acid rain, which would come as they rose higher.

The bathyscaphe propellers sped them toward the *Causapscal-des-Profondeurs*, which they found only a few kilometers off from where it was supposed to be. It was a remarkable bit of cloud sailing by Alexis for his first time, and his relief was palpable in the radio, as was Jean-Eudes's elation.

They moored beneath the *Causapscal*, recovered the oxygen from the inflated bags, and used pulleys to raise the cage up onto the gantry. There was no way to bring the four-meter-long probe into the *Causapscal-des-Profondeurs*. No airlock was big enough.

It took another hour for them to secure the bathyscaphe properly beneath the youngest and most buoyant of their trawler herd about two kilometers away. Pascal and George-Étienne had been in their suits for twelve hours before they finally covered the probe and resigned themselves to examining it tomorrow.

Jean-Eudes and Alexis waited with restless-footed impatience at the line in the floor as Pascal and his father did their second acid wipe-down and unsuited. The boys chattered excitedly about their adventure as soon as Pascal cracked the seal on his helmet. It sounded like an adventure, like Alexis had actually had to navigate more than they'd expected, but Pascal couldn't do more than smile appreciatively. He felt like he'd been scooped clean with a big spoon, experienced something that had hollowed him out.

Pascal smelled food. Alexis had even made supper. It didn't smell wonderful, but most suppers didn't. He stripped off his suit, threw one arm around Jean-Eudes and another around Alexis.

"Water. Then tell me over supper," he said.

He and George-Étienne listened to the story of a rogue wind that had blown the habitat off course and how he and Jean-Eudes had needed to change altitude to find a new wind direction and then pick a whole new course to get to their rendezvous point. George-Étienne, effusive and proud, eventually sent Alexis and Jean-Eudes to bed.

"Going to take us days to find all the herd back," George-Étienne said when son and grandson were in their rooms.

"More for you to teach Alexis," Pascal said.

George-Étienne smiled thoughtfully and nodded.

Pascal slumped into the bench and slid his pad into the middle of the table, followed by the camera and radio receiver that they'd used on the surface. Both were dented and sand-scoured. The lens of the camera was a web of fractured diamond, some pieces of which had fallen right out. But the tiny CPUs functioned, displaying their data on his pad. George-Étienne sat closer.

Pascal slow-played the darkness at the end of the tunnel. The first section wasn't completely dark. Faint light flashed, almost like the bioluminescence they found in nightside clouds, but he couldn't be sure. The camera had been moving fast and the light from the lamp might just have been reflecting from something.

Then came the darkness where they saw no walls at all. And then, stars. No sun nearby. Just stars. Both of them looked for a long time, rotating the pad, but neither could match the starfield to constellations in their encyclopedias. They didn't have any software to help identify them, but it didn't matter. It didn't make any sense. There shouldn't have been stars at all.

"What's the chance that we just found some kind of sophisticated visual projection?" Pascal asked. "Some sort of message, with information stored in a holographic image?"

George-Étienne looked at him dubiously. "Why would someone put a picture of stars under the surface of Venus?"

"Or the radio signal. It was so strong, and it's coded with something," Pascal said. "It could carry more than enough information to plant a virus or computer program in the operating system of the camera, and access the antenna feed directly, substituting in this star map."

"Why?"

"The star map is important," Pascal guessed. "Maybe it's a location, or maybe there's more information buried in the signal."

"So important that they buried it in one of the most inaccessible places in the solar system," George-Étienne said doubtfully.

"There's no way stars can be underground, Pa!"

He felt the elusive epiphany slipping away, pushed aside by doubts. He'd found something beautiful and mysterious under Venus, but it didn't mean that what he'd seen was true.

"Occam's razor, Pascal," George-Étienne said. "We have film footage of stars," he continued, tapping one finger. "We have multiple measurements of some kind of pressure sink below the surface of Venus, where there should be nothing but increasing pressure." He tapped the second finger. "We even followed the flow down and observed the drop in temperature and pressure, which match what we'd see in the neck of a balloon with escaping air. And we have a strong, coded radio signal," he said, tapping a third finger. "We don't know why such a strong signal should be coming from *within* the crust of Venus, but it's a lot easier to swallow if it's out in space, like a satellite, a habitat or a ship."

"That's not Occam's razor!" Pascal said. "Space can't be inside a planet. Some human group—maybe covert and secretive, but human—put this tech down there or lost it down there. They sent probes after it, following its distress signal. It's trying to send up some of its information, maybe as a program or a hologram, something where the information is buried graphically. But whoever sent all those probes down has stopped. Maybe they couldn't afford to send any more. Maybe they got what they wanted. Or maybe they're dead, and their secrets died with them. There was a lot of dust on all these probes."

George-Étienne's expression turned guarded, uncharacteristically cautious, as if reluctant to say something out loud that wanted to be out. He even looked away a bit shyly for a moment, making Pascal feel awkward.

"We could see the stars below the surface of Venus if there was a wormhole," George-Étienne said quietly.

"Nobody's ever made a wormhole," Pascal said with a sourceless frustration. "Nobody knows how to make a wormhole. They may be impossible."

His father shrugged. "We don't know if anyone knows how to make a wormhole. If a Bank learned how, do you think they would publicize it? Or would they build some first and try to get across the solar system with stock news before radio signals could make it? Insider trading. They could make millions. This was an early success. Or failure."

"Why would anyone leave a wormhole *here*?" Pascal asked.

"Maybe they built it in orbit, closer to the sun, and it was a success, but they hadn't figured out how to manipulate it and it fell?" George-Étienne mused. "They tried to recover it with the probes, but couldn't. Maybe they even buried it, but in the last decade the debris around it fell through, and I found the storm it causes."

"Occam's razor is supposed to make things simple, Pa."

"Mine's more simple than supposing lost holographic data."

Pascal brushed back his hair with both hands, unable to fully hold all of this in, feeling as if an epiphany danced at the edges of his awareness. He pulled his hands away when his palms met twelve hours of stubble. He shivered. His father eyed him sympathetically and then stared off into the distance for a while.

"Pascal, it may not matter what's down there. We may never know. But depending on what we find inside the probe we brought up, we might have it made. The D'Aquillons could be totally independent and live well, trading off the metal and parts in the probes. You and I could salvage all of them. It's like a gold mine."

Pascal nodded.

"Get some sleep," his father said. "Tomorrow we'll see what the probe's got in it."

George-Étienne went to his hammock, but Pascal didn't

follow suit. He drank more water, trying to rehydrate himself while he watched the playback of the camera entering the cave system, all the way to the end, to the stars themselves. Or to the pictures of the stars.

If he was right and the radio signal had planted a program or virus or data directly into the camera software, he should be able to find it. He linked the camera to his pad and started looking through the processor logs in the camera. Everything the temperature-hardened chip had done in the last day was in the log. He went through all the lines of operations. Very soon, he was able to skip vast sections of operations he recognized. He got to others that gave him a bit of pause until he saw where they fit. He went through the entire list this way until he got to the bottom.

No virus or strange program ran on the camera operating system or anywhere in the memory. But he wasn't as sanguine as his father about the possibility of an astronomical phenomena under a planetary crust. He didn't know how to figure out if an image was holographic, and the encyclopedia and teaching texts on the *Causapscaldes-Vents* probably didn't have anything that advanced. He sat quietly, listening to the radio playback for a while. It was pretty boring: every point two-two-three seconds, a tight radio burst. The same message over and over. A sped-up distress call, maybe? But from whom? What message was encrypted in the bursts, and how would they ever decode it? Pascal was training to be an engineer, not a cryptographer.

On a hunch, he opened the encyclopedia on his pad

and read an article twice before turning things over in his head. The camera had seen stars, but no sun. Granted, it might have been pointed the wrong way, but seeing no sun was a soft data point. The radio signal was a hard data point. High wattage. Very strong. An identical signal repeated over and over.

Then he realized what it was.

FIFTEEN

PASCAL RAN HIS hand over the ceramic. The triangular wing was three hundred and seventy centimeters from the lens at its nose to the row of little jet nozzles along its trailing edge. From tip to tip, its trailing edge was two and a half meters across, but it was only forty centimeters from dorsal to ventral surfaces, and these were flat, not aerodynamic. He sprayed compressed carbon dioxide to clean out pockmarks or dents that had collected silt. Some of the divots looked like fresh burns, artifacts of sulfuric acid exposure on the way up to the habitat. Other marks looked more like the scouring of wind erosion. Others were completely foreign to him: tiny burn marks or chipped hollows all along the leading edge of the wings that were absent on the trailing edges. What had it flown through?

"This is some pretty advanced material science," he said. "It survived atmospheric entry, the descent from one atmosphere of pressure to ninety, and all the chemical attacks. And somehow it maneuvered through the cave, *in that wind,* without getting smashed to pieces. We have a lot to learn about whatever this is. Maybe it's a good building material for *la colonie.*"

But it was more than building materials. Pascal had gone to George-Étienne with his discovery before breakfast.

"It's not a message, Pa," he'd said. "It's a pulsar."

George-Étienne had paused with one sock on and one sock off. Maybe all his arguing for a wormhole last night had been just words. Or maybe it was too strange. Pascal sat beside him on the hammock and showed the encyclopedia entry on neutron stars that emitted radio waves and x-rays. There weren't any nearby; the nearest one was almost 200 light-years away, and had a different period. This signal had to be coming from far away.

Faced with support for his wormhole theory, Pa had grown pale, like they'd found a magical doorway in a wardrobe instead of a powerful, tightly-repeating radio signal.

"It'll make your children rich for sure," George-Étienne had said, "but I've got to think about giving my children food right now. I want to see what's inside the probe. That at least we can sell."

And so they came out this morning to examine their treasure.

"Do you still have the Geiger counter?" Pascal asked.

"Somewhere, I guess."

Wrapped in thick clouds, solar radiation wasn't a problem for the *coureurs,* but at flotilla altitude, they had to be careful of solar radiation. Pa found their counter in one of the sealed tool boxes on the gantry. He dusted it with compressed carbon dioxide and handed it to Pascal. When he switched on the counter, it started registering little ticks. At the access port, the ticking shot up.

"Ha!" George-Étienne said. "Fissionables! Jackpot!"

It was a fair bit of radiation, enough that whatever was inside would eventually make them sick. The difference in ticking from inside to outside hinted that the ceramic was a strong radiation shield.

"We're going to need put the fissionables under the storage trawler so we don't get sick," Pascal said.

He would look up radiation in his textbooks later. With a bit of work, he put a rod-mounted mirror through the narrow port and into the low, hollow interior. He shone his light in and stared in stunned silence.

"What is it?" George-Étienne demanded.

Pascal handed him the light and held the mirror for him. His father shone the light on the mirror and moved his head around.

"*Sapristi,*" he swore. "Do you see gold?"

"I think I saw gold, copper, what could be platinum, silver or iridium," Pascal said.

Fine lines of bright metals had been laid into the ceramic in curving, overlapping lines.

"What is it?"

"It's like a circuit board, one big computer chip," Pascal said.

"It doesn't look anything like a circuit board. It looks like art."

Pascal took a deep breath, tried to collect his thoughts. The vastness of what he was thinking was like a piece of food too big to swallow.

"We make circuit boards with straight lines and angles so we don't get mixed up," Pascal said. "But there's nothing to say that solid state circuits can't be built with curving lines of conductors. It's the connections that matter. The makers of this thing deposited layers of ceramic, then layers of wiring with different materials, and then more non-conducting ceramic, then more circuit pathways. It might be one big chip."

"*Calvaire*," George-Étienne swore, peering closer. "Who the hell built like this fifty or eighty years ago? It doesn't look American. Or Russian. Maybe it's Chinese?"

"I don't think any human built this, Pa."

His father started, looked at him strangely. "What?"

"I may have grown up sheltered on Venus, but I know that no one on Earth or the colonies could build this thing. This isn't the way anyone on Earth builds circuits. There's a different kind of thinking behind this. It's all one piece. I think it's sintered, which means it was probably made in space, someplace like the moon or an asteroid."

"Little green men making probes?"

"Pa, I don't think this thing ever saw the upper cloud decks. It isn't shaped like an airfoil to generate lift by moving through the air." Pascal breathed. "I think it came from the other side. It came through that... wormhole... and found itself in an environment it wasn't built for—the Venusian atmosphere."

Pascal had to lean in to see his father's expression through the two faceplates. It was pensive. Calculating. His father had been poor all his life. That was part of why he'd come to Venus; on Earth, he had nothing to lose. And here, circumstance had forced him to choose between descending into subsistence in the lower cloud decks, or changing the kind of person he was. He'd worked all of Pascal's life, all of Jean-Eudes's life, looking for the lucky strike that might give his family some ease, to not be scrambling for their next meal. He'd lost a wife, a daughter and a son-in-law.

The wormhole—if it was a wormhole—was part of that lucky strike. This probe was part of that lucky strike. If this ceramic triangular thing was alien rather than human, its value was incalculable. And all those parts together made a strike too big for one man. Pascal had never seen a dog or a car, but his Pa's story of the chasing dog who catches the car was not lost on him. What could they do that wouldn't mean losing their one and only stroke of luck?

"Maybe it is, maybe it isn't," George-Étienne said. "Doesn't change our choices."

"What do you mean?"

"I mean, we cut this thing up and sell the pieces, including the radioactives."

"Pa! You can't scrap it! This is world-historical."

"Maybe so. I don't fault your idealism, *cher,* but I'll tell you one thing: the government is weak. They'll sell out to anyone with two dollars to wave around. And the Bank of Pallas has a branch manager up in our clouds who's looking to build her career. If word of this gets out, do you really believe that any real scientists will come down here, excavating and studying for the benefit of all humanity, much less compensating the D'Aquillons? Gaschel will sell access to any bidder, at under market cost, for a kickback no doubt, and our independent Venus suddenly becomes an armed protectorate or territory of the Americans or the Chinese or even the Bank of Pallas."

"Pa, we don't know what this is," Pascal said. "It looks like one big circuit. If we cut it up, it won't work anymore. This discovery might be one of the most important ones in human history!"

"It doesn't work now, Pascal," his father said, putting his hand on Pascal's shoulder. "Look, family comes first. Always. In forty years, do we really want Alexis to be riding around in trawlers like I did, or do we give him something better? I hope to hell that in ten years, you're doing something better than me. But we're never going to get any better, *la colonie* isn't going to get any better, without some sort of boost. This might be it. We'll never get confused or lost if we stick to what's important, Pascal. Family first."

Pascal huffed a sigh in his helmet, briefly fogging the area in front of his mouth. George-Étienne understood *la colonie* and its politics and where the D'Aquillons fit. "Family first," Pascal repeated.

"Take it apart. Photograph everything you can. Be a real scientist. And then we'll trade the pieces. If this is what we think it is, I've got buyers for this now. Tomorrow. After, we'll go back for more of these. And then we'll figure out what to do."

SIXTEEN

FRANÇOIS-XAVIER LABOURIÈRE'S OFFICE wasn't far from the hall where *l'Assemblée* met. It looked out onto the greenhouse layer outside the *Baie-Comeau,* so it seemed to be bursting with light and green. Marthe had been here once or twice with other delegates during negotiations. This time she was alone. So was Labourière. She wasn't in the habit of seeing the *présidente*'s Chief-of-Staff, so it seemed the *présidente* was annoyed enough to have her right hand deal with Marthe. She slid the door shut and sat in one of the plastic chairs in front of his small desk.

"Water?" he asked, unscrewing a dark jar over two cups.

She shrugged. He poured. Labourière was about fifty, lean, careful with his words and gestures, except for smoothing back his receding hair when he was nervous. He wasn't smoothing now. He smiled and toasted silently. She took her cup and drank. The sulfur was so faint that the water tasted almost pure.

"We probably should have given you more notice of the decision around the *Causapscal-des-Vents*," he said. "The math is a bit inescapable and we only got the final projections the day before."

"I would like to see those projections," Marthe said. "I'm surprised Gaschel didn't present them."

"I'll send them your way." He leaned back and drank again. "I hope some of the shock is wearing off."

"Pa doesn't know. We're not in comms range yet. So there's still shock to come."

"Let us know how we can help you through this process."

"I'm not going through a process," she said. "I'm protecting my home from somebody's bad decision."

"I've heard some of the noise you've been making. Some of it is understandable. Some of it is needlessly making people nervous without changing anything. In the end the *Causapscal-des-Vents* served over twenty-nine years, nine more than it was rated for, and now has to be used to keep newer habitats running."

"The life expectancies of habitats are guesses by engineers in Montréal. How long did they give the *Matapédia* before it sank? *Pointe-à-la-Croix* is three years older than the *Causapscal* and it's not being disassembled."

"*Pointe-à-la-Croix* has six people on it and is running a hydroponics surplus," Labourière said calmly.

"Our productivity is down because you've been starving us for parts. And although there are two of us, my brother Pascal just turned sixteen and he's likely to come up from forty-eighth. And Émile is getting serious with some girl and is probably getting married," she lied.

"If your little brother wants to come up, we'll find him a good bunk. And if your older brother gets married, we'll find him a couples' spot. When those things happen. Right now we'll make sure you and Émile get good places to stay."

Labourière was calm. Marthe was good at showing calm when her blood was up. She wanted to hit something—him, the *présidente*. But family came first, and that almost always meant sacrifices. They sacrificed for Jean-Eudes. She could sacrifice by pretending to be calm. She sipped her water.

"I've seen the bunk wait lists," Marthe said. "Me and Émile would get separated and one of us would get stuck on *Pointe Penouille*."

"You won't end up on *Penouille*."

"String-pulling?"

Labourière reached for the water jar, thought better of it, then smoothed back his straight, graying hair.

"You're valuable, Marthe. I could probably get you and Émile spots on the *Forillon*."

Her, valuable? She almost laughed in his face.

Forillon was supposed to be a habitat that had aged well, a second-generation dirigible that housed about twenty people. It wasn't part of the main flotilla; it floated seven thousand kilometers westward along the top of the clouds. Cushy spot.

"It's not a sure thing that the *Causapscal-des-Vents* is to be scrapped. I think I'll wait and see about bunking."

"I can put you and your brother into the *Forillon* now," he said. "But the wait list is the wait list. I can't keep the spots open while you try to delay things."

"As soon as we come into comms range of the *Causapscal-des-Profondeurs,* I'll tell Pa. I'll probably have to go down for a few days to see how he wants to handle this."

"I'd rather deal with you than your father."

She did laugh this time. Her father *would* be harder to deal with, but she could get them a better deal than he could. The thought didn't make her feel particularly loyal.

"I bet. He'll let me know what he thinks and I'll come back and tell you. In the meantime, I'm waiting for the committee schedule to open up. If you want things to go faster, get me scheduled at a committee meeting."

They argued a bit, but in the end, he couldn't deny her a chance to have this discussed in committee. She finished her water and left.

SEVENTEEN

THEY DIDN'T HAVE any lead to shield them from radiation, but the probe's shell was heavy. Pascal did a slow examination of the probe, mapping out the radiation. The count outside the probe was almost uniformly negligible. The ceramic must have been heavily doped with lead. Only through the pitted, glassy lens at the front did radiation shine out. Pascal began cutting through the probe with a circular saw. Dust flew off the gantry and rained darkly in the wind behind him.

He took pictures as he went, trying to map as much as he could of the lines of conducting metal, but his heart sank when he'd cut out a plate thirty centimeters on a side. Looking edge-on, the hull of the probe was filled to bursting with complex patterns of fine metal wiring. There was no way to map this without cutting it into thousands of sections and photographing each one. He hadn't the tools for that. Whatever it was, whether the toy of an alien intelligence or the epitome of human genius, he was destroying it for scrap. Very, very expensive scrap. He and his father would need to save one or two of these probes for proper scientific study later.

His father joined him by the time he'd sawed out seven such sections.

"They're filled with metals!" George-Étienne said.

"Gonna be hard to get the metal to market," Pascal said, sawing the section over the source of radiation, about two thirds of the way to the stern of the probe.

"We already grab volcanic dust from the clouds," George-Étienne said. "People expect us to be selling dust. If we grind these up, people will think we've had a lucky few months."

Pascal checked the depth of his cut, brushed at it, then resumed.

"There's nothing like this anywhere on Venus, Pa," Pascal said. "If they look at the dust they'll see it hasn't been acid-worn."

George-Étienne cracked two pieces together experimentally. They didn't break.

"So we grind them up and separate the metal from the ceramic dust."

He whacked the pieces together again with no more success.

"It's going to take mechanical grinding, Pa."

The eighth plate came loose. Pascal hung up the saw and passed the Geiger counter around the cut. It clicked a lot. He removed the plate, revealing a fist-sized ceramic block, pitted in a pattern he didn't recognize. The detector's clicking came so fast that it was a continuous buzz. Pascal blocked the source with the plate again and the counts diminished.

"What is it?" George-Étienne said wonderingly.

"I checked the detector's manual," Pascal said. "A counter like this can't distinguish between different materials, but uranium is common enough in space, and plutonium is a decay product. Could be cobalt or thorium too."

"That'd run a power plant for years," George-Étienne said. "Or power the engine of a thermal fission rocket. We wouldn't need the Bank for shipping. Can you imagine not needing the Bank?"

"We've got to do something safe with it until we can get some lead."

Pascal started making a box out of the plates he'd cut, fastening the sides with carbon filament. He pried the fist-sized piece of radioactive material out and used tongs to put it in his makeshift box before covering it. The radiation counter ticked slowly outside the box. George-Étienne helped by wrapping a bit of thin trawler skin around the box to hold it together better.

"The bathyscaphe is thick enough that if we put this in there, the radiation shouldn't make us sick," Pascal said.

"I'll fly it over."

They used the Geiger counter to look for more stray radioactive particles, scooped them into the box and sealed it. George-Étienne shouldered into a wing-pack and plunged into the clouds with their prize.

EIGHTEEN

BEING PRÉSIDENTE DE *l'Assemblée coloniale* was usually a thankless job. Doctor Angéline Gaschel had led the tiny Venusian nation for ten years. She had four thousand souls to care for, a predatory Bank as an ally, and equipment that wore down far more quickly than in any other place in the solar system. Any chance of becoming self-sufficient depended entirely on risky investments with overwhelming price tags. She'd mapped out a vision for the next forty years of Venus, ending in a home they could joyfully give their grandchildren. But that depended on how well she could shepherd the nation through the next years.

The *présidente,* along with a number of other key government personnel, lived on the *Baie-Comeau,* a huge floating habitat owned jointly by *la colonie* and the Bank. Art by schoolchildren and plans for new habitats and industries decorated the clean lines of the hallways. Today, she was fully suited and sealed as she stepped onto the busy roof port, where small drone dirigibles constantly carried supplies to and from the *Baie-Comeau*. The human traffic was almost as busy. One of the port workers helped her into her wing-pack, careful not to knock the bottle of brandy she carried.

She checked that no one was beneath the plank, double-checked her engine status, then leapt into the space above the clouds. The gee-forces gripped her as she swooped up and attained level flight. The Venusian branch of the Bank of Pallas was four kilometers astern, in the center of the main flotilla. It was a smaller habitat, housing some thirty off-worlders who staffed the branch office, along with offices for an additional ten to fifteen local Venusian staff for periods of heavier work.

Along with the Bank of Ceres, the Lunar Bank, and the Bank of Enceladus, the Bank of Pallas was a major economic power in the solar system, around which political, legal and even police powers had accreted. Without the Bank of Pallas, *La République du Québec* would never have been able to afford to become a space-faring nation. Without the Bank of Pallas, Venus would never have been able to declare independence. Partnerships with Banks were complex. Venus needed the Bank of Pallas, and with its investment already made, the Bank of Pallas wanted Venus to succeed. Few people understood the nature of debt and the two-way obligations and incentive structures that they created. Much of Gaschel's job was managing that relationship.

She landed on the roof and was buzzed down. Below the airlock in the stairwell, she shed her helmet and wings with one of the Bank security people. The stairwell led down to another pressure door and into a hallway with glass doors to the main lobby. The Bank employed a dozen Venusian citizens in good economic development jobs. From one of the offices, her niece waved to her and returned to her work. Cultivating the right relationships early was another key to stability. One day, perhaps one day soon, her niece would become a delegate in *l'Assemblée,* and maybe in her time would become *présidente,* ensuring stability of policies and a skilled hand in managing the relationship with the Bank. The next set of doors swung open on their own and Gaschel walked through to the offices of Leah Woodward.

Woodward was a black-haired woman with a confident smile and a PhD in Economics. She'd been one of the youngest supervisors in the Branch Office on the asteroid Hygeia. At thirty-four, she was among the youngest Branch Managers in the solar system, although Gaschel wondered how much profit or business Woodward could squeeze from Venus to propel her career forward.

"*Madame la Présidente,*" Woodward said, moving around her desk to shake Gaschel's hand.

Although Woodward had been here eighteen months, and had implants that gave her an extensive linguistic range, hearing her speak French was not pretty. Gaschel answered in the accented English she'd learned in Montréal during medical school.

"Good afternoon, Miss Woodward. Thank you for the invitation," she said, holding out the bottle. "I brought you an experimental variety of brandy. Our biochemists have been trying to see if blastulae can be turned into food or even soil. In one of their experiments, they made brandy by accident."

Woodward took the bottle formally, smiling.

"We'll have to try it over supper," she said, and waved Gaschel through to her suites.

In the small dining room, a cook had just placed a steaming pot in the middle of the table. A window gave a distorted view, fish-eying the clouds through hydroponic gardens and the curved plastic-and-teflon skin of the branch office. At the base of the wall, though, water had pooled a meter deep; in the brown murk, small shrimp and crab scavenged.

Woodward uncorked the bottle and sniffed experimentally.

"What are you going to call it?" she asked in English.

Gaschel pulled her eyes away from the bright green of the leaves outside the window.

"I don't even know if it's worth calling it anything," Gaschel said. "Some people seem to love it. Some call it vile."

Woodward filled two shot glasses.

"You could say that about Venus," she quipped.

"I've come to love it," Gaschel said.

"Me, too."

They toasted and sipped warily. Neither spoke. It was potent and bitter.

"You still love it?" Gaschel asked.

Woodward nodded. "It's an interesting flavor," she said, smacking her lips and smelling again. "On Hygeia, they produce a rough *aguardiente* a bit like this."

Gaschel tried hers again, then set down the glass. "They may need to keep working on the recipe."

"Still, for pure novelty, it might sell in some markets," Woodward said. "Who has ever tasted Venusian food or drink? The delta-V isn't prohibitive, especially if you have steady imports. Outbound traffic could carry something to sell."

"Let's look into it."

"You may like this better," Woodward said, lifting the lid on the pot. Garlic and seafood smells mixed in the room. "This is our first Venusian shrimp harvest, with our own vegetables and herbs."

Gaschel's mouth watered and she sat, accepting a bowl. She hadn't smelled anything so good in months. Years. She hadn't eaten shrimp in thirty years. The taste bloomed a tiny longing in her for the Montréal of her youth. They each silently, almost reverently, took a second helping, and there was no small talk. Only when they sat back over empty bowls, with water in their glasses, did the conversation resume.

"I listened to the session of *l'Assemblée*," Woodward said.

"Did you enjoy it?" asked Gaschel guardedly.

"It's a tough situation. Is there anything I can do to help?"

"I don't expect Marthe D'Aquillon to roll over, but the policy rationale is sound. We'll have the metal to reduce our imports so that we can cover our other credit."

"The asteroid will pay for itself after a few years, and

then generate income for Venus," Woodward said. She played a slow finger along the edge of her glass. "But maybe you don't need the asteroid that much?"

"I beg your pardon?"

"Or perhaps not in partnership with the Bank of Pallas?" Woodward looked at her meaningfully.

"I don't take your meaning, Miss Woodward."

"I'm wondering if you might have been looking for credit and supplies from another source," the branch manager said. "My directors wouldn't be happy if they found out you were working with one of the other Banks."

"What other Banks?" Gaschel said, her stomach going suddenly cold and heavy. "We're not working with anyone else. Just the Bank of Pallas."

"You don't have a lot of fissionables," Woodward said.

"I know."

"We detected radiation coming from Venus."

"If it's new, it might have been spit out of a volcano recently. We can see about sending something down there to try to recover it."

"A little bit of radioactivity in a magma flow wouldn't penetrate the clouds. This was hard enough to set off the radiation detectors on the branch office. We didn't have the detectors oriented to look downward. By the time we reoriented, the signal was gone. It had been moving."

Gaschel's mind spun. "On the surface?"

"In the clouds."

"What?" Gaschel demanded. Both her hands gripped the table of their own volition.

Woodward hadn't noticed. She rose, hot eyes on Gaschel. "Let me tell you what my directors will think," she said, walking around the table in a wide, predatory circle. "Either the Government of Venus is playing dumb with us while playing footsie with one of the other Banks, or one of your *coureurs* is working behind both our backs."

Gaschel had to turn her chair to keep facing the branch manager. A *coureur des vents* going to one of the Banks without her knowing? How? What would they trade to the Bank? Political power? Regime change? Resources on the surface that needed huge engineering investments to reach? Venus had little of value. That was their problem. The maybes and perhaps could spin for days. She didn't deal in maybes.

"Neither narrative makes you look good," Woodward said.

"You think a *coureur des vents* bought radioactives from your competitors?" Gaschel said, trying to keep the heat from her voice.

"Or you did."

"The Bank of Pallas is my only partner!" Gaschel stood angrily.

They faced each other across the office. Woodward wasn't tall, but she wasn't relying on height for menace.

"If it turns out I believe you, my directors will be gratified to hear that we can continue to count on this friendship. But the questions remain: why would your people be acquiring radioactives, and are you able to handle it?"

"*If* it turns out I believe you," Gaschel retorted, "I can only guess that they're starting their own industries."

"Or you're naive and they're making some messy weapons."

Gaschel's hands went cold.

"If that's the case, is the Government of Venus interested in buying weapons or police supplies?" Woodward asked neutrally.

"That won't be necessary," Gaschel said. "Send me copies of your observations right away."

Woodward moved to a side table and picked up a small pad. She handed it to Gaschel. "Uncertainty makes business environments expensive," she said. "For both our sakes, I expect this uncertainty to be clarified very shortly."

NINETEEN

IT WAS ON waking that Pascal felt the worst. In dreams he was never himself. In his dreams, he played the parts of men. He played the parts of women. He played the parts of things. And sometimes he was no one at all, just a cloudy façade, surrounded by firmament-bright clouds. Inevitably, he woke, and he became prickling flesh again, sweaty, hairy, and rough. Ugly.

He rose quietly, pissed without touching himself, and shaved in the dark. The only places he did touch himself were his scars. Wormy lines radiated up from the top of his left hand like a misshapen spider. Fine lines in parallel rows etched the inside of his right forearm. Scars spotted his neck where seals had failed and no beard would grow. The rippled welts inside and over his thighs were still healing.

He padded out into the main space of the *Causapscal-des-Profondeurs*. In his room, Pa was speaking quietly into the radio. Pascal walked to the galley and made enough noise for Pa to hear. George-Étienne's conversation resumed, even more quietly, and Pascal shut the oven door on a scattering of blastula chips. His father joined him shortly, sitting without looking at him.

"What is it?" Pascal asked. "Who were you talking to?"

"Marthe."

"Is everything okay?"

George-Étienne shook his head. "Fuckers," he said after a few moments.

"Is Marthe okay?" Pascal demanded. "Is Émile?"

"Marthe is fine. Émile is probably drunk." He finally looked at Pascal. "The fuckers are taking away the *Causapscal-des-Vents*."

"What? Who?"

"The fucking government. Fucking Gaschel."

Gaschel's name was not spoken in their home. If she had to be referred to at all, she was called the fucking mayor, the fucking bitch, or the fucking doctor.

"Why?" Pascal said. Where would Marthe and Émile live?

George-Étienne waved his hand dismissively. "Doesn't matter. The bitch is sticking it to us again. Surely she hates Marthe's guts as much as mine."

"But why?"

"Because Marthe is smarter than her and the fucking bitch couldn't get her way in *l'Assemblée,* I bet you. We'll find out soon. I asked Marthe to come down."

"Here?" Pascal said, suddenly elated. "She's coming here? When?"

"The *Causapscal-des-Vents* will be positioned to give her a good glide path in about four hours. I want to talk to her about what the hell we do with what we've found. The grinding is good—Jean-Eudes is good at it—but it feels small-scale. I'm trying to think about how to be more ambitious. Marthe will have ideas."

"What do you mean, ambitious?"

"How do we barter away all those probes?" George-Étienne said. "I've been thinking about what you said. Some of them are worth more whole, but we've got no access to anyone who could buy them, or bid on them."

His mood was black and the silence throbbed with frustration.

"I stayed up last night trying to figure out more of the probe," Pascal said. "You want to see?"

George-Étienne finally nodded. Pascal expanded the view on his pad of an engineering image he'd made.

"I've found its main thrusters and attitude jets," Pascal said, pointing to the lumps at the back and those on the underside, sides and top. "They're fed from a single tube system from..." he altered the view to show a small hollow just aft of the dorsal access port "...this tank."

"The tubes from the tank," he said, expanding that view of it, "run over the radioactive source. Solid reaction mass probably melts in the tank, boils and shoots through the jet valves."

"That wouldn't work in the atmosphere of Venus," George-Étienne said.

"Not at all," Pascal said. "But if this thing spent a lot of time in a vacuum, that's another story. Among asteroids, they could harvest water ice, or dry ice, or liquid nitrogen as a reaction mass for propulsion."

"This boosts your alien theory," his father said.

"It *is* alien!"

George-Étienne smiled at him and patted his arm. "I know, Pascal. Good work. You figured out it runs on fission."

"Not really," Pascal said. "The propulsion system is simple, with the fissionables used only to heat the reaction mass. I don't know what the rest of it ran on. Maybe the power plant was lost when it crashed in the cave."

"From the other side."

"Yes."

"Too bad we can't go down there," George-Étienne said. "I'd like to get the rest of those probes and explore the eddies to see what other high-tech debris might come out."

Pascal took a deep breath.

"We might be able to, Pa."

"Better probes?"

Pascal shook his head and leaned close.

"Air going from high pressure to low expands and cools," he said. "We could set up a cooling system in the caves by setting up dams at several points. If we let air through in a controlled way, it would cool. We could even generate electricity with turbines."

George-Étienne's brow lowered as Pascal spoke.

"It's brilliant," he said after a moment. "You're talking about building a base down there. Someplace to live. A way to explore that cave system and even the other side."

Pascal felt himself grinning to match his father's smile. But then it faltered.

"But how?"

George-Étienne patted his arm again.

"You eat, Pascal, and keep thinking. Start making plans. Don't worry about what it costs yet." He opened the oven and pulled out the hot tray of blastula chips. "Eat." He even gave Pascal a wondering laugh.

"Why are you happy, *papa*?" Jean-Eudes said sleepily as he emerged from their room.

George-Étienne hugged his eldest and then laughed.

"Be proud, Jean-Eudes! I think your little brother is a genius."

Jean-Eudes grinned and Pascal's cheeks heated.

"And Marthe is coming for a visit," George-Étienne said.

"Marthe is coming!" Jean-Eudes exclaimed. "Pascal! Marthe is coming home!"

Then Pascal laughed, realizing that he, too, was happy.

TWENTY

MARTHE WAS LEAVING Émile responsible for the *Causapscal-des-Vents*, whatever that meant now, and whatever that meant to him. He needed to keep it running and producing, if only for her pride and to spite Gaschel. She left him the same message in the habitat, on his suit comms, and in his *inter-colonie* inbox. Then, she leapt from the roof of the *Causapscal-des-Vents*.

She didn't wear the expansive, light, highly-curved wings used for flitting about the upper atmosphere. They would snap like matchsticks in the dense winds below, and they didn't have the acid-resistance of the wings she'd grown up with. She wore a wing-pack she'd built herself, modeled off the wing-pack her mother had used. She'd made the parts herself out of volcanic metals, the atmospheric carbon she'd turned into nanotubes in the depths, and the scrap around the *Causapscal-des-Profondeurs*.

The stubby deep-cloud wings had a low camber to

account for the greater lift that even a little airspeed could give at two atmospheres of pressure. They were tougher, too, the kinds of wings that could carry a flyer and their load even through hard turbulence if need be, and still resist the sulfuric acid until they could be cleaned.

She didn't unfurl them yet. Their design was next to useless in the tenth of an atmosphere of pressure at the flotilla altitude of sixty-five kilometers. And passage through the super-rotating winds of the upper atmosphere to the slower winds of the upper cloud deck could be violent. No need to wear a small sail through it.

So she descended, faceplate down, arms back, legs canted outward, in free fall. The wind hissed. Wispy yellow-white half-clouds, patches of condensed water or sulfuric acid, whipped past her. She judged the distance to the super-rotating winds and the next layer by looking kilometers away to see where the winds caught at the peaks of high clouds, tearing the tops away. Normally, rolling convection cells clouded, making a washer-board pattern that looked like river rapids from far above, but the weather was clear and what they called *Les Rapides Plats* weren't visible today.

She tucked herself into a ball. Seconds later, contrary winds buffeted her, slowed her, pushed her sideways, and spun her. Her free fall speed was such that after twenty seconds she'd punched through the turbulence. She straightened out as she plummeted into the upper cloud decks. Behind her, the flotilla of *colonie* habitats raced away from her, west-to-east. They would circle the whole planet on the high super-rotating winds in just four days.

She was entering the more sedately blowing world of thick, bright clouds filled with yellowing and reddening light. Droplets of sulfuric acid speckled her faceplate and beaded away in the wind.

At fifty-eight kilometers above the surface, she burst through the upper cloud deck into the clear space called *Grande Allée*. It was a transparent cushion of air a kilometer thick between the upper and middle cloud decks. In free fall she was past its beauty in about fifteen seconds.

After plunging ten kilometers, the temperature rose to about twenty-five Celsius, and the pressure was over half an atmosphere. It was starting to feel like home. The light became more diffuse, the visibility more restricted.

She extended her wings, but didn't switch to glide flight. She was at altitudes where rosettes and trawlers naturally floated. Hitting one of them, while highly improbable, would be lethal at terminal velocity. The clouds thinned and the light oranged further, giving the eerie impression of brightening below. At fifty-two kilometers, almost the bottom of the middle cloud deck, she turned her free fall into a steep glide. The buffeting wind, thicker than the air at sixty-fifth *rang* was exhilarating, renewing.

The clouds whipped past until she entered the second vast, clear volume of sky: *Les Plaines*. She pulled into level flight, speeding along the transparent immensity sandwiched between two sheets of yellow clouds. She raced past a flock of wild trawlers, nice mature ones with long tails and heavy bobs under them. Everything began to feel more real. Things were alive here.

The yellow-brown ceiling of the middle deck receded above her as she plunged into the ocher tops of the lower cloud deck. Beads of sulfuric acid rain whipped across her faceplate, and a small storm bucked and shoved her. Her suit pressed closer to her skin, and its cooling system activated.

The *Causapscal-des-Profondeurs* would be over the volcano Maat Mons at midnight, at an altitude around forty-fourth *rang*. She was at the fifty-first *rang*, nearly over the immense unseen shield volcano, having already bled off much of her falling speed. She swooped sideways, and dove joyfully into the lower cloud deck, her former nursery and her home.

The light took on a dreamy, polarized quality in the lower decks. The midnight sun, hidden by twelve kilometers of clouds, was apparent now only in the particular reddish-yellow color of the light. Each level of the clouds reddened sunlight differently: a product of the kinds of clouds and the concentration of sulfuric acid. So home had a set of colors, as did homesickness.

There was nothing like the heat of her first suit walk, the weightlessness of her first wing-pack flight, the triumph of her first collaring of a wild trawler, the pain of her first burn. Deep thunder rolled, a visceral boom that the upper atmosphere couldn't carry. Her heart thumped faster and she dove. Fine lines of sulfuric acid trembled on her faceplate.

The temperature outside her suit climbed to the boiling point of water, just as the lower cloud deck began to dissolve into a fine haze. At forty-eighth *rang*, it was now too hot for clouds, and the vaporized acid looked the same dark yellow in all directions. This sub-cloud haze was the shapeless chaos of home.

This deep, the timbre of sound changed again. An atmosphere and a half of pressure and increasing heat made sound faster. Sound felt omnidirectional and made the world closer and smaller in anti-intuitive ways.

She was now close enough to pick up the weak locator signal that Pa had turned on for her. He was a suspicious man and normally ran the *Causapscal-des-Profondeurs* in the radio quiet preferred by the *coureurs des vents*. Her home floated fifteen kilometers east and several kilometers lower. She angled into the wind and glided downward though a browned haze so hot that sulfuric acid was breaking down into water vapor and sulfur dioxide.

Soon, a single trawler began to resolve, at first just a fuzzy vertical line, hanging gray and still. She dialed up the zoom on her faceplate, and as she neared, made out the distended, over-sized bulb that could only come from bioengineering. This was one of the herd with a transmitter-repeater mounted on its crown. The engine of her wing-pack keened in an excitement she shared. She dialed down the wattage on her helmet radio so that her transmission would only carry a few kilometers.

"*Causapscal-des-Profondeurs,* this is Marthe. Come in."

Static sounded for a while, lightning echoes and cloud static of the kind that fed the trawlers.

"Marthe! Marthe! It's Jean-Eudes!" she heard, and smiled. "You're coming home!"

THE HOUSE OF STYX

Her heart grew bigger, but she waited until she could hear static again. Jean-Eudes sometimes left his thumb on the transmit button.

"I'll be home soon, Jean-Eudes. Wait for me."

"I know! I will! Marthe!" Then came the sound of her older brother whooping.

She throttled up, speeding herself along the last few kilometers, spotting in the distance a couple of trawlers from the family herd. Their slow propellers churned, keeping them close to the *Causapscal-des-Profondeurs*. One was unusually close, the old habitat they'd used to live in, the one they used mostly for storage. Curious.

The temperature had risen to a hundred and twenty degrees and the pressure to over two atmospheres. Her wings were sensitive now, reacting to her every movement. She circled the *Causapscal-des-Profondeurs* twice. On the gantry, under the wide head of the habitat proper, a figure stood in a survival suit. Her father. She was twenty-four and didn't need someone spotting her every take-off and landing, but here he was, watching her. She swooped, then angled up to the gantry, cutting her thrust so that she landed gently on the hanging nets, as if it hadn't been a year since she'd last done it. She folded her wings, clambered up and her father hugged her.

"Beautiful landing," he said as if she were fifteen.

"Careful," she said. "I'm soaked. I passed through a lot of rain on the way down."

"It's just acid," he said gruffly, but he helped her shrug out of the wing-pack and then they neutralized each other and her wings. They entered the airlock, wiped again, and then repeated one last time inside while Jean-Eudes and Alexis waited at the line, with Pascal waiting a little farther back, smiling. When she'd unsuited and crossed the line, Jean-Eudes and Alexis hugged her together.

"You're so big!" she said to Alexis. "What have you been feeding him, Jean-Eudes?"

Brother and nephew grinned and let her go.

"*Ostie!* You're bigger too, Pascal!" she said.

He hugged her shyly. He was ten centimeters taller, and his muscles had started filling out. He looked good with his hair grown out, too. They made small talk, asked awkward questions, laughed, and gave her food and drink. Her two brothers and her nephew stared at her.

"This is a better welcome than I ever get on the *Baie-Comeau*," she said.

"What's the *Baie-Comeau*?" Jean-Eudes asked.

"Is it big?" Alexis asked.

"Two hundred people live on it," she said.

"Whoa," Alexis said.

"Enemies all," George-Étienne said flatly.

"Enemies?" Alexis asked.

"Not all enemies," Marthe said. "Political opponents, some allies, and some people who don't even know who we are."

"The important ones are enemies," George-Étienne said.

"What's happening with the *Causapscal-des-Vents*?" Pascal asked.

The green of his eyes was very clear, not a Venusian color.

"What's happening to the *Causapscal-des-Vents*?" Alexis repeated, looking from one adult to the other.

George-Étienne shushed him with a gesture.

"The government wants to take it, basically for scrap," she said to Pascal and her father.

"Can they do that?" Pascal asked.

Marthe shrugged. "We don't own it. No one owns anything."

"The D'Aquillons own the *Causapscal-des-Profondeurs*," her father said bitterly. "We own our trawlers."

"They're leaning on the Hudon family for a bioengineered trawler or two," she added. "Maybe they're going to encourage some people to move deeper, go off the grid."

"The Hudons don't have to give shit," George-Étienne said.

"They might have to," Marthe said, "just like we might have to."

"Are you kidding me?" George-Étienne said. "It was always a lousy class of habitat and we were never given anything to repair it with. And now they're kicking us out?"

"Where are they going to live?" Jean-Eudes asked. "Marthe, come live with us. You can have my hammock."

She squeezed Jean-Eudes's hand.

"Their argument isn't dumb," Marthe said.

"You agree with them?" George-Étienne demanded.

"Nobody's going to think their political argument is a crazy idea."

"Are they likely to win in *l'Assemblée?*"

"Eventually."

"How long can you hold them off?" George-Étienne asked.

"Using all my tricks? Weeks. If they're stupid, maybe months, but they're not stupid."

"You'll have a place to live?" Pascal said. He looked at his father and added, "… and Émile."

"Émile and I will have some place to live," she said, "and so will you if you want to come up."

"Pascal isn't leaving!" Jean-Eudes said.

Pascal reddened.

"He's not leaving now, Jean-Eudes, but he's sixteen," she said. "At some point, he'll want to see other habitats, see different jobs. If he wants to be an engineer, he'll have to work with real engineers for a while."

"I don't want Pascal to go," Jean-Eudes said.

"Me neither!" Alexis said.

"The real effect of this is that the *présidente* is taking me off the table politically," she said. "I've been playing the part of loyal opposition and it looks like Gaschel got tired of it. Without a habitat, I'm no delegate."

"You can be our delegate from the *Causapscal-des-Profondeurs*," Pascal said.

Marthe shrugged. "No one cares what the *coureurs* think. They only care what people in artificial habitats think."

"That's bullshit," Alexis said.

"Watch your mouth!" Marthe and George-Étienne said together. Alexis flinched.

"Pa," she said, looking at him meaningfully, "you can't watch your mouth around Alexis?"

"Why does she want you off the table?" George-Étienne said.

"I've been opposing her debt strategy for years. She's trying to dig us deeper. She's negotiated a big new loan with the Bank to buy 3554 Amun."

"An asteroid?" George-Étienne scoffed.

"It's a good idea," Pascal said. "Venus needs a lot of metal."

"We shouldn't have to pay for an asteroid at all," George-Étienne said. "The asteroids don't belong to the Banks just because they landed robots on them. Nobody asked them to go squat forever on a claim. We should be able to go out and pick any one. They're not using them."

"Let's just take one," Alexis said sullenly.

"If you touch a Bank's stuff, they can see that your equipment fails," Marthe said, "or they can call in the money you owe them."

"That's not fair!" Jean-Eudes said.

"It's the way things are," George-Étienne said.

"I hate the Banks," Alexis said.

"You shouldn't have said anything," Jean-Eudes said. "We would still have the *Causapscal*. You shouldn't have made them mad."

George-Étienne clasped Jean-Eudes's shoulder. "Your sister did the right thing."

"It's not fair," Jean-Eudes said.

"I may end up visiting you more," Marthe said.

Her older brother smiled.

"Alexis, Jean-Eudes," she said, "in the inner pocket of my suit, you may find a data sliver with some new music and movies I brought you."

Brother and nephew went for her suit, found the data sliver triumphantly, and then went into George-Étienne's bedroom where there was a reader. George-Étienne smiled appreciatively.

"Do you mind if I smoke?" she asked.

"You said you were quitting."

She put away a small bag of tobacco and paper.

"So what's your plan?" George-Étienne asked. "Use all the procedures to delay?"

She shrugged. "I can't turn enough opinion to stop this."

"So the *Causapscal-des-Vents* will be lost," he said, without the anger she'd expected.

Pa had a strange look. From his room, the sounds of a movie playing emerged.

"Tell," she said. "There's something."

George-Étienne signaled Pascal, went to the cupboard and pulled out something square and blocky. Pascal scooted closer. The first image on his pad was a close-up of a chasma, from maybe only ten kilometers up.

"Artemis? Devana?" she asked.

"Diana," George-Étienne said, sitting on the other side of her. "Remember I told you I've been tracking a weird storm system there?" He put the block in front of her. It was about thirty centimeters by thirty centimeters, perhaps another eight or ten thick. She held it up. She didn't recognize the color. It was a weird mix of granular reds and blacks.

"This isn't a surface sample," she said. "Something you made?"

She adjusted the angle and light reflected from the ends of thousands of metallic filaments running through the material.

"We sent a probe to the surface," her father said. "We found a cave at the base of Diana Chasma. Wind was blowing into the cave."

"*Into?*"

"Show her the first recording, Pascal."

His pad showed grainy images from the surface, but possibly worth a bit on the black market all the same. And then things got strange. They'd found a cave. Not so strange. Venus was covered with the fragments of lava tubes. But then he showed a video of pebbles and stones flying *into* the cave, dislodged by the camera itself, on what was obviously a dense wind. It was astonishing. Its possible value was going up in her calculations. And the video became increasingly strange. The turbulence and wild swings made understanding harder, but the silt and wind made it look like pictures from underwater. The rock faces were inexplicably smooth. And then, the last images showed a triangular shape.

"Wind can't go *into* a cave, Pa," she said finally.

Pascal took back the pad, the image frozen on the triangular thing. His fingers raced over the pad, and he opened another set of images, of a big triangular shape on the gantry under the *Causapscal-des-Profondeurs*. Pictures of Pascal sawing into it, making square sections. She felt her eyes widening.

"You brought it up?" she said, peering harder at the section. "What is it?" The new, clear pictures made it look like some sort of... she didn't know what. Satellite? Plane? Drone?

"We thought it was a probe sent by the Russians or the Americans," George-Étienne said.

"What's it made of?"

George-Étienne tapped the thick plate she held.

"This is it. Some kid of ceramic," Pascal volunteered. "The metal inside is circuitry, I think. The whole thing is one giant processing chip."

"*Sapristi*," she cursed. "Who the hell builds drones like this? Who the hell is that far ahead of us?"

"Whoever it was, they were this advanced a long time ago. It spent a long time down there. We got it out by going down ourselves," George-Étienne said.

"What? You went down?" she said, staring at him. "You both went down?"

Pa didn't answer, feeling the heat in her tone. She slammed down the ceramic plate.

"Not in Duvieusart's old bathyscaphe? You put Pascal in danger and left the boys on the *Causapscal* by themselves?"

"We're *coureurs,* Marthe. It isn't as easy as up at sixty-fifth."

"This isn't about easy or hard, Pa! Do you know how dangerous that was for both of you? And Jean-Eudes and Alexis alone with the whole herd?"

The sound of the video from George-Étienne's room quieted. Pa didn't seem to care that they eavesdropped.

"They looked after themselves," George-Étienne said. "Alexis is ten."

"*Câlisse,* Pa! The world isn't the way it used to be. What

if something had happened to you? How long would it have been before I could have gotten to them?"

"Nothing happened, and Alexis held the *Causapscal-des-Profondeurs* over the RV point for two hours. He's as good as Chloé was at that age. He's better than you were at that age."

"And Venus took away Chloé as a full-grown woman, Pa!"

"Nothing bad happened to Alexis and Jean-Eudes," Pascal said gently. "Both of them were very proud of themselves."

"You both shouldn't be," she snapped.

"We got the probe," Pascal said. "Look at what else we saw when we got the camera deeper into the cave."

She still couldn't believe they'd left Alexis and Jean-Eudes alone, but she huffed and turned her attention back to the pad. Pascal zoomed in on another picture. In an eddy deep in the cave lay a dusted graveyard of shipwrecks, twelve or more wrecked drones.

"How many of these probes did you find?" she asked. "Who would send so many down in one place?"

"Pascal thinks the tech is alien," George-Étienne said, baiting her.

There was still no sound from Pa's room.

"You'd better be watching those movies or I'm putting them back in my suit!" she yelled. The sound of a movie restarted, louder than before. She squinted at the images, then lowered her voice.

"*Crisse*," she said. "You can't be serious! Little green men?"

Pascal slid the ceramic block to her. "No one uses this tech on Earth or on Venus."

"That we know of," she said.

"Look at this."

He swiped through the images, each one showing the dark of the cave with tiny circles of light from their lamp. Then, a starscape.

"What is this?"

"This is what we found at three hundred and twenty meters into the cave," Pascal said.

She looked at her father. He was poker-faced. This was a joke. She tossed the pad on the table. She didn't like these kinds of jokes. Pascal and George-Étienne watched her earnestly.

"At the bottom of the cave, we found a wormhole," George-Étienne said in a low voice.

A shiver of goose-flesh rose to her neck. "Wormholes don't exist."

"We don't know how it works," Pa continued. "We don't know why it's stable. We don't know why it's there. But it's been there for a while, and blowing carbon dioxide into space. We found a tunnel to another place, Marthe."

"I think it's around a pulsar," Pascal added. "We got repeating radio signals all the way down. We thought it was a distress call, or a coded message, but the wormhole opens onto a system with no star, just a pulsar."

She shoved at her father and he got up in surprise. She rose impatiently and walked to the galley, stood stiffly for long moments. What the hell? They believed it!

They both believed it. And while her home was being

185

confiscated, they were making up stories. No. Not exactly stories. Not to them. They believed. They had photographic, radio and physical evidence.

They weren't stupid. Either one of them. Even though Pa sometimes edged close to conspiracy thinking about the government. She took a deep breath. She faced them. They were looking at her as if awaiting a sentence. They needed her to believe them.

She leaned back, pulled out her tobacco and paper, and looked at her father, daring. He said nothing. She slowly filled the paper, rolled and licked it. She came to the table, struck the match on the section of ceramic hull, and inhaled.

"Get me a drink and show me everything again from step one," she said, sitting back down.

TWENTY-ONE

GASCHEL'S SUITES IN the *Baie-Comeau* were less expansive than Woodward's, although her view was higher. Her office looked down on the yellowed clouds and the white hazes as if from the tower of a great ship. Blobs and specks of green far ahead and to the side marked the positions of other habitats. *La colonie's* main flotilla was spread across a circle thirty kilometers off the *Baie-Comeau*. Smaller flocks of a few dozen habitats lay thousands of kilometers away, following the west-to-east winds over the top of Venus's clouds, so that every seven to eight thousand kilometers was a human flotilla.

Most of her closest aides lived on the *Baie-Comeau* or in attendant habitats. They met today in her office. Claude Babin, the *colonie's* treasurer, was standing. His news hadn't been good. They already had a trade deficit with the asteroidal corporations, as well as a sizeable debt, and they'd just gone through the list of what the *colonie* would and wouldn't import this quarter.

They'd again put off buying updated vaccines, as well as some cancer therapies, so that they could get some basic metals that had no substitutes. They'd also added a shipment of water and ammonia, because their closed habitat systems kept leaking away hydrogen and nitrogen, which were difficult to replace on Venus. And, with too much hesitation, she'd decided to acquire a set of higher-grade solar cells that would increase the *colonie's* industrial production of carbon nanofibers, which were durable enough to substitute for metals and cladding in some places. But they'd be paying for it for a while.

"*Merci,* Claude," she said, dismissing him. "I need the rest of you for a moment."

She was left with a small group of people. François-Xavier Labourière was the chief of her political and administrative staff. He'd been with Gaschel since the beginning of her political career. Thomas Bacquet was the fidgety, efficient Deputy Chief-of-Staff. Cécile Dauzat managed *la colonie's* industrial works, and Laurent Tétreau was a politically-minded Junior Engineer in industrial works who'd been doing more and more political work for Labourière. She sat. They did too.

"I need the locations of the *coureurs des vents,*" she said.

Labourière looked to Dauzat.

"All of them?" Dauzat asked warily.

"There aren't that many," Gaschel said.

The manager of industrial works wriggled in her seat.

"It's almost a hundred families, maybe more, *madame*, floating at many changing altitudes, across dozens of latitudes."

"Forty-five kilometers is the altitude," Gaschel said. "The latitude is the Atla Regio region. The time is four days ago."

"We don't track the *coureurs, madame*. They don't even track themselves," Dauzat said.

"You can narrow it down with this information," Gaschel insisted.

"Maybe," Dauzat said. "Historically, maybe. The *coureurs* do share meteorological reporting. We might be able to build up profiles based on where they tend to report from."

"What kind of a problem are we dealing with, *Madame la Présidente?*" Labourière asked.

Gaschel looked at each one.

"Just this room?" she asked.

They nodded.

"Someone down there is floating around with some hot radioisotopes," she said.

"One of the mom-and-pop operations found some on the surface and brought it up?" Dauzat asked.

"The signal was too hot for raw ore. And no one on Venus has the capacity to refine it," Gaschel said. Some of the faces, especially Tétreau's and Labourière's, started to show dawning realization. "The Bank of Pallas thinks that someone down there is cutting a deal with another Bank."

She let that sink in.

"Is this Marthe D'Aquillon? Or her father?" Labourière asked.

"Narrow it down," she said, with a finality that caused the four of them to stand, pay their respects and get moving.

TWENTY-TWO

PA AND PASCAL showed Marthe everything they'd learned or guessed or filmed or measured. It took an hour. She stopped them, made them back up, interrogating every observation. Pascal didn't drink, but she and Pa downed a quarter-bottle of his good *bagosse*. They hung on her expressions, and at the end, they watched her smoke as she considered it all.

She swore very deliberately "*Maudit câlisse de tabarnak de gros problème, papa.*"

Pa began to grin, his eyes defiantly alight.

"It's ours, Marthe! No one knows we've got it. We've got a tunnel to the stars ourselves. The government and the Bank can fuck themselves."

She rested her head against the wall, staring at the ceiling, blowing smoke in a cloud.

"What do you think?" George-Étienne asked.

"I'm having a hard time believing any of it. And what do you do with a wormhole in the ground? Who could we tell?"

"We don't tell anyone!" George-Étienne said vehemently. "So no one takes it away."

"We can't do this alone, Pa."

"Family first."

"I never forgot, Pa," she said, putting the cigarette back to her lips. With her eyes, she traced the rib lines of the trawler in the ceiling. There was something spiritually comforting about being inside another living thing. Protected. Enwombed.

"I thought I was coming down here to plan how to keep the fight alive with no seat in *l'Assemblée*. Not this. Stars inside Venus," she said wonderingly.

And it was a wonder. A road to hidden stars. A little nuts. A lot nuts.

"A seat in *l'Assemblée* might not be so important in the future," George-Étienne said, "but for now, we need you there."

"Why?"

"Pascal had an idea. Show her, Pascal."

Pascal smiled shyly and expanded an engineering schematic on his pad. Around a rough outline of the cave, he'd drawn a cap to go over the cave mouth, with a massive door in it. Deeper in the cave were other caps, each with airlocks, and some with turbines to generate electricity.

Under this design, in each successive portion of the cave system, the temperature and pressure dropped, like a series of refrigerators one inside the other, taking advantage of the final pressure drop into the hard vacuum. Two portions of the cave system had areas where eddies had scoured out voluminous caverns. Pascal had designed underground habitats in these, with bioreactors, tool shops, hydroponic areas, small living spaces, and even a tiny port from which they could use powered vacuum suits to explore the other side. Marthe blew smoke upwards and butted out her cigarette in a bowl.

"Good work, Pascal."

"It works," he insisted. "We can build it. This is all off-the-shelf tech."

She made a face. "How much steel do you need to hold back ninety atmospheres of pressure?" she asked.

"We don't need to hold all ninety-three atmospheres at once," he said. "Because the airlocks are nested, we can distribute twenty to thirty atmospheres across any given one. The steel we have will survive that."

"We don't *have* any steel, Pascal," she said.

"*Oui*," her father said, smiling.

She caught his meaning. Her mind raced, looking for any other possible meaning to his cryptic assertion. At the same time, her thoughts ran down rabbit holes of implications.

"*Non*," she said. "That's insane."

"What?" Pascal asked. "What's insane?

"There's lot of metal in the *Causapscal-des-Vents*," George-Étienne said.

Pascal's eyebrows rose. Then rose again. At any other time, it would have been funny. It wasn't any other time. Pa was grinning now. Marthe sighed. Pa took her tobacco case, rolled her a cigarette and handed it to her. Then he started laying out his ideas.

TWENTY-THREE

AFTER SO MANY hours of shocks, the family finally settled. Alexis had to go to bed. Pa broke out a jar of *tord-boyaux* he'd brewed a while ago. He and Marthe continued drinking together. Pascal had rarely seen Pa drink and didn't really want to now. And Pa and Marthe looked like they wanted to speak quietly between themselves anyway.

Pascal felt strange. Seeing Marthe woke weird feelings he couldn't put his finger on. He shepherded Jean-Eudes to their room and made Alexis get into his hammock. His older brother was breathless and smiling.

"So many movies!" Jean-Eudes said, yawning. "And music. I love it when Marthe comes! I wish she'd live with us."

"Help me with her hammock," Pascal said, holding out one side of the hammock ropes. It wasn't a job he needed help with, but he and Pa and Marthe all found things that Jean-Eudes could help with. Jean-Eudes was happiest when he was taking care of his family. And his elaborately overdone knots never slipped.

"What's a saint?" Jean-Eudes asked after he'd tied a fist-sized knot on one side of Marthe's hammock.

"Where'd you hear that word?"

"In one of the movies. Also, a lot of people are called saint something," Jean-Eudes said. "Saint Cyr. Saint Hyacinthe. There's more. Saint Siméon."

"In the olden days, people believed in lots of things that weren't true," Pascal said, sitting on his own hammock. The slow sway of the *Causapscal-des-Profondeurs* rocked him. "Saints are magical things, like fairies. In the olden days, they believed that some people were so great in life that they became magical after they died, and that their magic helped people who believed in them."

"You don't believe in saints?"

"No, buddy," Pascal said. "That's just make-believe."

Jean-Eudes began the fourth layer of his knot. It was now bigger than his fist. Marthe wouldn't fall. "That's too bad. If saints were true, *maman* would be a saint and we'd see her."

"Saints didn't always appear like fairies," Pascal said, laying back. "I think you felt them around you while they helped you."

Jean-Eudes had no more rope. It was all in his fat knot. He tugged to test it and moved into his own hammock. His breathing became deep and slow and Pascal thought he'd dozed off.

"If saints were real, *papa* could be a saint too," Jean-Eudes said. "And he would keep watching us, protecting us."

Pascal looked over. Jean-Eudes was making a face, and his eyes watered.

"What is it, buddy?" Pascal asked, sitting up.

"I don't want *papa* to go away like *maman*," he said with a trembling voice.

"Pa is young, Jean-Eudes," Pascal said. "He's going to be around a long time, so long that you're going to have to help take care of him when he's old."

Jean-Eudes gave a little laugh at the thought. "But he's older than me," he said. "Who will take care of us then?"

Pascal reached across the swaying space and put his hand on his brother's arm.

"Marthe will. She's like Pa," he said. "She's not scared of anything."

"Of anything?" Jean-Eudes asked.

Pascal couldn't imagine anything that would even give her pause.

Jean-Eudes laughed into the silence, answering his own question. "No. *My* little sister isn't afraid of anything."

They were quiet for a time, listening to the hushed voices outside, the barks of sudden laughter against the creaking of the trawler in the wind. Marthe and Pa had the same tone of laugh. After a time, Marthe came in.

"You guys are still awake?" she said. "I think it's only afternoon for Émile and me."

She swayed a bit and her cheeks had pinkened. She'd stripped down to shorts and a loose tank top, but she was still sweating. Pulling a small bottle from the pouch of her suit, she sat on her hammock and pulled one foot up.

A directionless longing rose in Pascal. His mouth was dry.

"How are you doing, Pascal?" she asked. Her elegantly raised eyebrow was a kind of compulsion he had trouble resisting.

"I'm okay," he said quietly.

She opened the bottle, revealing a tiny brush covered with red lacquer. How had she gotten nail polish? Had someone made it? With all the things that they couldn't have on Venus, his sister had nail polish.

"You're sixteen," she said. "You must get lonely here."

"I'm here," Jean-Eudes said. "He's not lonely."

"Shhhh, Jean-Eudes," she said, painting one toenail. "We'll get to you in a minute. We let the little brother talk first."

Pascal's face felt hot. He stared at the glistening polish.

"You've never seen a girl paint her toes?" she smiled.

He looked away, embarrassed.

"Chloé and I made our own polish as soon as we knew enough chemistry," she said. "Our first few tries were awful. Oils and resins from blastulae are good for the lacquer, but we could only make a puke color."

"Puke!" Jean-Eudes cackled. "Puke!" Marthe smiled at him, but kept painting.

"Chloé talked about boys," she said. "I talked about girls. We were going to go into business and sell our nail polish all over *la colonie* and make everyone beautiful."

Pascal thought he could remember those times, when Chloé had been fifteen and Marthe thirteen, Pascal had been just five or six and still sleeping in a room with Pa and *maman*. The *Causapscal-des-Profondeurs* had been new then, and they'd since changed the layout. Chloé and Marthe had shared a room that he remembered as immense, although it had probably been little better than a closet with hammocks. Jean-Eudes and Émile had hammocked in the main room. Pascal had wanted desperately to be old enough to share a room with his sisters, and Chloé had let him sleep in her hammock a few times.

"Did you?" Pascal asked.

She shook her head. "Chloé got her boy," she said wistfully. "And other people make better stuff than this. I make my own for fun."

"Can you paint my toes?" Jean-Eudes said.

"That's for girls, Jean-Eudes," Pascal said uncertainly.

"It's for anyone who washes their feet," Marthe corrected.

"I can wash my feet!" Jean-Eudes hopped from his hammock.

"Come on, Pascal," she said. "It's fun."

His churning stomach hollowed nervously, but he hopped off his hammock. She came off hers and sat on the floor. Jean-Eudes sat beside them.

"You have to dry them, silly," she told him.

Jean-Eudes hustled back to the basin, leaving wet foot prints. She motioned Pascal to give her his foot. It was scary and thrilling. He didn't understand why. The brush licked his big toenail, leaving red. Marthe gave two other strokes and then the first nail was done. It looked beautiful.

"You should come to the upper clouds, Pascal," she said, painting the next nail. "You need to see people your own age."

The idea terrified him. Two strokes and the next one was done too.

Marthe tilted her head, examining her work, blowing on the first three toes.

"Do you like girls? Boys? Both?" she asked.

The smell of Pa's homemade sipping whiskey was on her breath.

His answer slipped out of him before he had a chance to question it. "I don't even like myself."

Jean-Eudes looked at Pascal strangely, but Marthe had already told him to wait his turn and he was quietly attentive, feet drying. Marthe didn't look at Pascal strangely. She nodded at him as if what he'd said was the most logical thing in the world. She turned to the last two toes and finished them in one stroke each.

"Don't touch them to anything until they dry," she said. "That's good advice for toes and people." She capped the bottle. "You don't need to decide between boys and girls, but no brother of mine isn't going to like himself," she said, pulling him into a headlock and knuckling the top of his head. It turned into a hug, and for a moment he felt safe. He loved Marthe. And he was jealous of how comfortable she was in her skin.

TWENTY-FOUR

ÉMILE STUMBLED INTO the habitat area of the *Jonquière*. He'd been drinking. And smoking weed. For hours. He was actually hammered, and he'd still made it here on his wing-pack. The day he couldn't fly hammered was the day Venus really should take him. He'd nearly missed the upper landing platform. He'd fallen, bent one of his wing struts, but caught himself before he'd gone over the edge. He didn't know who lived on the *Jonquière,* or whose party this was, but he hadn't dented their stuff.

Thérèse had been moody and unresponsive. She hadn't answered his messages. Even Marthe, with whom he got on well enough sometimes, had gone. He was kicking about their shitty habitat alone. Sometimes cleaning. Sometimes fixing. Mostly just sitting around, smoking Marthe's cigarettes and fermenting a new batch of *bagosse* that couldn't be ready fast enough. He'd scrawled shitty lines of stilted, unimaginative poetry on his pad until he'd decided to crash this party.

He took off his helmet and hung it in the webbing under the ceiling. Beyond the door was drumming. He spun the wheel and opened the door. The drumming echoed loud in a haze of cigarette and hashish smoke hanging oily in the air.

Émile came face-to-face with Réjean.

"This your habitat?" Émile asked.

"*Oui*," Réjean said.

Émile swayed. Réjean's pupils were all fucked up. Émile clapped a hand on Réjean's shoulder and leaned in. "As long as you don't say anything about my family, we got no problems," he said.

Réjean's screwy pupils stared back. He had a huge bruise on his neck.

"Did I do that?"

Réjean looked puzzled for a second, then touched his neck. "Hoarders."

"What?" Émile said.

"Didn't break, but it was close," Réjean said, slurring a bit. "I'm a constable. We got called in to raid some black-marketing family, a big operation. I got hit with a bat right in the neck. Thought she broke it."

"*Sapristi*. I thought you guys had tasers."

"It was too close. I tasered one guy, but then hit one of my buddies. But we had back-up, Bank security."

"What the hell does Bank security care?" Émile said.

Réjean shrugged. "The government asked them to back us up 'cause it was a big operation. And I think the Bank guys need the practice. They haven't got much to do. And who knows? Black-marketing may cut into their profits."

"Quick mop up?" Émile said, swaying.

"Not so much. These guys were hoarding everything! Metal. Tools. Food. Liquor. Cigarettes."

"*Crisse!*"

"They weren't ready to give up. But the Bank guys had guns."

"Really?"

"Really. Gunpowder. Goddamn loud."

"They shot them?"

"One of them," Réjean said.

"Why wasn't it in the news?"

"I don't know. Maybe the Bank or the government didn't want to make a big deal of it. Maybe they think it'll make people nervous. Makes me feel better. Fucking hoarders. I got some of their stock. I don't have much, but there's enough for a shot or two for everybody," Réjean said, jerking his thumb to a plastic bag of clear liquid hanging on the wall.

Émile smiled. This might be a good party.

"I write shitty poetry," he confessed, swaying closer.

"I paint acid scars," Réjean said. "I did a lot of Thérèse."

Émile didn't trust the meaning, and rocked Réjean back and forth with hard muscles. "You did some really nice work on the vines," he said finally, then released Réjean and walked around him.

The gondola, all of the *Jonquière*'s habitat, really, was packed with partiers. Blinds blocked out the omnipresent sun, leaving hard straight beams of sunlight to cut through the gaps and across the smoky room. He put his empty metal flask beneath the spigot and filled it.

He turned, took a swig and shuddered.

Crisse!

Terrible. Coarse and bitter and sulfurous. It burned all the way down. Mouth. Throat. Stomach. It had already been diluted, but just with water. Nothing masked the awful taste.

In the corner across from him, under slashes of bright daylight, a young man drew a knife across the inside of his forearm. The angle of the light and the arm showed rows of scars from old cuts. Émile flexed his left arm self-consciously, where his acid burn in the shape of a trawler was slowly healing.

Venus only receives us with pain, Thérèse had said. He took another swig of *bagosse*, swayed in place uncertainly. He wanted to help the kid, but who was he to get between the boy and Venus? Who was he at all? His communion had not given him answers, any more than Thérèse's communion had. Émile stumbled forward, put his hand on the cutter's shoulder.

"I write shitty poetry," Émile said.

The young man regarded him uncertainly. Émile ran a fingertip across the many scars, dragging the new-welling blood across them.

"You already gave Venus her due," he said.

"Clouds don't touch anything," the young man said. His pupils were huge; he was so high.

"No," Émile said, drinking again, not taking his eyes from the man, "I guess they don't."

"We're all clouds," the young man said. Then he began to weep quietly.

Émile retreated.

Few people here had ever seen Earth. They had mostly been born here. Venus was their birthright, their home, but it often fit like an oversized survival suit. Or a suit with a wrinkle in it you just couldn't reach. Their home was a gift. Wondrous. Worth poetry, better than what he wrote. Worth more than the artful scars on their bodies. But it always felt like a gift that ought to have been given to someone else.

That's why people fell apart. He'd heard of it happening in the asteroidal colonies, on the moon and on Mars. People lost their shit when they left the Earth. A million years of evolution and brain wiring couldn't be undone so fast. Nothing wrote that fast. And so they couldn't deal with it. And they all couldn't deal with it in their own ways. This guy cut himself. Thérèse invented religion. Marthe got into political fights. What did Émile do?

Nothing. He drank. He put whatever he could find into his body. And he didn't know how to stop.

He chugged the flask empty and stumbled against the wall, wondering how okay it would be to go back for a refill.

People surrounded him, dancing, drinking, drumming on the walls and floor, but the noise and darkness was a cocoon of aloneness. The press of bodies hid the cutter, who wept alone. Émile hung his flask on his belt and pushed towards the tiny bedrooms. One guy looked up at him as he was pushing, and his face lit with recognition.

"D'Aquillon!" he yelled into Émile's ear.

"What?"

THE HOUSE OF STYX

"You're Émile D'Aquillon!" the man said. He was clean, in the way flotilla people were clean. Baby hands, with only spot-scars. "You guys are getting a shitty deal from *l'Assemblée*," the man said. "You don't deserve to lose the *Causapscal*."

"It's a box of holes floating under a bag of oxygen," Émile said. "What do you care?"

"I'm Laurent Tétreau," he said, extending a pale hand. Émile took it warily, conscious of the ropey scars on his hands. "I work for a member of *l'Assemblée*. There are more than a few people who think this could have been handled better. The *présidente* has made a little war with your father for no reason. I know people who want to fix it. And you have a role to play in making peace with your family."

Émile snorted. "If you want somebody my father trusts, talk to Marthe."

"You can have influence," Tétreau said. "You just need to try. Marthe is leading the D'Aquillons in a direction that isn't good for anyone."

"There's nothing I can do about it," Émile said. "Pa called Marthe back to *Causapscal-des-Profondeurs*."

"Do you know why?"

"They don't tell me."

"They should. You're a D'Aquillon. If they aren't giving you the respect you deserve, there are other jobs and places to live. I know places that could use a guy like you."

"A job?" Émile asked, still swaying.

"Keep me in mind, Émile," Tétreau said. "You have a

role to play in making peace, maybe more than Marthe."

He held out a cup of *bagosse*. "I think I'm done. You want it?"

Émile took the cup and poured it carefully into his flask, not losing a drop. Then he handed it back and drank deeply. Tétreau staggered past him and swung his arm over another guy's shoulder. Émile watched him for a while, the *bagosse* slowing him so that the world dragged for moments at a time, movement strobing.

When he turned to keep moving to the bedrooms, he saw Thérèse, her slim body swaying, making out with some guy. A sculptor maybe? Sculptor bullshit. Sculpt shit. Anything they made here was eventually going to be swallowed by Venus. There was no ground. No place to rest, ever. What the fuck were you going to put your sculpture on? The clouds? The clouds ate everything, down to the bone.

Émile grabbed the guy's shoulder, yanked him away, and punched him right where she'd just been kissing him. Émile stared at the guy, a little too drunk to do any more, waiting for him to do something. The guy wiped his bloody lips, looked up at the size of Émile, thought better of it, kicked at the wall and slunk away. Émile turned. Thérèse had her back to him, dancing by herself.

He unzipped the front of his survival suit and stripped to his waist, tying the arms around his hips. Then he moved close to her and showed his left arm, where he'd already taken the bandages off. The wound was scarring in exactly the trawler shape she'd made. He touched it. She eyed him with a kind of exhaustion, then melted and touched the wound too, leaning her head down to kiss it.

"I'm fucked up," she yelled in his ear over the drumming. Her breath smelled of hash.

"I am too," he said.

"Venus doesn't want us."

"Venus needs us," he said in her ear.

"We're puzzle pieces that don't fit here."

He rested his hands on her shoulders. "Nobody fits anywhere. The joke's on us."

She smiled, kept dancing, more slowly, swaying, independent of the raucous drumming and singing.

"It's not a very good joke," she said.

She leaned against him. Her body radiated heat. These two puzzle pieces matched. Her head was under his chin, until she looked up. He thought she wanted a kiss, but she avoided his descending lips and said in his ear, "I need to fit somewhere."

"Would you like to fit with me?" he said, half-teasing.

As soon as he said it, he knew he'd fucked up, missed out on something, some connection she was seeking and he could have made. But he didn't know how. She nodded anyway, like she hadn't expected better. They rested against one another, trees against the storm, rocking slowly to discordant music in the thickening smoke.

TWENTY-FIVE

PASCAL WOKE VERY early the next day. He swayed almost imperceptibly as the *Causapscal-des-Profondeurs* followed the contours of pressure at forty-fifth *rang*. Jean-Eudes was breathing softly, and Marthe snored in her hammock.

Last night seemed wonderful, like a weight had been lifted away. He didn't want to ruin the moment by moving, by bringing his body and the world into focus. But the idea of fresh stubble bothered him more and more. He couldn't stand the thought of hair standing stiff on his chin, over his lip, on his cheeks, touching his pillow. His hammock creaked as he slipped out. In the dark, he shaved by touch.

Scrape. Scrape. Scrape.

"You can turn on the light, Pascal," Marthe mumbled.

"I'm done," he whispered quickly.

He scraped the last of his face clean, toweled himself, cleaned the straight razor and hurried to the galley. Two cups smelling of *tord-boyaux* had tipped and rolled to the table edge in the swaying of the habitat during the night. He wiped and shelved them, then sat at the table and regarded his ten red toenails in wonder.

Marthe staggered out of their room soon after, adjusting her tank top and scratching at her hip. At the galley, she poured two cups of water and sat across from him.

His toes were so beautiful. For years, he'd never felt anything but ugliness, wrongness. It was a feeling that had taken a long time to sneak up on him, to realize that other people didn't feel the same way. He didn't mind being ugly, if only he could feel *right*. He desperately wanted out from under this feeling of wrongness.

"You're going through a tough time," she said, before sipping at her water with distaste.

He didn't answer.

"Jean-Eudes says you're sad." She tried swallowing more, but gave up partway. "He's worried about you, but he doesn't know what to do."

"He told Pa, too. It's not anything."

"Pa thinks everything that happens to teenagers is just adolescence," she said.

He laughed nervously and tried to look blasé. "He's right."

But she didn't say anything. She looked at him like Pa did when he was trying to figure out if he'd done anything wrong. His put-on smile melted.

"When I was about fourteen I think I realized that Venus doesn't want us," Marthe said.

"I love Venus."

"So do I, but when I was fourteen, I didn't think she loved us back."

It was an alien concept to him. He didn't feel unloved. Venus wasn't about love. She was about hiding and showing. Mostly she hid, but every so often, in a break in the clouds, a strange timbre of sound, she hinted at her true secret self.

"Do you still think that?" he asked.

"She can't physically eject us anymore," Marthe said, "so she attacks us psychologically. She makes us hate ourselves. Others. Our lives. She's hitting Émile too. Has been for years."

"Is he okay?"

She shrugged. "He's Émile." She pulled close the container of *tord-boyaux* that had been full last night. "He got a taste for this too early." She unscrewed the box, sniffed and pulled away. "Well, not this. *Bagosse* and weed are more his vices."

"He's been sending me his poems."

"He writes poems?" Marthe asked.

"They're beautiful."

Marthe's expression was hard to read. He didn't have a lot of experience and she was almost a politician. It wasn't hurt he saw in her eyes, but a kind of wistfulness.

"I'll ask to read them some time," she smiled.

"Is Venus attacking you?"

"No," she said. "Yes. It depends what you call an attack."

She sipped her water and he took up his. She set her cup down and leaned across the table, taking his hand in hers.

"It's okay to be sad, Pascal. I was. Sometimes I still am. But sharing makes it lighter. I've always got your back."

Even hungover, her half-lidded regard was penetrating.

She reminded him of *maman,* and Chloé, what he could remember of both of them. His throat felt tight. He pulled his hand away and tucked his feet out of sight. Plateaus, tesserae and coronae of scars, red-pink and bulbous, padded the backs of his hands, a reassuring erasure of an alien body. His breath felt thin and insubstantial. Her words terrified him.

"I feel wrong all the time," he whispered. "Everyone looks like they belong, like they're right in the world. I can't even look in the mirror." He took a deep breath and leaned over. The vision of his ten bright toenails split and wavered through tears. "I put on *maman's* dress."

She came around and knelt in front of him, taking his hands. She was smiling.

"How did it feel?" she asked.

"Really good," he whispered. His world was spinning.

"You didn't put it on because you missed her?"

Pascal shook his head.

"Put it on," she said, "as many times as you want. *Maman* would have done anything to make you happy, including giving you the dress off her back."

He nodded.

"It's stupid," he said, his voice thinning and tears falling. "It's just stupid."

"When I was growing up," Marthe said, "Pa was expecting me to like boys. Émile likes girls. Chloé liked boys. But I didn't and it didn't matter to him. Don't worry. Be whoever you want."

She was trying to soothe him, but making it worse. What if he didn't know what he wanted to be?

TWENTY-SIX

MUCH LATER, HER father and Jean-Eudes got up. Jean-Eudes was laughingly proud of his bright red toenails. They breakfasted, and Pascal's mood seemed to lift a bit in the morning energy of family.

"Jean-Eudes, Alexis," Marthe said, "you couldn't have watched all the movies yet. Why don't you chill while we talk engineering?"

The pair didn't need a second invitation, and scooped tortillas off the table and ran for George-Étienne's room.

"They're not going to get anything done today," her father said.

"Pascal, bring your pad," Marthe said. "I want to poke holes in your plans."

Pascal shared a smile with his father. He brought out his pad and thumbed through his designs. Marthe put an arm over his shoulders and opened the blueprints for the *Causapscal-des-Vents*.

"Pa, you propose using the metal from the *Causapscal-*

des-Vents," she said. "You're not stupid, so you're not talking about asking for it."

"Correct," George-Étienne said.

"So, we're talking about stealing a massive piece of kit from *la colonie,*" she said. "Right now, the metal is slated to offset some metal imports so that we can use real money on the cost of the asteroid."

"That bitch can fuck herself with her asteroid," he said. "She's shoveled us shit all our lives."

"*La colonie* has to pay for the loss," she said, "everyone who lives up at sixty-fifth *rang,* and all the *coureurs.*"

"How many habitats have we lost just because of wear?" George-Étienne said. "This is one more, that's all."

Pascal looked at her. She squeezed his shoulder.

"You're right, Pa," she said. "But even if we sink it, we don't get it. It's designed to run in a tenth of an atmosphere of pressure. By fiftieth *rang,* it'll start crushing. By the time it drops to twenty kilometers, it'll be a smoking raisin."

"Of course," George-Étienne said. "We have to catch it."

"With what?"

"We organize our trawlers," he said, "tie them to the *Causapscal-des-Vents* as it's sinking and use them to slow and stop its descent."

She looked at her brother. "Would that work?"

"If we use all of them and the *Causapscal-des-Profondeurs,*" he said, "we could just make it."

"With no margin for error and a big chance of

damaging some or all of our herd," Marthe said. "And our only home. Are Alexis and Jean-Eudes going to be in the *Causapscal-des-Profondeurs* while we try this, Pa?"

"This is the only way," George-Étienne said. "The math can work."

She shook her head. "Wild trawlers can't take that kind of extra stress for long."

"Ours are modified," Pascal said.

"She's not talking about you and I grafting some equipment into a wild trawler, Pascal," George-Étienne said. "She's talking about the big bio-engineered trawlers. Different breeders are designing bigger trawlers to be larger habitats."

"And they're all spoken for, or not ripe yet," Marthe said.

"Marie-Pier Hudon has a herd of four that should be mature enough," George-Étienne said.

"One or two of those will be confiscated by the *gouvernement*," Marthe said.

"All the better. She'll be more motivated to help us," her father said.

"Good," she said. "I thought you were going to propose that we steal her trawlers."

"They can help us," George-Étienne said.

"But why would they?" Marthe said. "Marie-Pier has her own problems."

"She'll have to trust us," George-Étienne said.

"No one trusts you," Marthe said.

Her father's face twisted momentarily, but he didn't seem capable of regretting what she'd said.

"And on that basis, we can't ask the Hudons to help us commit theft," Marthe said.

"Then you should go talk to Marie-Pier," George-Étienne said.

"And pitch a heist to her?"

"No one can talk better than you," he said. "You're right. She'd turn me away at the door."

"What's in it for her, Pa?" she said.

"We think we've found a wormhole under the surface of Venus," her father said. "It changes everything, even if we don't yet know how. She can be a partner."

"*You're* going to take a business partner?"

"A minor partner."

"No one will help commit a crime for second banana. Equal partners or nothing."

"It's ours!" he said. "We need it."

"Something this big can help both of you. You want half the big prize or all of nothing?"

George-Étienne huffed loudly, but didn't disagree.

"How do we know she won't just go to the *présidente?*" Pascal said.

Pa looked at her for long seconds.

"Marthe will know how far to talk, and what not to say," he said.

Marthe tried to imagine what she might say to Marie-Pier Hudon and came up with nothing. Pa wanted her to sell a hole in the world, based on trust. And they didn't have trust. They didn't have anything. Marthe was soon to lose any political influence when she stopped being a delegate to *l'Assemblée*.

"Even if Marie-Pier says yes, I don't know if that's enough partners," she said.

"No more."

Marthe gave him a doubtful look.

"Who's going to do all that work, Pa? Do you even have the tools to take apart the *Causapscal-des-Vents?* You and Pascal aren't going to be enough."

"You," her father said.

She gave him the look again.

"Émile," Pascal said.

George-Étienne frowned and ignored the remark.

"If I need to try to convince Marie-Pier, this is all going to come up," she said. "The *Causapscal-des-Vents* won't float in the clouds for a year while you take it apart and try to hammer its parts into different shapes. We don't have the equipment. And I'm not sure this can be done."

"Damn it, Marthe, that's why I asked you for advice! *La colonie* has been shitting on the D'Aquillons for twenty-seven years. Now we've struck gold! If we lose this chance, it'll kill me. To give our family something would make it all worth it. Show me how."

Pa was alone in many ways. Jeanne-Manse was dead. Chloé and Mathurin had been taken by Venus too. Émile had left because he was Émile, and because Pa was Pa. And here Pa still was, trying to keep his family alive and happy beneath the lower cloud deck, shrouded in acid mist. He wasn't a fool. He loved them. They were here because family came first for him. Jean-Eudes was alive and happy and laughing with painted toes because family came first.

How many families would have chosen differently?

In all the history of *la colonie,* none. So Pa didn't trust anyone else.

Faced with all the pressure the poor, fledgling government could muster, George-Étienne and Jeanne-Manse had still brought Jean-Eudes into the world. This wormhole, this cave in the wrinkled hide of Venus, was Marthe's Jean-Eudes moment. The easy choice would be to say no, to go back to sixty-fifth *rang* and find some way to make a life. She could. She was good enough to find another job and maybe even make her way back onto *l'Assemblée.* She didn't need to become a criminal. She didn't need to put her reputation and freedom at risk.

But that wasn't what George-Étienne would have chosen. And it wasn't what she would choose. She was George-Étienne's daughter, all the way to her painted toes.

"Give a girl something to drink if she's got to plot larceny," she said slowly.

George-Étienne grinned over an elation that burst almost visibly from his chest. He went to the dispensary. Pascal was looking at her, smiling. She squeezed him close and kissed his forehead.

"You and Pa are crazy, you know that?"

TWENTY-SEVEN

THE WALLS OF the *Causapscal-des-Profondeurs* vibrated in sympathy with the storm outside. Acid pelted with big drops, drumming the outer envelope of their home as thunder rolled outside. They'd come up to forty-eighth *rang* to avoid a bad cell of turbulence in the sub-cloud haze. They'd still hit a storm, but a storm at forty-eighth was better than the hotter, thicker weather at forty-fourth.

Pascal swung in his hammock as updrafts and cross-winds ripped at them. The skin of their habitat vibrated with the heaving effort of the propeller above their living space. Lightning had struck them twice so far, filling the trawler's electroplaques and charging all their batteries. Trawlers did most of their growing in the tail hours of storms, when fully fed and drenched with acid.

Marthe and Pa worked out on the gantry. In a storm like this they had to inspect everything every few hours. It would be Pascal's turn in the early morning, so he'd been trying to get some sleep.

Storms midwived Venusian life, broke apart the budding colonies of blastulae, rosettes and trawlers, and churned lower atmosphere minerals up to the cloud-living bacteria. Storms affected humans more ambiguously. A storm had taken Chloé and Mathurin. Caught outside when it struck, they'd sheltered in one of the domesticated trawlers, but the storm had been bad. The D'Aquillon herd had been scattered far and wide. Half the herd was never seen again, nor Chloé and Mathurin, leaving Alexis an orphan.

But sometimes the storms brought new life to people, too. More than once, a terrifying storm had thrown them clinging and sick into steady air, only to find that Venus had taken thousands of trawlers and pushed them into the same eddy as the *Causapscal-des-Profondeurs*. The family could rope and tag up to twenty trawlers in as many hours, which was subsistence and even wealth for a year. Sometimes the storms of the lower cloud deck punched so deep that they scooped up tons of metal-rich volcanic ash in their winds. And every so often, Venus did neither good nor bad, but just thrashed pointlessly at her new tenants, like tonight. Jean-Eudes groaned. He didn't like storms. Pascal never got storm-sick. In the soft light, he was watching his toenails, shiny and red.

His thoughts felt like the silt in the cave, obscuring, shaken about, needing time to settle. And Marthe was like a storm herself, never leaving anything untouched in her wake. She loved him, even if he didn't love himself. The force of her was like a prop, giving him a tiny boost of courage, direction in the storm. He didn't hate himself either, exactly. He hated his body. It was alien to him, distant, someone else's. He could avoid mirrors, shave his face clean every morning, shave his whole body, and yet not escape the oppressive weight of wrongness. Except the once, when he'd snuck into his father's room and put on *maman's* dress. In that one moment, in that single frame of a movie of his entire life, it was like he'd finally seen something right. He'd seen himself.

Like a storm, Marthe created and destroyed. She'd invented a painful, terrifying hope, even as she seemed to have stared right through to the center of him. He didn't want anyone looking at him. No one could understand what it was to stand in front of people, pretending to belong to the world, and feeling like a liar and a fraud. In the *Causapscal-des-Profondeurs,* he could pretend forever, with his father and Jean-Eudes. They loved him without reserve, but couldn't see him, couldn't see the unhappiness and in-turned acid and corrosive hopelessness of pretending.

Yet the only thing worse than pretending was being seen.

The disturbed silt in his mind hinted at a cloudy idea that terrified him.

What if Pascal were really a girl? What would that knowledge tell him? Tell her? He couldn't reveal himself to the world. It was his secret. Her secret. Her secret to keep. It might not even be true. Pascal was sixteen. Hormones. He could be confused about lots of things. He didn't know what was wrong with him, why he felt so bad about who he was, when even Jean-Eudes was so at ease with himself. The cloudy idea wasn't getting clearer.

The toes winked back at him, shining in the gloomy light. Pascal had that one image, the look of himself in the dress, looking back at him in the mirror. And he had stared through another piece of glass, through the layers of Venus, and found stars.

What could Pascal do? What could Venus do? No one would ever see the stars. They would only look at Venus and see her deceiving clouds, her ugly, wrinkled hide, never see what she really contained. And this was Pascal's body. He couldn't leave it, just as Venus couldn't leave hers.

Jean-Eudes sat up, groaning. "What is it?" he asked.

"What?"

"Are you crying?"

Pascal wiped at his cheeks and found tears.

"Are you sad?" Jean-Eudes said, hopping from his hammock and lurching over on the shifting floor. He clung to Pascal's hammock and brought his face very close. "Are you scared of the storm?"

Jean-Eudes was good. Jean-Eudes was never going to engineer new machines for them, or even be able to maintain a habitat on his own. And yet Pascal admired his older brother intensely. Jean-Eudes knew he was different, and he didn't care. He didn't care that he couldn't do everything his brothers and sisters could do. And Jean-Eudes was even getting used to being proud of his capable little nephew. Jean-Eudes just *was*, with an authenticity that was inspiring and terrifying. And Jean-

Eudes loved Pascal without any reservation.

"Yes, I'm sad."

"Why?" Jean-Eudes said, swaying over him.

"Something's not right with me, Jean-Eudes."

"Do you want water?"

"You were born a boy. You feel like a boy."

"Yes," Jean-Eudes said.

"What you feel matches your body," Pascal said.

"I'm a boy."

"And Chloé felt like a girl. She had a girl's body."

"And Marthe too. She feels like a girl. And she likes girls."

"I think I feel like a girl, Jean-Eudes."

His older brother stared down at him for a long time, his frown deepening. Then he suddenly burst out laughing. Pascal sat up in the swaying hammock.

"You wore a dress!" Jean-Eudes said.

Pascal wanted to smile, but he couldn't. Not now, not this time. He waited for his brother to stop.

"Jean-Eudes, what do you think it would be like if you felt like a girl, but had a boy's body?"

His brother's face sobered. "I don't know," he said finally.

"I never look in the mirror, Jean-Eudes. My heart expects to see someone like Marthe or Chloé or *maman*, but what I see is a man. If I look too quick, my heart is surprised. When I look, parts of me are missing and parts of me are extra."

Jean-Eudes was frowning again. "I think you look good," he said.

"My brain knows that I'm supposed to look like this, but my heart says that this is wrong. That's why I'm not happy."

"You would be happy if you were my sister?"

"Maybe."

"But you have this body," Jean-Eudes said.

"Yes."

"And you can't change your body."

"Not really."

Jean-Eudes stared at him unnervingly for long moments, and then lurched forward and gave him a crushing hug.

"You can be my sister."

Pascal wanted to shrivel and hide. Hope terrified more than despair. Pascal started crying, and Jean-Eudes held on.

TWENTY-EIGHT

MARTHE FLEW OUT of the *Causapscal-des-Profondeurs* as soon as the storm broke. It had taken them a few hours of asking through the *coureur* network to find out where the Hudon habitat was. The *coureurs des vents* could survive in bioengineered trawlers anywhere in the middle and lower cloud decks or even, as the D'Aquillons occasionally did, in the sub-cloud haze.

With less sunlight and smaller spaces, the *coureurs* were less independent than they said, and worked hard to live hand-to-mouth. They knew who produced what and had a laborious signaling system through their herds so they themselves couldn't be tracked, but they could still find each other as the winds blew them. The *Coureur des Tourbillons,* the center of Marie-Pier Hudon's calving operation, was about two hundred kilometers west of them, and about seven kilometers higher in the atmosphere, just beneath the layer of clear air of *Les Plaines.*

That was a significant hike, and her father had sold the family's homemade plane last year. So Marthe traveled the cheap way. They inflated a carbon-fiber balloon with oxygen, clipped her harness to it, and the *Causapscal-des-Profondeurs* slipped away beneath her, vanishing into the mist.

She rose for an hour through acid rain, into the clear air of *Les Plaines,* up past the middle cloud deck, until her little balloon carried her into the enormous vista of *Grande Allée.* The west-to-east wind was faster at this altitude, and from here her wing-pack would have a glide path to the *Coureur des Tourbillons.*

She unfurled her wings, hung herself upside down in her harness, and then unclipped. The exhilaration of flying seized her as she leveled out and followed the bottom of *Grande Allée.* The cloud tops of *Grande Allée's* floor were beautiful, with none of the mountainous stacking of the upper cloud deck. Forces in the atmosphere stabilized the winds and clouds here to cut a path right around Venus, as if someone had plowed the air clean. The engine of her wing-pack keened, carrying her fast as her altitude slowly bled away and she skimmed meters above the misty cloud heads with only her thoughts.

In the yellow-orange light, flying *Grande Allée* was a humbling experience. The cloud decks occupied a strange interstitial space, meaning different things to different people. To the *coureurs* who lived wrapped in clouds, the open skies were vast and vertiginous. To those living in the clear air beneath black sky and stars, the clouds induced a sense of drowning. Marthe could toggle between the two perspectives.

Flying in the clouds was also solitary in the best possible way. No politicking or romantic positioning here, no hunt for advantage, no blocking of opponents or seeking of the high ground. This was just her, small in the vastness.

She was worried about Pascal. She couldn't walk his path for him, or help him much more with his reflections. This all seemed sudden to her, but she hadn't been home in a year. He'd gone from fifteen to sixteen, with the confusion and awkwardness of adolescence, without even any hints of how to proceed. She ought to have been more present. Pa could teach Pascal how to run a herd of trawlers in the depths, but he couldn't guide him through the questions he had.

She worried about her Pa too. His patience was thinner than it had been. He'd been alone too long, struggling to keep them all alive. She saw him more clearly now, flaws, weaknesses and all. He had more flaws. He was quicker to anger. He carried more resentments and final words.

It might have been the calcification of self that came with age. The other, more frightening possibility was that he'd always been this way, and that Marthe had grown past him. It was an unsettling thought, one that forced her to consider the past of the family in the context of the flawed man her father was today. How many of the D'Aquillon hardships had been born of his intransigence, if he'd always been this way?

But those were hypotheticals, and she had more pragmatic concerns. She didn't know if she could carry the whole family. She knew someday she would have to, but didn't want it to be so soon. She couldn't even fix Émile. George-Étienne D'Aquillon and Jeanne-Manse had both been only twenty-four when they'd emigrated to Venus. She couldn't imagine making that kind of choice at this age. But Marthe wouldn't be alone in what Pa was proposing.

Pascal had come a long way in his self-studies as an engineer. He was fragile, but smarter than any of the family. His designs were sound and more inventive than anything she could have tried. And she herself was an able mechanic who knew tools and materials, as was Pa. But they needed something much more elaborate to turn engineering schematics into real structures.

She knew a lot of the mechanics and engineers in *la colonie*. Many had the right tools and far more skill than she had, but they were also the ones living in the best habitats, and therefore closest to Gaschel's party. She had an idea of someone who might be skilled enough, properly equipped, and who would have reason to help them commit a crime. But talking to him would be Pascal's job.

Marthe descended through the middle cloud deck and *Les Plaines* for three hours before her instruments told her she was close. Venus had some reasonable global positioning satellites; the problem was that everything kept shifting in the clouds, and weather fronts could interfere with positions. But she was in luck today. The positional transmitter in her helmet antenna picked up the intentionally weak signal of one of the herd of the *Coureur des Tourbillons*.

Coureurs lived like shepherds in winds that wanted to scatter their sheep. The peak of each domesticated trawler was mounted with a short-range transmitter, antenna and small propellers. When they drifted too far from their habitat, the propeller brought them back. It didn't always work. *Coureurs* lost their flocks to storms all the time.

Yet few ever mounted stronger transmitters. They didn't trust the government and preferred that the size of their flocks not be known. And to be honest, they didn't always trust each other. Her father suspected a few of his peers of finding his lost trawlers and not returning them, or of stealing them outright. She wasn't sure, but the fact of the matter was that it was difficult to know where a *coureur* was at any given time. And Marthe hadn't found the *Coureur de Tourbillons,* only a transmitting trawler, dark and small. She circled it in the shadowless orange light, looking at the direction its propeller was pointing, and winging in that direction. After a few kilometers, she started to hear the faint signal of the *Coureur des Tourbillons.*

The spraying acid of the clouds became a harder rain with fierce downdrafts. The engine on her wing-pack whined high and Marthe churned through the bright rain. Soon, a shadow loomed in the clouds. She was startled by its size. The bioengineered trawler was easily twice the diameter of the *Causapscal-des-Profondeurs,* maybe thirty meters across.

A wide gantry hung underneath, around a tail cable much longer and thicker than anything Marthe had ever seen under a trawler. She circled it once, ducked beneath, then slowed and stalled onto the hanging nets. She caught her breath for a moment. She was out of practice. Living in the high flotilla was making her soft. She felt heavy climbing onto the gantry, where she shucked her wing-pack. There was a spray and brush for neutralizing equipment and she was careful to get all the acid off her pack before hanging it in the wing shed.

"*Coureur des Tourbillons*," she transmitted, "this is Marthe D'Aquillon. Permission to come aboard."

While she waited for the answer, she turned to wiping down her suit and neutralizing the acid with only half her attention. The other half admired the immensity of the habitat. The woody exterior was brownish-black, slick with the basic, hydrophobic slime that protected trawlers from sulfuric acid. Within the slime, little bubbles formed where tiny stomata pumped gases out of the outermost envelope to maintain the habitat's buoyancy. The great tail cable flexed in the wind, at least one hundred meters long.

"Marthe," came the radio answer, although too staticky to identify the speaker, "come aboard."

Marthe climbed into the first chamber of the double airlock and applied another neutralizing spray to her suit. The inside and outside of the trawler were at about one atmosphere of pressure, so she cycled right away into the next chamber. From here, light flooded in from windows in the airlock doorways to both sides. The windows looked on the outer envelope of the trawler, filled with lamps and bright green thermophilic hydroponic crops, growing at fifty degrees in eighty percent humidity. It was a hothouse oasis in the clouds. She punched the button and this second chamber pumped out the carbon dioxide and hissed in nitrogen and oxygen.

The inner light greened and she wheeled open the next door and stepped through into a brightly-lit, torus-shaped space with brown, oiled floors. Three bioreactor tanks, side-lit, grew algae for food.

Standing before her with gloves, boots and a body apron was Marie-Pier, looking at her strangely. Two boys stood behind her, looking apprehensively. A man stood with crossed arms in the galley. He had Marie-Pier's eyes.

Marthe extended her arms and Marie-Pier wiped her down one last time with sodium bicarbonate, especially on her back and over her seals. When she was done, Marthe hissed open the seal on her neck and removed her helmet.

"I didn't expect you to visit personally, or for anyone to come so soon," Marie-Pier said. She was pretty for a woman in her early forties, although she wasn't exactly Marthe's type. Marthe mostly knew dramatic girls on the edge of not being able to hold their shit together. Marie-Pier had a speckling of acid point scars on her left cheek, just beside her eye, under a ponytail of brown hair. She gave the impression of respectability, despite the fact that she was one of the savviest black marketeers.

"I thought we might have some things to talk about," Marthe said, popping the locks on her wrist seals.

Marie-Pier stood back and let Marthe take off her own suit.

"Maxime and Florian," Marie-Pier said of the boys, who looked down shyly, "and my brother Marc." Marthe had never met him, but knew of him as a bioengineering technologist, part of the family business.

"*Bonjour,*" Marthe said, unsealing the front of her suit and peeling it down to step out. She hung it up, wiped her feet and stepped over the line. "Your home is beautiful. I've never seen a trawler this big."

Marie-Pier was a bioengineer who specialized in the weird genetic material of Venusian plant-life, playing with the metabolic pathways that controlled growth and maintenance. No doubt a lot of her attempts to build habitats out of trawlers had sunk into the atmosphere until incineration, but her successes were astonishing.

"*Merci.* You're not in the market for a trawler to replace the *Causapscal-des-Vents*, are you?" Marie-Pier asked.

Marthe shook her head, admiring the arching lines of the veining in the ceiling. "Not exactly." Brother and sister looked at her warily. "I was hoping to discuss political matters with you."

Marc made a face, pushed himself off the table and walked back into an area that looked like a lab. Marie-Pier put two glasses and a green juice on the galley table. The boys disappeared into a room. Marie-Pier poured.

"A bit shocking what happened in *l'Assemblée,* isn't it?" Marthe asked.

"You're going to have to be clever," Marie-Pier said.

"Clever isn't going to save me the *Causapscal-des-Vents*," Marthe said. "I'm looking for options, though."

She sipped. It was a mint juice, close to a cold tea.

"Do you have any?"

"I might."

"And you came here," Marie-Pier said. "You looking for a trawler?"

Marthe looked in the direction of the lab and the boys' room. She leaned across the table and spoke quietly.

"I have a business opportunity, but it's not the kind of opportunity I can talk about with many people."

Marie-Pier raised an eyebrow doubtfully.

"The D'Aquillons have found something very, very valuable on the surface of Venus," Marthe said. Marie-Pier regarded her patiently, the way she might wait out a barterer to see his opening price. "What we found could economically transform Venus, including our relationship with the Bank of Pallas."

"The Bank you've been criticizing for some time," Marie-Pier said.

"To be fair, I also criticize the government."

"You don't worry that I might run off and carry this news to *l'Assemblée?*"

"You don't know what we've found or where it is, and Venus is big."

"Why me?"

Marthe finished her mint juice, then played with the condensation it left on the table. "You're a straight shooter," she said slowly. "I think you have an incentive to help us. And I think you're smart enough to contextualize a small theft within the larger scheme of events."

"A theft?"

"A *small* theft, in the bigger picture."

"I trade on the black market, but I'm not interested in being a thief. Or in helping one."

Marthe nodded, sliding her glass into the middle of the table. "I understand," she said. "It probably wasn't a sound idea. You weren't the only partner we needed. I can go."

"You're not going to pursue your incalculable wealth?" Marie-Pier asked.

"You were my Plan A. I'll have to develop a Plan B."

"What was Plan A?"

Marie-Pier was staring at her. Marie-Pier the bioengineer and Marie-Pier the black marketeer were accustomed to being frank and being treated frankly. That's why she didn't like *l'Assemblée*. Empty words. Posturing.

"The government wants to take the *Causapscal-des-Vents*," Marthe said. "We need enough metal to build something on the surface. If it sank and looked like an accident, it wouldn't be the worst thing in the world."

"Steal a whole habitat?"

"It wouldn't be hard to make it look like it really sank," Marthe said. "No one gets blamed."

"Ballsy," Marie-Pier said. She hadn't said *reprehensible,* or *underhanded,* or *cowardly.*

"I'm sure I can come up with something after we lose the *Causapscal,*" Marthe said.

Marie-Pier eyed her unfinished juice. "What exactly does very, very valuable look like?" she asked.

"Unique," Marthe said, "hard to exploit, hard to hold onto, but I think incalculable is a reasonable valuation."

"Mineral?" Marie-Pier asked. "Animal? Vegetable? Technological?"

"Scientific and technological," Marthe said after musing on it.

"And everyone will want it."

"*Oui*," Marthe said. "But we're staking our claim."

"And the government has a right to it, just like they have a right to the *Causapscal-des-Vents?*"

"Just like they have a right to your bioengineered trawlers," Marthe said.

"And what kind of cut of 'incalculable' had you considered for me?"

"I don't know yet," Marthe said. "Do you want to talk about it with us?"

"You D'Aquillons are hard to trust."

"Have you ever known me or my father to be anything but plain-speakers?"

"No, and that's what got you into your trouble."

"And you?"

"Maybe," Marie-Pier said. "I never built the alliances I should have in *l'Assemblée*. But I'm not stupid either. I don't know your father except by deed. He hasn't got my back. If it's a choice between me and one of the D'Aquillon children, I have no illusions about the decision he'd make. That's no way to think about working together."

"Visit the *Causapscal-des-Profondeurs*," Marthe said. "If you can be discreet, we can talk there."

Marie-Pier slid her finger on the table, dragging condensation into thinning roads that she considered intently.

"No promises, no expectations," she said finally. "I'm just going for information."

TWENTY-NINE

THE FLOTILLA OF ninety-two habitats and factory floats around the *Baie-Comeau* was slowly crossing the terminator into night. The forward-most habitats were already in the somber starscape, like tiny, distant ships sailing on a curving reddened sea.

The *Baie-Comeau* had begun dropping in altitude. Although the lower winds were more turbulent, it was slightly warmer; enough that they needed less battery power to keep the greenhouses from freezing. Gaschel liked watching the habitats transition from forty-eight-hour day to forty-eight-hour night. The crops grew under lamps, the industries ran on low power, her people turned to indoor work and family time and enjoyed more sleep in what they called the long night.

The two men sat with their backs to the window.

"We did some looking, *Madame la Présidente*," Labourière said. "*Monsieur* Tétreau found some interesting things."

Tétreau turned a pad so she could see his display. He cleared his throat.

"It turns out that only three families regularly submit meteorological reports as deep as forty-fifth *rang*," Tétreau said. "The Mignaud family, the Cyr family, and the D'Aquillon family."

"Of course it might be Marthe D'Aquillon," Labourière said in exasperation.

Tétreau was looking for some sign from Gaschel's face. She didn't give one.

"The Mignauds and D'Aquillons herd and modify their own trawlers," Tétreau said, "just small stuff, not full bioengineering. They trade oxygen and water with other *coureurs* and occasionally with upper atmosphere families."

"Black market," Gaschel said.

"*Oui, madame,*" Tétreau replied.

Black markets were a necessary evil. Tétreau knew it. Labourière knew it. She knew it. She still didn't like it.

"What about the Cyrs?" she asked.

"Trawler breeders in the lower cloud decks," Labourière said. "They spend more time at fiftieth *rang*, but they also descend and have submitted met reports from lower altitudes."

"If we wanted to, how fast could you find them?" she asked.

"This wouldn't give us much more to go on," Tétreau said. "They don't submit the reports in real time, or from their central trawlers. They'll transmit upward through a transmitter-repeater setup on the most distant trawlers in their herds."

"But you can build up patterns over time," she said. "Where they've been, they'll go again."

"The D'Aquillons and the Mignauds are also volcano chasers," Tétreau said. "They've fitted some of their trawlers to drag nets of rosette fronds through the lower cloud deck, and especially the sub-cloud haze, where volcanic ash may be floating. They can harvest up to a dozen kilograms of metals and minerals in a good month of trawling. But this means that they'll go wherever they think volcanoes and really low storms have conspired to lift metallic and mineral dust into the sub-cloud haze."

Gaschel didn't look pleased.

"I pulled in some favors," Tétreau offered. "I have a cousin married to a *coureur* at fifty-fifth *rang*. He looked into acquiring some metals from D'Aquillon. They met up and he traded for some. He sent me up a sample."

Gaschel's eyebrows rose.

Tétreau produced a small plastic ziplock bag with about thirty grams of black powder.

"Very mildly radioactive," he said, "nothing that couldn't be explained by contamination."

She took the bag, squeezed it. The texture was wrong.

"This isn't volcanic ash," she said. "It's been processed?"

"I've seen processed ash," he said. "It's finer than this. This has been roughly ground."

"What does that mean?"

"I used labs on the *Petit Kamouraska*," he said. "These aren't the normal elements that come out of volcanic ash. It's heavily enriched with iridium, tungsten and platinum group metals."

"We haven't looked very hard for platinum metals on the surface," she said, squeezing the bag again, considering the grains.

"We don't think we'll ever find any," Labourière said. "Tungsten and platinum group metals bind strongly to iron. During the resurfacing of Venus half a billion years ago, iron sank in the molten crust."

"We should *never* see these metals coming out of volcanoes," Tétreau added. "We would expect to see them in iron-nickel asteroids. Not only that—there are fragments of clays mixed in this sample. Very few, but they're there. Venus has no clays because it has no water."

Her office had dimmed as they passed the terminator. Now the lights came on. She placed the bag on her desk between them.

"And how many ways are there to get asteroidal metal and fragments of clays down to the forty-fifth *rang*?" she asked.

Labourière made a doubtful face. "The same two ways Woodward hit you with," he said, finally. "One of the *coureurs* is trading with one of the other Banks in secret, or the Bank of Pallas is trading with the *coureurs* in secret and isn't telling you."

She sat back. The darkness outside had closed in. The approaching cloud tops gave the impression of being poised to swallow the *Baie-Comeau*.

"Since the Bank of Pallas brought this to us, we might assume that it isn't them," she said, "meaning the *coureurs* are playing with another Bank, violating our loan contracts with the Bank of Pallas."

"Unless the Bank of Pallas itself is setting up a false flag operation to find us in violation in advance of our next debt negotiations," Labourière said glumly.

Gaschel ground her teeth. "What made you focus on D'Aquillon?" she asked.

"George-Étienne D'Aquillon doesn't have any love for the government," Tétreau said, "and this happened just after Marthe D'Aquillon started posting her arguments in the flotilla web."

"The Mignauds don't love us either," she mused, "but George-Étienne's resentment is old."

"My talk with Marthe wasn't very useful," Labourière said. "I offered spots on the *Forillon,* but I don't think she'll be easy to buy off."

"Everyone has a weakness," Gaschel said. "Find out what theirs is."

"The second son, Émile, isn't rumored to be much of a friend to his father," Tétreau said. "Bit of a drunk and drug-head."

"Doesn't sound like getting him on our side would do much," Gaschel said.

"I made first contact with him. Now might be the time to try seeing what we can get from him," Tétreau said, "while Marthe is in the depths consulting with her family."

"I want to know where they are. Where they all are," Gaschel said.

She gently ground the powder in the plastic bag.

"If someone is getting radioactives from another Bank, or even from *our* Bank, we need to know and we need to know fast," she said. "Put planes and drones into the atmosphere. I want a real search. If we can't figure out who's doing it, and it puts the *colonie* in danger, we may need to arrest all three families and search their habitats."

THIRTY

PASCAL ROSE AND rose with a queasy, excited knotting in his stomach. He was in an emergency safe-bag, basically a hammock-chair inside a narrow plastic umbrella sheet sealed at the bottom. The whole thing hung under a flabby balloon of oxygen carrying him higher and higher.

Every *coureur* had enough of these for everyone who lived in their trawlers, for getting to urgent medical attention or to flee a sinking habitat. The balloon would only take him up to about fifty-eighth *rang*, but *la colonie* distributed itself so that at any time, some habitat of the flotilla was within a few hours and could provide a pickup. "Be careful," George-Étienne had said, assembling the safe-bag on the gantry for him.

"I will, Pa."

"Watch the storms," his father said. "If they get bad, drop and try again later. Or duck and find a *coureur* habitat."

"I've been herding with you for years, Pa."

"Don't trust anyone up there," his father said. "Don't tell anyone except Phocas that you're a D'Aquillon."

"I won't, Pa," Pascal said.

"That includes your brother," his father said, dropping the plastic around his survival suit.

"I know, Pa."

Pascal had dutifully lifted one foot, then the other, so that George-Étienne could seal him in. His father fussed with the wires, gave him a hug, and then inflated the balloon. It rose, bumping its way up the undercurve of the *Causapscal-des-Profondeurs*. When he was done, it tugged hard on its peg. His father looked through both their faceplates and the layer of plastic.

"Come home, Pascal."

"I will, Pa."

He gave his father the thumbs-up. George-Étienne pulled the slipknot and Pascal swung off the gantry. Before he could swing back, the top of the *Causapscal-des-Profondeurs* was already five meters beneath him. Two more swings and his home was a darker smear in the hot haze. Then it was gone, and he found himself peering futilely up through the acid-covered sheeting. But there was nothing to see except the balloon carrying him higher and higher. The haze was the same from every direction.

The altimeter in his helmet showed him rising fast: at forty-six kilometers, the temperature dropped below the boiling point of water. The altitude tickled in his stomach with vertigo. He'd worked with his father outside for three years in the suit and wing-pack Chloé had worn as a teenager, but always within a few kilometers of the habitat. He felt different now. He'd left home. For the first time. He was terrified—of what he would see, of what the world would see in him.

Was this what Émile had felt like when he'd left home? His stomach lurched, not from the wind. He hadn't thought about Émile's leaving for a while. He didn't like feeling that the family was breaking apart.

Five years ago, he'd been eleven, feeling odd in his skin, and his family had already been breaking for some time. *Maman* had been dead for five years, and Marthe had been in the upper atmosphere for a year. Pa and Émile yelling had woken him. The youngest of the children, Pascal had missed the beginning of many arguments, and didn't speak the shorthand adults used to fight. Jean-Eudes snored restlessly.

"How is that responsible?" Émile demanded. "No medicine. No rations. Who are you helping? What if Pascal gets sick? Or Alexis?"

"Or Jean-Eudes, *ostie?*"

Both of them had been drinking. Pascal slipped from his hammock.

"Jean-Eudes doesn't have medicine," Émile slurred. "That hasn't changed. All you've done is said that *you* won't let anyone in your family get medicine or rations."

"That's for your brother!" Pa yelled. Émile and Pa stood toe to toe. Émile's head almost brushed the inner wooden ceiling of the habitat, but Pa was bigger. His heart made him bigger. Being their father made him bigger, and there was a hesitation in Émile's stance in the face of Pa's heart.

"Nobody changed their minds!" Émile said. "We're just down here rotting, making your moral gesture. *Tabarnak!* We're not even doing that. We get rations now, thanks to Marthe."

"We're not eating goddamn government rations!" Pa said, stabbing his finger into Émile's chest. "Marthe grew every damn bean she sends us."

"Every habitat does that," Émile said, waving his hand dismissively. "We went almost twenty years with less food than we needed because you wanted to make your point."

"*Colon!* Jean-Eudes is the point. If you don't love him, go find some fucking medicine!"

Émile leaned closer. "I can, any time I want. So can Marthe. Even you can. You know who can't? *Maman,* because you brought us down here. You killed her."

Pa stood in white-faced shock. Pascal, in the shadows, stood by stupidly. Pascal had never connected Jean-Eudes and living in the depths and *maman.* Pa swung his fist at Émile. But Émile was fast. He caught Pa's fist in one hand and held it there, against all of Pa's force. They stared at each other over the shaking fist. Émile seemed to grow taller as his right arm drew back. Pa looked at Émile in eye-narrowed defiance.

Pascal ran out. "*Non! Arrêtez!*"

Émile's fist snapped forward, knocking back Pa's head, throwing him to the floor.

"Pa!" Pascal screamed.

He hammered his fists into his brother's arm and ribs. It didn't do anything but hurt his hands. Émile put his hand

246

on Pascal's head, gently, the way Jean-Eudes touched Alexis.

"You'll see one day, Pascal," Émile said slowly. A tear ran down his cheek.

Pa rolled up, holding his eye, looking up at Émile.

"Get out," he said coldly, quietly. "I wish you'd never been born. You're not a real man."

Émile turned, patting Pascal's head as he walked to the airlock.

"*Non!*" Pascal screamed. "Go where? He can't go anywhere! It's too hot to stay out! He has to come back to cool off."

Émile was putting on his survival suit. Jean-Eudes was groaning awake. Alexis mewled in his hammock.

"Émile! Don't go!" Pascal said. His brother sealed the chest of his suit. Pascal wiped his eyes. "*Papa! Papa!* Make him stop! Take it back! Émile! Take it back!"

Pa rose from the floor, still holding his eye. Jean-Eudes was up and didn't understand. Émile's back was to them and he fitted on his helmet, snapping the seals.

"Émile!" Pascal cried, and he ran across the line as Émile stepped to the airlock door.

"Pascal!" Pa yelled.

Pascal gripped his brother's waist and looked down, seeing his bare feet across the line. There was no burning. The acid burned inside him. Émile stroked Pascal's hair with a gloved hand, then gently picked him up under the arms and set him on the right side of the line.

"Émile..." Pascal said, but so quiet that Émile couldn't hear him through the helmet. Émile opened the airlock and stepped in. "Take it back..."

"Émile is going outside?" Jean-Eudes asked.

Pa came to Jean-Eudes, planted a kiss on the top of his head and then moved to the kitchen, still holding his eye and swearing.

Jean-Eudes neared. "You shouldn't cross the line," he said to Pascal. "You're a good boy, but you shouldn't cross the line."

Pascal began sobbing, and hugged Jean-Eudes around the chest. Jean-Eudes hugged him back tightly.

Émile had never come back.

His trip to the upper atmosphere was the exact one that Pascal was taking now. Clouds roiled, changing shape tirelessly. Most of the time he was inside them, and it was darker, but bubbles of clear air shot through the clouds, some of them kilometers across. He felt movement; he felt himself rising with a frisson of aimless terror. He would come back. Whatever he found up there, it wouldn't be home.

Suddenly, the world brightened and expanded. Ocher clouds laid a thin drizzle of rain over the plastic around him. Every so often in the middle deck, gusting east winds pushed his balloon westward. The higher he climbed, the faster the winds would carry him. He marveled at the size of the rain drops. They ran fat rivulets over the survival sack, cloudy with the acidophilic Venusian bacteria. The clouds were alive up here.

He became disembodied, one with the storm and with the cooling of the air. Layers separated him from the world, so that he could imagine himself bodiless, a creature of thought and feeling, detached and peaceful. This feeling lasted for a long time, until he floated up, out of the middle cloud deck, and into the big openness of *Grande Allée*.

He'd never been this high before. The light was becoming strange. The polarized yellow became directional and bright. Light definitely came from *above*, from a single source. Holding one glove over another made a fuzzy shadow, like artificial indoor lights did. As he rose, the world took on an unnatural quality, an unreal focus. He felt like an explorer, like everything he saw would be strange. The slowly moving ceiling of *Grande Allée* held its breath as his expanding balloon drew him into the brightness.

A few minutes later, his radio crackled. "Pascal?"

Pascal scanned the too-bright clouds.

"Émile?" he said.

"Pascal!" a voice said through the static. "Got a fix on you. Be right there."

Pascal's heart thumped faster with nervous excitement. He'd been sneaking brief messages to Émile over the last year, but he'd gotten back little more than unsettling poems. Haunting genius soaked his brother's poetry, a longing that frightened him by resonating with some unknown part of himself. But apart from that, he didn't know his brother.

Pascal's safe-bag lurched, rocked and began sinking. The ropes shook and feet stepped above his seat. Together, they sank. A knife came out, and the plastic ripped away and fell around him. Then the knife was gone and the sure feet slipped into footholds. A massive angel with great light wings grabbed Pascal.

"You got big!" Émile's blue eyes glittered behind his faceplate, over a bearded face. Pascal smiled and nodded.

"Stay there a sec," Émile said, letting him go and pulling something big from behind him. "You've never used upper-atmosphere wing-packs, eh?"

"No."

Émile hooked an arm through the seat as they sank and sulfuric acid rain started speckling their suits. One-handed, Émile levered the second wing-pack to Pascal's back. Émile was so big. He remembered Émile as a giant, but it was like Pascal was still a child compared to Émile. Pascal shrugged into the strange wing-pack, strapped it tight and plugged it into a pocket jack. A new dashboard appeared inside his faceplate.

"It's almost like flying with the lower deck wing-packs," Émile said, "but these are sensitive as anything. Steady hand. And they're like parachutes in a cross-current or updraft."

"I can do it," Pascal said.

Émile clapped him on his chest, grinning.

"Of course you can, little brother! Go. I'll follow to make sure the safe-bag doesn't snag us."

Pascal climbed up the ropes and freed his feet. The wings were huge. Furled, they went past his feet.

"Dive, straighten out, unfurl and then spin up your engine," Émile said. "If you haven't flown these before, you don't want to dive backwards."

Pascal leapt, trying not to shake Émile much. He

plummeted through the cloud. Pascal had been flying for years and he oriented himself fast, opening his wings. They pulled him into level flight at once. The engine roared to life, thrusting him forward, climbing.

"Right behind you," Émile said in his radio. "Be aggressive with the angle of attack. These things are hard to stall. If it gets bumpy, keep climbing. Getting above the turbulence of *Les Rapides Plats* will be choppy."

Pascal felt strangely young. It had been a long time since Émile had taught him anything. Not that he'd ever taught Pascal anything useful. Marthe and Chloé and Pa taught him all he knew about living on Venus. Émile taught him to make fart noises with his armpit, how to make spit-balls, and how to burn holes in scrap metal when Pa and Chloé were out of the habitat. But Émile's eager encouragement made the past touch the present, in a happy way.

Pascal got a feel for the wings, shifting his weight, testing the control surfaces before throttling up. The lift they produced was startling. And the air was so light around him. The wings from down home suddenly felt clumsy and poor.

But he wasn't underestimating what was coming. He'd read that from the cloud tops, *la colonie* could look down upon a washer-board pattern of clouds, rowed tubes going on forever into the distance. The wind moved too slowly in the depths to form rolling convection cells the *colonistes* called *Les Rapides Plats*.

Pascal was coming at *Les Rapides Plats* from underneath and even before he'd come close, the turbulence vibrated his whole body. He kept his throttle on full, increased his angle of attack and, with a terrifying shudder in his wings, he was swept violently upward. The straps squeezed him, twisting, and his wing-pack creaked.

"Throttle to full!" Émile called.

He already had, but it was hard to pick the right angle of attack, or even stick to one. Every few moments, one wind or another tried to tip him. An updraft lifted him dizzyingly fast and at the crest of his rise, the wind tried to claw back at the tip of his port wing.

"Bank right!" Émile said.

The mist churned. It was almost easy to see some of its invisible movements, but he didn't have an intuition for it. He banked right and exited the rolling convection cell at its peak. As he looked up, the clouds turned on themselves, vapor twisting into ghostly tubes, like a washer-board visible only against a certain angle of light. The upper winds blew so much faster that the next layer beneath acted like the rollers on a conveyor belt.

"Pick a cell," Émile said, "get the direction right, and then get in at the bottom and ride the updraft! Go on! Don't wait too long!"

Pascal timed it and flew straight into the bottom of a horizontal barrel of wind a kilometer in diameter, striated with filaments of cloud pulled into long, thin strings. A twisting wind wrenched him sideways. He struggled to level his flight. He swooped down, throttled and pulled up again, and winds buffeted him with no pattern. He was used to storms. He lived among them. But deep storms were immense things, with churning wind streams kilometers wide. For every meter he climbed here, the roaring, battering wind knocked him down half.

"Increase your angle of attack!" Émile said. "You just have to power through the turbulence."

He did it. It was hard, but he did it. Over the next torturous fifteen minutes, Pascal climbed two kilometers, before finally emerging from the invisible mob of windy fists wrenching him around. He felt like he'd worked an hour running new cabling off a trawler. His brother was saying encouraging things in the radio, but Pascal was almost too tired to hear, and the stars were all around, winking through the last layers of clouds.

Pascal throttled full again and plunged into what he thought was the bottom of another air cell, intending to climb. He entered poorly, the lower edges of it far bigger than he was expecting, as was its speed. His engine keened and he pulled up, following the rise of the cell.

"Beautiful!" Émile said.

It was dizzying. Thrilling. His stomach left itself somewhere down in the bottom arc. He climbed and shot out the top and the air, while still unruly, became manageable. Venus stopped playing with him.

The clouds above glowed a searing white. His faceplate tried auto-darkening, but he overrode it, craning his neck to look sideways at the bright disk forming behind the clouds. It was too intense to look at straight on.

The sun. He was going to see the sun for the first time.

The clouds broke and a terrible, burning whiteness stared back at him. His eyes watered and finally he had to look away, blinking at tears. The top of the upper cloud deck wasn't regular and flattened like the floors of *Les Plaines* and *Grande Allée*. Its bright surface sloped up over cloudy hills, dove into wide valleys and through shadowed caverns of mist. Vaporous cumulus foothills rose into towering mountains of cumulonimbus. In some places, fingers of moisture reached over transparent hollows of air, while in others bursts of cyclonic fury funneled columns of yellow-white towards the black sky. This textured, aerial world bore no correspondence to Venus's corrugated gray flesh below. It was enchanting and unsettlingly false.

"It's your first time seeing the stars, isn't it?" Émile asked.

"It's beautiful."

"Day or night, the stars are always shining." Émile darted ahead on a steep climb. "Come on!"

Pascal followed. They made for a habitat shining green in the distance. As they neared, others came into view, dozens, hovering like tiny emeralds in the cloudscape. The strange dirigibles with bloated, transparent envelopes contained more green than he'd ever seen.

Accustomed as he was to the organic shapes and cobbled-together grafting of the living trawler habitats, there was something marvelous about the smooth, straight lines in the habitats, even those with obvious acid damage and missing paint and discolored panels. In the far, far distance, almost out of sight, other humans flew on wing-packs like his. Strangers. He knew almost no one outside of his family, and those he'd met were all visiting *coureurs*. The thought of talking to strangers excited him, with an edge of panic.

They came closer and closer to a habitat, and finally circled it once and then landed. Pascal flubbed the landing. The wing-pack was too sensitive. In the depths of forty-fifth *rang,* they had to land under the habitat by stalling just before hitting hanging nets. Here, at the sixty-fifth *rang,* he had to land on a flat surface. When he flared to kill his forward speed, he overdid it and flipped onto his back and hit the deck before sliding into the crash netting. He didn't have time to sort himself out before strong hands lifted him entirely out of the netting.

"That was great, Pascal!" Émile said. "I've never seen anyone fly so well on their first time! You should have seen me when I first tried these stupid things, and I was older than you."

Émile set him on his feet. It felt strange to have nothing above them but black starry sky and the sun. And Émile's full size was apparent now. He was big, taller than Pascal by thirty or forty centimeters and much wider, heavily muscled under his suit. Émile was smiling down at him through the faceplate.

"Come here, little brother!" Émile said, hugging him close. "I missed you."

"Me too," Pascal said.

They got themselves out of the wing-packs, which wasn't easy. Pascal's wings were longer than he was tall and he had to bend over to furl them. After they neutralized and stowed the wing-packs, Émile put an arm around his shoulders and gestured wide.

"Welcome to the upper world," he said. "The sun, the stars, all the habitats." When Pascal couldn't think of anything to say, Émile filled the silence again. "I'm really glad you came."

"Me too," was all Pascal could think to say.

Émile dropped his arm. "I'm sorry I left you with the old man," he said. "I couldn't live with him anymore. It was for the best."

Pascal nodded.

"And I'm sorry I wasn't there to help look for Chloé and Mathurin."

"It wouldn't have helped."

He wanted to say something nice, about Émile's poetry, but he didn't understand where he fit into the verses. He didn't know yet how to untangle the sadness in the poems, the sadness in missing his brother, and the sadness that throbbed in him.

"It's good to see you!" Émile said, grabbing Pascal's shoulders.

At the edge of the platform on top of the habitat, fenced by netting, was a set of stairs down the side. The view from them was dizzying for no reason at all. It wasn't the faint sounds carried to his helmet on winds too thin to properly touch him. He'd lived his whole life on heights. But he'd never *seen* any of them. He'd lived in clouds without definition, life without shape, within a reddened darkness like a baby might have felt in a womb.

And now he was under the cold stars. The cloud tops reflected an eye-stinging white light, with no heat or pressure from Venus at all, like he was in a numb, deaf new world. He felt like crawling back into the gloom of the clouds. Pascal gripped the railing. It wasn't far. Three meters down, out of the ghostly wind, was an airlock door. Émile spun the handle and they stepped in.

Pascal reached for his neutralizing pad and wiped. Émile laughed when he saw the fraying carbon-fiber rag embedded with sodium bicarbonate. Émile took it and looked at it.

"How long have you been carrying this around, Pascal? Was this Marthe's or mine before you got it? Throw it away."

He pulled plastic-wrapped pads out of a pouch and gave one to Pascal. Pascal put his old cloth back in his pocket and unwrapped the pad. It might not be new, but it was newer than anything he'd ever seen.

"Turn around," Émile said, spinning Pascal with a big hand. The pressure of his brother's hand ran on the top and back of his helmet, around the neck seals, over his whole back and shoulders and under his arms, neutralizing the sulfuric acid.

"*Sapristi!*" Émile said, sounding eerily like Pa. "This suit is a walking wreck. You need a new suit."

"Jean-Eudes has been patching it for me," Pascal said nervously.

The hand on his back stopped.

"He's been doing a good job," Émile said, as the hand moved to the lower back. "You know *maman* and I taught him how to patch suits, eh? Took the little bugger years to not burn his fingers with the sealant. He got frustrated and cried." Émile's hands worked at the backs of Pascal's legs. "I taught him how to wash dishes so I wouldn't have to. Lost cause though. *Maman* didn't let me get away with it."

Émile's voice was distant, longing.

"I taught him and Alexis how to check the valves for leaks," Pascal said. "He likes that too."

"No shit! You're a good brother." Émile said, finishing the backs of Pascal's legs and heels. "So is Jean-Eudes," he said more quietly.

For a moment, awkward silence held them. Then Pascal turned and Émile turned his back and dutifully lifted his arms. Pascal had to reach for the top of Émile's helmet. His suit was almost patch-free, new and shiny, with good pockets sealed against the acid. They wiped down their own fronts and sides, and then their seals again while the airlock finished hissing in new air.

Finally, Émile wheeled open the next door, revealing a long interior hallway filled with drawers and shelves. Windows opened onto the bright greenhouse layer. They cracked the neck seals on their helmets. The air was cool and thin. He breathed deeply. It was like inhaling nothing. The atmosphere was a ghost. Émile pulled off his helmet and grinned down at him from a tangled brown beard.

"I can't believe how much you've grown up," he said. "You're a good-looking kid. We should show you to a nice girl."

Pascal's cheeks heated and he looked at his feet.

Émile laughed. "Oh, they're going to love you."

The lack of air felt suffocating. The heat in his cheeks. The cold air. His brother. The pressure of pretending. He took a deep breath.

"It's so big," Pascal said.

"This is just a work area. The living area is smaller."

They followed narrow stairs down the inside of the envelope.

"Everything looks so clean and new," Pascal said. "They're really going to scrap it?"

"Oh, this isn't the *Causapscal-des-Vents*," Émile said. "We're on *l'Avant-Gardiste*. A friend of mine is crashing here."

"I need to get to the *Marais-des-Nuages*," Pascal said, stopping.

"I know. This'll take just a minute. I wanted you to meet someone."

"Who?"

"Thérèse. She's special to me. I want her to know my family."

"Hasn't she met Marthe?" Pascal said.

A quick, furtive flinch darted over Émile's face, but he put on a smile that Pascal wasn't sure was real.

"Marthe is a handful sometimes. It wasn't a great meeting. And you're my little brother! I'm proud of you!" He slapped Pascal's shoulder and Pascal felt himself smiling. "Marthe showed me all the engineering texts she got for you. You're going to be somebody, one of the bosses who tells mechanics like me and Marthe what to do! Can you imagine? I can't wait to grab my deck-buddies and say, 'Look! Our boss is my little brother!'"

"I need to talk to Phocas," Pascal said.

"This won't take long. Come on!"

Émile led Pascal down the last stairs, through a single pressure door and into a small space that was kitchen, dining area and living area. No one was here, but Pascal marveled at the lines, the way everything fit together. Machine beautiful.

"She works night shifts mostly," Émile whispered, "and crashes in friends' hammocks when they're not using them."

Émile peeked around a curtain into a bedroom.

"What is it?" a woman's voice said. Not sleepy at all.

"I have a visitor, *ma chérie*," Émile said. "My little brother is here."

"He can't stay here."

"No, *bébé*. I just wanted him to meet you."

She sighed heavily.

"I don't have to," Pascal said as his stomach turned on itself again.

"No, it's okay. She's gonna love you."

Émile pulled on his arm until they passed the curtain into a gloomy room. A thin, black-haired woman rocked on a hammock, cigarette between two lazy fingers. Her undershirt was sleeveless and ornate images ran up her arms and over bony ribs. She was beautiful, austere, stormy and utterly unselfconscious. A sadness crept upon him, a kind of mourning envy for the self-possession this woman had, that he couldn't imagine ever having.

"He doesn't look anything like you," she said in a bored drawl.

Émile laughed. "No? Lucky him, eh? I take after my Pa. Pascal looks like *maman*. And he's smart. He's burning his way through the engineering curriculum and he's getting top marks."

Émile stepped awkwardly to Thérèse and kissed her cheek.

"Pascal, this is Thérèse. She's an artist, and my muse."

"I... I've read Émile's poetry," Pascal said. "You must be a good muse."

Thérèse looked at Émile, who looked sheepish and Pascal thought he'd said something wrong.

"It was really nice meeting your brother, Émile," she said finally. She turned to Pascal. "It was very nice to meet you, Pascal."

"Will I see you later?" Émile asked her.

"I'm working on a new piece," she said impatiently.

The room was bare of anything artistic.

Émile kissed her cheek again, took a drag on her cigarette and handed it back to her. Then he was shepherding Pascal out the door, back through the pressure door and up the stairs.

"She's an artist," Émile said apologetically. "She has an artistic soul, you know? Her muse strikes when it strikes. I think she liked you. She's great, isn't she?"

"Yeah," Pascal said.

"It's hard to be with an artist."

Pascal had to stop halfway up the stairs to catch his wheezing breath. Émile patted his shoulder.

"Happens to all of us, buddy," he said. "You'll get over it in about a month."

Pascal didn't say he wasn't going to be here a month. Émile must have known that.

"Thanks for saying something nice about my poetry," Émile said. "I might be getting better. You're the only one I've ever shown it to."

"Really? Why?"

"Poetry is something close, especially if it sucks," Émile said, smiling easily. "Who else could I show it to? Marthe? Think I need her judging me more? Thérèse? I'm trying to impress her. Jean-Eudes wouldn't understand. You're the only one I can trust."

He felt like hugging Émile. He felt for a moment like they were family. But he was a stranger too.

"It pisses off Thérèse that I don't show her. She might even wonder if I'm actually writing anything. Around every beautiful artist, you'll get a lot of guys who'll just pretend, just to be around her. I fucking hate poseurs."

· Émile was still smiling, his eyes bright, his sheer faith in the conversation dragging it forward. But the last statement was true. Pascal saw it. Émile hated people who pretended to be what they weren't. With a sinking feeling, Pascal turned, as if from a blow, and began trudging up the stairs. He slipped on his helmet, sealed it and turned the air to one and a half atmospheres.

THIRTY-ONE

PASCAL AND ÉMILE winged across the constellation of floating habitats. The *Marais-des-Nuages,* the Phocas habitat, was forty kilometers ahead and their wing-pack engines whined in the high, thin air. They climbed high enough that even the wayward white mists and snow clouds floated beneath them, with the habitats laid out like tumbled gems on yellow-white velvet. They flew among the stars now; stars extended in every direction, limited only by the gentle curve of Venus and the sun.

"Where's the Earth?" Pascal asked.

"Behind the sun right now, I think," Émile said. "We'll catch up to it in a couple of weeks."

Pascal was vaguely disappointed. He hadn't realized until now that he'd wanted to see the Earth. He was Venusian. That was the only certainty he had about who he was. But even the Venusians had come from somewhere. His parents had been born in Québec. His blood came from Earth. If he went there, he would find cemeteries marking the passing of the people who had come before. Ancestors.

People left no mark on Venus. His mother left no mark, other than her children and her husband. No Venusian had a grave. The Earth would only have been a tiny disk, perhaps just a blue dot, but he felt that it would have been something, to see his roots. Something to ground him.

"When are you going to move up to sixty-fifth *rang*?" Émile asked. "We could spend time together. I could show you around. How to live up here. It's weird and different, but so much better."

His brother sounded lonely, but Pascal couldn't see him. Émile was just a featureless winged figure ahead. Pascal wanted to bridge the gulf between them, but he didn't know how.

"Jean-Eudes and I talk about you sometimes," Pascal said, "when Pa isn't listening. He's going to want to hear everything about you."

"You're not going to come up?"

"Jean-Eudes and Alexis need me."

"You don't belong in the lower decks, Pascal. Pa has to take responsibility for Jean-Eudes. Bring Alexis with you."

Émile began a slow glidepath, aiming towards a habitat ahead and below.

"Jean-Eudes would miss us," Pascal said. "Like we miss you."

Émile was silent for a long time. "I miss you too," he said finally.

"Come back."

"I can't."

"Make up with Pa," Pascal said.

"I don't belong in the lower decks."

"Where do you belong, Émile?"

The habitat had resolved into a small dirigible, wrapped in black solar cells and a hydroponic greenhouse. It looked older than the *Avant-Gardiste,* patched like Pascal's suit, with seam lines running awkwardly like scars. To his engineer's eye, the lines recorded a history of failure and near-failure.

"I don't know," Émile said.

His older brother began spoiling his airflow, slowing, increasing his angle of attack and throttling down as he drifted lower and lower. Émile signaled him to approach first. It was hard to copy Émile's expert flight exactly. Pascal wished he could have used his own wing-pack here, but it wasn't designed for air this thin. Stall alarms kept going off in his helmet, despite what Émile had said. Clumsily, he swoop-flared, swoop-flared, and came down too fast on the platform roof, but did what he was supposed to: get feet and hands on the deck and furl his wings. He came close to the crash nets, but hadn't needed them this time.

"Are you okay?" Émile called in his helmet, alighting gracefully on two feet beside him.

Pascal got his knees under him and tried to stand, but fell forward when the furled wingtips touched the deck.

"Whoa, little buddy," Émile said, catching him with one arm on his chest and the other holding up his wing-pack. "Unstrap."

Pascal popped the straps and walked free. Émile held

his wing-pack in one hand, opening a long case in the floor to rack both sets.

"When I first got here," Émile said, "my baby sister had to teach me how to use these things."

Pascal laughed. The outer envelope of the dirigible and the port side of the habitat had the same type of stairs. Pascal cautiously stepped down.

"Do they know we're coming?" Émile asked.

"No."

"You didn't call ahead?"

"From the lower cloud decks?" Pascal said. "Marthe and Pa want to keep this discreet."

"What do you need from Phocas?" Émile asked.

"It's... political, something I'm cooking up with Marthe."

"*You're* cooking up?"

Pascal faced his brother on the landing in front of the airlock.

"What is it?" Émile asked.

Pascal switched to a low frequency unused by the main habitats and reduced the wattage on his transmitter. He made the *coureur* hand-sign for switching to that frequency. Émile hadn't been so long under the sun that he'd forgotten where he'd come from.

"What are you cooking?" Émile asked again on the new, quiet channel.

"I can't tell you. And I need to talk to Phocas privately."

"What?" Émile demanded, loud enough that Pascal heard him though the faint air. "I'm not good enough to listen to what concerns *my* family? I'm losing my home too!"

"It's not that, Émile," Pascal said. "What we're trying may be dangerous. The less you know, the safer you are."

"I'm not afraid! If there's danger, I want to be in on it."

"Maybe," Pascal said. "For now, we go this way. We're probably going to need help in a few days. Weird help. I need to talk to Marthe."

"Marthe and Pa?" Émile asked. "You can't decide on your own? You can't tell your own brother?"

Pascal stared up at Émile. His brother's faceplate was fogging over his beard.

"You know what?" Émile threw up his hands. "Fuck it! Talk in private all you want. Fuck you! I'll wait out here. And after this don't ask for my help again!"

A sick feeling of regret welled in his stomach, like Venus herself was bleeding into him. Pascal had messed this up. He'd pissed off his brother because he didn't have the right words, the right skills to deal with people the way Marthe could. Pascal wasn't like *maman*. Pascal was like Pa.

Pascal turned to the airlock and spun the wheel. He stepped in and looked back at Émile, who had turned to stare up at the starred black sky. Pascal shut himself in. In one pocket, he had the neutralizing pad he'd gotten from Émile. In the other, his old scraggly one. He pulled out the old one and neutralized himself. When he had finished and air had hissed in, he cracked the seal around his neck and inhaled. Stale air. Cool, unnaturally so, like everything up above the clouds. He spun the wheel and passed into the habitat.

At the bottom of the stairs, he knocked on the big pressure door. He heard nothing behind it, and went to knock again when the wheel in the middle of the door started turning. He stepped back. After a moment, someone tugged on the door, needing a couple of tries to get it open. An old woman in a dress and a robe stood on the other side, looking up at him suspiciously.

"Eh... *Bonjour, madame*," he said. "I'm looking for Gabriel-Antoine Phocas."

She grunted and moved back to let him in. He stepped over the rim of the pressure door frame and looked about in some bewilderment. The walls of the *Marais-des-Nuages* were thin, as if layers of metal had been scraped off them. Machine pieces and tools lay everywhere. This was a scrap collector's dream. An older man in pyjamas and robe sat in a carbon-weave swinging chair. He looked at Pascal but didn't say anything.

"*Bonjour, mon oncle*," Pascal said awkwardly, using the honorific one used with old people in the clouds. Two childish faces looked out from one bedroom, but apparently he wasn't interesting and the faces disappeared.

An attractive man came out from a storage room. But behind him, Pascal saw that it wasn't storage. It looked like a whole machine shop in there, filled with pieces of equipment he recognized, and others he didn't.

"Who are you?" the man asked.

Pascal unsealed his wrist, took off his glove and extended his hand. The man shook it.

"I'm Pascal D'Aquillon, the brother of Marthe D'Aquillon."

The man made a doubtful face.

"I thought you were taller."

"That's my brother Émile. He's waiting outside."

The old woman sat in her own swinging chair and tsked.

"I didn't want to intrude with many people," Pascal said. "Are you Gabriel-Antoine Phocas?"

"What do you want, *monsieur?*"

"Could we talk in private?" Pascal asked.

"Are you from the government?"

"No. I'm coming on behalf of my sister Marthe. And my father. We're *coureurs.*"

Phocas looked at him strangely for a moment, then moved back into his workshop. Pascal followed and Phocas closed the door—a real door, not just a curtain. Phocas's arms were well-muscled, and pristine, without acid scars. He had other kinds of scars that looked like they came from cuts and heat burns, but Venus hadn't touched him.

Pascal's cheeks heated as he realized that he'd been staring.

"You don't have any acid scars..." he said weakly.

Phocas looked at his hands. "I don't go outside much." He waved his hand to take in the workshop. "I have all this."

"That's why I've come."

"The workshop? You can't have it. The government's been trying to take it away from me for years."

Phocas didn't look old enough to have been doing anything for years. Marthe's description of a kind of nineteen-year-old engineering *wünderkind* was hard to reconcile with the physical *presence* of the man, his easy certainty.

"Why?" Pascal asked.

"The metal. Why else?"

"Don't we need tools?"

"The government workers have tools. Mine are extra. A waste of metal. But I do good business fixing things on the black market because the government mechanics take forever. Always something higher-priority for them to do."

"Oh," Pascal said.

Phocas looked at him strangely again for a moment, and sat, evidently not taking him that seriously anymore. On the shortest wall, a rack of different wing-packs hung, four of them the long, light wings of the upper atmosphere. The positioning of ailerons and spoilers differed on each, and as he looked more closely, the same was true of camber and wing angle. The other two wing sets were more familiar, with the stubby, low-aspect-ratio shapes that were used in the depths. But the designs were still odd. The material was shiny, but not carbon filament.

"You've made the control surfaces on this one too big," he said. "It'll be too sensitive. It'll be like the wings here. Not something to carry an awkward load."

"I don't want to carry a load," Phocas said. "These are for aerobatics."

Pascal regarded them more carefully, guessing at the way they'd maneuver at higher speeds, higher angles of attack. They would be sensitive, maybe stomach-lurchingly so.

"How low have you flown them?"

"Down to *Grande Allée*. Deep enough for you?"

Pascal nodded. "I've lived all my life below *Les Plaines*.

Today is the first time I've ever seen the sun."

Phocas whistled in appreciation and leaned back against a loaded workbench.

"What are you here for?"

"I came to see you."

"I don't get that line very often." Pascal's insides twisted as Phocas smirked. His face became hot. Even his ears. Phocas laughed, and Pascal wanted to shrivel away and hide.

"My sister and my father have a business deal they want to talk to you about. It's kind of secret," Pascal said, trying to get the conversation back on track. "It's engineering. A big engineering job."

"You got metal?"

"Maybe," Pascal said. "Maybe a lot. We might need some help in getting it."

"You offering me a cut?"

"Marthe and my father think you'll be interested."

"Is that why they sent you?"

Pascal felt his neck and cheeks heat again.

"I'm the engineer," he said. "That's why they sent me. I want to build something on the surface."

Phocas arched an eyebrow. "What the hell for? Mining?"

"Something like that."

"Why? Are you the next one to think you can find anything in the basalt while you're cooking at four hundred and fifty degrees? How close you gonna get for remote working? Or have you made high-heat solid state chips? Take a whole lot of machine thinking to run a full mining operation. The asteroid miners found that out the hard way."

Pascal felt a bit dumb, partly because he didn't know anything about asteroid mining programming code, but also because Phocas wasn't taking him seriously. He pulled a heat-resistant carbon weave bag out of his pocket, cracked the seal and gave it to Phocas.

Phocas looked inside, then poured the dust onto his work bench. He frowned, peering close at the shiny grinds, leavened with ceramic dust Pascal hadn't been able to clean away in a hurry.

"Where'd you find copper?" Phocas asked.

Pascal said nothing. Phocas pulled an electromagnet out of a drawer and plugged in the battery. He passed it over the pile of dust, but only a fraction leapt up to it.

"There's iron and nickel," Phocas said. He looked closer. He saw the same bluish tinge that Pascal had first seen. "You found cobalt with the copper vein?" He took some from the magnet and rubbed it between thumb and fingers. "Some of this cobalt is refined, isn't it?"

"I think so," Pascal said.

Phocas set down the electromagnet and turned his attention back to the remaining pile. He spilled the silvery grains between his fingers. "Platinum," he said, "and lead sulfide. Are you scraping the frost off Maxwell Mons? They've done that before and gotten lead sulfide, but never anything better. You found a surface vein in the mountains?"

Pascal regarded Phocas silently. The conversational shoe was on the other foot now. Engineering and chemistry were easier to talk about.

"We don't know exactly what we've found," Pascal said. "We think we need someone like you to see what it is."

"Doesn't Gaschel have a say?" Phocas asked. "Why isn't she coming to see me about this?"

Pascal met his eyes challengingly.

"I didn't expect her to know," Phocas continued. "But *I* expect to know."

"Marthe and my father invite you to come down to the *Causapscal-des-Profondeurs* to talk about it."

"Where is it?"

"Probably eight hundred kilometers east of us already," Pascal said. "Our next window will be in three days."

Phocas's lips quirked and he looked at the deep-cloud wing-packs.

"Unless we fly back," he said.

"Eight hundred kilometers is going to feel like twelve hundred when you factor in winds," Pascal said.

"These packs can do two hundred kilometers an hour," Phocas said. "Want to fly with me? We deep dive to match wind speed and then fly for her. We'll make up a lot of distance just on the glide path. Twenty kilometers is a big drop."

Pascal was dubious. He wasn't looking to run out of fuel and cook in the atmosphere. The *coureurs* respected Venus.

"What do you think I made these things for if not to fly?" Phocas said. "And most people are too chicken to fly with me. You're not chicken, are you?"

Pascal wasn't sure.

Phocas came closer, pulling one of the wing-packs out of its rack. "Do you like flying?"

Pascal nodded.

"Ever flown with someone, just for fun?"

"We don't do a lot of things for fun below the lower deck," Pascal said.

Phocas laughed and shoved the pack into Pascal's chest.

"You're going to start. I live for flying."

Pascal turned away while Phocas stripped to get into his survival suit. Increasingly uncomfortable, Pascal opened the door, slipped awkwardly out, and closed it behind him. *Ma tante* and *mon oncle* sat rocking in their swing chairs, looking out the glass, through the hydroponics and onto the cloudscape. Pascal held his helmet uncertainly, cleared his throat, and then said nothing. A girl of about twelve giggled at him from the doorway of her bedroom, made kissy sounds and then disappeared. Pascal's cheeks heated again. Then the door to the workshop opened and Phocas strode out in a clean new suit, two heavy wing-packs slung over his shoulder.

"Louise, I heard that," Phocas said.

The girl giggled, as did a little brother, although neither emerged.

"Louise, I'm going on a trip. It might be a couple of days. You have to do the chores."

The girl sighed heavily from the room. That seemed to be answer enough for him.

"I'm going out, *grand-mère*," he said, kissing the old woman on the crown of her head. He did the same to the old man.

"Those aren't the right wings," the old man said.

"Every wing is the right wing, *grand-papa*," he said

274

loudly, as if the man was hard of hearing.

Grand-papa Phocas tsked.

Phocas spun the wheel and Pascal followed him onto the stairs, a bit numbly. He hadn't actually thought that Phocas would give him the time of day. He hadn't thought that he'd offend his own brother. He hadn't had time to imagine any of the upper world. Not that it would have helped.

They sealed their helmets and cycled through the airlock. Pascal tried not to look at Phocas, but the airlock wasn't large. Phocas turned Pascal around and pushed the wing-pack onto his back. Pascal slid his arms in, strapped it closed and jacked in. A weird dashboard lit in his helmet. Fuel consumption he was used to, but he saw a fuel efficiency reading too, as well as solar cell input, internal engine pressure, and a number of other things Pascal had always thought standard and unadjustable.

Phocas spun the outer door and bright sunlight cut into the airlock. Émile was on the roof of the envelope, staring at the cloudtops, arms crossed, apparently unaffected by the cold. Émile turned and saw the wing-packs.

"Where are you guys going?" he said, a little testily.

"This must be the big brother," Phocas said.

"What does that mean?"

"*Monsieur* Phocas is coming down to meet with Pa and Marthe," Pascal said.

Émile's glare through the faceplate said all he couldn't say in front of Phocas.

"Well, you can't go now," he said finally. "You got two or three days until you've got a good glide path."

"We've got one now," Phocas said.

"What?"

Phocas stepped to where the platform began to curve down, at the edge of the nets. He tapped his wing-pack. "I built these," he said. "They can get us farther than your house."

"They cannot!" Émile said. "I'm not going to let you risk my little brother. Wait the three days and do a safe descent."

Phocas turned to Pascal. "What's it going to be?" he said. "You believe me or the big brother? You either think my skills are great or you don't. Are we flying or not?"

Pascal's heart thumped. Phocas and Émile both watched him. He wanted to disappear. He wanted to fly away just to stop them from looking at him. He didn't know if Phocas's wings would work. It seemed awfully far. He stepped closer.

"Émile, it'll be okay. I'm flying with *Monsieur* Phocas."

His brother's jaw set behind the beard and faceplate. Pascal wanted to do something to reconnect them, but he couldn't take the last three steps to his brother.

"I'll talk to Marthe, Émile."

"Yeah," Émile said sourly. "Thanks."

Pascal turned so as not to have to face him and stood beside Phocas.

"Follow me," Phocas said. "Stay on channel twelve. I'll help you. Don't open your wings until I say so."

Pascal nodded. Phocas leapt high off the habitat, over the netting. Pascal took the same heart-lurching leap and plunged after.

THIRTY-TWO

In the fifth hour of flying, Pascal and Phocas came close enough to try pinging the *Causapscal-des-Profondeurs*. If a radio check came from one of the family's suits with the correct encryption, the habitat would signal back, using a directional antenna and only enough wattage to reach the traveling family member. George-Étienne was no more suspicious than any of the other *coureurs*, or at least not by much.

Many in the upper habitats had interpreted the *coureurs*' decision to live off-grid as a repudiation of the government. In the beginning it hadn't been, but each group had begun circulating its own stories about the other. But contrary to what the upper cloud *colonistes* said, the *coureurs* followed no unified philosophy, and families established safeguards to hide not only from the government, but from each other.

"We've got a problem," Pascal said into his radio.

Phocas was a hundred meters ahead and below,

sweeping through the thin, featureless haze where raindrops almost boiled. He seemed to revel in the depths. They'd pirouetted through the orange grandeur of *Grande Allée,* and used *Les Plaines* like a great red-lit race-track at two hundred and twenty kilometers an hour. Phocas had laughed as he buzzed a wild trawler so closely that arc discharges snaked off the hanging cable, to stroke his suit.

"What's the problem? You don't really live down here?" Phocas joked.

"I got a ping-back from the *Causapscal-des-Profondeurs.* They're not at forty-five kilometers, but forty. At that altitude the winds are even slower, so they're another hundred kilometers east."

"We don't have enough fuel," Phocas said.

"We still have enough to climb and blow our safe sacks."

"It'll take us days to hop back to the *Marais-de-Nuages* on borrowed wing-packs."

Then they would still have to wait for another window, later than the one they could have taken in the first place. They didn't have that much time, not if the government wanted to confiscate the *Causapscal-des-Vents* now. Marthe could delay, but they really needed their plan to be working already.

"Are you willing to take a risk?" Pascal asked.

"With you?"

Pascal didn't feel himself blush.

"We're off by about half an hour," he said. "I can get us a half hour."

"How?"

"Is your suit good?"

"Of course."

"Follow and don't talk," Pascal said, putting the shoe on the other foot.

He set a steeper glide descent to give them more airspeed, but not enough to make up the missing hundred kilometers. As he descended, he changed the frequency of his helmet radio to a band filled with static. He listened carefully while doing some buoyancy calculations in his head.

Trawlers didn't get all the electricity for their metabolism from lightning; that was just the most spectacular way they nursed on the clouds of Venus. Their cables were forty to sixty meters long, enough to bridge two close layers of clouds. Static built up naturally on clouds, and running the trawler's long cable through the clouds could collect the charge. This steady feeding on static was actually ninety percent of the trawlers' diet, and their feeding made a quiet noise, but not in a way ears could hear.

A nearby trawler feeding on static could squawk in the radio band. The only problem was that far-off lightning, natural cloud-to-cloud discharges, and other trawlers all made the same radio noises. It took good ears to find trawlers. Chloé had been a prodigy. His father could do it. So could Pascal.

He cast a glance behind him. Phocas trailed him by a hundred and fifty meters, and didn't give off any signs of panic, even though it was a hundred and twenty degrees

Celsius and the pressure had climbed to almost three atmospheres. Their suits were rated to one hundred and fifty degrees. After that it was like wearing a cooking bag.

There.

A long, drawn-out squawk lifted above the white static on this band, like running nails along a wall. It was a very weak radio interference that only transmitted a few kilometers, and Pascal began to turn, following a circuitous flight pattern about five kilometers in diameter. Shoulder-checking, he made sure Phocas was still behind him. He listened for the sound, hearing it again and again, and after three circuits, he got a sense of direction and narrowed his search, still descending.

Venus pressed harder and hotter, but this was home, and he was hidden in the haze, enshrouded, without body, touching nothing. Then he saw the obscure outline, a kilometer below, a dark circle in featureless orange haze. He switched back to the common channel.

"How good are you at point landings with these wings?" Pascal asked.

"I don't think I've ever landed with them," Phocas said, an edge of tension creeping into his voice. "How small is your home?"

"We're not landing on the *Causapscal-des-Profondeurs*. We're landing on a trawler."

"A wild one?"

A hundred meters lower was a mid-sized trawler, about seven meters in diameter, with six lobes pressed against one another like fat orange slices. Its surface was overgrown with slimy black plants that threaded roots into a silty paste in the center pit on its top. Lank vines hung down the bulbous sides, looking like stringy hair.

"You go first," Pascal said. "Be ready to fly if you miss. I'll catch you if you damage your wings."

Phocas's labored breathing sounded in his helmet as if he was about to say something pithy or funny, but in the end, the seriousness of the situation seemed to have sunk in.

"*D'accord.*"

Phocas swooped lower, slowing his airspeed. The keening of his wing-pack dropped off every few seconds as he experimented with his approach. Finally, he slowed, swooped up beside the trawler, flaring into a stall. He splashed onto the muck of its peak, falling over, but clinging to the center pit, stopping his momentum before he went over the other side.

"Brilliant!" Pascal said.

It was astonishing that he'd done it on his first try. His weight was now sinking the trawler. That was the reason Pascal had wanted to go second. It was one thing to land on a relatively stationary target. It was another to juggle a landing swoop onto a sinking platform only seven meters wide.

"Not very graceful," Phocas replied.

"Get down," Pascal said, swooping in faster than Phocas had done.

This wing-pack was more sensitive than his own, but he could do this maneuver injured or tired. He flared, bleeding away his airspeed, then swooped down, stalling and extending his spoilers, cutting his lift at the moment he was over the trawler. He surprised himself by landing shakily on his feet.

Pascal sat and put both feet in the puddle of sulfuric acid in the hollow of the trawler roof. Trawlers and the epiphytes that grew on them secreted chemicals, forming a filmy membrane over the collected water that raised its pH and turned it into a gel with a much higher boiling point. The gel eventually overflowed over all of the trawler, protecting the hard, woody exterior from the harshest effects of sulfuric acid. Pascal wiped some of the slime off the surface of the trawler and spread it over his suit.

"Scoop up the scum on the edges of the trawler," Pascal said. "Put it on your feet and then put at least one foot in the middle to keep from slipping off."

Shadows hid much of Phocas's expression behind the faceplate, but he ran his fingers over the mucus with distaste and wiped it off slowly as Pascal had done. Then, doubtfully, he dipped one foot into the puddle in the middle.

The trawler sank more quickly, emerging into a hollow in the sub-cloud haze, a small clear space of maybe two hundred meters.

"It's hydrophobic and basic?" Phocas said, as if dredging up a memory.

"When flying down, we covered our suits in acid, but at this depth water evaporates and concentrates the acid. The mucus won't stop everything, but for now..."

Phocas looked all around. The temperature was a

hundred and forty degrees now, and close to three and a half atmospheres.

"Remember to breathe deep," Pascal said, "and keep at it."

"This is going to get us back a half hour?" Phocas said.

"We're deeper now than the *Causapscal-des-Profondeurs*, so we're riding slower winds. The habitat is approaching our position every minute, and we're not using any fuel."

"Ow!" Phocas said, swatting at his thigh.

A tiny hole had formed there. Phocas's suit wasn't as good as he'd thought. It wasn't lasting as long as it should have in the sulfuric acid. Phocas pulled a kit out of a sealed pocket, broke it, and dabbed at the opening.

He was doing it wrong, and not quickly enough. He was quick enough for the world above the clouds, but not here. Pascal's hands moved fast, thought-free, swiping open his own old kit. He made one quick neutralizing wipe, goopy, a second wipe away with fingers, making certain the bicarbonate squished through the tear, before slapping a patch and sealing it quickly with epoxy. Ten seconds. Done.

Phocas looked at him strangely.

"What was that?" Phocas asked.

"The pressure is thirty times what you're used to, and it's a hundred and seventy degrees hotter. Acid chemistry is different here. You can't be slow. And I don't even know that your kit is strong enough."

Phocas's eyes widened as Pascal spoke.

"You shouldn't get your legs scarred up on account of a visit," Pascal said awkwardly.

"Thank you," Phocas said after a moment. "Thank you." Then he smiled.

"What?"

"I didn't even ask you to play doctor with me yet."

"I'm not a doctor," Pascal said.

Phocas looked at him strangely and Pascal wondered what he'd missed. He began wiping up more of the mucus off the surface of the trawler and spread it on Phocas.

"What are you doing?"

"I don't trust your suit," Pascal said.

"You're going to put that goop all over me?"

Pascal applied more and more until Phocas's suit was shiny with slime.

"It looks like somebody sneezed on me!" Phocas said.

Pascal laughed and slimed his own suit. "You really haven't done this much, have you?"

Phocas shook his head. He prodded at the patch over his leg. "It still stings. Will it scar much?"

"The acid is neutralized, but you still burned yourself. That's just a small one, though."

"You do this a lot."

"*Oui.*"

"You have scars?"

"Lots."

The pressure was over five atmospheres now. Phocas looked like he wanted to say something, but he also looked a bit red-faced.

"Breathe," Pascal said. "Deep, slow breaths."

"I see something," Phocas said, pointing down.

The haze below them was thinning.

"Wow," Pascal said. Lumpy, dark shapes moved below, indistinct. "We shouldn't be able to see this, not from thirty-fifth *rang*."

The haze thinned and melted, revealing the black and gray of Venus without her diaphanous mists, derailing whatever Phocas was going to say. Venus's ugly hide wrinkled beneath them, like the planet herself had shrunk but kept the same skin. Like a great sore, Maat Mons stared back at them, the volcano standing nine kilometers high on Atla Regio, a highland a thousand kilometers wide. The surface leaked with other volcanoes. To the west was the shriveled stub of Sapas Mons, and the other great volcanic peak Ozza Mons, standing over seven kilometers tall. To the north, the highlands narrowed and tumbled deeply, down to Ganis Chasma, with innumerable channels carved into the sides by lava.

Phocas's hand reached out and took Pascal's. Pascal felt hot, like he himself was Venusian stone, radiating heat. But he didn't pull his hand away. They'd lived all their lives in and over clouds. Solid rock was a strange, magical thing, hypnotic and deeply touching. Phocas leaned over, mouth gaping. Then he was smiling.

"I've never seen the surface."

"And today was the first time I'd seen the sun," Pascal said.

"It's kind of a special day."

They looked at each other, making Pascal awkward. He was going to slip, and probably needed to grab onto something, but wasn't quite ready to let go of Phocas's hand. Gabriel-Antoine's hand. He had a beautiful name.

"This is the true Venus," Gabriel-Antoine said, as if sensing Pascal's thumping heart.

"This..." Pascal said, then, like an idiot, forgot what he wanted to say. His brain just shut off. "We shouldn't be able to see it from here. The haze usually only clears at thirty-second *rang*. But sometimes it rises or even clears when the volcanoes are really active."

The words came out in a know-it-all tumble. He breathed deeply, feeling the warm air in his lungs in a way that he hadn't felt the cool air of the habitats above the clouds. This was more than a lucky sighting of the surface. This was special.

"This is... only a part of it. Venus hides important parts of herself from us."

"Poetic," Phocas said.

"My brother is the poet," Pascal said quickly.

"The big guy?"

"The poems are beautiful."

"There are different kinds of poets," Gabriel-Antoine said. "We can make poetry with machines. We can make poetry out of flying, turning it into dance."

"I'm not anything," Pascal said.

"I saw the way you looked at my wing-packs," Gabriel-Antoine said, moving a bit closer. Even in the gloom and even shuttered by the faceplate, his eyes were a piercing pale blue. "I saw the way you flew in the depths, the way your body moves like you belong down here, like you're seeing things I can't see and adding them to some cloud dance."

Pascal looked away, but left his hand in Gabriel-

Antoine's. The words were beautiful, and Pascal couldn't believe that Gabriel-Antoine was saying them. Here. Standing on a cloud creature above Venus in recline, a sight that only a few hundred people in all of history had ever seen with their own eyes.

Gabriel-Antoine edged closer uncertainly, and almost slipped. Pascal grabbed him with both arms and steadied him. Gingerly, Gabriel-Antoine stilled in his grasp. Pascal swallowed.

"Nothing on a trawler is flat," Pascal said weakly. "It takes practice. I'm surprised you haven't fallen yet."

"Maybe I'm close," Gabriel-Antoine said. Pascal's stomach lurched, but Gabriel-Antoine's flashing grin was looking over the wrinkled hide of the goddess of love, not at him.

"What does she hide from us?" Gabriel-Antoine asked.

"I'll show you at *Causapscal-des-Profondeurs*," Pascal said, and reddened when he realized how suggestive that sounded.

"It takes someone who has something hidden to see what's hidden," Gabriel-Antoine said. "Will you show me what you hide?"

Pascal went cold. "Do you hide things?"

Gabriel-Antoine smiled behind the faceplate of his helmet. Then he shook his head. "I rarely hide anything, and even if I do, it isn't for long."

Pascal swallowed nervously, as if Gabriel-Antoine had thrown the ball back to him, launching a challenge: *Be brave*. How brave was he? Did he even know what to be brave about?

The trawler wouldn't sink much more. The atmospheric pressure was so thick that buoyancy was double or triple what it would be at fifty-fifth *rang*. Trawlers didn't like being this low and this hot. Valves under the hard, woody skins would already be pumping gasses from the interior, lightening the load. The whole world seemed to hold its breath. The haze hung in stillness around them. The ground was unmoving far below. And the pair of them froze in place, in nervous, exciting confusion, at least until the faster winds above them blew the *Causapscal-des-Profondeurs* nearer.

THIRTY-THREE

MARIE-PIER HAD A small carbon nano-fiber airplane, its fuselage printed from the carbon dioxide of the atmosphere over the course of months. Marthe and Marie-Pier pulled it out of its storage case, fueled it, and locked the wings into flight position. Marthe knew the *Causapscal-des-Profondeurs's* course and despite the cluster of storms raging fifty kilometers above Aphrodite Terra, she could lead them to it.

The flight was bumpy. Immense bolts of lightning punctuated fierce, sudden updrafts, pockets of downdrafts, and showers of sulfuric acid. It took them an hour to get out of the storm and into a slow, steamy rain, and another two hours before Marthe received the chirping family response from the *Causapscal-des-Profondeurs*. They finally, with some exhaustion, got close enough to begin circling the big family trawler, looking for a good approach. Marie-Pier was a good pilot, even for the depths, but Marthe would almost always have preferred something that depended on buoyancy rather than airspeed, or better yet, just to fly with her own wing-pack.

The hot winds buffeted the plane far more than anything they might have felt in the frigid heights above the clouds. And matching airspeeds to the habitat was not easily done in the depths. Their home floated and bobbed, occasionally running a few small propellers to change bands and avoid distant storms. But it was no runway.

Marie-Pier climbed a little bit, slowed almost to stall speed, and set herself on a tangential path to the *Causapscal-des-Profondeurs*. Then she punched the emergency inflators on four big oxygen balloons, two over the wings, one over the tail, and one just behind the cockpit. As the engine idled, the drag cut their airspeed and they were suddenly floating. The black bags strained upwards, slicking immediately with sulfuric acid rain. The plane began to sink and Marie-Pier gave each of the bags a bit more oxygen. A hazy half-kilometer separated them from the *Causapscal-des-Profondeurs*—in other words, a pin-point 'landing.'

Sulfuric acid speckled the glass, becoming rivulets. Marie-Pier turned on wipers and gunned the props to give them a bit of forward movement.

"A welcoming committee?" Marie-Pier asked, pointing into the light rain.

Marthe squinted. Two shadows resolved into fuzzy shapes: people on wing-packs.

"I don't recognize the wings," she said. "The smaller one flies like my little brother."

Running lights over the D'Aquillon home and spotlights underneath illuminated the gantry. The two figures on wing-packs flew by at high speed. Marie-Pier watched them go.

"I haven't seen wing-packs that fast," Marthe said.

Marie-Pier slowly maneuvered the plane beneath the *Causapscal-des-Profondeurs* as the pair of flyers alighted on the gantry. One of them—Pascal, by his suit—slid carefully down a cable and stepped onto the wobbling plane, locking the hook at the end of the cable into a ring on the tail. By the time Marthe and Marie-Pier exited the plane from the cockpit floor hatch, Pascal was already done tying ropes to the four balloons.

Marthe touched both sides of her faceplate to both sides of his in greeting. Marie-Pier did the same.

"Marie-Pier, this is my brother Pascal. He'll take care of the balloons and cover the plane with a tarp."

She led Marie-Pier up a rope ladder to get out of the spitting rain. On the gantry, her father was out, applying bicarbonate to what had to be Gabriel-Antoine Phocas's suit.

Marthe didn't start any more introductions. Courtesy was courtesy and acid was acid, as the expression went. Venus always came first. Marthe spread a bicarbonate solution on her guest, head to toe, and felt the heat where it neutralized pockets of acid. She held out the container and extended her arms so that Marie-Pier could do the same. By the time she was done, Pascal had finished removing the four balloons from the plane. It hung, nose down, under a waterproof tarp.

George-Étienne would have neutralized Pascal, but Gabriel-Antoine seemed to be getting into the deep rituals and took the container to apply the bicarbonate to her brother. Marthe watched him work and led his hands back where he had missed spots. It was funny how upper-clouders could look so helpless in the depths. As funny as it was to be a *coureur* making all sorts of errors of manners in sunlight.

They made light introductions and cycled in through the airlock. Marthe was sensitive enough to those who lived above the clouds to know, even before she saw their expressions, that the D'Aquillons were going to look like country bumpkins or very poor cousins to their visitors. Marie-Pier was not wealthy, but her bioengineered trawlers were popular on the black market. And Marie-Pier's were newer and bigger, not beaten and worn like the *Causapscal-des-Profondeurs*. She didn't know what it was to live this deep in the clouds.

Gabriel-Antoine's expression was unexpected. At first, it was simple surprise, perhaps that anyone lived under such rustic and improvised conditions. While Pascal tended to a small acid burn on his thigh, Gabriel-Antoine examined the walls with eyes and fingers, tracing the ribs, finding the tiny pumping valves in the trawler shells. He whispered questions to Pascal in wondering tones.

And then Jean-Eudes came out with Alexis, both pasty-faced with unfinished sleep, and an underlying, infectious eagerness. At least, she hoped it was infectious. Neither Marie-Pier nor Gabriel-Antoine would have ever met anyone with trisomy-21.

George-Étienne clapped Jean-Eudes on the back, then shook his shoulder. "This one is my eldest, Jean-Eudes," he said, smiling, inviting, but with an expression of holding his breath. "And my grandson, Alexis."

Marie-Pier kissed Jean-Eudes on both cheeks. "A pleasure to meet you, *mon grand*," she said. "*Et toi aussi*," she said to Alexis.

This seemed to satisfy her father. And Marthe too.

Gabriel-Antoine looked away from the walls distractedly. "Jean-Eudes?" he said, shaking her brother's hand. "Pascal told me you keep the pressure right in here."

Jean-Eudes brightened, stood a bit straighter. "Alexis helps."

Gabriel-Antoine gravely shook hands with her nephew, who was equally serious.

George-Étienne gripped Gabriel-Antoine on the arm. "Good," he said. "Good."

Marthe's brief tour of the *Causapscal-des-Profondeurs* ended around the galley table. Gabriel-Antoine had never been on a living habitat, and he had many questions that Marie-Pier, George-Étienne, and Pascal answered in turn.

It was late, and after a time, George-Étienne shooed the protesting Alexis and Jean-Eudes back to bed. The rest of them remained around the table with homemade *bagosse* that Marthe poured into small, lumpy glasses. If neutralized with enough base, the wood fibers from some parts of trawler envelopes could be fermented and distilled into a stinging *bagosse*. George-Étienne screwed together two more worn carbon stools and set them down for himself and Pascal.

"*Santé,*" Marthe said, toasting.

They drank. Pascal sputtered. Gabriel-Antoine complimented the still-maker. The conversation finally flagged.

"Thank you for joining us," Marthe said after smacking her lips at another sip. "We're looking for some help."

"Engineering help," Gabriel-Antoine said.

Marie-Pier regarded her and her father silently.

"A few kinds of help," Marthe said. "But to talk about it, I need your word that whatever we discuss tonight, it stays here."

"You'd trust our word?" Gabriel-Antoine said, smirking. Her father looked uncomfortable.

"I know you both from a distance," Marthe said. "Everything I've seen leads me to believe that both of you are honest. Enough that I would trust my family's secrets to you."

Marie-Pier lifted her glass and toasted her.

"And you're no friends of the government," George-Étienne said grimly.

Marie-Pier arched an eyebrow at her. "Rebellion?" she joked.

George-Étienne made a derisive sound. "The government isn't legitimate," he said. "This isn't what we founded. This is government by Bank puppets."

Marie-Pier didn't look convinced. Gabriel-Antoine was slowly turning his shot glass, looking at the misshapen bubbles and yellowed impurities frozen within.

"The D'Aquillon family's old disagreements with the government are not what this is about," Marthe said quietly. "Because of those disagreements, we've chosen to work the lower cloud decks, and even occasionally the surface, for things to barter. Now we've found something valuable. We don't want the government or the Bank to take it away. But we need help exploiting it."

"And what is it?" Marie-Pier asked dryly.

"Your word, please," Marthe said.

Marie-Pier considered the *bagosse* and fished out flakes of blackened wood fiber. "I promise to keep whatever is discussed tonight a secret, whether we decide to work together or not."

"If it's criminal and we don't do anything or say anything, doesn't that make us accomplices?" Gabriel-Antoine asked.

"If it ever came up, you could say you didn't believe us."

Gabriel-Antoine shrugged. "I promise," he said, waving a hand carelessly.

Marthe looked meaningfully at her father, urging him silently to keep his peace and take them at their word. This wasn't his strength, and she wasn't sure what he'd finally do. He held her stare a long time, then cleared his throat.

"Some parts of this are going to be hard to believe," George-Étienne said. "Some weeks ago, I found a cave on the surface, a really strange cave. Wind on the surface was going *into* it."

"Are you joking?" Gabriel-Antoine said.

"Pascal and I sent a probe down."

"Your probe survived the surface of Venus?" Gabriel-Antoine said.

Pascal activated his pad, played the video from the

remote probe, and turned the pad to Marie-Pier and Gabriel-Antoine. They both frowned. Gabriel-Antoine magnified the view, tapping the screen, looking for more data.

"What's the scale?" he asked.

"The cave mouth is twenty meters across," Pascal said.

"I've never heard of any wind like that on the surface," Marie-Pier said. "But this isn't valuable."

"We sent in the sensors as far as we could," George-Étienne said. "The cave went deep. And the wind went as far as we could see."

The video kept on rolling. Marie-Pier and Gabriel-Antoine, and even Marthe, leaned close to each other to frown into the screen.

"You tied a camera to a light to a rope and just hoped it would hold in that wind?" Gabriel-Antoine asked.

"He improvised," George-Étienne said, clasping Pascal's shoulder, missing Gabriel-Antoine's tone. The engineer was impressed. More.

Gabriel-Antoine paused the video near the end, when the image had settled fuzzily on the triangular shape. "What's that?"

"We couldn't tell from the video," George-Étienne said. "Pascal and I needed to get a better look, so we went down ourselves."

"You went to the surface?" Gabriel-Antoine said in astonishment. "How?"

"Duvieusart's old bathyscaphe," George-Étienne said. "I acquired it some time ago."

"I thought it was lost," Marie-Pier said.

"Or scrapped," Gabriel-Antoine said.

"It's gone from *coureur* to *coureur*," George-Étienne said simply. "We've modified it over time. Pascal and I went down in it."

"To the surface," Gabriel-Antoine said wonderingly.

Pascal took the pad back from them and switched to the video they'd taken when he and Pa had gone down. He turned it back to them. They watched it as minutes went on, with Pascal providing technical comments.

"What's the cage?" Marie-Pier asked.

The video showed their cage spinning wildly in the current of supercritical carbon dioxide.

"Sample return container," George-Étienne said.

Gabriel-Antoine and Marie-Pier watched in rapt silence. The video's sound was low, but it still moaned in the subsonic, like listening to a hurricane. The operation to crate the triangular ship entranced the newcomers.

"They're a spacecraft of some kind?" Marie-Pier asked.

"We don't know," George-Étienne said. "Russian? Egyptian? Chinese? American? It doesn't make sense that any of those powers would have sent so many down without ever having told anyone about it, or colonizing Venus themselves. No one has staked a claim to this."

"To what?" Gabriel-Antoine asked.

"Watch," Pascal said.

The camera followed the current deeper. Marthe watched Marie-Pier and Gabriel-Antoine see the part that gave her shivers every time she saw it.

Stars. Clear as any picture they could have taken from

sixty-fifth *rang.*

"What the hell?" Marie-Pier exclaimed.

"This video has been spliced together with some starscape," Gabriel-Antoine said peevishly. "Poorly."

"Look at the star patterns," George-Étienne said. "Tell me where in the clouds of Venus, or even in the solar system, we could have filmed those stars."

Gabriel-Antoine squinted at the screen, moving the video backwards and forwards, zooming.

"In the solar system?" Marie-Pier asked.

George-Étienne nodded.

"What are you saying?"

"Our best guess right now," George-Étienne said, "is that under the surface of Venus is a wormhole to somewhere outside the solar system."

Gabriel-Antoine looked up doubtfully.

"I think it might not even be a real solar system," Pascal added. "It may be a pulsar system."

Marie-Pier looked at Marthe again.

"A pressure sink under the surface of Venus," Marie-Pier said, "and a picture of stars deep underground."

"And a bunch of probes whose technology we don't understand," Marthe said. "*Vas-y,* Pascal."

Pascal pulled a carbon-weave bag from the shelf and pulled out the thirty-centimeter section of probe hull. He dropped it on the table with a thud.

"Here's a piece of it," Marthe said as Gabriel-Antoine lifted it and eyed it from different angles.

Marie-Pier slid her glass across the galley table. Marthe refilled it.

THIRTY-FOUR

THE TABLE WAS quiet but for the moaning of the wind in the video, but Pascal felt electrified, buzzing. Marthe was giving him a cautioning look. She touched his arm.

"Why don't you make some coffee, Pascal?" she said. "Let's take a break to absorb things a bit?" she added to the others.

He stood. Marthe always knew what to do. She stood too. Gabriel-Antoine was still frowning at the hull section. Marie-Pier met Pascal's eyes and he felt suddenly shy. She smiled.

"You went to the surface, Pascal?" she said, rising too.

He nodded and moved to the galley.

"Do you have anything more than video?" Gabriel-Antoine asked. He'd set down the hull piece and was replaying the video. "And the unedited video? This stars-under-the-surface is a hoax."

"Never mind. I'll make the coffee," Marthe said. "Pascal, can you take Gabriel-Antoine to see the sample we retrieved?"

Pascal turned. Marthe took the press from him and smiled. Butterflies fluttered in his stomach, but Gabriel-Antoine was still frowning, his teasing manner gone.

"Outside?" he asked.

"He's asking a fair question. Show him the proof."

The young engineer was silent as they suited up and cycled into the slow, sweltering hundred-degree wind. The electric lights under the habitat shone on the gantry, making the clouds seem somber.

"Come on," he said to Gabriel-Antoine, leading him around the ring of platforms and railings woven of tough carbon nanotubes. Pieces of equipment and piles of supplies were lashed down against the weather. Almost at the other side of the gantry from the airlock was a long triangle shape under an acid-proof carbon tarp. He undid the lashings and pulled the tarp away.

The probe lay on its dorsal side, exposing its underside. Pascal felt bad about the saw marks in the hull, but there had been no other way to really see inside. Broken manipulator arms, or just stubby remains, lay limp. Gabriel-Antoine ran his glove along the ventral side, hunching to look at the surface from an angle.

"This is a small sample intake hatch, and here's the camera lens," Pascal said, indicating both the open space near the attachment points for the manipulator arms, and the abraded glass lens on the front.

Gabriel-Antoine gratefully accepted an offered flashlight and peered into all the holes.

"I couldn't find the camera's guts," Pascal continued,

a little more comfortable inviting Gabriel-Antoine's attention to the engineering puzzle, "although there's a lot of space in there. For all we know, before it shut down in that cave, it might have ejected its memory and some of the more valuable equipment."

"That doesn't make sense if it's Russian or American or Chinese," Gabriel-Antoine said.

"I don't think it is."

Gabriel-Antoine straightened, his eyes narrowing. "Someone out there?" he mocked.

"Humans didn't build this."

"Did aliens help your bad video splicing?"

Pascal opened a drawer and took out a block of ceramic about two centimeters thick and ten centimeters on a side. It was inlaid on one surface with metal fibers, while the cut edges showed cross-sections of other metallic threads, edge-on.

"This is part of the ventral section of the hull," Pascal said. "It's ceramic. I think the metal running through it is circuitry, but not laid out in any way that humanity has ever printed its circuits."

Gabriel-Antoine looked at the sample from different angles.

"How would they have laid down conducting metals before firing?" he asked.

"It's not material science we're familiar with," Pascal said.

"Just 'cause we don't know doesn't mean it's little green men," Gabriel-Antoine said. "Venus will never catch up to the tech the Banks are producing, or the Chinese. How far ahead of us is everyone else?"

"If whoever it was knew about the cave, why didn't they establish a research presence in the clouds before Québec ever colonized Venus?" Pascal asked.

Gabriel-Antoine shook his head doubtfully, peering into the cut in the underside of the little probe.

"Stars!" he said contemptuously. "What do you take us for?"

"It's a wormhole!" Pascal insisted.

Gabriel-Antoine stood straighter. He was breathing hard, almost panting. Sweat sheened his face. Pascal put a hand on his shoulder, feeling something electric in the touch.

"Take it slow," Pascal said. "You've been under two atmospheres and high heat for hours. I don't know how good your suit is. You could be risking heat exhaustion."

"Look," Gabriel-Antoine said, taking a deep breath. "I get the whole 'rugged intellectual outdoorsman' cute thing you've got going on. I'm into it, and I'm really impressed with your talent for living in the depths, and that you made it to the surface. But I don't buy the stars. There are no such things as wormholes. So just tell me what your family is really looking for."

"You saw the video of the wind!" Pascal said. "Going *into* Venus. How else would you explain that?"

Gabriel-Antoine huffed, fogging the inside of his faceplate.

Pascal turned him around. "Come on. Let's get you inside before you pass out." He felt strange taking the lead, touching Gabriel-Antoine, even through their suits. He felt like another person was running his body, speaking confidently. He kept one eye on his guest as he covered the probe again.

They hadn't been under the sulfuric acid, but Gabriel-Antoine's instincts weren't bad; he was already slicking the front of his suit with bicarbonate paste again. Pascal came up behind him and rubbed the paste on his back. Gabriel-Antoine did the same and his hands felt like they were stroking Pascal's legs and back and arms, making him tingle.

They cycled in and Pascal felt like Marthe was looking at him, even though she probably wasn't. He felt exposed and flushed. He helped Gabriel-Antoine out of his helmet and touched his forehead, then his neck.

"Everything okay?" George-Étienne asked.

"Pressure and heat can get to people when they first come down," Pascal said, "and I already brought Gabriel-Antoine deeper today than we'd planned."

Gabriel-Antoine pushed at fussing hands and took off his suit. Marthe gave him water and a soup from the cold box. At the table, George-Étienne picked up the piece of ceramic from the probe.

"What did you think of it?" he asked Gabriel-Antoine. He passed the piece to Marie-Pier.

"The probe is very nice and well worth studying," Gabriel-Antoine said. "I'm half convinced of it. But I certainly don't buy the stars."

"What do you mean?" George-Étienne said.

"You saw the film!"

"Video can be doctored," Gabriel-Antoine said dryly,

trying the soup. He made a face.

"Deep cooking," Marthe said apologetically.

"Well, this one wasn't doctored," George-Étienne said.

Gabriel-Antoine shrugged. George-Étienne's face screwed tight.

"*If* it was true," Marthe said calmly, "what then?"

"*If* it was true?" Gabriel-Antoine said, leaning back. "If you really found a real wormhole, in violation of the laws of physics, then this is a discovery on the scale of the invention of agriculture or fire. Its value would be incalculable."

Pride swelled in Pascal's chest. He'd known that it was that big. And Gabriel-Antoine did too, despite his outward flippancy. Marie-Pier squinted uncertainly. This was new to her. Even Pa looked a bit taken back. He knew what they'd found, but had focused on the immediate possibility of feeding his family, giving them what he thought they deserved. And vindication. But the wormhole itself eclipsed anything they could selfishly imagine.

"Let's park your objections for now," Marthe said. "Let's just talk about what we *could* do if it was true."

"If something of incalculable value was in the surface of Venus," Marie-Pier said, "the government would nationalize it, probably without paying those who found it."

"And quickly realizing that they have no idea what to do with it," Marthe said, "the government would invite the Bank to lease it."

"For whatever pittance the Bank of Pallas offers,

because they know the government has few options and cash problems," George-Étienne said.

"Hence the secrecy," Marie-Pier said. "But what can you do with it?"

"We," Marthe said.

"We can go down there," Pascal said, "and really mine the surface, and if there are asteroids on the other side, those too."

George-Étienne slapped the table with his palm. "Asteroids that no Bank has staked out! For us, right here around the table."

"Mine the surface at ninety atmospheres of pressure and five hundred degrees?" Marie-Pier asked.

"We've got the wormhole," Pascal said. "If we cap the cave, we can create a vacuum, or any pressure we want."

Gabriel-Antoine frowned.

"Even if you had the materials to cap the cave mouth," Marie-Pier said, "you'd have a vacuum on one side and ninety atmospheres on the other. Even the strongest metals wouldn't last long, especially at those temperatures."

"We'd have several caps, one after the other," Pascal said, "each one dropping the pressure ten or twenty atmospheres. And we could connect them with turbines to produce electricity."

"But it would still be too hot," Marie-Pier said. "Hell."

"*Non.*" Gabriel-Antoine looked at Pascal suddenly, smiling. He explained to her how the refrigeration would work.

"And if there are metals in the crust around that cave, we could mine them," Pascal said.

"Even a little bit," George-Étienne said.

Pascal took the ceramic hull plate section from Marie-Pier. "We found radioisotopes in these probes," he said. "They might have used them to heat reaction mass for propulsion, and maybe even run the electrical systems. We could do the same, taking compressed carbon dioxide and heating it to use as a propellant on the other side."

"The other side?" Gabriel-Antoine said dubiously, but he seemed to be fighting the communal enthusiasm.

"The government is going to notice metal circulating in the black market," Marie-Pier said. "People will know and wonder where we got it all. Legally, they have a right to it."

Marthe tipped her hand side-to-side in a *comme ci, comme ça* gesture.

"I've checked the laws," Marthe said. "They're vague. *L'Accord de Colonisation* says that the surface of Venus can't be owned, but some kinds of prospecting and exploitation are legal. I doubt they ever expected anyone to try to mine the surface."

"They can and will withhold permits if they'd rather do it themselves," George-Étienne said, "or to screw the D'Aquillon family."

"Is that what you're looking for?" Marie-Pier asked. "Legal cover?"

George-Étienne shook his head.

"I have a couple of bills that I think would change the laws to our benefit if you and Gabriel-Antoine would support me in *l'Assemblée,*" Marthe said.

"But secrecy is better," George-Étienne said.

"We need a different kind of help," Marthe continued. "We need engineering help from Gabriel-Antoine. Pascal is good, but this kind of job needs more than one engineer." Marthe paused, almost shyly. Pascal's guts readied to somersault. "And we can get the metal for one, maybe two caps by dismantling the *Causapscal-des-Vents*."

"What?" Marie-Pier demanded. "It isn't yours."

"We risked ourselves to find it," George-Étienne said.

Marie-Pier regarded him calmly.

"That's your view, George-Étienne," she said, "but that won't be everyone's view, and certainly not *l'Assemblée's*."

"*L'Assemblée* can fuck itself," he said.

"It doesn't matter," Marie-Pier said. "It's not like anyone would fail to notice you float-docking the *Causapscal* and dismantling it."

"We're going to sink it," George-Étienne said. "Do the work down here, out of sight."

"In the acid?" Gabriel-Antoine said.

"We can cover it with enough acid-resistant tarps," Pascal said.

"They'll still see it by radar," Marie-Pier said. "Whatever balloons you inflate to keep it from sinking are going to be pretty damn obvious. They'll look for it."

"It will be harder to find if it's hanging under a few of your trawlers," George-Étienne said. Marie-Pier's eyes widened slightly. "The ones the government is trying to take away from you."

Pascal leaned forward, drawing her attention. "We can cover the tarps with the kind of epiphytes that grow on trawlers, to further mask the radar profile."

"That's phenomenally dangerous," Marie-Pier said. "A controlled sink, even one that survived the descent through the turbulence above the clouds, could go wrong as soon as the acid rain hits. And if you hook just one or two trawlers, you might just end up ripping them apart. It would take three or four to hold up *Causapscal-des-Vents*. The wood shells will crack if they're constantly colliding with each other."

"I didn't hear that it was impossible," George-Étienne said cajolingly.

"You heard 'phenomenally dangerous'," Marie-Pier said.

"Could you do it?" Marthe asked, turning to Gabriel-Antoine, who was stirring around his cold soup, probably repelled by the sulfurous smell and taste.

"Not enough information," he said. "Even barring the ridiculousness of your wormhole idea, I would need measurements to know if capping the cave is even possible."

"Why don't I take you down?" Pascal blurted, surprised at his own words, thinking as much of those hidden stars as being cramped in the tiny bathyscaphe with Gabriel-Antoine.

"To the surface?" Gabriel-Antoine said disbelievingly.

"You'll see the stars yourself and we can map the cave accurately," Pascal said, looking imploringly at his father. "We need both the engineers to see it."

George-Étienne smiled slowly, proudly.

THIRTY-FIVE

PASCAL TOSSED AND turned before finally falling asleep. Jean-Eudes had set up his hammock with Alexis and George-Étienne in his father's room. Marie-Pier had a hammock over Marthe's in the storage room, leaving Gabriel-Antoine to share Pascal's room. His nerves were electric with Gabriel-Antoine's presence, and he guessed that Gabriel-Antoine was feeling something too. But Pascal felt ugly, unclean, unreal.

Marthe had pulled him close by the back of his neck into a hug before bed, whispering, "Good job. You've done good with Gabriel-Antoine. You speak his language." As she smiled and let him go, her palm brushed lovingly along his cheek. Her fingers had scratched along the bristle on his cheeks, sending a shiver down his spine, like nails on a chalkboard.

"What's wrong?" Marthe whispered behind him. She put her hands on his shoulders. "Are you nervous about Gabriel-Antoine in there?"

309

He shook his head, but shrugged too. She rubbed his shoulder.

"You're just sharing a room," she whispered. "But I think he likes you."

His cheeks got hot.

"And it looks like it's mutual," she said.

He shrugged again.

"If it isn't, no big deal," she continued. "Just go to sleep."

He made an uncertain smile and backed away. He was ugly. So ugly. He was exhausted, but it had probably been thirty hours since he'd last shaved or washed. He rubbed his arms, feeling the light bristle of hair. He'd shaved there too. He hated it. He wanted to scrape it all off now, but Gabriel-Antoine was already in the room. He felt sick to his stomach.

He moved the curtain aside and stopped in the doorway. Gabriel-Antoine had stripped down to underwear and was laying in Jean-Eudes's hammock, pale muscled legs and arms shining with sweat. Pascal felt sick again. Gabriel-Antoine looked up and smiled.

"You guys seriously live in this heat?" Gabriel-Antoine asked lazily.

"It's only twenty-eight degrees," Pascal said, side-stepping in.

"This is the temperature of a habitat when something is broken."

Pascal sidled over to the wash stand and brushed his teeth silently, trying to be as small and inconspicuous as possible.

His hands shook. He wouldn't look at the mirror. Even thinking about what he probably looked like made his face hot. He looked at the tiny sink and his hands hidden there, with the beginning of dark stubble on the backs and on some fingers. If he rubbed, he'd feel it.

"Do you mind if I turn off the light?" Pascal asked.

Gabriel-Antoine laughed. It was an easy sound. "Are you shy?" he asked. "I'll close my eyes."

He looked behind him and Gabriel-Antoine made a show of closing his eyes, allowing Pascal's eyes to linger. Gabriel-Antoine was beautiful. His pale skin was nearly unscarred, bandaged over one thigh, where Pascal's fingers had brushed as he'd neutralized and disinfected. Pascal shut off the light.

"I had my eyes closed," Gabriel-Antoine protested.

Pascal made a grunt of agreement, taking off his shirt.

"I wouldn't have opened them."

"Right," Pascal said. He ran a bit of water, moistening his face and arms with little taps, fast and gentle enough that he couldn't feel any of the growing stubble.

"What do you care if I see?" Gabriel-Antoine asked. "We're all just guys here."

Pascal's face heated again, but he gave a tiny laugh. He lathered with a bit of soap.

"You're really good-looking, Pascal," Gabriel-Antoine finally said. "I wouldn't mind seeing you."

Pascal scraped at his face with quick strokes, feeling a weight lifting as the ugly bits of beard left him. But he wasn't so focused that he didn't hear Gabriel-Antoine's words. They summoned an uncertain elation in his chest.

"You're shy," Gabriel-Antoine said into the silence. "I get that. You've been down here all your life. Maybe you've never had anyone court you."

The scrape, scrape, scrape continued. His face was done. Pascal remoistened one arm and scraped the razor down its length, feeling around raised scars with leading fingers.

"Or who knows? Maybe you're rolling in boyfriends or girlfriends," Gabriel-Antoine said. "How many *coureurs* live at this depth?"

"Not many," Pascal said, feeling the smile creeping warily onto his face.

"Or maybe you think I'm some Lothario, cruising down every cute guy I see," Gabriel-Antoine said. "That's not what I'm like. My life is kind of what you saw on the *Marais-des-Nuages*. A lot of drafting. A lot of machines. A lot of trying to recover scrap and turn it into something else."

Pascal finished his other arm and then stroked it, feeling for any ugliness he'd missed. None. He dabbed with a wet hand at his chest and then lathered.

"I go to parties sometimes, maybe some of the same ones as your older brother," Gabriel-Antoine said, "but I'm kind of lonely."

Pascal took a deep silent breath, happy for the sound of Gabriel-Antoine's voice masking the scraping of his shaving.

"If I'd known your big brother had a cute little brother, I would have made friends with him," Gabriel-Antoine said.

The smoothing of his skin and the dark started to let a weird confidence leak in.

"You talk like you've said these words a lot," Pascal said.

"They slide off my tongue when I'm inspired," Gabriel-Antoine said.

"*Sapristi!*" Pascal hissed. "Does any boy above the clouds fall for that?"

"I've never said it to anyone else," Gabriel-Antoine said. The hammock squeaked and Pascal heard the sounds of bare feet touching the floor.

"Stay there!" Pascal said with a bit of panic.

His hands started to shake. He couldn't use the razor flustered like this. He rested it against the sink, while passing the fingers of the other hand over cheek, throat, chest, arm. He was smooth. The hammock creaked again as Gabriel-Antoine settled back on it.

"You're really shy," Gabriel-Antoine said, "and I'm coming on strong. I'm sorry."

Pascal waited for long breaths. "I *am* shy," he said finally.

"If you're shy about scars or something, don't be," Gabriel-Antoine said. "I don't acid myself, but I think scars are hot."

He didn't know what Gabriel-Antoine was talking about, but at least his own hands had stilled. He wiped the razor and folded it. He crept to his hammock in the dark and hopped in. Gabriel-Antoine's hammock creaked. Pascal froze, but didn't say anything. Gabriel-Antoine's feet padded uncertainly closer. Then a warm hand was on Pascal's shoulder. Fingers ran along his arm, leaving tingling awareness in their wake. He stayed perfectly still. The fingers traced up his shoulder and over the damp smoothness of his chest. His heart thudded in his ears. Gabriel-Antoine's fingers traced lower, to the waistline of his light pants.

Pascal's hand snapped down and caught Gabriel-Antoine's wrist. The other froze. With shaking hands, Pascal drew Gabriel-Antoine's hand up to his lips and, cautiously, he kissed the calloused fingers. Gabriel-Antoine cupped his face and, slowly, in the dark, neared, their breaths mixing. Gabriel-Antoine's face bristled with a day's stubble, teasingly rough. Pascal inhaled as the kiss deepened. Gabriel-Antoine's other hand drifted lower, sneaking along Pascal's side, down his leg, over his pants, before sliding up the inseam. Fear surged in him and he caught Gabriel-Antoine's arm in his hand again.

"*Non*," he whispered.

Then he kissed up tentatively, seeking Gabriel-Antoine's lips. Gabriel-Antoine's hands wriggled from their captivity and cupped Pascal's face, and he kissed back for a long time.

THIRTY-SIX

ÉMILE ALIGHTED AT the busy port on the roof of the *Baie-Comeau*. The biggest of the habitats didn't just house the government and important industries, but the hospital. Landing crews serviced the wings, fueled and racked them, while a different crew slowly reeled in drone-bins with incoming supplies from different habitats. A half-dozen people in survival suits were either shucking their big wing-packs or putting them on. Émile unstrapped his wing-pack, tied it to the rack, and cycled through a big airlock with five others.

He didn't know the upper decks of the *Baie-Comeau* very well. The envelope nestled a warren of offices, meeting rooms and the hospital, but the corridors of black carbon nanotube paneling, pressed strong and light, all looked the same. At the end of a corridor he spotted a sign with a red cross on it. He'd never been here. Whatever medical help he'd needed, his father and mother had given it to him, consulting decades-old medical encyclopedias on their datapads.

It was cool and clean. The waiting room was half-full of adults and children in survival suits. Beyond that was a nurses' desk and a ward of closely-packed hammocks behind a curtain. He entered uncertainly, then went to the nurses' desk, where two big men with unscarred arms argued over a medical report.

"I'm looking for Thérèse Jetté," he said.

One man frowned. Checked his pad.

"Jetté?"

Émile nodded.

"Outer waiting room," the man said, pointing. "Out the door, to the left, down the hall."

Émile followed the directions and arrived in a small, foul-smelling room. Four chairs were affixed to the wall. Thérèse's thin, sweaty body was draped across two of them. A waste bin was near her head. She'd obviously needed it. A damp cloth had fallen on the floor. Émile knelt and touched her.

"Thérèse!"

Fine blue veins showed in cool, papery eyelids.

"Thérèse, where's the doctor?"

She moaned and looked at him with dilated pupils. A shallow sigh escaped her lips as she recognized him.

"No doctors," she said.

"There are doctors and nurses," he said.

She shook her head, swallowed as if about to be sick again, then moaned.

"I'm getting a doctor."

She gripped his hand tightly. For the first time, she

looked ashamed. Embarrassed.

"No," she said weakly. She made a visible effort not to be sick again. "They don't waste meds on ODs."

"You ODed?" He stroked her face, felt the temperature of her wrist, the way *maman* had taught him to look after Marthe and Pascal when they were young. He felt like he was going to cry. "It doesn't matter. They have to."

"I'm not dying. The best they could do is give me a lot of water and a bucket." She was crying. "I made a mess."

She had. The vomit hadn't all hit the waste bin, and it smelled like she'd soiled her suit too. He stroked her hand and kissed her cool forehead.

"Don't worry, *chérie*," he whispered. "I'll clean you up."

She breathed easier and closed her eyes.

"Where is everyone?" he asked. "Why did they leave you alone? Why didn't they call me sooner?"

"Réjean brought me," she said in a weak voice. "He left."

"What about the others? Your artist friends? The sculptors?"

She shrugged. He brushed the hair away from her face. Her breath came shallow and sour. He got water and knelt, wiping her face, cleaning the sweat and sick around her mouth. Then, what was on the floor. He sat, exhausted, although he hadn't really done anything.

"Did you do it on purpose?" he finally whispered.

Her tears came harder and he thought of the kid with the knife at Réjean's party, and even Marthe, who'd carved her own marks into her wrists.

"I don't know," she sobbed. The spiritual helplessness in her voice shriveled all his other concerns. A terror seized him. He might have lost her because... because of what? Because she'd given up on Venus? Because she couldn't fight anymore? He lifted her head and hugged her as her sobs came stronger and louder.

"We belong," he whispered in her ear. He whispered it over and over. "We belong here. We belong to each other."

"Don't let me go?" she pleaded against his chest.

"Never."

THIRTY-SEVEN

PASCAL HAD SET his alarm to vibrate on his wrist and he crept to the floor. Gabriel-Antoine was snoring in Jean-Eudes's hammock. Pascal's eyes were scratchy from lack of sleep and his lips felt raw from kissing. He ran through his dark rituals nearly silently, scraping himself smooth again.

In the galley, he found Jean-Eudes and Alexis trying to whisper. They were excited at all the guests and wanted to hear everything they'd talked about. Pascal made them a quiet breakfast, but his mind was elsewhere, not just on Gabriel-Antoine. They were about sixteen hours from a point where he and Gabriel-Antoine could conceivably drop to Diana Chasma. Their next window wouldn't be for eleven or twelve days, and if Gabriel-Antoine still didn't believe them, by the time they could prove anything to him, the *Causapscal-des-Vents* might already be confiscated. The bathyscaphe would need about six hours of hard work to prepare, and they'd have to change course, too.

By the time Gabriel-Antoine got up, everyone else had risen and they were all talking in the galley. Gabriel-Antoine and Marie-Pier were slick with sweat, and even Marthe was wilting in a tank top and shorts. Her time above the clouds had made her forget the heat of home.

"You still want to see the stars?" George-Étienne asked Gabriel-Antoine. Marthe handed him a coffee.

Gabriel-Antoine had the pattern of the hammock pressed into his face, and Pascal had the urge to massage the marks away.

"I see stars all the time," Gabriel-Antoine said. "How safe is the old bathyscaphe?"

George-Étienne shrugged. "It's overengineered. You can help Pascal prepare it and see for yourself."

Pascal felt himself flush when Gabriel-Antoine smiled at him. He caught Marthe eyeing him and smiling knowingly, but he didn't know if anyone else had seen the strange, brief smile.

Marthe had gotten her hands on some spices. Over a spare but tasty breakfast, they discussed the descent to the surface. They hadn't been planning another one, but two engineers, or at least an engineer and a student, could do a lot. They debated objectives and the equipment they would need. They dug out old lasers and checked the ratings to see whether they would survive the surface. Pascal and his father laid hands on another few hundred meters of carbon cabling to see how far they could send the camera. Gabriel-Antoine had ideas on how to mount a better motor onto the camera frame to get more controlled vision. He also had far better ideas about how to program the camera instructions once it was out of radio range, and how to stabilize it in the wind.

Jean-Eudes took to the task of looking over Gabriel-Antoine's suit, and tsked loudly about how it wouldn't do, even though it was smooth and largely unblemished and unpatched. They had a spare survival suit, one of the hand-me-downs that Émile had outgrown, but Pascal hadn't yet grown into. Gabriel-Antoine tried it on and Jean-Eudes cleaned, tested and patched it while the rest of them made plans. Alexis watched all the busyness from the safety of Marthe's lap.

By mid-morning, Pascal, Gabriel-Antoine and George-Étienne were winging over to the supply trawler about two kilometers off. Pascal felt safe in the clouds, safe in his suit, as masked and unidentifiable as anyone. In the hand-me-down suit, Gabriel-Antoine was now looking as rumpled as any *coureur.*

The clouds glowed spongy orange and brown, the last remnants of bright sun attenuated by twenty kilometers of mist and rain. Gabriel-Antoine rolled in the thick atmosphere, testing the performance of his wings. The supply trawler wasn't much of a sight. Black and brown tendrils overgrew its roof and outer walls. Broken tools, salvage and spare equipment were stored on a small gantry in a ring circling the trawler's head. Poles and winch arms projected off the top in four directions and carbon-fiber nets hung. Epiphytic growth festooned them: slimes, black-leaved vines, roots and molds.

"You used to live here?" Gabriel-Antoine said in the radio as they flew closer.

"Until ten years ago," Pascal said. "The woody layers and valves can't sustain the temperature gradients anymore, but it's still buoyant enough. We gather electricity on it and crack oxygen and water out of the rain. And store stuff."

"All that growing stuff is Venusian plants," Gabriel-Antoine said. "Gross."

"That's our garden. Some of it can be made into food," Pascal said.

"Blech!" Gabriel-Antoine said.

"It gets better when enough sulfur is taken out," Pascal said, wanting to impress him with something, but not sure what to say. After what he'd seen at sixty-fifth *rang*, everything down here looked suddenly poor. "We use everything. Chunks of Venusian plants go into our bioreactors, or we bake the plants to ash to get water and nitrogen and some heavy metals."

"That's pretty rough," Gabriel-Antoine said.

"*La colonie* turned its back on us," Pascal said, "so we turned our back on *la colonie*. All the *coureurs* did." He didn't know why he'd said that. It wasn't a political conversation, and yet nervousness drew his father's words out of him.

They alighted on the gantry, three close, accurate landings. Gabriel-Antoine was an excellent flier and was adapting quickly to the new depth and pressure. In response, the trawler started slowly sinking. Pascal uncovered the bathyscaphe.

"Wow," Gabriel-Antoine said, running a hand along the beaten, dented, acid-scarred surface "This is it."

"*Oui*," George-Étienne said proudly. "It would have been recycled long ago, or confiscated by the government for some nonsense. A lot of the *coureurs* thought it belonged down here with the people who actually followed Duvieusart into the wild."

"It looks so primitive," Gabriel-Antoine said. "How depth-worthy is it?"

George-Étienne slapped it. "I've been to the surface four times in it. Pascal once. If you go, you'll join a club of less than a dozen people who have ever made it all the way down."

"We believe enough in the equipment to go down, but you never know," Pascal added.

Gabriel-Antoine looked at him with a silent *thanks a lot* expression.

"You would never know," George-Étienne said. "If something went wrong at those pressures, you'd be dead before you could feel it."

George-Étienne opened the hatch and pulled out the metal box in which they'd been storing the radioactives they'd pulled from the probe. Pa had already traded some away for metals, batteries and chips Pascal thought they would need to dismantle the *Causapscal-des-Vents*. He stowed the radioactives in the middle of a stack of old batteries. It wasn't a lead-lined container, but the batteries had enough lead to block most of the radiation for now. If the clouds didn't cooperate, it was possible that the radioactivity would be detectable at a higher altitude, so neither of them wanted to leave it too long out of the bathyscaphe, which blocked the particles better. Pascal handed Gabriel-Antoine a multi-spectrum light and various filters to hold. "Pa and I maintain the bathyscaphe pretty well," Pascal said, "but you probably want to check it."

Gabriel-Antoine found far more than its depth-worthiness to check. The centimeter-thick steel seemed strong enough to him to withstand the ninety atmospheres of pressure, although he doubted the Stirling engines. He tutted at the backwardness of the software, the limitations of the hardware, and started making lists of upgrades he would make.

"Don't think too fancy," George-Étienne said at one point. "Few things work right at four-hundred and eight degrees. It's primitive on purpose."

"It's primitive because it was built of leftovers thirty-five years ago," Gabriel-Antoine shot back. "I've built pretty good deep-dive chips and processors for rescue and salvage drones. They want to automate mining of the surface. But they haven't got enough capital to launch something self-sustaining. And as far as I know, no one has found any likely mining sites in the basalt, so I doubt they're in a hurry."

"They can have the sun and sky," George-Étienne said finally. "This is for us."

Pascal rechecked the manipulator arms, spooled on the additional carbon cabling, mounted the camera and lights onto small motorized platforms of Gabriel-Antoine's design. The engineer argued with George-Étienne about software fixes. In a moment of quiet common industry, Pascal came to his father and signaled for him to switch to the family frequency.

"Pa, are you trying to annoy him?" Pascal asked softly.

"We don't have to change everything!" George-Étienne said. Pascal shushed him. Loud enough voices carried through the helmets and travelled without radio.

"Pa, he's a really good engineer," Pascal said. "I'm learning a lot just by seeing what he asks about."

"*You're* good, Pascal."

"I can't do it all, and there are lots of things I can't do at all," Pascal said. "And he knows a lot of the new engineering and programming they're doing above the clouds. We're offering Gabriel-Antoine a partnership and he obviously doesn't trust us. Arguing doesn't make it better. We have to show him."

"I don't want anyone around I can't trust," George-Étienne said. "And if he isn't ready to trust me, why should I trust him?"

"He's only known us for a day, Pa. He's not a *coureur*, but I think Marthe got us the right person."

George-Étienne hmphed. He could be worn down eventually, but using Marthe's name was a bit of a rhetorical shortcut, an appeal to authority that sometimes ended debates. In the end, they didn't change any of the software anyway, not because George-Étienne didn't want it, but because they didn't have time for the inevitable debugging. They had to be ready by the time they reached the drop window.

THIRTY-EIGHT

DESCENDING THROUGH THE gloomy lower cloud deck, breaking into the open haze beneath, and then finally seeing the naked Venus inspired no less awe in Pascal the second time. Perhaps more, even, because this time he was the one who had to decide everything: descent rates, Stirling engine rotation and power, wind drift, and hot sulfur dioxide chemistry. And maybe some of the awe came from sharing the descent with Gabriel-Antoine. His companion's silence was answer enough to how Pascal felt as they sank towards the heavily deformed highlands of Alto Regio and the snaking depths of Diana Chasma.

It was very unlikely that Gabriel-Antoine would be able to recognize the surface features, and Pascal didn't want to name them. Pascal had a bit of his father's suspicion in him. If Gabriel-Antoine didn't decide to work with them, if he couldn't be convinced to help, Pascal didn't want him to know enough to lead anyone back. Pascal adjusted the fins, putting them onto a steep glide-path south and west over the dark flatness of Rusalka Planitia.

"That's a tessera," Pascal said, pointing to Nuahine Tessera on their right, a lighter-colored area of hundreds and hundreds of kilometers of terrain heavily deformed by repeated contractional folding.

"Everything looks destroyed," Gabriel-Antoine said, "like after a disaster."

Something *had* destroyed Venus half a billion years ago, something so catastrophic as to melt the planet's crust, and maybe explain Venus's slow, backwards rotation. The sterilizing heat, blistering volcanoes and cracked, blackened rock added to the impression of something damned, as did the unnaturally transparent sky.

"It's a world without even ghosts," Pascal said.

Gabriel-Antoine turned in his helmet to smile at Pascal. They were cramped side-by-side in the berth made for one, but neither seemed concerned with being pressed together. Nervous and comforted at once by the contact through two layers of survival suits, Pascal searched for words to keep impressing Gabriel-Antoine.

"Across the plain are coronae," Pascal pointed, showing raised, pancake-shaped plateaus: Khabuchi Corona and Nirmali Corona to the left, and ahead, the massive Atahensik Corona, its stone surface baked gray and black.

"From a distance, Venus is beautiful and bright," Pascal continued. "From space. From Earth. From Mars. But she doesn't want to be touched. She knows she's not beautiful, so she pushes us all away with heat and acid, because when we finally break through all that, we find out she's not what we thought. She's hideous and she doesn't want to feel like we're stuck with her."

"That's a strange way of looking at Venus," Gabriel-Antoine said. "At sixty-fifth *rang,* people say Venus hates us, hunts us."

"She doesn't want to be seen like this because this isn't who she is."

Gabriel-Antoine squeezed his hand through the gloves.

"You're not stuck with her," he said. "You fly through the clouds like an angel."

"I pretend, like she does," Pascal said, steering them westward, towards high Ceres Corona.

"I've seen you," Gabriel-Antoine said. "You're beautiful."

Pascal sighed, wanly, wanting to believe, knowing that Gabriel-Antoine thought he spoke the truth. But Gabriel-Antoine hadn't seen the inner Pascal. He moved his hand free to work the controls.

They flew over Miralaidji Corona at only ten kilometers. The rough plateau was wrinkled like a popped blister, all sharp edges. The pressure outside the bathyscaphe had climbed to forty-eight atmospheres, and the temperature to almost three-hundred and ninety Celsius. The bathyscaphe creaked under the stresses. Gabriel-Antoine tried moving his head from side to side to get a better perspective on Miralaidji.

"There are no shadows," he said plaintively.

"That's part of crossing from her illusion to the body she wears," Pascal said, continuing the gentle turn towards Ceres Corona, and the chasma that cut for hundreds of kilometers across its feet. "Nothing looks right in an in-between world."

"I've heard the mysticism that some people above the clouds have about Venus," Gabriel-Antoine said. "Is that what this is?"

Pascal shook his head in his helmet.

"I'm not mystical about Venus," he said. "Lots of *coureurs* are, though. Pa almost is, although he won't admit it."

"What do you think, then?"

"Venus isn't just a mirror. She's every mirror. We all see ourselves in her."

"Longing?" Gabriel-Antoine said. His tone was half question and half statement, like he might be longing too. Pascal dared not look at him. Gabriel-Antoine's voice was potent, more powerful now that it was disconnected, whispering to him through an earpiece, so intimate that Pascal could hear his breathing.

"Seeing something mystical in Venus isn't incorrect," Pascal said. "Marthe, Émile and I all grew up where the deep clouds play tricks on our senses. Sounds come from nowhere. The world casts no shadows. Shapes and lights emerge from the clouds and vanish. Storms swallow habitats and return them months later, like ghost ships. Some *coureurs* see the bioluminescent clouds and call the lower cloud deck a fairy world. Instead of calling themselves *coureurs des vents,* they call themselves *coureurs des fées.* Émile and I come from the same world, but I can only see some parts of Venus through his poetry because he sees something different in his mirror."

Pascal dared a glance. Gabriel-Antoine was smiling softly. Pascal's heart turned to mush. He wished the survival suits weren't between them, and yet he was glad they were.

"He's not the only poet," Gabriel-Antoine said. "I think I would like to live in a world of magic and fairies."

Pascal was dripping sweat now and looked away. Despite all the insulation, the interior of the bathyscaphe had reached ninety degrees and the pressure had risen to four atmospheres. Their suits worked hard to keep their interiors below body temperature, but that wouldn't last long.

The regular wrinkles on the upper surface of Ceres Corona now appeared sharply defined, rows and rows and rows of broken stone, mounted by sharp, unweathered edges. The lead sulfide and bismuthinite clouds hovered at two kilometers, partly obscuring, partly silvered. Pascal spoiled their lift, but even on full spoil, they sank through the thick atmosphere as if through water.

"Even if the fey existed, they would be in the clouds," Pascal said. "They couldn't survive where we are now. This is a world without wind, without rain, without life. There's no erosion here, no marking of time except the volcanoes."

"And your cave," Gabriel-Antoine said. "You've found the one place on the surface of Venus where something is happening."

"You believe me now?"

"You're showing it to me."

"Yes," Pascal smiled.

The flat slope running from the mountain peaks on the north canyon wall down to the base of Diana Chasma was clear ahead. The sense of overwhelming scale was difficult to put aside for two people who'd grown up in contained habitats. Certainly Gabriel-Antoine must have lived with wide skyscapes above the clouds, but a vast open space was not the same as a vast physical thing, like an unmoving stone of uncounted quadrillions of tons thrusting itself into this baking ocean. They both knew storms that towered kilometers high, but that was just acid and carbon dioxide. This was stone. They had no comparator. Those who worshipped Venus need build no monuments. Venus built her own.

Gabriel-Antoine sighed lightly at the sight, and with the earpieces, it was as if he'd sighed next to Pascal's ear. Pascal's heart thumped faster. Gabriel-Antoine had something of the poet in him too, something that *felt* Venus.

Pascal increased their descent angle. Diana Chasma itself was a monument as well. Serpentine, snaking for a thousand kilometers, the web of the chasma system was a hundred kilometers wide, each trench clawed two to three kilometers into the crust. The chasma walls seemed improbably steep, and all the more massive for that. The floor of the chasma was broken in some places, flat and even in others, littered with boulders and landslide rubble, which seemed sand-grain tiny from this altitude.

"Can we see it yet?" Gabriel-Antoine asked in a small voice.

"Almost," Pascal said. "Another fifteen minutes."

"Until we get there?"

"Until we come within sight of it," Pascal smiled. "We're descending at almost terminal velocity, which this close to Venus isn't much."

"This thing has never had a leak?" Gabriel-Antoine asked.

"We don't use it much," Pascal said.

Gabriel-Antoine looked at the outer and inner pressures. The difference was eighty atmospheres. If they did get a leak, it would be like an explosion inside the craft.

"It's never had a leak with me in it," Pascal added.

"You're a good luck charm."

The brown and black edges of the chasma rose above them and they entered an even gloomier world, richer in grainy detail than the clouds they knew, vaster than their habitats, and spectral in the deceptively perspective-deadened shadow-free light. The thick air moaned outside the bathyscaphe, differently from the high, frantic whistle of wind over wing-packs and suits, or even the thrumming of storms outside habitats. Pascal had meant what he said. This was an underworld, lifeless even beneath the strangeness of Venusian cloud life and its human colonists. An underworld without ghosts.

They slowed in an environment that had more in common with the sea floor than an atmosphere. Pascal turned their creaking bathyscaphe onto a final approach. On their last journey, Pascal and George-Étienne had decided to land farther from the cave mouth to be safer. Boulders on the smooth ground loomed only ten meters beneath them and Pascal spun the prop for a few moments to kill their descent speed. Then, they sank, meter by meter, second by second. Venus neared to give them a gritty, dry kiss. They bounced once, very gently, with a weird buoyancy so that the slow wind carried them forward. They stopped on the bathyscaphe's wheels and held their breaths.

"Welcome to Venus," Pascal said quietly.

Gabriel-Antoine might not have trusted himself to speak, or perhaps he wanted another touch, because he took Pascal's hand for long seconds as he craned his neck awkwardly to peer up through the fish-eye diamond porthole. Above them, gray clouds hid a yellow glow like a cooling ember. The walls of the Diana Chasma felt prison-like. The wind, perhaps five kilometers per hour, but powerful at ninety-three atmospheres of pressure, made a low hum around them.

"It's real," Gabriel-Antoine whispered.

"Venus?"

Gabriel-Antoine was still peering up at the walls and the all-too-solid eighty-ton boulder about thirty meters away.

"I've never touched a planet," he said. "Before today I'd never even seen a planet this way, only in pictures."

"I never believed pictures, not in my heart," Pascal said. "I don't know that anyone born in the clouds can."

"Thank you for showing me this."

Gabriel-Antoine turned. He had a nervous smile replaced every few moments by an awe Pascal knew. Pascal was younger than Gabriel-Antoine, but here, he was the experienced one.

"We're probably effectively breathing five atmospheres,

and heat exhaustion is going to hit us before the Stirling engines fail," he said. "We'd better get cracking."

Gabriel-Antoine exhaled heavily. He was sweating as much as Pascal. He turned to the new control panel that they'd installed. The bathyscaphe vibrated as the tool bay door on the outer hull opened.

In preparing for this descent, Pascal had been elated to have another engineering mind to throw ideas at, someone with whom he didn't need to hold back any of his mathematical or geometric shorthand. In fact, Gabriel-Antoine sometimes had to slow down for Pascal, which was both embarrassing and exciting. Between them, they'd designed and 3D-printed a half-dozen torpedo-shaped drones, none longer than a half-meter. Made almost entirely of carbon nanotubes, the drones could move for hours on the surface of Venus like little submarines before the heat wore down their control mechanisms.

Gabriel-Antoine activated all six, sending them on pre-programmed courses. They needed to measure the wind speed and direction in the three-dimensional volume around George-Étienne's cave. The drones had simple course-correction software, which would collect data and give them a 3D map of the local winds.

In the meantime, Pascal drove the bathyscaphe forward on its spindly carbon wire wheels to the boulder ahead of them. Their little craft rocked slightly and skidded sideways on the slow, heavy wind.

"There's a lot of wind," Gabriel-Antoine said, looking up from his display. "Like a storm, but no clouds or anything in the air."

"It's only a few kilometers per second."

"It's a wind of super-critical carbon dioxide," Gabriel-Antoine said. "I'm changing the routes of the drones. I just about lost one. What's making that wind?"

"The true heart of Venus," Pascal said. "The stars."

Then they had to focus on their tasks. Despite the changes, one of Gabriel-Antoine's drones couldn't correct its course in time and was dashed onto rocks and swept into the cave mouth. Pascal tethered the bathyscaphe to the boulder and swung it around to the lee side so that they faced the cave. For long moments, they stared in wonder at its impossibility.

They'd mounted a heat-resistant laser and linked it to a mapping program. Centimeter by centimeter, it scanned the ground, the rim of the cave and as far down the throat as it could. This would give them a detailed topographic model of the cave entrance. They had a radar they could have brought down, and software that could have analyzed the chaos of input within the cave, but radar waves bouncing up into the clouds would have been the quickest way to give away their location to *la colonie,* and to the Bank too.

Pascal spooled out a cable with a small chemistry payload that they'd jury-rigged the night before. The rock was far too hard to sample with the tools they had, and any acids or reagents they had would have boiled at these temperatures. But decades of scientific prospectors had faced the same problem, and they had carried down two sulfur-silicon-oxygen powders in the little payload.

Or, more correctly, they were solids at forty-fifth *rang*. Somewhere on the way down the two solids had melted in their containers. When mixed, they formed a high-temperature sulfuric acid variant. Pascal poured the hot acid onto the stone, and filmed it etching the surface. The wind blew blebs and drops of the acid-stone slurry into a collection container. Pascal zoomed the camera, photographing the morphology of the stone that had resisted the acid, and very carefully lowered the chemistry payload into the wind torrent running into the mouth of the cave, repeating the process inside twice.

By the time he'd finished that and left a spidery drone clinging to a hollow of the cave wall, it had been ninety minutes and Gabriel-Antoine looked like he was succumbing to heat exhaustion. He'd lost two more of his drones. They landed the other three in the lee of larger boulders nearby, where they could be recovered.

Pascal pulled in all the equipment, inflated their oxygen balloons and released their cable. The launch was rough, and frighteningly sideways at first, but within a second their buoyancy shot them up like a bar of soap from a fist. The bathyscaphe creaked and the surface shrank beneath them, Venus becoming once again the hideous, inscrutable, distant lover. Approaching Venus had burned them. Not just their souls. The bathyscaphe had not been able to keep the internal pressure below four atmospheres. It had barely held it at six. And the internal temperature had risen to one hundred and fifty degrees, the heat tolerances of their survival suits. But the decompression of the oxygen tanks had cooled the inside by two degrees already. They continued rising without any leaks.

"You okay?" Pascal said.

Gabriel-Antoine nodded weakly. He was dripping with sweat and had puked in his helmet.

"Soon we'll be high enough for me to deploy radiator vanes to cool us off faster," Pascal said.

"I don't know..." Gabriel-Antoine said, "... how you do it... I come from the cold."

"I'm a *coureur des vents.*"

Gabriel-Antoine sipped water listlessly from the straw stub in his helmet. The wind of their ascent hummed outside, already down to three hundred and ninety degrees Celsius. Pascal deployed the radiator vanes vertically along the hull.

"Not a *coureur*," Gabriel-Antoine said. "An angel."

THIRTY-NINE

ÉMILE WATCHED THÉRÈSE kneel in the bay of the *Baie-Comeau's* oxygen-cracking factory. Réjean, Mylène, and Anne-Claude sat on battery stacks. Cédric's arms were draped over Anne-Claude's shoulders. Bénoit knelt beside Thérèse, holding a breathing mask connected by tubing to one of the big atmospheric tanks. The factory was solar-powered, and during the forty-eight-hour day, it pumped atmospheric carbon dioxide into tanks to crack it into oxygen and carbon monoxide for life support and jet propellant. During the forty-eight-hour night, the factory idled, but the collecting tanks were still full of Venusian air.

Bénoit was a dick from the *Val-Bélair* habitat on the other side of the planet, on a training course on the *Baie-Comeau*. He'd been sniffing around Thérèse since he got here. He put his face into the breathing mask and inhaled deeply. He kept it on, and his breath came faster and faster. It was just carbon dioxide.

Idiot.

Finally, he took it away, close to passing out. As he passed it to Thérèse, he stroked her back and she didn't pull away. She put the mask to her face, and breathed for twenty, thirty seconds, her breaths turning into panting. Her face took on a bluish tinge.

Émile pushed Bénoit out of the way, put his arm around her and tried to pull away the mask. She shrugged violently at his arm and elbowed his reaching hand. She closed her eyes again, and the blue tinge beneath her papery skin dropped to her neck.

She swayed and he wanted to support her again, but didn't. Anne-Claude and Cédric came close, watching her eagerly. Thérèse dropped the mask and fell forward onto hands and knees, taking great gasping breaths. She groaned. He put his arm on her shoulder, and she flung it off again. She gathered enough strength to sit up, then glared at him and kicked him. Her bony heel didn't hurt, but he felt the heat of flushing on his face.

"What?" he said softly.

"Stop getting between me and Venus!"

"I'm not! I thought you needed help."

"There is no help with Venus! I do this. I choose."

He took the mask off the floor. "I want Venus too." The plastic was warm against his face, moist with exhaled breath. Hers. Bénoit's. A primal panic raced from lungs suddenly heavy with carbon dioxide. His panting came quickly. To slow it, he held his breath, the carbon dioxide of Venus's atmosphere. His heart thumped. Thérèse stared dubiously at him. He closed his eyes. He tasted the faint bitterness of sulfur. Exhaled. Breathed. Panic throbbed. Chest burned. Spit thickened in his mouth. He forced another breath, but instead of strong, it came quick and shaky, panting. The parched air of Venus tasted of unquenched thirst. Push out. Pull in. He just wanted to last longer than Bénoit.

When his vision was more black spots than plastic floor, he dropped the mask and inhaled. Even breathing real air wasn't enough. He needed to change all the air in his lungs. Venus—choking, killing, spiteful Venus—filled his chest like an ocean filling a drowning victim. He didn't pass out, but it was close.

Anne-Claude and Cédric took the mask and knelt in front of one another. Like he should have with Thérèse. He dragged his eyes to hers. She watched him, tight-lipped. Then her hand rested on his leg.

"What are you doing, Émile?" she said. "Why are you even with me?"

All the panic that had risen out of him splashed back in, washing away all the good things. He gripped her hand, held it there. He didn't know how to answer in front of people, all watching.

"I want to be with you." He felt the stumble.

The palpable failure of his answer.

"You don't like the real me, Émile," she said. "Humanity here needs a connection with Venus. I'm going to find how to reach her. What are you doing here?"

"I want to be part of that," he whispered.

"If I wasn't doing this, would you be here? Drinking of Venus's oceans? Touching Venus's skirts? Feeling her bite?" she said, not lowering her voice at all. Everyone was listening.

"I'm running from one connection and looking for another," he said quietly, leaning close to speak just in her ear, choosing his words. But like his poetry, none of them ever felt right. "I don't know what will make me feel like I belong, but I think it will be through you."

"I thought you were a poet," she said, "but you don't make anything. I thought you wanted Venus, but you only go through the motions. You know what I like about you? You're lost. Lost is the right start, but it's only a start."

"You're lost too," he said, the first thing he could say with conviction.

"I'm not lost," she said, withdrawing her hands. "I know exactly where I want to be. I just don't yet know how to get there. I'm questing. Purity of vision is what will get me there."

He swallowed down bitter spit. She rose, touching Anne-Claude and Cédric on the tops of their heads like a benediction. She sat with Mylène and Réjean on the battery stacks. Bénoit joined them and they shared a joint.

FORTY

DESPITE HAVING BEEN on the surface less than two hours, it took four hours to decompress as they rose to the *Causapscal-des-Profondeurs* forty-five kilometers higher. Marthe and George-Étienne stowed the bathyscaphe while Marie-Pier brought Pascal and Gabriel-Antoine inside, and stripped their suits to let Jean-Eudes clean them. Jean-Eudes made a gagging face at the puke smell of Gabriel-Antoine's suit, which sent Alexis into a giggling fit.

Pascal was well enough once he'd wiped himself down and put on coveralls. This wasn't the first time he'd overheated, but Gabriel-Antoine needed an hour of slowly sipping water while Marie-Pier sponged his torso under a fan. Pascal imagined sponging Gabriel-Antoine's hard chest, and resented that everyone else was here, that Marie-Pier was taking care of him. If they'd been alone— if they'd flown to some other habitat, just the two of them—it would have been Pascal's responsibility.

The outer door of the airlock to the garden torus slammed. Jean-Eudes and Alexis dropped the cleaning and repair of the suits and ran to wait at the line on the floor for Marthe to come through. Marie-Pier smiled as she observed this and shared a glance with Pascal. The dull carbon wheel spun and Marthe and George-Étienne stepped in.

Both were careful and disciplined, the way all *coureurs* had to be with the acid and heat and pressure. They didn't step past the line. They closed and locked the airlock door. They put down the equipment they'd been carrying, then checked each other's suits, applied a bit more bicarbonate, and re-wiped the seals on their necks before removing their helmets. Jean-Eudes put on dark gloves, wiped the helmets diligently, and strapped them to the wall. Alexis, who normally left this to Jean-Eudes, begged to be allowed to help his aunt.

Pascal came over, put on a pair of gloves and wiped down the packaging around the instruments they'd pulled out of the bathyscaphe. They were just cool enough to touch for a few seconds at a time. He brought the instruments to the table.

"*Ça va?*" George-Étienne asked, jerking his chin to Gabriel-Antoine.

"I'm good," the engineer volunteered.

George-Étienne stripped off his suit and handed it to Jean-Eudes.

"You were down there a long time," he said. "How did it go?"

"It was incredible," Gabriel-Antoine said wistfully.

They stowed the suits, dressed and came to the table Pascal had folded down. He'd hooked the instruments to the computers and unrolled a screen. Pascal took the three solidified acid-dissolved rocks out first. They smelled of sulfur and were stained faintly yellow. They passed them around.

"A sample," Pascal said. "We expect that the rock is like most of the rest of Venus's surface, basaltic with no water to speak of."

George-Étienne put his arm around Jean-Eudes, who stared at the ugly yellow-veined black blob in wonder. "Your brother brought you a real piece of Venus," he said. "If Venus were a proper planet, we'd be walking on that stuff all day long."

The thought of standing on rock seemed so ridiculous to Jean-Eudes that he laughed. Alexis took the stone, weighing it in his palm.

"Rock as far as we could see, going on forever," Gabriel-Antoine said to Alexis. "No rain. No wind. Just heat."

"Can I go, *grand-père?*" Alexis said. George-Étienne shushed him.

While they'd been talking, the computer had finished calculating a three-dimensional view from the laser topography data. The rock face, the cave mouth and about twenty meters of the floor of Diana Chasma were rendered in yellow lines on black. The detail was excellent. They could have probably shaped a cap to go over the mouth with just this study.

"That's going to take a lot of steel," Marthe said.

"And we're going to have to have layers of caps," Pascal said.

"That isn't the only channel, though," Gabriel-Antoine said. "Did the wind map turn out?"

Pascal changed the display, showing a three-dimensional volume where the drones had moved. At every meter, arrows of different sizes showed the wind direction and speed. There were gaps in their measurements, but the picture showed that the cave system was more complex than they'd thought.

"I don't know how to read this," Marthe said.

Pascal turned the display and hid all the vectors except those that pointed at the rock. This thinned the blizzard of arrows and showed at least six openings. The main cave mouth was the largest. About twenty meters rightward, the photograph of a small opening, barely large enough to fit a person crawling, matched to a series of arrows indicating wind speed. Photographs showed another opening twenty meters to the right, hidden behind a boulder, and smaller rocks that seemed to be held in place by the force of the wind. Far to the left, almost three hundred meters away and about forty meters off the floor of the chasma, was a cave opening under an overhang of rock. It was about two meters in diameter. The drone scans had found two other minuscule channels, also connected to the main channel.

"I don't understand how you can cap a cave in all that wind," Marie-Pier said. "The pressure and wind force are stronger than anything we ever see in the cloud decks. Why isn't the atmosphere of Venus emptying in all that?"

"They say that five million years ago, it took a hundred thousand years for the Atlantic Ocean to fill in the Mediterranean Sea through the Straits of Gibraltar," George-Étienne said. "This cave is tiny compared to the Straits, and the surface of Venus is far larger than many Atlantics."

"We've been working on different plans," Pascal said. "With proper mapping of the tunnels, we can prepare caps for various parts of the cave, and either lower them in or assemble them in the caves. They'll be hinged, and once they're fixed into position, we can swing them into place, let the wind hold them there. That will stop the wind enough for us to work."

"But you'll cook down there," she said. "Do you have enough robots to do all that?"

"As soon as we've got two or three caps in sequence," Pascal said, "we'll run high pressure atmosphere down to low pressure spaces, making electricity and cooling the interior, like a refrigeration unit."

"The rock will still be four hundred and fifty degrees Celsius," Marthe said, "even if you can get the air down to a couple hundred degrees."

"We can get the air colder than that," Gabriel-Antoine said. "We're starting with a vacuum on one end of the cave. That will be the coolest area. The rest depends on the pressure drops and insulation."

"You'll need good insulation," George-Étienne said.

"Vacuum is a good insulator," Gabriel-Antoine said.

"It'll take a lot of steel to double-jacket that whole cave," George-Étienne said cautiously.

"Or we play with the rock," Pascal said. "We'll have unlimited electricity and a vacuum. We could melt and reshape rock to have hollows. Air will insulate too."

Marie-Pier shook her head, doubtfully.

"It's an enormous undertaking, for what?" she said.

"The heart of Venus," Pascal said.

"Independence," George-Étienne said. "The stars."

Marthe regarded Marie-Pier. "Whatever is at the bottom of the cave, whatever it is that leads into a vacuum in some other solar system, nothing like it has ever been found before."

Marie-Pier waved her hand, not dismissively, but she seemed to be struggling with her argument.

"If that really leads to another solar system—and I'm not disputing that—" she added quickly "—then it does have unique value. But none of us are eminent scientists. I'm an applied botanist. He's an engineer. And we have no tools or instruments, not the kind needed to really discover anything. And even if we did, if we can't tell anyone, then what?"

"Understanding comes later," George-Étienne said. "In cooled tunnels under Venus, we could mine, really mine. Pull our own ore out of the ground. We know what iron, aluminum, nickel, hydrogen, carbonates and minerals are worth."

"Metals, yes," Marie-Pier said, "and then what? How do we explain where we came into tons of steel?"

"We don't need to trade more than a fraction of it," Marthe said. "Only what we have to, for what we can't make ourselves. We'll build a sturdy habitat in the caves.

Greenhouses. Bioreactors. Lots of space to live."

"And among the stars," Pascal said. "We know how to build spacecraft. We know how to print solar panels and robots to go mine the asteroids in this new solar system. We know a lot of basic vacuum industry. We have energy. We have metals. We have a base to start from."

His enthusiasm was catching. He saw it catching among them. But Pa's expression was becoming more sober.

"Access to mining and space will change Venus, not just for us and all the *coureurs*," he said. "It will eventually help even the people living above the clouds, being strangled by the Bank monopoly and an incompetent government. But it's more than that. We've found a bridge to the stars like the ancients tried to build. We've found the Axis Mundi."

FORTY-ONE

TÉTREAU HADN'T SEEN his girlfriend in days, and saw his family only before he slept. But this was the time in life to make a mark. He could get into *l'Assemblée* soon and still be one of the youngest members... but lots of members turned that step into nothing. He would show his dedication and talent and, although young, would be a prime candidate for a seat in the cabinet. And who knew, with enough supporters and favors owed, in a decade or two, maybe *président?*

Labourière waved him in. Tétreau closed the door and sat.

"We've got twenty aircraft in the upper cloud deck equipped with radiation detectors," Tétreau said, "as well as eighty drone planes. We have more drones, but no more radiation detectors for them. Industry section is calling it a new wind-mapping exercise, as well as a test of new comms systems."

"What are the odds they actually find something?" the

Chief-of-Staff asked.

"It's a big planet and the atmosphere is thick enough to scatter-blur even strong signals. We're focusing on the equatorial band, which gives us overlapping sensors in a lot of places," Tétreau said. "If something is in that strip, we'll be able to triangulate on it."

"Then you can use radar."

"If we use radar now, we'll just draw attention to ourselves," Tétreau said.

"And once we have a source pinpointed by radar, the constabulary can go down. Maybe even with some Bank guards."

"Really?"

"Woodward wants to get to the bottom of this as badly as *la présidente*," Labourière said.

"I'm going to talk to Émile D'Aquillon again," Tétreau said. "I've thought of a way to get in."

"How?"

Tétreau explained his new idea.

FORTY-TWO

DIFFERENT FAMILIES ADAPTED to the close quarters of the habitats in different ways. Some yelled. Some shut down. Some developed body language cues to tell the others when they wanted privacy. Marthe had learned all the cues young. She'd always been curious about the unspoken, and when she'd moved up to the *Causapscal-des-Vents* at sixteen to be her father's representative to *l'Assemblée,* she'd had to learn a whole lot more body languages fast. *L'Assemblée* was the watering hole of every upper habitat and even some of the *coureur des vents* families. And everyone reacted differently to conditions that would have made rats eat each other in behavioral experiments.

Marie-Pier hadn't said anything yet, but had stayed at the table, rerunning the video Pascal and George-Étienne had taken, the one that had revealed the cold vacuum beyond the hole in Venus. Marthe had watched Marie-Pier many times in debates in *l'Assemblée,* watched her expressive, space-consuming conversational gestures. And while she seemed intent, her body language wasn't closing. She wasn't afraid or defensive.

Marthe sat across from her. She pulled out a dark, thin paper made of hammered trawler fiber and tapped in coarsely chopped tobacco. She licked, rolled and held it out to Marie-Pier. The older woman hesitated.

"Anything good in it?" she asked.

"I didn't bring any with me."

Marie-Pier took the cigarette and the electric lighter. Marthe rolled herself another, lit and inhaled. Faintly sulfurous. Acrid. Satisfying. They smoked in silence, eyeing the little image. Finally Marthe rotated it. It didn't make it less inscrutable or sharpen any of the blurred stars caught by the vagaries of focus.

"I wish we had a better picture," Marie-Pier said.

"In a while, we'll be able to build a telescope," Marthe said, "to explore whatever is out there."

"Never thought of myself as an explorer."

"You weren't born here, were you?"

Marie-Pier shook her head. "I was born in Havre-Saint-Pierre," she said, hooking her thumb over her shoulder as if pointing at Québec, "but I don't remember it really. My parents brought me here when I was three."

"I was born at the base of the lower cloud deck, at forty-eighth *rang*, over Arianrod Fossae," Marthe said. "Three trawler habitats ago."

"Tough primitive trawlers back then. Arianrod is north, isn't it? Why so far north?"

"The prop trains on the old trawlers weren't as reliable.

Pa followed the winds a lot more, steered a whole lot less."

"Fossae are named after war goddesses, right?"

Marthe nodded.

"That's funny," Marie-Pier said with a smile. "And very *à propos*."

Marthe smiled, shrugged and drew on her cigarette, making the end glow.

"Tough life this deep," Marie-Pier said.

"It's not an environment that encouraged us to look more than a few weeks, or months ahead," Marthe said. "We don't choose. We endure."

"But you went sunside," she said, jerking a common thumbs-up that the *coureurs* used to indicate the main ships of *la colonie*.

"Bright lights, pretty girls," Marthe said. "And I was never in any control down here. Winds blow you where they want."

"Good life?"

"I don't carry Pa's baggage about the Bank and the government, but I can see that *la colonie* is heading nowhere. We're never going to get out from under these debts. The Bank will make sure of that. We're never going to steer our own destinies."

"I have two young children," Marie-Pier said. "I don't have a lot, but we're okay for now. They have to grow up. I have to give them something certain." Her hands shaped something, cupping whatever it was that she would give her children. Neither woman knew what it was.

Marthe nodded slowly. "I'm not saying what we're proposing isn't risky."

"Very risky. Stealing a habitat, and a few of my trawlers."

"Those don't belong to the government."

"The law says they do."

"We both know who writes the laws, and who's funding them," Marthe said. "We're losing the *Causapscal-des-Vents* because the *présidente* doesn't like us, and you're losing trawlers you built and were going to sell because you don't give gifts to the right people."

"It's going to get worse when they find out that we sank a habitat on purpose. My kids need the same medicine, all the other things kids need."

"Did you like Jean-Eudes?" Marthe asked.

"This isn't about Jean-Eudes," said Marie-Pier. "He's sweet."

"The government would rather he didn't exist."

"How did you grow up with no medicine or vitamins or any of the other food supplements you needed?"

"It wasn't easy," Marthe said. "I got sick a few times pretty bad. We all did."

"And you lost your mom."

Marthe dropped the butt of her cigarette into the ashtray, watching the coiling smoke.

"Yeah. But she didn't die because of our choices. Any *coureur* could have died just from being too far away from hospitals, including you. We were just too far from help."

Marie-Pier leaned forward. "My kids can't lose their mother, or have their habitat confiscated."

Marthe turned the image again. The stars moved.

"Playing it safe will probably get you, them and your habitats into the future, ten, fifteen years. Then what? They'll be paying for debts they didn't make, debts that weren't fair to start with because the Banks stacked the deck."

Marie-Pier looked at the stars in the image.

"They'll be alive and probably healthy, but they'll be trapped in the clouds forever," Marthe said, "just like Pascal, you, me and Alexis. Can we go where we want? To Earth or the other colonies? We'll never be able to afford to leave. *La colonie* will have less and less habitats, and more and more families will be forced into living subsistence lives in trawlers. That's for your children and your grandchildren."

Marthe tapped the display.

"This is scary. This is risky. But I have a chance to offer Pascal and Alexis and even myself the stars," Marthe said. "The wealth of the asteroids with the safety of a planet means we could turn Venus into a paradise. Towns and cities in the clouds. Space for us to live and thrive."

Marie-Pier had pursed her lips.

"But I'm scared," Marthe said, "not just of succeeding. I'm scared that we will find out, after all we've thought and planned—that we can't do it. That would kill me more than anything Venus could offer."

"Hope is terrible sometimes," Marie-Pier said.

FORTY-THREE

PASCAL WAS HYPER-AWARE of Gabriel-Antoine as they went into his room. Gabriel-Antoine brushed his teeth, washed himself with a sponge as Pascal turned away, hot-faced and awkward. He wanted the light off. He needed to have his face smooth. He wanted to be invisible. But he also wanted to touch Gabriel-Antoine. Feet padded up behind him. A hand touched his shoulder.

"You okay?" Gabriel-Antoine asked in a low voice.

Pascal nodded, then looked back and smiled nervously. Gabriel-Antoine's face was close.

"I'm going to clean up," he said, and felt his whisper flounder and fade.

Gabriel-Antoine didn't follow him to the head. Pascal shut off the lights.

"What are you doing?" Gabriel-Antoine whispered.

"Just a sec."

With shaking hands and clenched eyes, Pascal lightly lathered his face, and stroke by stroke, scraped away stubble with the straight razor. It was the worst sound in the world, and he couldn't imagine Gabriel-Antoine not being disgusted with him. It wasn't a sound Pascal could run from. He *felt* the sound. His skin felt it. His bones felt it like a fork scratching across a plate. He was so aware of Gabriel-Antoine that his hands shook until he cut himself.

"Hey, cutie," Gabriel-Antoine said. "You already shaved this morning."

"I'm almost done."

"Leave it on."

Pascal's stomach turned. "I'm almost done." But he wasn't. He lathered his chest and arms quickly, scraping himself smooth with swift strokes. But Gabriel-Antoine was listening. Thinking he was strange. As strange as Pascal really felt.

"I'm, uh, really happy we went down," Gabriel-Antoine said into the awkwardness. "You don't know what that was for me."

"I'm sorry you didn't see the stars," Pascal said.

"One day I will," Gabriel-Antoine said.

His voice was closer, although Pascal hadn't heard him approach. In a panic, he wiped off the last of the lather, and self-consciously touched his face and neck, looking for ugly stiff patches he might have missed. Then, his chest and stomach and arms. Tiny patches of soft stubble found his fingers and he felt uglier.

"You believe us?"

"One day we'll see them together," Gabriel-Antoine said from just behind him.

Pascal's hands trembled so much that he dropped the case of tooth polish instead of shutting it. Gabriel-Antoine's fingertips touched Pascal's arms, sliding up the smoothness, making Pascal shiver. Pascal jammed the toothbrush into his mouth and tried to move casually. Gabriel-Antoine's mouth was behind Pascal's ear.

"I've seen the stars my whole life without seeing them," Gabriel-Antoine said.

Gabriel-Antoine's warm chest pressed against Pascal's unshaved back. He dropped the toothbrush and turned against him. They were of a height and their noses were close. Pascal swallowed his toothpaste.

"You really didn't use that line before?" Pascal whispered.

Gabriel-Antoine shook his head. His grin was bright in the gloom. The sounds of quiet conversation in the main area drifted in through the curtain, along with weak light.

"You seem to have a lot of words to turn someone's heart," Pascal said.

"I only want to turn yours."

Whether it was true or not, Pascal wanted it to be. Gabriel-Antoine was handsome. Smart. Funny. Daring. And they'd gone to the surface together. Pascal felt his nervous heart beating so fast he wanted to scrunch into a ball, and he didn't want any of this to end. He neared his mouth to Gabriel-Antoine's and touched hesitantly. Gabriel-Antoine responded, pressing back more tentatively than his words. And Pascal pressed back at him, harder, putting his arms around him. After a few moments they parted. Pascal was hardening. He pulled away in embarrassment. Gabriel-Antoine leaned against the wash station beside him and stroked a thumb across Pascal's smooth face.

"You want to help me build the caps?" Pascal said, to fill the air with something other than his awkwardness. It sounded stupid.

Gabriel-Antoine nodded, an inscrutable gesture in the three-quarter darkness.

"It's upside down," Gabriel-Antoine said. "Wind and stars beneath the ground. It's magic. You've shown me the magic Venus has been hiding from us. And my life has been upside down since you walked in."

"Sorry," Pascal said, smiling sheepishly.

"I was tired of life being right-side up. I didn't know it but I'd been waiting for some angel to come along and save me from fixing ovens."

Pascal laughed low. "I'm no angel."

Gabriel-Antoine neared again, pressing his chest against Pascal's, and his lips to his.

"You have wings," he whispered. "You make me feel like a live wire."

"I feel like I'm close to getting electrocuted," Pascal said, resting his forehead against Gabriel-Antoine's.

"The tough cutie from the lower clouds in danger?" Gabriel-Antoine scoffed. "I feel like I want to protect you, but that you could keep me alive down here with one hand behind your back."

"I'll protect you."

Gabriel-Antoine's hand slid down Pascal's flat stomach, looking for the hardness down there, but Pascal's hand caught his wrist.

"I just want to make you feel good," Gabriel-Antoine whispered.

Pascal shook his head against Gabriel-Antoine's.

"You like men, don't you?"

"I like men," Pascal finally whispered.

"So do I. You like me, don't you?"

"I like you."

"Then let me make you feel good."

Gabriel-Antoine's hand tried again, but Pascal was strong enough to hold him back, barely. Then his other hand shot out, tickling, and Pascal twisted and caught the other hand too, and they were stalemated, breathing harder, trying not to make any noise that would be heard in the main area.

"I don't like me," Pascal finally whispered in terror, "down there."

"I've seen you," Gabriel-Antoine said. "You're beautiful."

Pascal shook his head. His heart pounded in his throat. He didn't want this night to end. He wanted to be more to Gabriel-Antoine. He didn't want to poison anything forming between them with all the blackness and wrongness inside of him. He gently released both of Gabriel-Antoine's hands.

"Let's move to your hammock," Pascal said. "Teach me to make you feel good."

"That's a bit one-sided."

"This is what I can do. Please be patient. Please. This is what I want."

"Okay, *chéri*," Gabriel-Antoine whispered in his ear before he began nibbling and kissing there.

They walked awkwardly, a four-legged thing clinging desperately to itself, before Gabriel-Antoine fell back into his hammock.

FORTY-FOUR

"WHAT DO YOU mean by that?" Émile said into the microphone. Thérèse's grainy expression in the monitor reacted a second later, melting from belabored patience into boredom. The delay from the Phocas' habitat to wherever Thérèse was bunking today wasn't from the radio signal. The processors and antenna were lo-fi pieces of shit.

"I feel like you pull me away from what's important to me, Émile."

"I'm a..." he said, then lowered his voice. He was in Gabriel-Antoine's workshop, but it wasn't soundproof. "We're both artists. Things aren't going to be easy."

"Are you?" she said after a second's delay. A look of pity crept into her eyes.

"Fuck you..." he said. "Fuck you and your stupid... acid burns! Who gives a shit about what the fuck you burn on your body? Stupidest fucking 'art' I've ever heard of. Acid is acid."

The pity in her eyes was still there. "Goodbye, Émile."

The transmission ended. He swore and was about to grab something, anything, and smash it into something else, but everything looked valuable and neat in the little workshop, and *Madame* Phocas was swearing too, out in the main room.

Émile was about to swear back at her, but realized she was really worked up at someone else. He was going to clock whoever it was if they didn't stop pissing the old lady off. He wrenched open the door. *Madame* Phocas was arguing with a guy at the open doorway that led from the gondola up through the envelope of the *Marais-des-Nuages*. The new arrival stood there, genuinely perplexed, as the old lady got her second wind.

"Get off this habitat, you piece of government shit!" she said in a reedy voice, before succumbing to a coughing fit. "Bring a goddamn warrant if you want to try to set foot here!"

Émile put his hand on her shoulder, but she shook it off.

"I'll take care of this, *ma tante*," he said.

"I'm just here to talk to *Monsieur* D'Aquillon, *ma tante*," the government guy said.

Grand-papa Phocas had struggled up from his hanging chair and was trying to straighten his back to face the newcomer. He was red-faced and Louise ran to help him stand.

"*You* brought him here?" *Madame* Phocas demanded, poking Émile in the ribs.

"I don't know this guy from *crisse*! Calm down, *ma tante*! I'll kick his ass if he doesn't leave, but sit down, *ostie*!"

Grandmaman Phocas didn't seem used to being spoken to that way and her thin lips pressed tight. Émile didn't wait for her response but marched to the door. He stepped into the stairway in the envelope, closing the heavy pressure door behind him.

"Who the *crisse* are you?" Émile said.

"I'm Laurent Tétreau," the man said, holding out his hand. Émile took it warily. "We met at Réjean's party."

Émile had a fuzzy recollection. "Did I punch you?"

"No."

"Good."

"I'm an assistant to Dauzat and Labourière in *l'Assemblée*. I mentioned before, I think the D'Aquillons are getting a shitty deal under the leadership of Marthe and your *papa*. It's a shame you got caught in it. You're probably the one who could make peace."

"Oh yeah." Émile looked back at the metal door and patted his suit pockets. "You got a cigarette? They don't let me smoke around here."

Tétreau produced a pocket flask. "I don't smoke, but is this good enough?"

Émile hadn't had a drink since yesterday. After the latest shitty conversation with Thérèse, the prospect perked him up. Tétreau unscrewed the top, took a sip and passed it to Émile. He drank too, cautiously, not sure of where he stood with this guy.

He was surprised. It wasn't *bagosse*. It was smooth. It warmed his throat and chest, instead of burning. "Is this real whiskey?" he asked. There was even a trace of sweet— rare—and a hint of sulfur, like everything on Venus.

"It's an Irish recipe we're been adapting to Venus," Tétreau said. "We'll never get it perfect, because the chemistry is different, but we built casks out of the sides of trawlers."

Émile held up the flask. "Can I?"

"Drink it all. I've got a few bottles in my bunk."

Émile's mouth watered and he sipped slowly this time. "Shit," he said wonderingly. There were more flavors than he could name, good ones, uncertain ones, but it kicked as hard as *bagosse*.

"You're a hard man to find," Tétreau said.

"Splitting my time between here and the *Causapscal-des-Vents*."

"Yeah, I had to track your suit's transceiver."

Émile spotted the badge on the outside of Tétreau's suit. Not just a constable. A lieutenant. He lowered the flask. The suspicions bred into him surfaced.

"I thought the cops weren't supposed to use transceiver data unless they needed to."

Tétreau shrugged. "Who cares, right? I just wanted to talk, and we got to share a bit of real whiskey."

It was hard to argue with his reasoning. Émile sipped.

"What have you got on the Phocas family to get *ma tante* all freaked out?" Émile said, hooking a thumb behind his shoulder.

"We know Gabriel-Antoine Phocas is hoarding a lot of metal scraps and tools," Tétreau said. "Some official channels have been pressuring him about it. Hoarding's no good."

"So why not bust him?"

Tétreau shrugged. "Some small-time stuff is okay to let go. Little crimes excite people, like they're pulling one over on the inspectors."

"I don't know what I can do to help you," Émile said.

"Like I said before, I think you're being wasted. You ever thought about joining the constabulary?"

"Me?" Émile demanded. "I punched a constable once. And they don't give good jobs to families like ours."

"It's not about family," Tétreau said. "You're a big guy who can fly up here as well as in the depths, right? We don't have enough *coureurs* on the force. Constables get first pick of bunks. Better rations, too." Tétreau tapped the flask meaningfully with a fingernail.

"What do I have to do?"

"It's a part-time job," Tétreau said. "We get called up when we're needed. We knock some heads. It's always better to have another big guy on our side."

Émile laughed low. "My Pa would have a stroke if he heard I joined the constabulary."

"You and your Pa don't get on anyway. Marthe doesn't treat you great. She's downcloud with your Pa, right? The two of them are just going to get each other angrier and angrier about something they can't change. It should have been you to go sort things out with the rest of the family. I don't know why they treat you like they do, but I'm not going to make that mistake."

Émile sipped. He would love to see Pa's face when he heard the news that the constables wanted his son, and not the way he expected.

"I mean, they got you being errand-boy over here?"

Tétreau said. "Why isn't Gabriel-Antoine taking care of his own habitat?"

The whiskey, so good, took on a bitter taste.

"Phocas is with them," he said. "Him and my little brother flew down after Marthe had gone."

"Why?"

Émile shrugged. "Something about extracting metal out of trawler tail cable."

"There's almost no metal in trawler tails. Is that another pipe-dream?"

They didn't really tell him. He wasn't part of the family. Not in *that* way, when it counted.

"One of many," Émile said, tipping the whiskey up.

"Think about the constables," Tétreau said as Émile handed him back the flask. "I'll call you in a couple of days."

FORTY-FIVE

MARTHE CLOCKED IN only a few hours of hammock time. After Marie-Pier turned in, she smoked at the kitchen table. She slept fitfully and got up before anyone else. The smells of hard sulfur-laced wood, of sweating bodies and growing green things dragged her back in time.

She remembered Pa, much younger, *maman* and Chloé, both still alive. She remembered Émile as a teenager, working the trawlers with Pa. She almost always remembered Jean-Eudes as big, even though she was taller now. As just a little girl, she'd taught Jean-Eudes to count and read with the patience of very young children, an effortless patience she couldn't imagine anymore.

She remembered Pa's fights. With the government. With Émile. Sometimes with *maman*. Even as a teenager, Marthe had been his confidante. They'd stay up late, talking about politics, about raising the family. She might have been as happy living down here, riding the winds, helping raise Pascal, Jean-Eudes, and Alexis.

371

But in those late-night conversations, Pa hadn't just taught her to roll cigarettes. He decided that she would go to the upper atmosphere to live on the *Causapscal-des-Vents*. She would represent the family in *l'Assemblée*. It had pissed off Émile. It had scared the shit out of her. But Pa was right too. They both knew she would be good in *l'Assemblée*, even if they were both nervous about it. There were things she was good at, things she could do that Pa couldn't.

But she wondered if she'd left too early, before she'd learned everything she'd needed. Marthe still woke up beside walking disasters like Noëlle. For that matter, so did Émile. What had they missed? What hadn't Pa been able to show them? Maybe they'd left home too early, or maybe something hadn't translated from Québec to Venus.

Pa and *maman* had been born on Earth and they'd stayed together until Venus took *maman* away. George-Étienne and Jeanne-Manse had even left *la colonie* for the lower cloud decks to keep their little Down syndrome baby. And against all odds, they'd made a family.

Sleep eluded her not just for these thoughts, but because of time lag. The high flotilla raced on winds that circled the planet every four days. But in the deep habitats of the *coureurs,* not only might there be a hundred or more hours of day and an equal amount of night, but the day-night rhythms were distended. Day and night blurred.

In the depths, clouds made high noon arrive yellow and diffuse. And nighttime was always lit by spongy red light scattered all the way from the terminator. *Les coureurs* and *les colonistes* from the flotilla meant different things by the words "night" and "day."

She found one of the ceramic plates that Pascal had sawn from the space probe. It was pockmarked and weathered. It was riddled with wiring that seemed chaotic but that Pascal said was alien circuitry. She believed him. There was wealth in knowledge, in resources, and although an antique and surreal concept to Venusians, there was value in land. She left the piece of hull on the table as she rolled another cigarette. She considered all that piece of ceramic meant to them, lines of possibility spinning out into futures she couldn't know, futures among the stars that Alexis might grow old in, and his children in their time.

Marie-Pier and Gabriel-Antoine were not family, but they needed that kind of bond to build this bridge to the stars. If circumstances blew the D'Aquillons apart from the Hudons and the Phocas, they would all lose. They needed to make a family, but it wasn't the kind of family Pa knew how to build. They needed to make a political family.

An hour later, people slowly woke up and began joining her at the table. Pa was gentlemanly and courteous to Marie-Pier, less so to Gabriel-Antoine, who was obviously smitten with Pascal. Gabriel-Antoine was glowing and Pascal was shy and quiet at the table, hiding a half-smile. Did they have the makings of a family? If they did, she still might not be the right one to make it. But if Pa tried to negotiate, he would blunder about, the way he might hammer the corrosion off a lock. And Pascal was too uncertain of himself to weld different political interests together. Marthe crushed out her last cigarette. "I've been thinking," she said, gesturing to the piece of hull on the table.

Pa slid a bowl of soup and a cup of coffee in front of her. He took up the hull fragment, ran his scarred fingers across its pitted outer surface and smooth inner surface, and handed it to Marie-Pier.

"Ceramic minerals," he said, "and iridium, platinum, silver, gold and other metals. We're going to grind them up for some quick resources to help bootstrap us."

"That's small potatoes, though, Pa," Marthe said. "If we do more than sell scrap—if anybody finds out we may have found traces of alien technology—Venus will become the new gold rush, fought over by the Banks. We lose it all. *La colonie* loses it all."

"Are you thinking of a broker?" Marie-Pier asked. "Someone not traceable to Venus?"

Marthe shrugged. "Can you imagine anyone who would fit the bill?"

Marie-Pier pondered the heavy fragment in her hands.

"I've thought through all the risks I can think of," Marthe said, "and I still want to do this. I think rolling the dice is worth it."

Gabriel-Antoine poured himself a cup of coffee and put one foot on the bench, leaning over the table. He took the hull fragment from Marie-Pier and turned it in the light, seeing things that the others probably didn't.

"I'm not going to lie," he said. "I'm bored up at sixty-fifth *rang*. I'd love to take on a big engineering project.

I'd love to figure out what this is and how it works."

Marie-Pier was still pensive.

"Sometimes I think the D'Aquillons have been kicked around not just by the government, but by the *colonistes* too," Marthe said. George-Étienne stared at his hands. Marthe rubbed his shoulder. "The D'Aquillons stick together. We don't trust easy. We put a lot of weight on family. Not just blood. Any of us would have dived into the clouds to save Mathurin, my late brother-in-law. Jean-Eudes would have done it."

Jean-Eudes looked sheepish and teary at once. Pascal nudged him with a shoulder and gave him an encouraging smile.

"Émile, for all his differences with Pa, would have jumped after Mathurin too," Marthe said, "because family is family."

She jerked her head at her little brother.

"Show us the stars, Pascal."

Pascal came to them awkwardly and unrolled the display over the table as Gabriel-Antoine moved dishes out of the way. Alexis, unaccustomed to the seriousness of the tone, and the strangers, snuck behind the bench and draped his arms around George-Étienne's neck, peeking from behind his grandfather's head.

"I don't know why we found the stars," Marthe said, "but we can't reach them ourselves, and we're offering to share them with you. But do you trust us to be straight with you? And what are we really offering? A corporation? A business partnership with the sharing of dividends? Those don't make any sense here. We can't involve the government or the Bank. And notarized pieces of paper don't make trust." She paused. "The only thing I can think of to make a real partnership is marriage."

George-Étienne's head jerked up. Marie-Pier's cheeks pinkened. Gabriel-Antoine, still cocky, looked back at Pascal.

"Your sister moves fast, eh?" Gabriel-Antoine said. Pascal flushed to his hairline. Gabriel-Antoine winked at him. He grinned at Marthe. "You and I don't swing the right ways, Marthe. Who's proposing to me?"

"I'm talking about three families, Gabriel-Antoine," Marthe said.

"Polygamy?" he said.

"Not exactly," Marthe said. "Marriages bind families, because they have something at stake together. A joining of the D'Aquillons with the Phocas family and the Hudon family would be a real alliance, something serious."

"Hard to imagine," Marie-Pier said.

"You, Pa, and Gabriel-Antoine enter into partnership, to join the three families into a single house," Marthe said. "The three of you share the leadership of the house, or it goes through turns. Pa, then Marie-Pier, then Gabriel-Antoine. The ages happen to work out for a succession of leadership every ten to fifteen years."

"Not you?" Gabriel-Antoine asked.

"Pa is the head of the D'Aquillon family until he doesn't want to be," Marthe said.

Gabriel-Antoine's face was turning serious. Marie-Pier's lips twisted in thought. Jean-Eudes had taken an uncertain step closer to Pascal. George-Étienne looked at her with melancholy.

"I just want to give my children something," George-Étienne said, reaching up to give Alexis's arm a squeeze. "Something more than they're getting now." Alexis didn't understand what was going on, but he squeezed his grandfather back.

"Something for Maxime and Florian," Marthe said to Marie-Pier. "And something for Louise and Paul-Égide," she said to Gabriel-Antoine. "And all their children in turn."

"Are you looking for George-Étienne and I to make children?" Marie-Pier asked.

George-Étienne reddened again.

"Don't ask me to help!" Gabriel-Antoine laughed.

"We'll raise our families together as a house," Marthe said. "Work together. Pool our resources. Share."

"Sounds like a tribe," Marie-Pier said.

"Families come in all shapes," Marthe said. "Gabriel-Antoine, don't you need help to give you more time to do real engineering?"

"*Oui,*" he said.

"We can help raise Louise and Paul-Égide and give Alexis a brother and sister at the same time. And we can help you care for your grandparents."

Marie-Pier was quiet.

"It's a big step," Marthe said to her. "I think we can trust you, and I think you think you can trust us. And you're right. We're risking a lot. And without you, I don't know how we'd do this. If we go for it, it'll be hard. We're talking years of sending out drones to mine the asteroids of that other system, building habitats, growing food, manufacturing, industrializing, all in a place that has never seen a Bank flag. It'll be a new start. We'll be the first humans to leave the solar system."

Marie-Pier looked around at them all, then back to the strange alien technology in her hands.

"Sink the *Causapscal-des-Vents* on purpose, eh?" she said. "And carry down four of my trawlers with it? The stresses might break one or all of them, and then your habitat really will be falling into the abyss."

"We have engineers to make the plan," Marthe said, giving Pascal a quick, reassuring smile.

"And if they find out? The Bank and the government?" Marie-Pier continued. "That'll be hard to explain."

"We'll have to be fast," Pascal said.

"If they find out, I join George-Étienne in the doghouse," Marie-Pier said. "Maybe they take the *Coureur des Tourbillons*. Maybe I go to prison. And my children and my brother start from zero, begging for bunks in the common habitats."

"You don't know that they won't be begging for bunks in ten years," George-Étienne said. "*La colonie* can't afford metals. Habitats are going to fall on their own. And if this works, your children will be some of the richest people on Venus."

Marie-Pier took a deep breath. "I'm not used to these kinds of risks."

"We'll take care of you and your children," Marthe said. "That's what family does."

Gabriel-Antoine nodded slowly. "I will too. My

grandparents are old. I don't know what I can give Louise and Paul-Égide other than a stake in a black-market repair racket. And they probably would like a brother." He winked at Alexis who smiled from behind his grandfather.

Marie-Pier regarded the young engineer, one of her prospective 'husbands,' for a long time. But she reserved a longer look for George-Étienne. He looked back at her evenly, not challenging, not pushing. Marthe was proud of him. The future of his whole family was riding on the decision of this woman.

"What do you think, Jean-Eudes?" Marie-Pier asked. Jean-Eudes reddened and smiled shyly.

Marie-Pier extended a hand to George-Étienne and clasped it. Then she shook hands with Gabriel-Antoine. Then the two men shook.

"What do we call ourselves?" Gabriel-Antoine asked. "I don't want to change my name."

"We keep our family names," Marthe said.

"But we have to call the house something," Pascal said, taking a step closer. "To belong. We're founding this house in the Hadesphere, but our bridge to the stars is in the Stygian layers of Venus. Maybe we should be the House of Styx."

"Venus protect fools in the wind," Marie-Pier said.

George-Étienne and Gabriel-Antoine smiled and repeated the curse and invocation used by mothers in the clouds for decades.

FORTY-SIX

AFTER NINE O'CLOCK at night, Gaschel's office was mostly empty. She was reading the interesting bit of Tétreau's report about the visit of Gabriel-Antoine Phocas and Marie-Pier Hudon to the *Causapscal-des-Profondeurs*. For extracting metals from trawler cables? She'd never heard of anything like that. There couldn't be more than trace amounts recoverable. Unless they'd found some new process. Or unless they hadn't been open with the brother.

She was also scanning the terse reports of non-sightings from the planes and drones that Dauzat and Tétreau had sent out. The planes had covered about half the equatorial zone so far. She was impatient. Woodward was impatient. Gaschel had been in Woodward's office earlier in the day, receiving ham-fisted threats about debt interest, but there wasn't much Gaschel could do to make things go any faster. Labourière knocked at her glass door. He had a beautiful black woman with him.

Gaschel signaled them in.

"Noëlle Lalumière, *Madame la Présidente,*" Labourière said.

The Lalumière woman looked a bit awed by the office and by Gaschel. Labourière retreated and shut the door. Gaschel came around the desk, shook hands and guided her to a small seating area.

"Thank you for meeting me, *Mademoiselle* Lalumière."

"They said I wasn't in trouble."

"You're not," Gaschel said, pouring the younger woman a glass of water. She had juices and spirits to offer, but she didn't want to give this woman more reason than she already had to brag about this meeting to anyone. "I've asked you here discreetly as part of a criminal investigation."

Lalumière's brown eyes widened and she leaned forward. She didn't touch the water.

"It's about your girlfriend."

"Délia?"

Gaschel squirmed.

"I've maybe been misinformed?" Gaschel said. "I'm talking about Marthe D'Aquillon."

"She's not my girlfriend. I don't hang with criminals."

"It's an investigation," Gaschel said. "We don't know if she's involved, or if her family is."

"I don't know Émile, but he's a dick."

"You have some influence over Marthe?" Gaschel asked.

Lalumière considered the question, looking away, then pushed aside a coil of curly black hair. "Maybe."

"There's a reward involved if this goes as far as a conviction," Gaschel said. "Any conviction. Right now our investigations have led us to three families. Some other lines of evidence put the D'Aquillon family at the top of our list."

"How much?"

"How would you like to live on the *Forillon,* or the *Baie-Comeau?*"

Lalumière's eyes narrowed. "What are you looking for?"

"No one can know you're helping us," Gaschel said. Lalumière nodded. "Has she talked to you of any political plans? Does it seem that she's angry enough to do something illegal? Or her family?"

"She can get mad," Lalumière said.

"Marthe is down at the *Causapscal-des-Profondeurs* with her family. I'd love to know what she is doing there. I'd also like to know exactly where the *Causapscal-des-Profondeurs* is in case we need to make arrests. They probably communicate by maser. If you're in Marthe's habitat, and you can find out where it's been pointed or where it's going to be pointed, that will help a lot."

"I can do that," Lalumière said.

"Good," Gaschel said, smiling at the young woman.

FORTY-SEVEN

THE COMMS LIGHT blinked on and the buzzer sounded.
Émile jerked up, knocking over a bottle and a pile of
dirty plastic dishes. He'd fallen asleep at the galley table.
He stepped over the clutter on the floor. It was a message
from the *Causapscal-des-Profondeurs* by tight maser.
He didn't usually answer those, but Marthe was down
there. She was probably calling to ask if he'd cleaned the
habitat. He flicked the toggle.

"*Quoi?*" he said.

"How tight is this?" Marthe's voice said quietly.

He sighed, rubbed his eyes, bent to look at the controls.
He turned a knob. Marthe's maser beam looked to have
been scattered to a diameter of about eight centimeters,
more than tight enough for no one to be able to intercept.
He focused his beam on hers.

"You're at eight. Am I good? What do you want?"

"You're at six," Marthe said. "The carrier wave is clean
at two hundred twelve watts. I wanted to talk."

"Are you whispering?"

"A little. We have guests."

"Phocas? Yeah, I know." The line was quiet for a moment. Marthe might have been counting to ten, or composing her thoughts, or swearing to herself. He put two fingers between the blinds to peek out at the blinding brightness of sun on puffy yellow-white clouds extending past the horizon.

"We've got an idea that will really help the family," she said. "It's not safe, and it's not something we want to share with everyone else."

"You and Pascal are turning black sheep?"

"We might need your help," she said. "You want in?"

He scratched his belly, found the bottle, uncorked it and rinsed and swallowed. "Does Pa know we're having this conversation, or is that why you're quiet?"

"Think about it, Émile."

He *was* thinking. About his holier-than-thou sister, his jackass father, and his little brother under both their thumbs.

"What's the idea?" he asked.

"Let me know your answer. We'll talk when I come back up."

"Tell Jean-Eudes and Alexis I said hi."

"I will."

Émile stood for a while, wondering what they might be cooking up, why Marthe thought it was a good idea to try to convince Pa to change his stripes. A knocking and hissing sounded way up in the envelope; the airlock on the roof of the *Causapscal-des-Vents*. Then footsteps on the stairs. Other than Marthe, only Thérèse knew the lock code.

His inside went mushy at the thought of her. What did she want? Crawling back. Or just exploring if there was a way back together. How did he want to play this? He gulped a mouthful of *bagosse* and used it to rinse out his mouth. He picked up some of the dishes as the lower airlock spun. He stood straight, then leaned back casually.

"Oh fuck, it's you," he said.

Noëlle stood in the stairwell, helmet off, hair tied tightly back. Her expression was as unimpressed as his must have been. Then she looked around the mess of the kitchen and living area, the tumbled stacks of unwashed everything. He might have felt a tiny bit self-conscious if this had been Thérèse.

"Where's Marthe?" She stepped in, looking around.

Émile picked up a jar that might have a bit left. He swirled it, sniffed. It smelled vile. He upended it into his mouth and swallowed in distaste.

"Downcloud," he said.

"Oh?"

"Downcloud," he repeated.

"*Causapscal-des-Profondeurs.*"

Noëlle looked for a place to sit and seemed to think better of it. Then she realized how hot it was and began fanning herself.

"*Tabarnak,*" she said. "Normally it's too cold here."

"I'm fixing it," he said. He waited. "What do you care? You're not with Marthe."

Her withering look was impotent. "Where exactly is Marthe?"

He shrugged. "Down. I just masered with her."

Noëlle looked at the comms equipment. "So she's not far? Can I maser with her? You can just set it up."

"I'm not setting it up," he said, crossing his arms.

"Why not?"

"She's busy. And you're boning Délia the beauty queen anyway. And my Pa's a dick and I don't want to chance him picking up."

"I just wanted to talk to her," she said. "Things with Délia aren't good. And I want to talk things out with Marthe."

Her expression was earnest, a little overeager, but people were dumb in love. And Marthe would probably want to talk with her. He looked at the comms pack for a second, then did a quick calculation in his head.

"I think even if I wanted to, I couldn't connect you. The angle she contacted me at was about as horizontal as it gets. The *Causapscal-des-Profondeurs* is probably slipping behind the planet right now."

She looked at the time on her wrist display. "What *rang* are they in?"

"I don't know," he said impatiently. "They don't tell me and I don't care. If there's been lots of eruptions, they might be low. If they're catching or calving, they might be higher. It's wind, *ostie*."

She frowned. "I guess I... I was wondering when I could see her."

"Did Délia dump you again?"

Noëlle pursed her lips tight and stepped back into the stairwell. "Tell her I came by," she said, and then swung the airlock closed as hard as she could, which wasn't hard, but still made noise. He found the stub of a joint crushed under a plate. He tapped it back into his dwindling supply, wiped his sweaty forehead and opened the blinds with his fingers again.

He really had thought for a second that it was Thérèse coming down the stairs to see him. And maybe he understood, a tiny bit, why she hadn't. The cloudscape drifted a kilometer beneath him, too bright, too clear, too cold.

This wasn't home. He could understand what Thérèse was trying to do. Seeking a home was all anybody ought to be doing. Who could feel at home in a tin can floating under a balloon? And he was slowing her down. He had been keeping her from making the clouds home. He kind of knew what home was. He'd had a home once, in the gloom of the cloud decks. He missed Chloé and Mathurin. He missed *maman*. He missed Pascal and Jean-Eudes and Alexis.

FORTY-EIGHT

Pascal wasn't sure what to feel. Now that they'd agreed to do it, the job seemed too big to think about. And people were looking to him and Gabriel-Antoine to figure out how to turn their sacrifices into success. Bubbling excitement tickled inside his chest every few minutes. At other moments, weight left him, as if the *Causapscal-des-Profondeurs* were dipping in a downdraft.

And he was going to work really closely with Gabriel-Antoine. The thought thrilled and terrified. His feeling of deep wrongness still loomed in his mind. Not about Gabriel-Antoine; he was wonderful. The black feeling of being wrong was about himself, of being something he was not, of being trapped. And even in this moment of elation, spurred by people believing in the true heart of Venus, that feeling was trying to crush him.

By the galley table, Gabriel-Antoine talked animatedly with George-Étienne and Marie-Pier over the piece of hull. Alexis and Jean-Eudes had scooted close to the buzz.

Marthe came over to Pascal and put an arm around his shoulders. She steered him away from the conversation. They walked slowly, wordlessly. She pushed aside the curtain to Pa's room and they entered. She closed the curtain and smiled at him.

"The House of Styx, eh?" she said.

He smiled back uncertainly.

"I like it," she said. She winked at him. "You helped build the House of Styx. Gabriel-Antoine came over pretty enthusiastically."

He didn't trust himself to speak. The thrilling soar and crushing doom warred inside.

"Nice work," she said, offering him her fist. "He seems into you."

His cheeks went hot, but he fist-bumped her with a sheepish smile.

"You seem taken too," she said. "First love is scary. I hope you do better than me."

"Why?"

"I was sixteen, living without Pa for the first time, sitting in *l'Assemblée*, cocky as hell, and I met Ghislaine. Twenty. Gorgeous blonde. *Folle, folle, folle en ostie,*" she said, her moving hands punctuating: crazy, crazy, crazy as fuck. "I stayed with her on and off for two years. I was *folle* too, wound completely around her finger," she laughed. "Don't worry. Gabriel-Antoine seems to be a lot more stable."

He nodded uncertainly.

"Hey," she said, cupping his chin with her hand the way she had when he was just a boy and too shy to look at her. She ducked her head to look up at him. "It's okay. I was just joking. Gabriel-Antoine really does seem decent, and there are worse things than having a cute, smart, decent guy wanting to know you better."

"There's something wrong," he said.

"Yeah?"

He didn't offer anything else. He didn't have anything else. She rubbed his arm. "You don't like guys? You like both?" she asked. "It's all good. Swing any way you want. Or don't swing at all."

"There's something wrong with me," he whispered.

"There's nothing wrong with you, Pascal. You're wonderful."

He pulled away from her touch. She held her hands at her sides. The silence lengthened. The conversation outside broke into laughter, even Jean-Eudes's deep, fast laughter.

"I feel detached. Disconnected. I feel like I shouldn't be here. Anywhere." He swallowed. "I like when I get acid burns. Sometimes I let myself get burnt. On purpose."

She held out her left arm. Three parallel scars lay across the pale wrist. Too clean for acid scars. Too straight and narrow. Long faded.

"Fifteen," she said. "Before I left for the sixty-fifth *rang*. I didn't know what the fuck we were doing down here. I didn't know that any of us had a future. Pa and Émile fought all the time. *Maman* had just died. I thought that the best I could hope for, after all my struggles and living, would just be getting dissolved by Venus, like everything else. Nothing mattered."

He took a deep breath. This wasn't coming out right.

"I love Venus," he said. "I love the clouds. The heat. The chaos. The shapelessness. I wouldn't want to be anywhere else. I don't think I could live in the cold and bright of sixty-fifth *rang*. It's *me* that's wrong."

She took one cautious step forward, then put a hand on his shoulder.

"Wearing *maman's* dress wasn't about missing her, was it?" she asked.

"I don't know," he whispered. His eyes were hot. He couldn't look at her.

"Are you a girl, Pascal?" she asked.

He didn't know what to answer. He didn't know, and it ached. Tears dripped along his cheeks. His throat was painfully tight. He felt something about to break in him, something holding back a river.

"Sometimes girls are born into bodies that don't match," she said, taking his hand.

He felt a crushing hopelessness and an overwhelming relief. He nodded, although he didn't know at what, and he wiped at his cheeks with the back of his hand. He didn't pull away from Marthe. He squeezed her hand harder.

"If it's true I'm trapped here," he said. "In a meat prison."

She hugged him. Then she wiped the tears from his face. She smiled.

"Little sister?" she asked.

His throat constricted, and more tears came, and he nodded... she nodded. Elation and despondency swirled like debris in a storm.

"Don't cry," Marthe said. "I know who you are now."

Pascal knew too: free and trapped, eyes opened to the perfect curse. Marthe hugged him tight as he cried silently. After a time, the tears slowed and he wiped self-consciously.

"Does knowing matter? I'm still trapped."

"We're all going to help."

"There's no help."

"There's hormones."

His brain felt like it stopped. "What?"

"You're not the first, Pascal. If your body is producing the wrong hormones, we can give it the right ones."

His terrified heart expanded, unsure of what to do faced with hope. "Really?" he whispered.

"Yeah."

The tickle of hope squeezed in somehow, too deep to be taken seriously.

"We can't afford hormones."

"Black market."

"We can't afford hormones."

"That's not your problem, Pascal. Leave that to me."

He didn't trust himself. He didn't trust her. It was too big.

"Turn me into a girl?"

"Part way. The rest is more involved. I know somebody who changed."

Hope settled in his heart, like a weed that would be hard and painful to pull out. The stress of its growth made his soul creak to accommodate it. She sat them on

Pa's hammock and they checked encyclopedia entries on hormones. He'd had no idea. He felt so stupid for never having found out about any of this. He felt like he'd wasted so much time. After a while, she helped him clean his face, wiping away tears, letting the blotchy redness calm until it looked like he hadn't been crying.

Not he.

Not he.

She? What did it feel like to be she?

Marthe opened the latches on the top drawer of Pa's storage and found his tobacco. She rolled a cigarette and stood nearby while Pascal just thought. What was it like to be a she? He would love to be like Marthe. So comfortable in her skin. Insides and outsides matching.

Part of it made so much sense, felt completely right. But the relief inside made how he... she was built so much worse. The full weight of... her prison was crushing. The hope now, with even a moment's thought, seemed absurd. Ridiculous. How could anyone escape their own body?

She'd shaved her chest and stomach and arms and face every day, twice sometimes, to find smooth skin, but that smooth skin was drawn tight over the muscles of a man. And dangling between her legs was... something strange, not entirely hers. Something had conspired to humiliate her, to make her unrecognizable to the world, a disguise that had covered her so completely that no one could see who she was, or even think to look. Marthe stood beside her and rubbed her back.

"I'm Pascale," she whispered with a weird, questioning realization. "Pascale with an E."

Marthe hopped back into the hammock, not easy with Pascale's inches and weight over her. The hammock pressed them together. Marthe held out her hand.

"I'm very happy to meet the real you, little sister."

A feeling of warmth, of impossible relief, washed through Pascale. The real Pascale. She held Marthe's hand, callous to callous, scars to scars.

"I'm so scared," Pascale said. "I'm buried."

Marthe shook her head and smiled and Pascale began crying again.

"We know where you are, little sister. You're not lost anymore. We'll come get you."

Marthe hugged her as she went through deeper tears with terrifying moments of sudden, irrational elation so big she thought her chest would burst.

After a while, they emerged. Marthe rejoined the conversation, but Pascale went to her room. *Her* room. It was time to shave; she had the faintest of stubble, but she didn't look at it with the same sense of hopelessness. She left the light on, and washed her face, looking in the mirror for real for the first time in a long time. The person looking back at her was still alien, disconnected. She combed her fingers through shoulder-length hair. She made a tentative smile, trying to see who she might be under this disguise of a sixteen-year-old man, all the way down to Pascale. Pascal was just the outside of Pascale. Pascale was in there, the Pascale who felt things, who reflected on herself and the world. It wasn't Pascal all the way down. The relief in that simple realization was almost too much to hold inside.

Yet even the relief wasn't easy. It was one thing to find herself. It was another to find herself trapped in an impenetrable prison. Marthe wanted to help her, but how far could Marthe help? And what would Pa say? Or Gabriel-Antoine? Her stomach lurched in terror at the thought. What could she tell him?

As if he'd heard her thinking, Gabriel-Antoine appeared in the parting curtains at the door. He smiled at her. Pascale let her hair go and wiped her hands self-consciously with a damp cloth. He stepped in.

"*Ça va?*" he asked.

"*Oui.*"

"You looked upset when you came out of your talk with Marthe," he said, leaning against the wall, crossing his arms.

Pascale cleared her throat.

"It's a little overwhelming," she said, "and fast. We're really going to the stars."

"That's not it," he said.

"It's not?" Pascale said stupidly. Her heart thumped. Fear rose.

He leaned closer. "You can't hide it," he said, smiling conspiratorially.

"What?" she squeaked.

"You're worried about me being your step-daddy," he smiled, running his fingers through her hair.

Pascale huffed in relief, and then laughed in a way she was sure had an edge of hysteria in it. She pulled away, not sure what to do with her hands, not sure where to look. Gabriel-Antoine didn't follow. He was still smiling.

Like he didn't know that what they had was about to be ripped apart, like a herd of trawlers in a storm. She didn't have to make decisions yet. She didn't know. She didn't want to ruin this. His smile was fading, and his look became more penetrating. Pascale felt the shoe about to drop, and held her breath.

"I've been thinking," he said, "of whether we want a hinged door at the opening, or whether we want an airlock. An airlock will take more steel, and will have a smaller opening, but it will be more stable."

Pascale smiled wide enough to feel the muscles of her face. It was relief. Things weren't good yet. But at least Gabriel-Antoine was still here. Pascale got her note pad and showed Gabriel-Antoine that she'd already been thinking along those lines. It was easy to engineer, and fun, and they talked all morning in a way that felt like what she imagined dancing must feel like.

FORTY-NINE

NOËLLE CIRCLED THE *Causapscal-des-Vents,* bleeding off
speed, cutting back the thrust. From the outside, the
habitat looked abandoned. A third of the hydroponics
bays were white behind opaque windows, growing
nothing because of pressure leaks or missing piping. In
other habitats, bright green leaves would show in the
other outer cells, but here algae filmed the inner surfaces,
obscuring whatever was growing there, giving the old
habitat a sickly, blinded look.

Nervousness tickled at her stomach as she flared and
landed. She was self-consciously quiet about her steps
and she looked around the sky to check if anyone had
seen. No one was flying nearby, and the odds of someone
watching her with a telescope were a bit silly to consider.
Habitats tried not to approach each other closer than six
or eight hundred meters, so only a handful were in naked
eyeball range. She unstrapped her wing-pack quickly and
went to the airlock.

It was locked. She entered the code Marthe had shared with her once, when she'd been flying here in secret instead of visiting her mother like she'd told Délia. The same excitement and fear hit her now. The panel greened and she turned the airlock wheel. Cycling through, she crept down the stairs and through the lower airlock. She cracked the seal on her helmet.

"Marthe?" she said softly. "Marthe?" She peeked around the airlock door. Sun shone through the blinds, warming the galley, but only the soft creaks of the gondola hanging under the envelope sounded, punctuated by different machines in the floor turning pumps and fans on and off. Dishes were everywhere. Old clothes. The remains of joints and cigarette paper.

"Émile?" she said, stepping out of the airlock. "Marthe?" she said louder.

Still nothing. The two rack rooms were quiet and unlit. She peeked into each one. No one was here. She went to the communication set and called up the call logs in the tiny display. She tried downloading the log, but it didn't look like the comm set's Wi-Fi still worked. She tsked in frustration.

She took a picture of the display, then toggled through the whole log, taking a picture of each call, the direction of the antenna, the strength of the signal. She didn't know if this would be useful, but she hoped it was.

She snapped a few more general pictures of the galley, then moved to the rack rooms. She knew Marthe's big hammock, the neatly netted clothes and bagged or boxed tools. She'd had more than a few pleasant trysts in here, with the excitement of the forbidden, and the rough, rugged beauty of Marthe, so different from Délia.

Noëlle took pictures and opened small drawers. She found a few knick-knacks. Cheap nail polish. Some old datapads that wouldn't power on. A stash of weed. Then, she pulled out a locket that might be silver. She'd never seen Marthe wear it. It was pretty.

A tiny LCD inside the locket displayed different pictures every time it was opened: babies, old people, young adults, even pictures of people on Earth. She'd never seen real silver. The links of the chain were blackening. Maybe it wasn't silver. It sparkled against the sunlight slipping past the gaps in the blinds.

She unzipped her collar and slipped the necklace into an inner pocket of her suit.

She took a picture and closed the drawers. She noticed the floor plates and lifted those up, exposing the drive shafts of the main propellers. Oily. Dirty. Nothing hidden there. She took pictures anyway, feeling a growing sense of urgency. Either of them could be back anytime. She looked under more floor plates. Just spare parts and tools.

She took pictures before moving to Émile's room. Piles of old clothes, a datapad and even some paper were everywhere, under old carbon-fiber jars that stank with the sour scent of dried *bagosse*. The paper wasn't real paper. Nobody was rich enough on Venus for real paper. The *colonistes* made something filmy out of rosette envelopes and some people wrote on that with pencils made of fused atmospheric carbon or artisanal inks, but it was an affectation more than anything else. Everyone used datapads. Except Émile.

The faux paper scraps were endless, with scribbled lines, crossed out, substituted, erased and rewritten pieces. She tried to read some, but it wasn't complete sentences, just random thoughts. She hoped he didn't show this to anyone. That would have been pathetic. She took a few pics anyway. The datapad worked and was filled with poems from Earth and Mars. A directory held a bunch of files that looked like poems written by Émile. They were cleaner than the handwritten things, but clumsy to her eye. Émile was at best a deckhand, when he even showed up for work. He was grasping, trying to be something he wasn't.

Then her eyes widened when she found pictures of gorgeous, naked Earth women. She wasn't an innocent. She'd seen racy things, Venus-produced sex videos, amateur films and stills under gloomy lighting, or worse, blinding white light. Depressing more than anything, especially when she saw someone she knew. The women in these pictures from Earth were beautiful, well-fed, shapely, with flawless skin that had never felt the least touch of acid. They were photographed under soft lights or even daylight. Her mouth went dry looking at them.

The pad was old, not Wi-Fi enabled, so she slipped it into her suit. She could download the pictures on her own habitat and then toss the pad into the clouds later. Her search of the galley was desultory. There was nothing here but old dishes. The floor plates in the galley didn't show anything interesting.

She took her helmet off the table and snapped it back into place. Being a spy was far less interesting than she'd thought.

FIFTY

ÉMILE'S POETRY NEVER came out the way he wanted. He had a vision in his head, the images he would evoke, the emotions that would rise in response, the truth he would wake in readers. He felt things, but how many hacks had written of clouds and winds, here and on Earth? How many second and third-rate poets had tried to describe moving to a new world?

The poetry of other times and places gave him no guidance. The Chinese poetry of colonizing the asteroids was brisk and austere, like starshine on powdery regolith. The Arabic poetry of the colonization of Mars was lively and lonely, with tones of dislocation in the airless, sandy rustscapes. He read ancient Hmong refugee poetry, of dispossession and displacement in distant jungles. But the poems of Earth all felt remote, antiseptic, tangential to him and his experiences.

He hadn't heard from Thérèse, and he missed her. He thought she needed him. He needed her. He'd heard

Thérèse was fucking Réjean. He'd fucked Hélène. Spite fucks were an acid with which to scar a lover's heart, raising ropey red marks that never went away. He sent Hélène bits of his poetry, lines that he felt worked. No whole poem worked, but Hélène couldn't keep her mouth shut. She would eventually mention his poetry to Thérèse and she would be jealous he'd never shared with her.

A few days later, he was on shift, fixing a drive-shaft problem on the *Plamondon*, sent there by maintenance control, when he got a text from Thérèse. It was a line he'd written for his poem about the singing of the trawlers in the depths, and the singleness of each of their notes. She followed the line with a question mark.

He texted back. "What are you doing?"

"Going to go flying."

"Want company?" he messaged.

"Are you still going to get in the way?"

"No."

"I'm on *l'Avant-Gardiste*."

"Be right over."

He left *Plamondon* and his tools, jetting on the high winds, racing against itchy feelings and amorphous insights. The lumpy ocher cloudtops were like the rolling hills in Earth poems, but he felt like he was having trouble understanding solidity. He'd seen the skin of Venus, and he'd seen pictures of Earth, but never really understood either. The idea that anything would ever feel hard and unmoving was strange. Venus was the shapeless, vaporous possibility of being everything at once and nothing at all. And shapelessness infected everything.

What was he? A D'Aquillon? Was he Thérèse's former lover? Was he his shitty job? Or his shitty poetry? Or was he just a container into which Venus poured herself from time to time? She could empty him just as easily, the way she had emptied *maman* and Chloé.

A single twitch of the controls could cut his wing-pack's engine, plunging him into the acid clouds. If he descended long enough and far enough, Venus would accept his offering, his shape, all definition and selfhood. He would leave no more of a mark than anything else they'd done on a world that rejected shape and definition, on a world that went out of its way to erase them.

He was questions without answers, existence without meaning, attempts without successes.

L'Avant-Gardiste floated three kilometers ahead. The small dirigible was the home of Isolde Livernois, the only artist among their small crowd who was consistently recognized as talented. No one had to lie to appreciate her silent, screaming masks. *L'Avant-Gardiste* was bigger than the *Causapscal-des-Vents,* growing more food on its inner layers. The electricity from its solar panels cracked carbon dioxide into breathable, buoyant oxygen, and solid carbon used to grow carbon fibers. *L'Avant-Gardiste* could support a larger family and give carbon fiber to the rest of *la colonie* for building materials. In another life, in another shape, it might have been the D'Aquillon family living here.

He slowed, circled more steeply, and swooped over the flat platform of the roof, alighting with only a few extra steps. He stowed his wing-pack and cycled into the habitat.

When he found the storage room and spun the door, the smell of weed wafted out. Thérèse's survival suit covered her legs, but her chest and arms were bare, pimpling in the cold. Her ribs showed, stretching her skin like a canvas.

He stepped in and spun the wheel shut again. She eyed him languidly, blowing smoke at the ceiling.

"Did you have trouble getting out of your shift?" she asked.

He shrugged. "I just left. They'll figure it out."

He popped the gloves off his suit and took the joint from her mouth.

"They're going to be mad," she said.

He sucked and inhaled. Waited. Three. Five. Seven. He blew his smoke into the clouds of hers.

"What are they going to do? Demote me?"

She sat up, rubbing her hand against the chest of his suit. He stepped back.

"I didn't neutralize," he said.

Her look was pensive as she considered her open palm. She turned it back to him. "She didn't hurt me."

"You might have gotten a burn," he grumbled. He kicked listlessly at a storage crate. "Somebody's offering me a better job, better place to live."

"Why aren't you there?" she asked.

"Hasn't come through yet, but when it does, everything will be different. I'll have space."

She smiled wanly and hmphed. "If you get a place, a bunch of girls'll be looking to bunk with you," she said coyly.

He handed her back the joint. "Yeah," he said.

She turned it in her fingers, then squinted up, like she was looking for deception or irony. His gut tensed, waiting for the flare of fickleness, the shift of winds, the sign she was changing her mind again. Earth and Venus were written on her. Red scars formed leafy vines and the trawler on her left shoulder. Venus was written into the rows of knife-lines on the insides of her arms.

"You're a canvas upon which we paint Venus," he said. "You're the map showing us how to live here."

She pursed her lips pensively, then hooked her fingers into the neck of his suit to pull his lips to hers. They were hungry, aimlessly unsatisfied. She released him and shook her head.

"I haven't found it yet," she said dreamily.

He rubbed the raised outline of the trawler on her shoulder.

"I wish I saw myself the way you see me," she said.

"So do I."

Her smile contained an infinity of exhaustion, like she'd seen something in her seeking that was too big to tell. She hopped off the hammock, slipped her arms into the sleeves of her survival suit, and sealed the long seam of the chest. "Come on," she said. She led him back through the living areas, back to the ladder leading to the top of *l'Avant-Gardiste*.

"Where are you flying?"

She didn't answer. They climbed the ladder and sealed their suits before emerging from the airlock onto the platform on top of the shiny habitat. Émile unracked her wing-pack and helped her into it. He shrugged into his,

411

snapped in and plugged in the control feeds. Her unfolded wings stretched out two meters on either side of her. His extended three. She was grinning in her faceplate, and backed up to the downward curve where the platform followed the far outline of the dirigible envelope.

"I'm an angel," she said in the crackling radio, leaping backwards off the platform.

He leapt after her. Her fall followed the line of the envelope and then she was hurtling through the thin air, righting herself, starting the little jet on her back and swooping downward, away from *l'Avant-Gardiste*.

They flew fast and his heart lifted. They were angels. A few times, he pressed the transmit button on his helmet radio, but said nothing. He didn't know how not to ruin the moment. They soared onward, the sun bright and warm on their suits. A rare water cloud haze hung over the brown and yellow acid clouds, like a spattering of snow, or the dusting of an angel's passing. Their world had a soul. It was inscrutable and strange, but it was here. He could feel it.

He wanted to tell her, "*Je t'aime. Je t'aime, ma muse.*"

And he did. He did love her. It wasn't just the magic of this moment. He loved her.

She laughed, something bright and cheerful and Venus-touched, like him.

"I feel it," he said. "I feel Venus. She has a soul. You were right."

The glaze of white over the clouds dropped behind them and she dipped. He followed. The cloud tops resolved into umber mountains and valleys speeding beneath them. As they descended, rounded, misty peaks loomed up beside them.

"She's all around us!" she said.

Then he laughed, unable to contain himself.

"I'll show you the three cloud decks," he promised, "all the way to the bottom of the lower deck, so you can see the surface of Venus yourself."

Her wings angled, and she spun and flew upside down, dropping as she waved at him. He was close enough to see her beaming at him in the full sunshine. He felt like flying loops. But he couldn't stop looking at her. He was hypnotized.

Then she was unsealing the front of her suit.

"What are you doing?"

"Let's touch Venus for real!" she said. "Real aciding! We're so close! We have to touch her, even if only for a minute."

She was descending faster and faster; flying upside down gave her no lift. The front of her suit flapped, exposing her upper chest and sternum and finally her navel. She'd unsealed her suit, exposing her pale skin to the icy, thin air of the upper clouds.

"Come on!" she said, angling her wings to right herself, before plunging towards the acid clouds beneath.

He dove after her, his heart thumping, finding himself thinking like Marthe or Pascal instead of like an artist. He knew how hot sulfuric acid worked at depth, but didn't know how fast it might work in the chill above the clouds, or if she went into a cloud bank. Worse right now was probably the cold and lack of pressure. Her neck seal would only hold in so much air while her suit was unsealed. Yet her grace was perfect. She banked in lazy pirouettes around her wing tip to bleed away altitude. She touched Venus in a way no one else dared; jubilant, reveling.

His hands twitched near the seals at his chest. No one else was here with her. Just him. She had contacted him to share a very different spiritual experience with her. If he didn't open his seal, too, her communion with Venus would be a lonely, unshareable wisdom. He moved his hand to the seal at the top of his chest.

But then she dove. Gravity and airspeed plunged her through the rolling convection tubes of *Les Rapides Plats*, where the slower wind swept her back, far behind. He furled his wings and plunged through the thickening air. Changing winds buffeted him. He unfurled his wings and pulled into level flight, his speed launching him after her, his wing-pack engine a high-pitched keening over the rush of wind.

They'd dropped out of the faint haze and flew only dozens of meters above banks of yellow mist. The world felt dreamy and inchoate, chaos prior to definition, a vital soul without body, spirit waiting for the word. They all sought a word, *the* word, the language and rhyme that would bring this world to life for them. They quested for a first morning.

Thérèse spread her arms wide and swooped down into a bank of lazy cirrostratus.

Émile throttled hard behind her, plunging into the *faux* darkness of limited vision and spongy light. His suit would protect him from most of the acid, probably for half an hour or more at this altitude. The engines on their wing-packs weren't meant for much acid, though. Tiny droplets formed on his faceplate, running sideways with the speed of his pursuit. Two hundred meters ahead, Thérèse rose, then swooped lower, wobbled, then pointed her arms downward and plunged deeper.

"Thérèse!" he called on the radio. "Not so deep!"

Maybe she heard him. Maybe her radio was off. Maybe she was flying her spiritual journey alone. Could angels really share anything with mortals? He found his hand at the seal at the top of his chest again. The spray of mist thickened into big drops that trembled sideways off his faceplate. Thérèse vanished into the lobe of a cloud bank, and he followed. The sunlight dimmed, and beyond, he found her, not flying straight, but bending, curling herself under her wings.

"Thérèse! Straighten out! Start climbing!"

But she didn't. Her curled posture pitched her forward, dropping her altitude even more. He came above and behind her and grabbed the hand grip, usually used for racking the wings or tying them down in a storm. Pulling up with both hands as he flew, he corrected her angle of attack, but slowed his own flying. Their packs whined in the acid mist. He couldn't see very well what she was doing.

"Thérèse! Seal your suit. Can you seal your suit?"

She didn't answer. Her arms and legs dangled, jerking and bouncing with the buffeting of the wind.

"Thérèse! Are you okay?"

He angled up, using both their engines to climb slowly. They'd dropped about nineteen hundred meters in total. They had to climb back through *Les Rapides Plats*. A side wind gusted against them, ramming him into her. Their wings clattered together and the wind shear of her wing-pack exhaust tore his survival suit above the knee.

He righted them with difficulty. Cold bit through the cloth covering his knee and he couldn't tell if it was just cold and low pressure, or if the thin, vaporized sulfuric acid was getting to him. He couldn't worry about that right now. Thérèse could be going into shock or be passed out because of hypothermia. The worst might be if somehow she'd run out of air. The neck sealed pretty well, but that didn't mean the suit was meant to be run with the chest open.

The buffeting worsened, knocking them side to side, and he wrenched his shoulder holding onto her. A downdraft plunged them hundreds of meters in seconds. He couldn't steer them right out. The shear would fold their wings like sheet metal if he tried. They rode a side-cyclone, spinning like a roller on a conveyor belt.

He'd grown up in vicious, thick currents, knew tricks to seeing their invisible movements. Some currents moved so fast that they created rows and sheets of low-pressure vortices in their wake, where unseen moisture became cloudy fingers. Along their rapid trajectory, faint edges of spinning white showed against the darker clouds below. He aimed them at the bottom of a big convection cell.

He could see approximately where the wind turned back up, and he angled them towards that narrow steadiness in the turbulence. His wingtips trembled, and his arms ached from holding onto Thérèse while keeping his legs from catching in her pack exhaust. Why wouldn't she say anything?

The shaking became worse, tight vibrations resonating across his wingspan. He extended his spoilers, cutting his lift, but setting up a different vibration along his wings, breaking the resonances that would have torn them to pieces. Then he shot into the sheet of air that narrowed flat before turning upward.

They rocketed up, propelled by the wind, gaining back their lost three hundred meters. But the wind began to slack and turn, to plunge back down again in the great eddy. Émile throttled his wing-pack to maximum, set a challenging climb angle, and using the momentum of the wind, broke out, through the next layer of turbulence, into the thinning air above. This upper wind moved much faster from behind them and he struggled to keep them from stalling with their lost wind speed, until he could turn them into the wind without snapping off their wings.

Their engine turbines shrieked as metal pieces scraped against one another. In the distance, a couple of habitats floated away from them. The *Avant-Gardiste* was one of the foremost habitats in the flock. Twisting his head in his helmet, he found five more habitats eastward, including the *Baie-Comeau*.

He climbed, slowly accelerating to intercept the *Baie-Comeau*.

The big habitat approached, looming bright emerald,

its shiny, transparent plastic like a sheen over black solar cells, thick aerial greenhouses wrapping around. Émile struggled with shaking arms to hold Thérèse and steer her unguided wing-pack, ignoring the cold pain above his knee.

It was so hard. It was so hard sometimes to live here. And the exuberant green of bursting life around the outside of the *Baie-Comeau* was philosophically shocking, as shocking as opening his eyes every morning and seeing clouds unmoored to any ground at all. Thérèse was hurt, maybe worse, because she'd sought to build a bridge across that dysphoric gulf, seeking a soul for her adopted world and for all of them, when everyone else built gardens in soap bubbles and didn't even try to touch their new world.

The *Baie-Comeau* neared, but not fast enough. The pain in his leg and arms tunneled his world down to that bloated bit of emerald. He listed downward, but caught himself. He was coming in too fast for a good landing, even if he had been the only one flying. On the top of the *Baie-Comeau*, people ran this way and that, clearing the landing platform. People, rescue workers maybe, shrugged into wing-packs. Around the roof edges, they unfolded struts, supporting nets. He couldn't cut Thérèse's power. He couldn't reach her controls, nor did he have strength in his hands even if he could.

They cleared the edge of the roof. He pulled one numb hand free and fumbled on his chest for the emergency shutoff. He was halfway across the landing platform before his clumsy hand found it and his weight dragged them both down, head first. The jet exhaust from her pack ripped at his legs again, but the drop of ten meters ended that as her wing-pack engine burst screeching into a spray of hot fragments. A webwork of cracks filled his faceplate and air hissed.

People rushed to him to help. Pain seared his legs.

Down in the wards, they gave him oxygen and x-rayed him and, after not too much waiting, had him in an emergency room. The bright lights and straight lines jarred his shocky thoughts.

His suit was off. Big nurses bandaged his arm and worked on his leg. The pain was still excruciating, but they didn't have painkillers. *La colonie* couldn't afford to import many or produce many of their own. He would have killed for a joint right now. Or a drink.

He smelled the characteristic odor of sulfur-burned skin, overlaid with the salty smell of neutralizing sodium bicarbonate paste. His knee was almost numb. For that much burn, the acid must have melted his nerves. His stomach lurched. *Crisse. Please don't make me lose my leg.* No one would tell him. He grunted in pain as they did something else.

Thérèse lay on a low gurney a few meters away, but no one was treating her. They'd taken off her suit. Her skin from collarbone to navel was badly burnt, dark over her sternum, lightening to ugly red-purple blisters away from that central line of chemical charring. The burns wept clear fluid and her body trembled.

Émile pushed the nurse off him. His right arm was working. His left shoulder felt like dead weight. The skin at the base of his left thigh was abraded and covered with angry red swelling, but no black.

"Stay still!" one of the nurses said. He was a bullet-headed man of fortyish with a bristle of sandy hair.

"What about her?" Émile demanded, hobbling to his feet.

"Nothing we can do for her," he said. His face was sympathetic, although his eyes were not.

"What do you mean?" Émile demanded.

"Doctor said she's over her health care limit," the nurse said.

A tall blonde woman looked up from another patient a few gurneys away. She pursed her lips and came to him.

"Come on," she said, hands on his shoulders, "down on the gurney. The nurses need to finish bandaging you. You got banged up pretty bad."

"She's hurt worse than me!" Émile said, desperation clawing its way up from his stomach. "Fix her!"

"*Mademoiselle* Jetté has used up her health care rations," the doctor said sadly, shaking her head, "twice over."

"She's dying!" he pleaded. "Look at her burns!"

"Are you family?" the doctor asked.

"Yes, kind of."

"I'm sorry, *monsieur. Mademoiselle* Jetté has a history of self-harm: cutting, acid. She's been in a lot, and we've used a lot of drugs and bandages and even blood. Other people need those things to stay alive."

"That's art," Émile said. "She's an artist. That's her art."

The doctor leaned in and spoke more quietly. "We've also pulled her back from drug overdoses."

"Once!" he said. "And you didn't even help!"

"Four overdoses in the last two years," the doctor continued. "Do you know the kind of meds we need to save someone's life when we barely know what she might have OD'd on? There's only so much medicine, and she's been warned. More than once. I can't take medicine from people trying to live to save someone who's trying to kill herself."

Émile wiped at tears with the backs of his hands.

"She has problems," he whispered. "If she's got a..." he waved his hands in the air helplessly "... mental disorder, you need to treat that."

The doctor's expression didn't soften.

"Please," he whispered.

He was Émile. And he was George-Étienne. He was standing in his father's shoes, twenty-eight years later. Had it been a blonde doctor telling George-Étienne to abort Jean-Eudes? His father could have said yes, and Jean-Eudes would never have been born. And then George-Étienne's wife and daughter Chloé would both be alive today. And Émile would have grown up above the clouds, in the bright sun.

Émile loved Thérèse. How much had George-Étienne loved an unborn Jean-Eudes?

"We've done everything we could. There's nothing we can do for her emotional problems. We ran out of medical rations for her," the doctor said, waving her hand to take in the full emergency room.

"Take my med rations," he said.

Émile hated his father. And he hated himself. George-

Étienne should have listened to the doctor twenty-eight years ago.

"That's not how it works," the doctor said.

"That *is* how it works!" Émile shouted. "My brother was born and my family got shit for the rest of our lives! We used nothing. For twenty-eight years, we've used nothing. You owe me. You all owe me!"

He was George-Étienne. Twenty-eight years ago, and now. A man could save his loved ones if he was willing to pay the costs. The doctor stepped back. Émile stepped towards her. The bristle-headed nurse was beside Émile, almost as big.

"You owe the D'Aquillons," Émile said. "Fix her."

The doctor took another step back, and Émile lunged. The big nurse grabbed his bad arm, and his shoulder wrenched. Pain fired up his arm and seared his shoulder. Émile turned, and punched the nurse in the eye, and the man went down. He spun. The other nurse was there, both fists ready. The man on the floor struggled, dazed.

"Stop!" the doctor said. "Get out! Take your girlfriend with you. You're cut off for now. Any more trouble and the *Sûreté* will be here to press charges."

Tears blurred his vision, but he couldn't wipe them away. He had only one good fist. The nurse still faced him. Neither of them advanced.

"Please just fix her." His throat convulsed and he was sobbing. "I love her."

The second nurse put down his fists, offered a hand to his companion on the floor and pulled him up. Émile's own fist sank. The bristle-headed nurse kicked Émile's leg hard, on the burn, and Émile collapsed in agony.

"*Viens!*" the second nurse said, pulling his companion away, following the doctor.

Émile gasped. The kick had displaced his bandages, tearing the fragile, burnt skin, exposing the raw, weeping flesh beneath.

"Émile," a soft voice said.

Gingerly, he shifted his burnt skin back into place and rewrapped his leg. Then he dragged himself across the floor to Thérèse's gurney. He pulled himself up with his one good arm and his one good leg. She trembled. Cold and clammy. Shocky. In agony. The front of her was hard to look at. Clear fluid squeezed through cracks in her horrific burns.

"You're always fighting," she whispered, putting a shaking hand over his. He leaned on the gurney and kissed her forehead. "I'm not worth fighting for."

"You are," he said.

"Stop trying to save me, Émile. I touched Venus." She began to weep. "You keep stopping me. I'm empty and nothing will fill me."

"Let me fill you. I'll give you my soul."

She turned away. Her hands shook with the agony of her burns.

"You're not enough, Émile," she said. "No one is."

His throat tightened painfully and all breath left him. He was empty too.

Her head turned to him and her eyes opened. She took a deep breath. "Leave."

FIFTY-ONE

MARTHE AND MARIE-PIER stayed at the D'Aquillon habitat another thirty-six hours, conferring about the mechanics of stealing the *Causapscal-des-Vents*. Trawlers' woody shells could withstand acid, heat, and pressure differentials, but their envelopes wouldn't endure sharp lateral forces, like collisions. If they used four trawlers to hold up the *Causapscal-des-Vents*, the winds would knock them together until they cracked.

Marthe had thought that they might get around this by having trawlers connected by different lengths of cabling, but Gabriel-Antoine pointed out that as soon as the winds twisted the cables, the forces would become unbalanced and unpredictable, like trying to fly tangled kites. So Pascale and Gabriel-Antoine had designed a set of four harnesses to keep the trawlers apart.

They would probably need to build the harnesses out of cables they'd salvaged from older trawlers in their herd. They might even need to cannibalize their healthy trawlers. It wasn't a pretty thought. If this didn't work, the D'Aquillons would have nothing, no ability to produce oxygen and water, no ability to filter metals and minerals from the clouds. But they were all sacrificing. The whole House of Styx was. It felt strange to say it. And good. The House of Styx. A new family.

But it was fragile yet. Marthe got George-Étienne in his room in a quiet moment while the rest of them were cooking. She and Pa were both a bit hungover and he offered her a cup of water. Despite his bleary-eyed exhaustion, he was almost bouncing on the balls of his feet, animated like she hadn't seen him in years. He was a man with hope again. Marthe took the tough little cup carved out of trawler ribbing, and sat on Pa's hammock and sipped. She made a face. She was no longer used to how much sulfur was in everything down here.

"Émile," she said finally.

Pa's face soured. "What about him?"

"We need him."

"We have enough people."

She shook her head. "Extra hands, Pa. Even with Émile, it's still a coin toss."

Pa drank his water, set down the cup and looked at her very deliberately. "I would rather pull in Marie-Pier's brother, even though I don't know him, or his loyalties. He can't be worse than a *con* who couldn't climb out of a bottle long enough to find his ass."

"You haven't talked to him in five years, Pa."

"Is he drinking?"

Marthe forced the water down.

"He won't fuck this up. This is about family, Pa. He's your son. And he's my brother."

"He turned his back on us."

"He never turned his back on me or Pascale or Jean-Eudes," she said. "He's a D'Aquillon."

"D'Aquillon is just a name to him."

His eyes were intense, daring her, but she wasn't a girl anymore. She couldn't be pushed around.

"Why'd you send me up to *Causapscal-des-Vents*, Pa?"

"You were right for the job, and you were ready, even at sixteen."

"Why didn't *you* go up, Pa? Speak in *l'Assemblée* for yourself?"

He smiled, but not with humor. Grim imaginings. "I don't think either of us think that I have the patience for all their posturing and alliances and payoffs and smiling insults. They didn't accept my son. That's all I need to know about them or anyone else."

"Do you think I'm a bad person for holding my own in *l'Assemblée*?"

"*Non!*" he said waving his hands a bit like Marie-Pier, catching his emphatic negative in the space they outlined. "Use their own tricks against them! You're better than them, and you can beat them at their game."

"The difference between you and me is that I can let a grudge go," she said. "Not every slight needs to be answered. Not every slight is even really a slight. Sometimes people are just idiots and they can't help it."

"A slight?" he said, raising his voice. He darted a glance at the curtain between them and the galley and stepped closer to Marthe and lowered his voice. His frown deepened. "'Jean-Eudes can't live' is a slight?"

"Neither of us are talking about that anymore, Pa. You dealt with that in your own way. We left. We became *coureurs*. That's not why you didn't go deal with *l'Assemblée* yourself. You didn't want to deal with every other friction that comes up, inevitably, between people."

"Hypocrites, you mean," he said.

"Sometimes people are stupid," she said. "Sometimes people are fed up and explode. Sometimes people are tired."

"And that's when they show their true colors!"

"That's when they fuck up," she said. "That's when they make a mistake they can't take back."

"Telling me to kill my son is not a mistake anyone can take back!" he whispered violently.

"I'm not talking about Jean-Eudes, *ostie!* He's born! He's here. He's healthy and we love him. No one is coming for him. I'm talking about your other son."

"Pascal is just fine, thank you very much," he said sarcastically.

"Émile," she said in a low voice. "This is what you haven't dealt with, Pa. This is why you sent me up sunside to be in *l'Assemblée*. You love us, but you can't let go of grudges."

"What I can't do is forgive someone who crosses a line, who hurts my family," he said.

"Émile *is* family."

"He gave that away!" Pa looked at the curtained opening. The sounds of pots knocking and Jean-Eudes's low voice laughing sounded outside. "He gave that away."

"Émile learned not to back down from his father," she said. "To never give in. And one day, both of them got too angry."

"This is my house and my roof!"

"And your son isn't welcome?"

"He's never even tried, so we'll never know," Pa said.

"He's going to try now, because I'm going to get him to try," she said. "I need him here. Pascale needs him here. Jean-Eudes needs him here."

"We're good enough together," Pa said. "I don't need him teaching bad habits to any of the boys."

"We need him here because he's a full-grown man. If this gamble with the House of Styx fails, we've got nothing. Not the *Causapscal-des-Vents*. Maybe not even the *Causapscal-des-Profondeurs*. We need him here to improve our odds. This is your legacy and mine. What gets left to Pascale and Alexis will be decided in the next few months. Grudges are a luxury that you and Émile have to sacrifice."

George-Étienne gestured dismissively. "If he apologizes and stops drinking—"

"There won't be apologies," Marthe said flatly.

"What?"

"Neither of you are capable," she said. "If you can't forgive, you just have to put things behind you."

"I don't have to do anything," he said hotly.

She rose from the hammock and put the cup on the table beside his. She paused at the door as his eyes followed her.

"You said family comes first, Pa," she said. "Now we get to see what's more important to you: the future of

Pascale, Jean-Eudes and Alexis, or you wanting to keep old hurts." The muscles of his jaw were bunching tight beneath a beard more salt than pepper. "I love you, Pa. We all do."

She pressed past the curtain. They'd finished their cooking and Marie-Pier was packing a basket for her and Marthe to take in their plane-ride back up to the *Coureur-des-Tourbillons.* Jean-Eudes saw her emerge from Pa's room and ran to hug her. He felt small. Muscled and older, yes, but needing her. Needing Pa. Needing Émile too.

"Tell my grandparents I'm good," Gabriel-Antoine said.

"I'll take care of them," Marthe said, "and of your habitat. Émile will have to do more on the *Causapscal-des-Vents,* but we can handle two habitats."

"I'll stop in too," Marie-Pier said, "when I'm up for *l'Assemblée.*"

"Maybe they'll miss me in *l'Assemblée*?" Gabriel-Antoine mused. They would and wouldn't. He'd never taken strong sides in any discussion, and his attendance was already spotty.

George-Étienne passed them by, suited up to go outside to crank Marie-Pier's plane up from under the gantry. He didn't give her a look. Not a good sign. At Pa's appearance, Jean-Eudes got back to work in the corner, doing final checks on everyone's survival suits.

Marthe shepherded Gabriel-Antoine to the wall on the other side of the habitat. She leaned. He leaned too, smirking, crossing his arms.

"Is this what I think it is?" Gabriel-Antoine asked.

"Don't hurt Pascal," Marthe said in a low voice. "And don't pressure him. He's young. He's never had a boyfriend."

"I want the opposite of hurting him," Gabriel-Antoine said.

"You're a grown man."

"I'm only twenty-one."

"And he's sixteen. Do right by him."

"Threatening?"

"If I thought you'd ever hurt him on purpose, yeah, you'd have to watch your back," she said, "but I don't think you're that kind. Just don't forget how young he is."

"You guys are good family," he said.

"We're all family now."

"Say step-daddy."

"Eww!" Marthe punched his arm.

He flinched and laughed. "I'll bring him flowers every day."

Marthe left him there, crossed the habitat, hugged Pascale.

"We'll talk soon, just you and me," Marthe whispered. "I'll get the hormones."

Pascale nodded, forcing a smile. Marthe kissed Jean-Eudes on the top of his head before taking her suit from him. Marie-Pier was almost suited up. Her brother smiled and backed away as soon as she crossed the line to put on her suit. Alexis raced up and wanted a hug, but wouldn't cross the line either. Marthe relented, crossed back, hugged them each once more and then suited up.

The pressure and heat hit them in the outer torus and then ratcheted up again when they cycled through to the gantry. Marie-Pier's plane hung nose-down, wings affixed. They floated in a high-pressure system today, a bubble of calm air in the spongy orange glow of Venusian night, so the plane barely swung on its cables.

"Keep an eye out," George-Étienne said, his tone giving no hint of the words they'd exchanged. "Word is going around that the government is acting funny. They've got lots of planes in the air. Drones too."

Marthe thought she must look just as puzzled as Marie-Pier.

"Radar?" she asked.

"No. Just silent flying. No one can figure out what they're doing. Air Traffic says they're testing comms and mapping sensors."

"That makes no sense," Marthe said. "I'll see what I can find out when I get back up."

"You're storm-free, all the way up to fiftieth *rang*," George-Étienne said.

"Thanks, Pa," Marthe said. "I'll be back in a few weeks."

"*Merci, ma chère.*"

"*Merci*, George-Étienne," Marie-Pier said. "I'll be back too."

Her father made a brief, courteous bow to Marie-Pier, something Marthe had never seen him do before. She and Marie-Pier climbed down the rope ladder, opened the hatch and slid in. Marie-Pier started doing internal checks. Her father detached the cables from the wing tips. They hung from a cable loop by a single retractable hook. The propellers turned fitfully, ready to come to full power. The plane turned slowly with the breeze. This was the start of the roller-coaster. Marie-Pier pulled the hook release and they plunged into the clouds. Marie-Pier pulled up, turning their fall into forward airspeed, and started the propellers.

Marthe looked back at the gantry and the wide diameter of her family's home. A bigger family now. And she felt a pang. She was returning to a cramped habitat that could have fit more, that could have felt more like a home, if there'd been more of Émile and less of Noëlle.

FIFTY-TWO

THE HABITAT WAS quiet and hot. Émile had left the windows unshuttered. The hydroponic bays had overgrown, and some of the produce would spoil soon. He flipped on the radiators and slumped in his hammock. Marthe's cigarettes lay on the galley table. He'd smoked half of them, mostly laying around. The acid burns on his legs hadn't infected and were healing. He vacillated between taking it easy and stiffly trying to suddenly do *something*.

He could use a cigarette, or something harder. He probably had some hash in his room. But the idea of getting high, or even getting another shot of nicotine, both called and repelled him. He wanted a drink, but the idea was distasteful, poisoned as if acid had leaked into his mind.

Thérèse had survived, barely. He hadn't heard from her—Hélène had told him. Thérèse was with Anne-Claude and Cédric, recovering slowly. Her followers came to her with food, and some medicine they'd hoarded. And they apparently listened to her talk of touching the soul of Venus.

He rubbed his eyes. It was all meaningless. Venus had no soul. He had no soul. This was all there was. The creaking, slow-rolling habitats in the upper atmosphere, or the living, storm-thrown habitats in the lowest cloud deck. Farming in the heights or scavenging in the depths, choices no different from the ones facing the teeming, nameless billions who'd scraped the ground for most of Earth's history, never walking more than thirty kilometers from where they'd been born. His parents had crossed hard vacuum to reach a world where most of them would be subsistence farmers. It didn't matter if Émile existed or not.

He turned to writing again, putting words to paper with slow, halting difficulty, in ones and twos, without rhyme or elegance. He wrote of himself, in tones and words that seemed self-absorbed and petulant. He tried to write of Thérèse, toggling between heroism and folly, vaguely prophetic, but mostly as if he were Quixote's dreaming, fractured descendant. She'd burnt like a Venusian Icarus and left him bitter and betrayed. She lived because of him and hated him for it. The words went on and on, transforming to everything he loved of her, and more, spilling from his fingers in crude images, repeated themes and amateur rhymes, until the sun had dropped from its noon height.

He set the paper aside. He trembled with a spiritual dampness like a larva emerging from its cocoon. Nothing felt right. Nothing he could do would take away the ache.

His hands shook. He needed a drink. He really needed to be stupid drunk. And high.

Instead, he climbed stiffly into the steamy hydroponics chambers on the inner surface of the envelope. The air was thick with oxygen and water, dank with the smell of mold and algae he ought to have cleaned long ago. He harvested, chopped, cleaned, cut, and emptied whole rows of trays with carrots, potatoes, Brussels sprouts, asparagus, beans and hemp.

He carried them mechanically below, sorting what they owed *la colonie*, setting aside the freshest for himself and Marthe. The vegetables that needed some ripening he set aside for *Causapscal-des-Profondeurs,* and what he'd left to ripen too long, he pickled, or cooked, or stewed. He cleared and planted more bays, cooked and stewed and pickled again, storing all that could be stored in the cold cellars below the gondola.

This was the life Thérèse was fleeing, the life they might have shared. At the thought of the two of them living some other set of choices, standing side by side, canning and cutting and pickling, he began to cry, like he hadn't in the hospital. This was what he'd lost: all the possibilities, not just the exciting ones, but the shared drudgeries her presence might have transformed and hallowed. Here a muse might have bettered him, and he might have been *her* muse, or her rock, whatever she needed. But she didn't want him. That's what she meant by saying he wasn't enough. He slumped to the floor, his fingers stained orange with carrot, but his thoughts and hopes inky black.

Marthe did not return until almost bright midnight. She came down the ladder and through the ceiling hatch. Her eyebrows rose slightly at the tremendous pile of vegetable waste to be shipped to a habitat with a bioreactor. The rows and rows of jars strapped into shelves also piqued her curiosity. She stood by the table, rolled herself a cigarette and lit it with a click of the electric lighter. She puffed silently, considering him.

"Thérèse dumped me," he said finally. "Twice."

"Oh."

She sat down opposite him.

"She got a bad acid burn," he said.

The corners of Marthe's eyes crinkled and her lips pressed tighter.

"They wouldn't give her medicine or treat her," he said.

Real anger flickered on her face, an old anger they had all inherited, and then it was gone, washed away by a deep sadness. She put her hand on his. It was warm and small. Émile was always the biggest. Even the biggest scars. She was clumsy, but she'd always been more careful than he was. Smarter. But they were still born of the same crucible. He turned up his hand and held her fingers.

"Do you ever wonder what Pa must have thought?" Émile asked. "What *maman* must have thought, when they said they wouldn't ever give medicine to Jean-Eudes?"

Marthe nodded.

"It's not fair," he said, "to live here. To have come here at all. Wouldn't we have been better off to have been born in Québec?"

"We wouldn't have been who we are," she said. "We would have been different people. Pascal and I might not have even been born."

He held her hand, waiting to feel a pulse, but his fingers weren't that sensitive. Marthe was warm. Marthe was real. Like Pa, she never changed shape. She lent solidity to the world. If only he were ready to pay the price of assuming a single shape forever. At its core, that had been most of what he and Pa had fought over. Émile didn't want to be just a *coureur des vents*, filtering ashes from the clouds. He wanted more than that. He didn't know what more would look like, but he knew he *could* be more, and he couldn't yet put his finger on his ineffable, aching faith.

FIFTY-THREE

MARTHE DIDN'T SLEEP. She didn't need it. Everything felt electric. The alliance, a new house and new family. The possibility of changing all the rules. She liked unwritten rules, politics. Governing was a Byzantine game of trust and mistrust, sleight-of-hand and showman's magic. And she saw the pathways she needed to lay down, the distractions to set up.

She squinted against the sunlight. The big sun would only redden in four hours, when the horizon of Venus had half-eclipsed it. In the meantime, hot white light shone closer and closer to a horizontal, and around them, the wispy clouds above sixty-fifth *rang* would glow ghostly yellow and white. The *colonistes* called the effect sunsight. Unless they deliberately shut it out, that sideways light felt all-penetrating, making the invisible visible, like being stared at. Sunsight was a time to shuck self-delusions. She was too pragmatic to entertain many. She was usually only fooled when she wanted to be fooled, like by Noëlle.

She had been a little more blind to her brother. That was a kind of self-imposed delusion. Marthe hadn't realized that Émile had been that serious about the woman Thérèse. Despite living on the same habitat, Émile's resentment of Pa—and maybe her own attitude, too—had made them ships in the night. In a lot of ways he was a stranger, more so than Marie-Pier or Gabriel-Antoine, but they needed him. Where were his loyalties? Was he, despite all his failings, still a D'Aquillon?

The windows darkened a bit more, the solar film absorbing more sunlight, but the great white eye still shone too bright. She lowered a second curtain over the first, making weird shadow patterns, putting off sunsight a little longer. She needed some of her illusions to be able to hope.

On her pad, she did four things.

First, she went fishing for hormones for Pascale. The med programs had already told her the different hormones and variants she could use, and gave dosages, treatment courses, with tutorials. The black markets ran on layered, anonymous, encrypted boards that shifted in location on the Venusian web. Most of it looked like herbs and handicrafts and other nonsense that people could produce and trade legally, as well as oxygen, which traded cheaply, and water, which traded for more, but was still legal to trade. But each of these actually represented something different. Mint sprigs might mean a rotor shaft. A child's doll might be electrical cabling. The bartering language was very much like the encrypted signaling used by the *coureurs*, although the ciphers had diverged as time went on.

It was also certain that government inspectors and constables had posted some of the listings as sting operations. For every real listing, three false ones were posted, or out-of-date ones popped back online weeks or months later due to obfuscation viruses black marketeers had running on dozens of servers throughout the *colonie*.

Marthe knew the surface cues, and even some of the intermediate ones. She clicked on an innocuous expired listing, clicked on a logo, entered a password, and was through to the intermediate levels. Not all of them—she didn't do enough trading to have deep access—but what she needed would be in this kind of Venusian dark net. This was where she unloaded a lot of the metals Pa's herds filtered out of the atmosphere. Here, someone could find rarer parts, as well as nitrogen and hydrogen compounds for bioreactors, unauthorized bunk spaces, and off-record work the government preferred to regulate, like encryption, programming, illicit engineering and such. Deeper levels of trader interactions ran below this one, probably organ donations and drug production. She didn't need those.

She found two listings that finally led her to sets of estrogens, progestogens and antiandrogens that the medical program confirmed could be combined into a hormone replacement therapy. The problem was that the person who had them wasn't asking for anything she had. Acceptable payments were hydrogen or nitrogen compounds, which was no surprise; hydrogen and nitrogen were so in demand that they were almost a

Venusian currency. The rest of the asks were for high-end electronic components, laser-grade optical fiber, and parts for x-ray diffraction devices. Nothing she had or could get. She wasn't sure how much of this stuff the *colonie* even had. After a little more looking, she gave up and sent a private message to Marie-Pier about the hormones. Marie-Pier's black market network was more extensive than Marthe's.

Second, she voted in support of a bill sponsored by Marie-Pier in *l'Assemblée*. Right now, because no one actually mined the surface, or could go there in practice, the right to commercially exploit and own land was vague. Old treaties still made it sound as if the surface of Venus was international space, and yet the law was far from clear. No one had ever seemed to care before now. The House of Styx would work in secrecy, but if they were ever discovered, they wanted to have legal title to anything they developed.

Marthe had written the bill, but Marie-Pier had tabled it, because Marie-Pier wasn't in anyone's bad books. Pascale and Gabriel-Antoine had come up with an ostensible need for the new law: Gabriel-Antoine and Marie-Pier proposed producing carbon fliers that could descend to the peak of Maxwell Mons, scrape off the galena and bismuthinite snows, and float the metals back to the surface. The proposal envisioned a cycle of metal recovery fliers, but it depended on a business environment where they could keep their profits.

Third, Marthe resubmitted the replacement parts list for the *Causapscal-des-Vents*. She attached a note that told the parts committee how long she'd been waiting, that she was disputing the seizure of the habitat by the government, and that these parts had been urgently needed months ago, critically so now.

And fourth, she lodged a report with Air Traffic Control, indicating that the station-keeping prop on the *Causapscal-des-Vents* was acting up and requesting a trailing position in the flotilla. She wouldn't act on anything today; no one was ready. But she wanted her distractions ready long in advance.

Émile padded in silently, ducking under the hatchway to his rack. He scratched at his shoulder, looked out at the sun through the layers, and took a carrot from the cold box.

"What's on your arm?" she asked.

He looked self-conscious, like he'd completely forgotten about it, then touched the stretched skin.

"It's like a tattoo," he said, sitting.

She took his hard arm in her hands and made a face as she looked closer.

"You burned yourself with acid on purpose?" she said, holding up her scar-spotted hands. She didn't touch his, which were far more roped with scars. "It's a workplace hazard, not a cosmetic."

"I like it."

She huffed and moved to the cold box, found a few carrots. They didn't get carrots often. They were hard to grow hydroponically. She crunched. "Thank you for all the crops," she said. "I half-expected them to have turned on the vine while I was gone."

He shrugged, then sat and rolled himself a cigarette. His hands shook a tiny bit.

"Got another one of those?" she asked.

He slid a small black case over the rough table.

"Gotta get in my butts before I'm with the two asthmatics on the *Marais-des-Nuages*," she said.

"How long you staying over there?" he asked.

"It's going to be a few weeks more at least."

Émile was examining the smoke coiling up from his cigarette.

"That's a lot of help Gabriel-Antoine is giving you. I went over to the *Marais-des-Nuages* with Pascal. He wouldn't even tell me what they were doing. Little shit. Pa got to him good, didn't he?"

"It's not that," Marthe said. She sucked a relieving rush from her cigarette. "Pascale loves you."

"He didn't show it. Pa can still go fuck himself, but Pascal and Jean-Eudes never stopped being my brothers."

"They don't need me down there either, Émile. We aren't engineers." She exhaled, working up some courage. "I may need you for other kinds of work."

"Yes, boss," he said sarcastically.

"I'm not fucking around, Émile. We're close to losing the *Causapscal-des-Vents*. We have a plan to keep it. There are parts of my plan that only you and I can do."

"What's the plan?"

She took a long drag on her cigarette.

"It's illegal."

"You think I can't keep a secret?"

"I don't know, Émile. This is the first time I've seen you

446

sober two days in a row in the last five years. You just burned a picture into your arm with acid. What the hell am I supposed to think?"

"It's not for you to judge me."

"*J'm'en câlisse*, Émile! We're not kids anymore. We're both grown-ups, and one grown-up can tell another that he's been acting like a jackass."

"*Mange d'la marde.*"

Marthe leaned across the table, looking up to meet Émile's eyes.

"I need you, Émile. We need you. Pa needs you. Pascale needs you. So do Alexis and Jean-Eudes. We're doing this for them. I can try to make things right with Pa, but you need to get a goddamn grip and be patient. I'm not the one *qui s'est emmerdé* with Pa."

Émile glared at her for a long time, and finally he looked away and butted out his cigarette. He rested his elbows on the small table, closed his eyes, and rubbed his temples with his palms. His hands trembled.

"How long since you've had a drink?"

"Few days."

"You quitting?" she asked.

"I don't have a problem." His hands still trembled.

"Don't talk to Pa yet," she said.

He regarded her, then looked away, very similar to her father's habit when confronted with something he didn't want to look at. But like Pa, this only lasted moments. Émile's stare swiveled back to her.

"Still trying to play *maman*?" he said.

Marthe blew smoke above them.

"*Maman* wouldn't have stolen the *Causapscal-des-Vents*."

It took a moment for his face to go through all the possible expressions until he realized she wasn't joking. "Are you crazy? You can't steal the *Causapscal*. Where would you take it?"

She pointed down. Her brother's eyebrows rose. Then rose again. "We're sinking it."

"Sabotage?" he said incredulously.

She explained the plan, to his utter stupefaction. She told him what Pa and Pascale had found on the surface of Venus, their Axis Mundi. She explained the new alliances and the creation of the House of Styx. She spoke at length, and Émile's interruptions faltered by turns, until he was just staring, dumbfounded.

When she finished, he wiped his forehead. He checked his pockets for his tobacco case. She slid it back across the table to him.

"This is insane," he said. Then he laughed grimly. "You know they offered to make me a constable, eh?"

"What?" she said with a queasy feeling that maybe she didn't know her brother at all, and that she'd just told him everything.

"A D'Aquillon as a goddamn cop."

"That's insane," she said.

"*Oui*. They offered me more rations, first choice of bunk space."

"*Ostie*, Émile. You can't support the government and the Bank by joining the *Sûreté*."

He shrugged. "I didn't say yes," he said. "I just think

it's funny that I haven't even started and I'm already a dirty cop."

"They're all dirty cops," she said. "And it's also awful suspicious."

"That they'd ask me? I'm big. I can knock heads."

"That they offered you this while they're trying to take away our home. It's a bribe."

Émile looked like he wanted to argue, but then that look diffused away.

"I need you here, Émile. The original plan was to let the *Causapscal-des-Vents* sink on its own, while I went off as a decoy. But it might not work unless somebody guides it. I think I need you to keep it safe on the way down."

He shook his head and finally worried out a single rolling paper from the others and started to tap in the last bits of tobacco. "I'll be the decoy. You go with the habitat."

"The decoy has to be fast," she said. "You're too big. A wing-pack will fly me faster. And I don't want you blamed for losing the *Causapscal-des-Vents*. We need the investigators to blame it on the lack of parts."

"You're no one's favorite either," he said. "You've caused so much trouble that they might think you're committing sabotage. Which you are."

"If we get caught, I don't even know where they'd start," she said. "Even if we don't get caught, if we don't nail this, the *Causapscal-des-Vents* will sink like a smoking can."

He licked the paper then laughed bitterly. "No one really knows you, do they? No one in the government can see what you're capable of, can they?"

"Are you in?"

"Does Pa want me in? Does Pascal?"

"Pascale certainly does. I'm working on Pa."

"Shit, we're all going to jail."

"Pascale and Pa found a way to the stars," she said. "This is for us."

He rose, inhaled, blew smelly smoke into the cabin. He moved aft to his rack and shut the curtain. She heard him moving around back there.

She gritted her teeth, finishing her cigarette.

"If you become a cop, I'll fucking kill you, Émile," she yelled after him.

"Yeah, yeah," he called back.

FIFTY-FOUR

MARTHE FLEW TO the *Baie-Comeau* an hour before she was to testify to the Resource Allocation Committee. She wanted to prepare. As much as their plans depended on Pascale and Gabriel-Antoine designing something sturdy and functional, and in Marie-Pier having the trawlers ready to catch their fall, if Marthe couldn't delay the seizure of the *Causapscal-des-Vents*, it was all for nothing.

The Resource Allocation Committee was not one of the more exciting committees. Lots of people wouldn't be watching what was happening, and she needed to get the public mood on her side. Gaschel needed it on hers, too. Marthe got to the committee room in the bowels of the big habitat about forty-five minutes early. She was surprised to find Noëlle cleaning the benches and folding desks with a cloth.

"Oh!" Noëlle said, with more ingenuousness in her expression than she normally brought to flirting. "Marthe. What are you doing here?"

Noëlle was sweating, adding a shine to her dark forehead and to her bare arms showing below sleeves rolled to her elbows. She was beautiful.

"I'm testifying here soon," Marthe said neutrally. "What are you doing here?"

Noëlle shrugged enchantingly with the rag.

"The concierge is sick. They needed the chambers clean. Wouldn't want *l'Assemblée* to clean their own rooms or anything," she added derisively.

Interesting that Marthe's on-again, off-again lover had replaced the concierge on the day Marthe was testifying. Someone was trying to rattle her? Or to get some dirt on her before the committee sat? The committee chamber had cameras, and it wouldn't be complicated to run them without Marthe knowing. She didn't look up.

"It's nice to see you," Marthe said, moving to one of the benches. She folded down the table and turned on her pad. "I'd better practice my lines."

Noëlle might have been expecting more. Maybe she and Délia were on the outs again. She huffed loudly, and wiped at tables with palpable pique.

"What are you going to do if they take your habitat?" she asked.

Marthe had to assume that she was being filmed right now, with or without Noëlle knowing, to turn public opinion or to sharpen the government's side of the debate. Noëlle was an unlikely femme fatale, but certainly capable of being an unwitting tool.

"I don't know," Marthe said.

"Shitty."

"*Oui.*"

"It's a shitty habitat," Noëlle said.

"It's home."

"You can't stay with me," Noëlle said.

"Fine. I'll send Émile to shack up with you and Délia."

Noëlle snorted and turned back to wiping the benches half-heartedly. "We're making it work."

Marthe gave her a doubtful look. "I know."

Marthe turned to her pad, and after a while, Noëlle took the hint. Maybe she thought Marthe was playing hard to get. Noëlle didn't do any chasing herself. She preferred the thrill of being chased, and she lived on scandalized adrenaline. In some days or weeks, Noëlle would tire of Délia again, and detonate an explosion of drama, with Marthe, or someone else. Dealing with Noëlle was like riding a storm in the fifty-first *rang*—dangerous and exciting, easier with practice, until overconfidence caused something bad to happen. Marthe wouldn't mind riding a storm right now.

But now wasn't the time. *L'Assemblée* was more dangerous. Unlike Noëlle or a storm, intent lurked behind its dangers. And those dangers knew enough about Marthe to engineer Noëlle's presence here today to throw off her concentration. They were taking Marthe seriously.

Noëlle left in a sulk before members of *l'Assemblée* started to come in by ones and twos. Félix Lévesque, the committee chair, was one of Gaschel's allies, as were a few others, like Laurent Tétreau, the secretary.

The other committee members were indifferent,

swingable one way or another, unless Gaschel had already gotten to them and engineered a foregone conclusion. Some witnesses filed in too. Catherine Nadeau, Charles Hébert, Boniface Lortie, and Éric Turcotte, none of whom had a stake in this fight. Marie-Pier Hudon entered shortly with her brother Marc, sitting a few rows behind her, not making eye contact.

Marthe wasn't exactly nervous. She could play these cards. And she understood viscerally why her father could never have done what she'd been doing for eight years. He couldn't hide his resentment and anger. He couldn't store it for another time. He was all heart, and couldn't set that view aside, even for an instant. She was better at this because she could hide what she thought.

Lévesque gavelled the meeting to order. Tétreau reviewed the agenda and witness list. Lévesque and other members had minor statements, points of order and records adjustments from previous meetings. It was fifteen minutes before they called Marthe. She rose, moved to the witness bench, and made eye contact with each of the committee members in turn. Most were neutral to her. Others did a poor job of disguising their loyalties.

"Thank you, *monsieur*, for giving me time to address the committee," Marthe began. "You may imagine my state when I heard that the government intended to confiscate my home. I've taken some time to absorb the news and consider the rationale. My questions are more about the long-term plan for the confiscation of other family habitats by the government."

"There is no plan to confiscate other family habitats,"

Lévesque said, frowning.

"Will you put that into law?" Marthe asked calmly. "Will you guarantee that no other family will ever have their habitat confiscated like this?"

"The *Causapscal-des-Vents* is in terrible shape," Lévesque said. "It's almost not atmosphere-worthy."

"The government had a large hand in bringing it to this condition," Marthe said. "The government has systematically refused to supply parts and materiel for upgrades or even repairs. I have a list here of the standard parts I have requested over the last twenty-four months using the procedures set in place by this committee. Only ten percent of the requests have actually been fulfilled. To compensate, I've had to trade away my own food, clothing and vitamins to other habitats to get the basic parts needed to keep the *Causapscal-des-Vents* floating. I've kept it afloat, and now you're taking it away."

"Parts and materials are directed to the highest-priority needs."

"Your neglect made the *Causapscal-des-Vents* a high-priority need."

"Parts get recycled and repurposed all the time," Lévesque said. "The *Causapscal-des-Vents* is a big part, but its dismantling will provide materials for a dozen other habitats. Better accommodations are available to you on other habitats."

"You haven't answered my question, *Monsieur*. What is the long-term family habitat confiscation plan? Who is next?"

"No one is next." Lévesque's irritation was growing.

"You claim not to have enough parts to keep the *Causapscal-des-Vents* floating, so it gets cannibalized into parts for other habitats," Marthe said. "Conveniently, you don't need to import more materials from off-world. But the policies of the government are not getting us any closer to being able to import new materials or to produce them on Venus. So, logically, in a year or two, the government will need to identify another habitat to confiscate and dismantle."

"That's a complete fabrication."

"The pattern of denial of parts and materiel to the *Causapscal-des-Vents* is systematic, going back at least two years," Marthe said. "But when I looked, I was surprised to find we're not alone. The same pattern has been playing out over the last twenty-four months on *La Mitis, Témiscouata, Mont-Joli,* and *Lac-Édouard.*"

The last habitat housed Manon Dubé, the committee member sitting on the right, aligned with neither Gaschel or Tétreau. Émile wasn't the only one in the family who could punch.

"What assurances will you give to the people living in those habitats that you will not be confiscating them?" Marthe asked.

"No one's habitat is being confiscated!" Lévesque said.

"Will they believe you after you've just announced your intention to confiscate the *Causapscal-des-Vents?*"

"The *Causapscal-des-Vents* is a poor-quality, poorly maintained habitat that would cost the entire *colonie* too much to sustain." A hint of stridence crept into

Lévesque's voice. "Should every habitat donate parts to keep it afloat?"

Marthe's voice stayed even by comparison. "The government has also been denying parts to *Batiscanie, Coucoucache, Lac-aux-Sables,* and *Cap-de-la-Madelaine.* Not as bad yet, but if this continues, in four to six years, these habitats will be looking like the *Causapscal-des-Vents.*"

"That's a lie!"

"It's all in the public records of this committee," Marthe said. "Is this the long-term plan? First *Causapscal-des-Vents,* then *Témiscouata,* then *Batisc—*"

Lévesque's gavel hammered over and over as more voices on the committee and in the audience rose in irritation.

"No one in the fleet should have to sacrifice their well-maintained habitat to keep your piece of shit afloat! This witness is deliberately endangering other habitats by protesting the reallocation of surplus resources to higher-need habitats!"

Some of the voices supported Lévesque, and glares focused on Marthe. But others in the audience and on the committee looked less certain. Sometime during their exchange, both Marthe and Lévesque had come to their feet. Marthe slowly sat, keeping her face impassive. He didn't. He was still yelling, partly at her, partly at people sitting behind her.

The amount of shouting would ensure that the video would be replayed at supper tables and evening smoke breaks all over *la colonie.* The official minutes and recording would be heavily edited. But Marie-Pier had recorded the whole hearing. And once the testimony had gotten heated, a few others had surely pressed record too.

Maybe after this was done, she'd see if Noëlle was in the mood for being chased.

FIFTY-FIVE

MARIE-PIER CAME UP from the *Coureur des Tourbillons* and met Marthe on the roof of the *Marais-des-Nuages*. The day was clear, with warm high-pressure cells pushing vast valleys into the cloud-tops, all the way down to the rolling yellowed vortices of *Les Rapides Plats*. Marthe would have invited Marie-Pier into the Phocas habitat as would have been customary and polite, if only to offer water, but Gabriel-Antoine's grandparents were cranky and tired. She clasped Marie-Pier's forearm briefly and they soared on wide wings towards the *Détroit d'Honguedo*, a big, aging habitat fifteen kilometers north, on the outskirts of the main colonial flotilla.

They didn't speak. Marthe found herself mildly paranoid now that she was the architect of such a clearly criminal plan. It hadn't been announced, but it was clear to anyone paying attention that more planes and drones had been patrolling most of the equatorial zone. A lot more. It might be as innocent as remapping, but unless the government had come into new sensing equipment, that wasn't likely. She hadn't found out what it was all for, but her suspicions were on a hair trigger.

If Marie-Pier was feeling any of this, Marthe couldn't tell. So Marthe did the only thing she could. She breathed deeply, traced the bright cratering of the cloudscape with her eyes, and dipped here and there, following thin downdrafts and riding updrafts. The tirelessly-moving surfaces of the upper clouds were beautiful in the way make-up and jewelry could be beautiful. Even though she'd lived up here for eight years, Marthe still felt like a transplant. That she was indelibly a *coureur des vents* at her core comforted her. Someday she would move back down to take care of Pa and Jean-Eudes. Perhaps even to the surface, near their Axis Mundi. Whatever troubles they had upcloud, there were ways for *coureurs* to hide in the depths.

The *Détroit d'Honguedo* revealed its shape as she crossed layers of haze. It was one of the last original habitats, the big communal ones they'd sent from Earth for the first immigrants. The loss of a couple of them, like the *Matapédia* and the *Montée de Corté-Réal,* had changed the strategy to smaller, more easily managed habitats for three families, two, or even one, like *Causapscal-des-Vents.* The trend had only reversed recently, with better material science and engineering experience. Big habitats like *Baie-Comeau* might be the future, especially if some of the frames and the envelopes could be built on Venus with indigenous materials.

The outer faces of the *Détroit d'Honguedo's* envelope

had clouded with age and acid, making of it a blind eye floating above the clouds. It probably still housed eighty or ninety people and carried some of the machine and electronic shops to service the flotilla. It was unsurprising that this might be one of the places where the black market flourished.

They alighted on the roof port, stowed their wing-packs and neutralized before descending through an airlock into the envelope. They cracked the seals on their helmets when the stairway opened onto the wide arcade. Little one- or two-person shops—machinists, electricians, small-electronics repairs, all government-run—ran along the arcade, framed by transparent layers of envelope filled with greenery and even suited gardeners.

"I've never seen this part of the flotilla," Marthe said. "When we get authorized for repairs at all, we get assigned to the *Baie-Comeau* or the *Escuminac*."

"I come here often. The inspectors are all bought off, unless you do something really stupid," Marie-Pier said, leaning her head close as they walked. "Can I ask you something?"

"Anything."

"Did your father shave and comb his hair after you proposed the marriage?"

A fit of giggling burst out of Marthe. "He did!"

Marie-Pier was laughing too.

"Don't worry," Marthe said. "It's not that kind of marriage. He can be very correct, though."

"It's not bad," Marie-Pier said. "I wouldn't have made the same choice he made about Jean-Eudes. I don't think

I'm strong enough. But I admire someone who did."

"He's not an easy man in many ways, as a father—or as a husband, I imagine, although *maman* seemed happy enough," Marthe said. "Sometimes I don't want to be like him. But other times, when I know it's something that really matters, I worry that I'm not enough like him."

"You are," Marie-Pier said.

At the end of the arcade was a small hardware depot. The light beside the doorway shone red over hand-painted letters that said *Present Requisition Forms*. Marie-Pier showed her wrist computer and the light greened. The depot was small, but the parts in here could have helped run the *Causapscal-des-Vents* for years. Marthe understood that hers wasn't the only habitat, but it didn't make the bitterness pass easily. At the back of the depot was a door leading into an old repair bay. Machinery and scraps were piled high in rude Venus-made shelves and netting, but that wasn't the main purpose of the room.

Within that circle of scrap sprouted rows of small stills, fans, fume hoods, a miniature bioreactor, and what looked like a homemade centrifuge. A few people in survival suits and regular clothes were cooking, measuring, jarring, labelling. The drafts carried scents of yeast and fermentation and sulfur and ammonia. Marthe got a few strange looks, but people seemed to know Marie-Pier. She and an older man kissed on both cheeks.

"This is Marthe," Marie-Pier said. "She's okay." She didn't introduce the man.

Marthe and the man kissed on each cheek as well. She tried not to gawk at the operation, although she ought not to have been surprised. A lot of things the *colonie* officially didn't have, but really did, had to come from somewhere. Homemade. And the pervasive black market fed the raw materials for illicit industrial processes.

"How's Laurette?"

"Pregnant."

"*Grandpère!*" Marie-Pier exclaimed, grinning, slapping his arm. "You're getting old."

"I'm not the one asking for hormones," the man said.

"I've got a friend."

"Your friend has expensive needs."

"You can give me a fair price."

The man considered Marie-Pier, cast a glance at Marthe and then back.

"Your brother said you figured out how to get forty percent less lignins in your trawler cables."

"Hard to grow," Marie-Pier said, "but I'll have a batch ready. It'll yield a couple hundred kilos of fiber."

"You want an ongoing supply of the hormones?"

Marie-Pier nodded.

"Can you manage a hundred kilos of low-lignin trawler cable per month?" he asked.

Marie-Pier seemed startled. Marthe didn't understand what was being offered or what he would do with it. Lignins, along with carbon nanotubes, made cables hard enough to support the weight of the bob and cable and the heat of the depths. Trawlers with mutations to produce less lignins would be harder to grow.

"I can probably do seventy-five kilos per month," Marie-Pier said finally. "Nobody else has this."

"I hear they're cutting into some of your operation," he said.

"Some of it," Marie-Pier said. "What the government takes won't affect this."

The man rubbed graying stubble on his chin, and the rasping sounded despite the other noises in the bay.

"All right. Seventy-five," he said.

They followed him to a fridge and he rummaged among small tied-top carbon-weave sacks, reading the handwritten labels. He finally put two into her hands. Marthe peeked into the bags with Marie-Pier. Dozens and dozens of little misshapen white pellets lay at the bottoms.

"They aren't pretty, but they're dosed right," he said. "Four months' worth. I'll expect your shipments to start right away."

"They will," Marie-Pier said, kissing him on both cheeks. "*Merci.*"

Marthe kissed his cheeks again too and they made their way back into the small depot. As soon as the door was closed behind them and she'd assured herself that no one else was in the depot, Marthe leaned close.

"Thank you, Marie-Pier. This means a lot to me."

"It's expensive, but your little brother... your little sister is worth it. I was ramping up operations anyway."

"What did you give him?"

"The lignins in trawler cabling make them useless for feeding bioreactors. Carbon nanotubes we can break down, but not lignins. I've engineered trawlers to produce a lot less lignin."

"You'll be able to grow something in the clouds that we can use to make real food?"

"I'm halfway there."

"And you still threw in with us?" Marthe said in some astonishment. Something like this, if the government didn't get in the way and nationalize it, could make Marie-Pier wealthy—wealthy for Venus, at least.

Marie-Pier looked shy for a moment. "The clouds are our home," she said. "I can engineer all I want and I'll still be part of *la colonie,* still living in the clouds. But I can dream of stars too."

"I never thought I'd be able to," Marthe said.

Marie-Pier handed her the little bags.

"No. You hold onto them," Marthe said. "You're going to see Pascale before me."

Marie-Pier put the bags of pills in an inner suit pocket. Then frowned. "Is somebody waiting for you?" Beyond the door to the depot, Noëlle waved.

"I'll have to take care of this myself," Marthe said. Her paranoia didn't feel so paranoid anymore.

"We'll be in touch."

Marthe opened the door and stepped through. Noëlle looked uncertain. Marthe grabbed her arm and led her through the arcade.

"Hey!" Noëlle said.

Marthe kept on marching her along. She'd never treated Noëlle like this. Marthe was always the one chasing, persuading, seducing. Maybe the change in behavior surprised Noëlle. It surprised Marthe. At the other end of the arcade, she found an alcove behind the stairwell into the envelope. She pushed Noëlle's back against the wall. The air smelled of machine oil and ozone.

"Why are you following me?" Marthe said. "First the committee chamber. Now here."

Noëlle mouthed some words, but couldn't make anything come out.

"You're no femme fatale, Noëlle."

"What?"

"Who asked you to spy on me?"

"No one!"

"The *présidente* already had me into her office," Marthe said. "Was it her, or didn't you even get to see her?"

Noëlle's dark brown eyes widened.

"What do they want to know? Who I'm seeing? Where I'm going?"

Noëlle's expression shifted to humiliated anger. "I'm not following you. I saw you and decided to say hi."

"Seeing as how neither you nor I have ever been here before, that's kind of hard to swallow, *ma chère*."

"Why are *you* here?" Noëlle demanded indignantly. Marthe was enjoying the role reversal, of not looking for approval, for scraps of Noëlle's affections. There was something bigger than her, their Axis Mundi, and she was more than just some mechanic on a shitty ship. Dreams had power.

"I need a place to live, Noëlle, because they're taking away my home."

Noëlle pursed her beautiful lips.

"You don't have to tell me who sent you," Marthe said. "Just tell me if you were going to go all the way."

"What do you mean?"

Marthe's lips swooped in, smothering Noëlle's with powerful need, and after a moment of surprise, Noëlle responded, her fingers reaching up to caress Marthe's cheeks.

Between breathless kisses, Noëlle spoke. "What happened to you?"

In answer, Marthe pushed Noëlle along the wall, to where a tool closet opened easily. She shoved Noëlle in and followed, closing the door behind her. Her femme fatale was hardly dangerous at all, but she was certainly warm in the darkness.

FIFTY-SIX

ÉMILE FLEW OUT to *Baie-Comeau* just after sunset, the hour-long period when the sunlight no longer touched the flotilla, but still lit the higher-atmosphere clouds into strings of luminescent mist. Vapor arched ten kilometers above him, glowing in soft whites, yellows and even pinks. Piles of puffy clouds above sixty-fifth *rang* were torn to shreds by intangible winds, suspended in airless, soundless stillness.

The stiffness from the chemical burn on his leg was ebbing. His shoulder ached a little less. His heart did not.

He hadn't told Marthe about Tétreau's messages. The *Sûreté* lieutenant had asked Émile for his decision a couple of times, politely enough. Émile wasn't sure how much he ought to hustle on the answer. Even if he did say yes, he didn't want Tétreau to think he was one of those hop-to-it types.

He'd spent a lot of time thinking about Pascal and Jean-Eudes, too. He was still steamed that Pascal hadn't trusted him with the family secret. He'd trusted a stranger rather than Émile. Would he have even believed Pascal, though? If it had been anyone but Marthe telling him their plan, he'd have called prank on them. But Marthe's sense of humor was shit.

Émile didn't want to lay this all on Pascal. The poor guy had been eleven when Émile left. No Émile. No Marthe. No *maman*. He'd been raised entirely by the old man. Émile knew well enough George-Étienne's force of will. All defects aside, the old bastard was unrelenting. Eleven-year-old Pascal wouldn't have stood a chance. Neither would Jean-Eudes. Émile had left them with George-Étienne. He owed them.

His choices shifted and evaporated and reformed faster than he could keep up. Everything had felt like a dead end before he'd met Thérèse; five years of shitty jobs and loser friends while the *Causapscal-des-Vents* slowly decayed around him and Marthe. And then, all of a sudden, he was on some new path.

Artists gave a shit about things beyond the day-to-day and getting high. They thought about the eternal and the essential, about philosophical questions. And Thérèse was... Thérèse. And it seemed like being something, someone other than just a hammer and ratchet monkey, fixing plumbing and venting. He didn't just have one unchanging day after another.

And when Pascal came up, it had been like opening a door long closed. His own little brother, back in his life. Émile had been serious about Pascal coming up to live. They could have shared a room, or even made a single rack space work with two hammocks, if need be. He'd done it before. Having Pascal here would have been making a family again.

And maybe Alexis could come up too. Émile was his goddamn uncle. He could raise his sister's boy. He hadn't really thought so far, but hell, there'd even be room for Jean-Eudes. Marthe was a good negotiator. She could get him a rack too. It was one thing for the *colonie* to tell a family to abort a fetus, but Jean-Eudes was a grown man with rights now. But that dream, the family whole again, had vanished in minutes. Pascal was George-Étienne's son. And when he disappeared into the clouds with Gabriel-Antoine, the might-have-beens followed him down.

A few weeks ago he'd been at the point of committing to Thérèse. He'd all but given her his whole soul. When he'd offered to take her down, to make a place for her to live in the depths, as a *coureur,* that hadn't been talk. He didn't know where that came from; it hadn't been all about her.

He was done with needing people's permission and approval for every little pot to piss in. Offering the depths to Thérèse had been desperate, but sometimes desperation blew away obscuring clouds. The idea of just being a farmer, a herder, came from somewhere. No approvals. No laws. Just muscle and brains against the power of Venus, a trawler of his own, and a family of his own, scrawling lines of poetry while Thérèse made art out of the living things of Venus. But all that had been yanked painfully away, like burnt skin pulled free, exposing the seeping soft pink beneath. It stung.

Even the offer to be a constable was sudden, dizzying and frankly ridiculous. He didn't know what they were smoking to think he'd be good. He was big, but there had to be more to it than that. Most of the *Sûreté* had to be more than hired goons taking bribes. But that looked like it would all evaporate too. Maybe Marthe was right and it was a bribe. A dumb idea.

But was it any dumber than what Pascal and Pa had cooked up? *Câlisse*, this was all nuts. A road to the stars, underground, that they couldn't touch? This was how he had to make things right with his brothers? Could he even?

The *Baie-Comeau's* rooftop, where he'd last crashed with Thérèse, lay beneath, striped with reflective paint and edged with runway lights and flashing lamps on the safety netting. He spoiled his airspeed, flared and landed right in the middle of the roof with only a few extra steps, stiff as he tried to avoid bending his knees too much with the healing skin. He furled his wings and stepped closer to a small crowd of people. Tétreau broke from the group and shook Émile's shoulder, hand-signaling that he was on channel twenty-four. Émile dialed himself up to twenty-four.

"Thanks for the invitation," he said.

"No problem," Tétreau said. "Nothing like a raid."

"What d'you want me to do?"

"It's a simple one," Tétreau said. "We got a tip on somebody sitting on a shitload of stockpiled parts on the *Batiscanie*. We go in. You watch. Other than domestics or theft, hoarding and black marketing is the major thing we go after."

"These all *Sûreté?*" Émile asked.

A lot of people wore the same survival suits as him, a little worn, but obviously woven in the clouds. They carried carbon night-sticks, and a couple had crowbars. Two of them were bigger, close to Émile's size, in sleek suits that looked lightly armored. Lumpy holsters showed on their waists.

"This is one of the *Sûreté* crews," Tétreau said. "A couple are Bank guys, doing a ride-along. They haven't got much to do otherwise except sit around the branch office."

Tétreau signaled to one of the *Sûreté* with chevrons painted onto his chest and arms. The NCO got everyone's attention, said a few things on another channel, then he led them off the roof and into the sky. Tétreau slapped Émile's shoulder and they followed, the starlight creating blurred ghosts of the wispy clouds to left and right.

"My main job as an assistant in *l'Assemblée* is getting busier," Tétreau said conversationally as the thin air whistled past them. "I probably don't have enough time to keep up with the *Sûreté*. Boniface could lead for me, but someone will have to fill in for him as sergeant."

"Yeah?" Émile said.

"Most of these guys are good enough for raids and following orders, but I don't know that any of them are good enough to whip the other guys into shape," Tétreau said. "Boniface tells them where to go and what to do and they do it, but he can't be lieutenant and sergeant both."

The *Batiscanie* resolved in the darkness, tiny running

lights coming nearer. Boniface was just a dark figure against back-lit clouds, a green light winking on one wing, red on the other. Three guys formed a triangle ahead of him. The two Bank guys flew farther back. Tétreau and Émile were back and high.

"Why don't you watch and tell me what you think of the op?" Tétreau said.

"Sure."

The wing tips banked and the three guys swooped in, one landing quickly on the roof of the *Batiscanie,* one pulling a close circuit, the third tracing a wide circle. The first clipped his safety wire, dropped his wings and put a screw gun to the hinges of the roof doorway as the second landed. Then the sergeant touched down and the main doorway was open. Their billy clubs were out. Émile itched to be closer.

"Nice landings," Émile said. "Can I listen on their channel?"

"Fifty-seven," Tétreau said.

Émile's radio didn't even go that high. "Can I land too?"

"Just do what they did," Tétreau said.

He and Tétreau set down. Émile found himself grinning. The Bank guys circled. Their flying wasn't so smooth. Maybe not surprising. They were just cycled in for a four-year posting, then off to some other Bank assignment. Lucky bastards.

Émile didn't bother asking permission; he just went down the stairs. Tétreau followed. The *Batiscanie* was about twice the size of the *Causapscal-des-Vents,* with a lot of burnt-out light bulbs, walls stripped of metal, and thickets of exposed wires. Noise sounded through the airlock. Tétreau and Émile jammed themselves in and cycled themselves through. Émile noticed Tétreau wasn't bothering with neutralizing. So be it.

The airlock opened onto a tight galley, behind which four curtained doorways led astern. The three cops were bunched at two of the openings. Émile still couldn't hear any of the chatter through his radio because he couldn't tune to channel fifty-seven, but there was plenty of air, and he cracked the seal on his helmet and lifted it clear. The air smelled of yeast and fermentation.

A couple of people were yelling *"Sûreté tabarnak,"* *"espèce de crisse de colon,"* and *"rendez-vous!"* They were too tightly bunched to swing their clubs effectively. Boniface got knocked back by someone.

Tétreau yelled at them all, pulling them back. Boniface had a bloody nose. Another guy's club was wet with something. Beyond them, two angry guys and a woman stood in the doorways, holding makeshift clubs made out of bars that looked like they'd been taken out of the structural struts of the habitat. Behind them were illegal stills, scattered metal scraps, tools, and what looked like old or spare parts, more than even Phocas was hoarding.

Émile wondered if he'd be able to take any of them. He was bigger, but unarmed.

Somewhere a baby started crying. The two guys and the woman leapt forward ferociously, striking fast and hard with their improvised clubs, forcing back the three cops, spilling the fight into the slightly wider galley area.

Boniface went down, stunned with a loud knock to the head. One of the cops pinned the woman. Tétreau joined the fight with a club in one hand and a taser in the other. There was a lot of quick radio talk and shouting. The baby screamed louder. Tétreau had one guy cornered, but the cop with him took a hit to the eye. His opponent pulled a knife.

Émile caught the guy's wrist and wrenched his arm back. The guy grappled with him over the knife, but Émile swung him into the door frame, once, twice, three times, before twisting his arm back so far that his hand opened senselessly. Émile wrestled him to the floor and got onto his back. The woman's hands were tied behind her back. The guy in the corner had his hands up. Tétreau was grinning at Émile and tossed him plastic wrist ties. Émile tied the guy's wrists together and stood. Their last cop opened the airlock and came in.

"Bit more fight than we expected, eh?" Tétreau said, helping Boniface to his feet.

"A bit short," Émile joked. The adrenaline rush made the ache in his leg feel more distant.

Émile lumbered towards the crying. In a low hammock in a small room, a wet-cheeked toddler fell silent when Émile came into view. Pascal had been this small once, running around their old habitat in a diaper. If things had worked out differently, maybe he and Thérèse might have been minding a toddler in a few years. The thoughts stirred wistful mourning. The child's lip trembled. Émile neutralized his arms and chest quickly and picked him up. The toddler squirmed and whined.

"*Voyons, mon vieux,*" Émile said softly. "It's after your bedtime, isn't it?"

He bounced the toddler in his arms, but the child wouldn't settle. A couple of the bound people swore at him.

"*Viens,*" Tétreau said beside him, reaching for the child.

Émile handed him over. The woman was sitting against the wall, her face bruised, her hands unbound again. She glared at Émile and Tétreau, but Boniface was near her with his club ready. Tétreau gave her the toddler and after a bit of fussing, he settled.

One of Tétreau's crew was in the back room. "*Crisse!*" he said. "There must be two hundred kilos of steel in here!"

"Oh man," another cop said. "Get a load of their still!"

The boiling barrel looked like it was made of carbon weave. The same materials might have made a lot of small parts, but he couldn't fault them the still. Beneath it was a solar stove where the window could provide hard sunlight to focus. Part of the wall had been stripped of insulation so the vapor could run against the cold outer skin of the gondola. Rows of collecting sacks bulged full. Down in the depths, the *coureurs* ran stills the other way: they boiled by putting pots and boil sacks outside, and cooled by running their tubes into the living areas of the trawlers.

"Is this any good?" the cop said, taking one of the sacks. "Or is this methanol?" He opened it and took a sip, swishing it between his cheeks. He made a face. "Oof. That's strong!"

Émile and Tétreau tried it. It wasn't bad. Wasn't good either.

"Evidence!" Tétreau warned, and the cop hung up the sack.

The business of charging the people with hoarding and resisting arrest got boring fast. Floaters were on their way to the *Batiscanie* to cart away the metals for redistribution. A foster sitter was also flying over to take care of the toddler and the habitat while these three were transported to detention on the *Baie-Comeau*. And there was the matter of what to do with the other inhabitants of the *Batiscanie,* who were on shift right now. Émile could see why some of the guys didn't want to be sergeants. It was dull. He would have let these people off on some of the charges—it was too much trouble. Eventually Tétreau walked Émile up to the roof again. As they sealed their helmets, Tétreau handed Émile one of the heavy sacks.

"Here. Thanks," Tétreau said.

Émile hefted the bag. "Evidence?"

"We got enough with one sack and all the metals and the hoarded scraps that ought to have gone to the bioreactor," Tétreau said. "And although being in the *Sûreté* is fun, it doesn't pay much, and some of it is dangerous. This is the least *la colonie* can do to thank you and the other guys. Besides, we can't do anything else with it."

Émile emerged onto the roof and strapped the sack to his chest after putting on his wing-pack.

"I'll call you for the next one," Tétreau said.

Émile nodded slowly in his helmet. "Yeah."

FIFTY-SEVEN

THE STARS, WRAPPED in vertiginous spaces, glared down hard and cold and endless. Marthe had come up to the roof in her suit to take one last look. The *Causapscal-des-Vents* was ending, no matter what happened next. If they were fast enough, her home would be chopped up for parts by her little brother... sister. If they weren't, *la colonie* would get its chance to scrap it.

The truth hadn't penetrated all the way to her heart. It was like rain on a suit, looking for cracks to creep in. Did she know how to say goodbye to a home? At the top of Venus, on her floating island, alone with this beauty, she didn't know how to put any of it into words. She wanted something concrete to make this experience hers and enduring, in the way the habitat had been hers.

Could Pascale and Pa, with their strange, impossible Axis Mundi, possibly replace this? Ten to twenty kilometers of attenuated atmosphere rose above her, making the stars wink unpredictably. What would naked stars look like in a real vacuum? She was a little terrified and a little excited by the thought. She turned in a slow circle, regarding the whole horizon, her feelings still unnamable. But all this she promised to one day give to her family, including Marie-Pier's children, and Paul-Égide and Louise.

She went back inside. Past the airlock, a small light was on in the kitchen. Émile sat sideways at the table, legs out straight. He had some bandages under his pants, but hadn't said anything. He held a datapad in one hand and a smoldering cigarette in another. Two lumpy shot cups sat on the table beside a black jar. She cracked the seal on her helmet.

"Inviting me to my own *bagosse?*" she asked.

"Scored my own stash," he said.

She sat and zipped down her suit. She sniffed at the cup nearest her. It wasn't subtle. The transparent liquid was still near the lip of his cup. "That's your second?"

He sucked on his cigarette. Handed it to her. She took a drag.

"Waiting for my little sister," he said. She couldn't tell if he was being ironic.

She blew smoke and lifted the little cup in two fingers for a toast. He raised his and they drank. It tasted the way band-aid glue smelled. "*Ouach!*" She shuddered, sucked another drag on his cigarette to drown some of the taste in the tobacco sulfur. "What is this?"

He shrugged and downed his.

"What's the occasion?"

He shrugged again.

"Are you writing?" she asked. His eyes assumed something of the startled animal. She averted her eyes, sniffed distastefully at the jar and poured them each another shot. "Pascale says you're good."

Émile snorted. "He's just a kid."

"I'd like to read your poems sometime."

He reached across the table, took his cigarette out of her mouth and lifted the next shot. They toasted and drank. Both shuddered.

"I'm in," he said.

"Why?"

He made a face. "What do you care?" He looked at the remains of the shot, but didn't drink and avoided her eyes. He shrugged. "Family is family, isn't it? In the end?"

She nodded. "All the way?"

He nodded, flicked the burning ash off their cigarette with big, acid-melted fingertips. He rolled the butt in his fingers to drop the remaining tobacco back into the box.

"'All the way' means I need some help making peace between you and Pa," she said.

"Did you ask him for the same?"

"Yeah."

He reached for the jar, but then screwed the lid on instead of pouring more. He rose.

"I'm going to finish cleaning out the greenhouses," he said. "No matter what happens, we aren't going to grow much more in them." He spun the airlock and carried his helmet into the envelope.

The *Causapscal-des-Vents* bucked in an updraft, but settled before too many chirping alarms went off. Down in forty-fifth *rang*, that would have been just a love tap. She sat for a bit, feeling the buzz. When she was younger, she'd been better with her liquor. She'd gone a bit soft. Had she stopped being a *coureur?* Was there such a thing as a *coureur* in the heights? If there was, she was it. She silently toasted her father and Jean-Eudes and emptied the cup.

She went into her room. Beneath the decking was a door into the small but powerful electric engines. Two propellers ran more often than not, keeping the habitat properly oriented in the wind. In a pinch, they could run for days to try to avoid a storm. She shut them off and opened a panel. Inside, the propeller shaft touched the drive train with a gear plate full of worn gears. She'd been asking for gear plates for over a year and had made do. She'd even traded away part of a door frame to get a third-hand gear plate for one of the shafts. And that was still better than the worn-out one it had replaced.

She pulled out that old gear plate and began wearing down the teeth even more with a brush and a small bit of acid. There wasn't much to do before it would be unsafe and ineffective. Then she unsecured the shaft, lifted it, and switched out the gear plates, storing the third-hand one under her bed, and installing the ineffective gear plate where it wouldn't do any good in the assembly. She closed the casing, put away the tools, closed the door and wiped her hands. In the kitchen, she switched on the radio.

"*Causapscal-des-Vents* to *Baie-Comeau* control," she said.

"*Vas-y, Causapscal-des-Vents.*"

"Control, our port gear plate, part 2288C, has given out," she said. "I've shut off the port prop. We can probably do a few kph on the starboard prop and full rudder, but we'll need a new position in the flotilla."

"Roger, *Causapscal-des-Vents.* Permission to drop downstream. Do you need immediate assistance?"

"No. I need a 2288C. I've had it on order for eighteen months with no response from *Baie-Comeau* Resources."

"Talk to Resources. Permission to drop downstream granted."

"Roger, control. *Causapscal-des-Vents* out."

That was the first step. The wind carried the flotilla, so it would take a day or two for the *Causapscal-des-Vents* to fall to the back, and then another day or two for it to fall out of sight of the flotilla. Control would probably assign a few habitats to slow down to keep pace with it.

That morning, she'd written a similar message to control from the *Marais-des-Nuages.* Normal maintenance would take the engines offline and the Phocas habitat would also drift back. Either she or Émile would do the maintenance and follow the navigational instructions. In a few days, the *Marais-des-Nuages* would also be near the back of the flotilla.

And radio was open chatter every habitat had to listen to. Everyone would have heard, again, that the

Causapscal-des-Vents was having problems because Resources wasn't giving them parts. Whether Resources had parts to give wasn't the point. What mattered was how many people on how many habitats now looked nervously at their own unfulfilled parts requests.

FIFTY-EIGHT

MARIE-PIER'S HABITAT, THE *Coureur des Tourbillons,* down at fifty-first *rang,* was just coming into range. A little electronic chirp let Marthe know that they'd established a maser line: cloud-penetrating and very difficult to intercept. After a few moments, Pa's voice crackled in Marthe's earpiece.

"*Ma chère?*"

"I'm here, Pa," she said quietly.

"You ready?" he asked.

"*Oui.* You?"

"*C'est beau.*"

"I've been thinking through things a bit more, Pa. I can fly fine, but I don't want to leave the *Causapscal-des-Vents* alone too long. I'm going to get Émile to mind it."

"I'll send up Pascal," Pa said. "Or come up myself."

"You have too much work down there, Pa," Marthe said reasonably. Nothing would be served by letting her temper into this conversation. "This is what were were talking about, Pa. Émile is good. He can do this."

A long period of white noise crackle sounded in her earpiece, the popping echoes of lightning halfway around the planet.

"*Crisse,*" he finally said. "I should have put you in charge of the House of Styx."

"You're the head of the family, Pa."

"And you're going to be *la présidente* of Venus someday."

"I swear too much for the old ladies," she said.

"*Tabarnak!* They won't care when we free Venus from the Bank."

His voice sounded like there was a smile in it. There was a dream in it.

"See you soon, Pa."

FIFTY-NINE

MARTHE AND ÉMILE spent the next day picking all the mature crops and sealing the immature ones in composting tanks. The nitrogen and hydrogen were valuable. They stowed and stored everything else on the *Causapscal-des-Vents* as if the inside of their home was going to fill with sulfuric acid. Packing all their things was a strange job. They didn't have a lot. They'd recycled almost everything they couldn't use anymore. Marthe couldn't find her locket with pictures of *maman,* no matter where she looked, and she lost long minutes turning things upside down. Acid would eat the silver quickly. But in the end, she gave up. Émile couldn't find everything he was looking for in his disorganized mess.

The *Causapscal-des-Vents* had fallen about thirty kilometers behind the main flotilla, fifteen behind the *Jonquière,* which was also trailing with small repairs. In a pinch, a powerless habitat could mount emergency sails and drift. Secondary flotillas circled the equator at intervals of about seven or eight thousand kilometers. The next one would catch up in about twenty hours. And even lone habitats would be tracked by satellites. But satellites couldn't see beneath the *Causapscal-des-Vents,* where she and Émile had stowed the ingredients for their plan.

Fifteen kilometers below, and about fifty kilometers downwind, Pa and Marie-Pier waited with the harnessed trawlers. The difference in wind speeds between sixty-fifth *rang* and fiftieth *rang* was about fifty meters per second today, so Marthe and Émile were about fifteen minutes ahead. And they had to count descent time and the speed they would lose as they descended into slower winds.

It was common enough to drop supplies to the lower decks in powered drones, but drones were small and maneuverable, and their carbon nanotube construction was designed to work from sixty-fifth all the way down to fortieth. A habitat was just a big balloon made for cold, low-acid environments. It was going to be a hard descent.

Sixteen kilometers ahead, the *Jonquière* was just a silvery-green speck, and they needed binoculars to see the rest of the flotilla. They had to avoid the satellites. And their chance was coming up soon.

Most of the atmosphere at sixty-fifth *rang* was clear down to two or more kilometers, with some haze. But sometimes weird low-pressure eddies formed, and columns of cottony cirrus clouds rose like great fingers, almost high enough to brush the habitats. Visibility in those cloud banks dropped to a few hundred meters. Marthe sat on the bench in the kitchen beside the pressure system controls. She stared out at the cloud columns, rechecked their locations, and drew a deep breath in her suit, briefly fogging her faceplate. This was the line of no return, her Rubicon. From opposition and protest voice to criminal was a bigger step than she'd expected. She squawked her suit radio once and then activated a new buoyancy program.

Her new program was basically the reverse of what every habitat had to do to stay afloat. Pumps sucked the buoyant, breathable air in the habitat into pressurized tanks. The struts in the envelope and the seals in the habitat proper began to creak under the weird pressure. At the same time, carbon dioxide was let in from the thin atmosphere outside and into the habitat.

They slowly began to sink, and their course angled straight for the cloud bank. The atmosphere was so faint at this altitude that even a little bit of carbon dioxide in the envelope made a big difference. After a few minutes, Marthe switched to the long-range antenna comms system.

"*Baie-Comeau* control, this is the *Causapscal-des-Vents*. We're losing altitude. Looks like an envelope leak. Going out to assess. Our patch materials are low and we've already requisitioned more. Do you have a crew to run us out some?"

Let the rest of the flotilla hear that.

The radio crackled momentarily.

"*Causapscal-des-Vents,* we can get a crew there. Give us a leak assessment."

"I'm topping up and putting on wings right now, control. Émile is going into the envelope. Stand by."

The cloud bank neared as they sank. The pumps whirred,

pumping more and more carbon dioxide into the habitat. Marthe spun the handle on the door, went up the stairs, and cycled through the airlock. Gusts of wind stroked faint fingers along her suit. She put on her wing-pack, clipped herself to a cable, and lowered herself over the side. She belayed in a complete circuit of the envelope, from bow to stern and back along the other side, as if looking for a leak. Later, a crash investigator might examine computer-enhanced satellite footage and see her climbing over the *Causapscal-des-Vents,* and would hopefully conclude that she'd done everything she could. The habitat's dip put the cloud column dead ahead.

"Control," she said into the radio, "it's a big leak. Looks like a lower starboard strut broke. The snap point tore the skin over sections C and D, and the port support struts are bowing. Émile is going to try to reinforce the port struts and then see if the starboard support can be fixed. We'll need patch materials, probably struts and temporary clamps. I'm going to check the stern struts and envelope skin. We're sinking too fast for it to be just the two tears."

"*Câlisse,*" control said. "Crew leaving now, *Causapscal-des-Vents.*"

"*Merci, Baie-Comeau.* See you when you get here."

Now the clock was ticking. They drifted into the clouds. In a few seconds, they would be too deep for the satellites to see. Marthe cranked the pumps to full. This was going to wreak havoc on the filters soon. The pumps were fitted with filters covered with different bicarbonates to neutralize the acids, but they had now sunk into a hazy yellow mist of sulfuric acid. The acid would soon fill the filters with salt, and then they'd be useless. Their descent accelerated and the clouds above them blurred the shine of the sun. She switched to the short, private habitat channel as she belayed all the way down the cable.

"*Enweille, Émile!* Let's get cracking!"

Her brother unscrewed the emergency hatch under the floor of the kitchen and emerged. It was an airlock of last resort, and he'd stretched three layers of webs of carbon fiber soaked in bicarbonate across the gap. They didn't need to worry too much about acid getting in from underneath, and the living cabin was now naked to the pressure of Venus. The gondola's full weight would be pulling it down.

A big bale was strapped beneath the *Causapscal-des-Vents,* but they couldn't open it yet. They hadn't gone through the dangerous part yet. Marthe swung herself under the bale and clung there, slowly strapping herself to it. Émile climbed up the rope she'd just descended. Marthe switched to the long channel.

"*Baie-Comeau,* this is *Causapscal-des-Vents,*" she said. "Tell the crews to hurry. I just found the big problem. The bowing of the port struts tore the envelope skin on the starboard side just above the cabin. Atmosphere is pouring in. We're dropping fast. Émile is disassembling one of the inner envelope walls to patch the outer envelope. I'm deploying emergency balloons."

She was too Venusian to avoid a twinge of remorse at the lie. Venus was always trying to kill them.

No *coloniste* ever joked about an emergency. Yet here

she was doing just that, initiating a response that would mobilize dozens or hundreds of people. *La colonie* had lost habitats before, big ones like the *Matapédia*. People and families had died. *La colonie* had adjusted, making smaller targets of themselves, just family-sized habitats, but those too sometimes sank when they got too old or too damaged in a storm. It wasn't just acid that scarred them all. Losses scarred them too.

"The planes and crews are scrambling. What's your altitude, *Causapscal?*" Control said. Crackles whispered in the radio.

The *Causapscal-des-Vents's* descent slowed. On the top of the envelope, Émile had obviously inflated the emergency oxygen balloons.

"*Ostie!*" she said. "We just dipped into a cloud. Acid's gonna get into the inner envelope."

"Focus on saving yourselves and the habitat first," Control said. "We'll fix it later. Pulling you up on satellite."

"We're already down to sixty-third!" she said. "Getting a little chop. I'm going into the envelope to help Émile get inner patch material."

That was another lie. They'd already dropped to sixty-second *rang*.

"We've got nothing on the satellite," control said. "What's your location? Where's your transceiver?"

"I'm not in the cabin! I'm on top of the envelope. If you can't pick up the *Causapscal-des-Vents*, use my personal transceiver! How soon are you going to get here?" Marthe said.

"The first crew should be there in nine minutes."

That was cutting it close. The crews might actually make it in time. They had to add to that time.

"*Câlisse!*" she swore. "The bowing of the starboard struts is unbalancing the whole thing. The hole on the port side with the missing strut is getting bigger. It might tear the ribs of the entire envelope."

"Hold it together, *Causapscal-des-Vents,*" Control said. "It will hold."

"No, it won't," she said. "I can see *Les Rapides Plats* just beneath us."

She didn't need to explain. The rolling convection cells, laid out like a warped washerboard in the sky, were punishing on the best of days. The best way to get through *Les Rapides* was to be small and heavy, plunging through as quickly as possible. A plane could do it, but it was rough. A person with furled wings could cross it pretty quickly. A big dirigible habitat—buoyant, with lots of surface area—was the worst thing to take into *Les Rapides*. And if any of what she was saying was true, then the emergency balloons really would be another stress, and would rip even an undamaged habitat.

"I'm cutting the emergency balloons!" Marthe cried into the radio.

It was a sign of whoever was manning Air Traffic Control that they didn't argue. They knew how habitats worked. Émile was listening in, and abruptly, the *Causapscal-des-Vents* pitched forward before righting itself. Two emergency balloons floated free, evidence of their emergency. She switched to the private channel.

"Get to shelter, Émile. This is going to be rough."

The transition layer rose towards them.

"*Causapscal-des-Vents!* Are you all right?"

"Hang on!" she said on the flotilla channel. "About to hit *Les Rapides*. Keep a lock on my transceiver."

Control didn't bother them on the radio, but there were lots of side orders to the rescue crews, position updates and so on, enough to distract her. The habitat lurched up, and then, with a gorge-raising drop, a downdraft swept them down, like going over a waterfall. The wind howled around them, whistling in the wires and grasping for the edges and corners.

Marthe's straps jerked her body as the habitat creaked dangerously, metal bending somewhere. They spun, and then all of a sudden, she was flung upward, on top of the upside-down dirigible. Parts of it collapsed, the struts unable to bear the weight up of the gondola. If she'd been there for even a few seconds more, the struts would have all deformed, bursting all the buoyancy chambers. But the habitat spun back to right with a shriek of metal and plastic. *Crisse.* She'd expected chop, but anxiety rose, like she was a teenager again. All their plans were just plans that Venus would test. And they couldn't do anything but wait and try to hold down the animal fear.

Turbulence buffeted the *Causapscal-des-Vents* and snaps sounded above her—big ones, otherwise she wouldn't have heard them through the fierce, thin wind. She tasted blood in her mouth where the jostling had made her bite her lip. Her head ached. Somewhere in the bumping she'd whacked her head against the bale behind her. Then the *Causapscal-des-Vents* lay on its side, rattling in place for a fraction of a second, long enough to count as stillness, before plunging a hundred, two hundred meters, maybe more, in one of the big rollers in *Les Rapides Plats*. The rattling and vibrating in her sideways drop became painful until, like wet soap flying out of a crushing fist, they burst out into thick yellow cloud.

She swung beneath the *Causapscal-des-Vents* as if under an unwieldly parachute. The habitat shook and creaked and sank. She swallowed blood and the thick saliva that preceded vomit. Two minutes of punishment had passed. She toggled the private channel.

"Émile," she said unevenly. "Where are you? Émile?"

"*Causapscal-des-Vents!*" Control was cracking. "Status report."

"Émile!"

She started unstrapping herself.

"*Causapscal-des-Vents!*"

"*Sapristi...*" Émile finally answered.

"*Ça va?*" she said.

"Good enough," he said.

"Control, we're below *Les Rapides*," Marthe said, switching to the flotilla channel. "Have you still got a fix on my transceiver?"

"*Causapscal-des-Vents*, we've got a strong signal from your transceiver. Looks like sixtieth. Are you alright?"

"The habitat is in one piece," she said, as she pulled the knots free of the bales she'd been strapped to. The tarps and ropes came apart and a weird umbrella-shaped parachute hung there. Its surface was silvery. "Checking for additional damage. How soon to the crews?"

"Emergency crews," control said, "you're authorized to drop below the transition layer. Do it as quick as possible, before we get too far ahead."

Good advice. Between sixty-fifth and fifty-ninth, the windspeed would have already dropped by about twenty meters per second. Every minute, the *Causapscal-des-Vents* dropped behind the flotilla by another kilometer. And as they sank, the differential would build. Air Traffic Control wanted the crew to get down to the same level as soon as they could, so at least they wouldn't be carried away on winds with the rest of the flotilla. With aching arms, Marthe scaled the ropes up the gondola and envelope.

"Probably ten minutes, *Causapscal-des-Vents*."

She reached the roof of the envelope. Émile was strong-arming frayed, ropey nets out from the stairway. She got behind him and they started tying corners of the net to the cleats on the roof. When they'd gotten half of the ends tied down, they stood at bow and stern and started throwing the nets over the edge. The ratty material was made of old fragments of trawler cable and bits of Venusian plants. The uneven shape and hardness would blunt their radar reflection.

The clouds thinned to a fine mist and the view suddenly widened. The kilometer of clear air of *Grande Allée* stretched for as far as they could see. The bottom of the upper cloud deck loomed above them and the top of the middle cloud deck extended away like a floor. The wide view gave them a visceral sense of the speed of their descent. They were still eight kilometers higher than their rendezvous point with the *Profondeurs*, and crews of planes were racing their way. If any of the pilots were daring, they might have already ducked straight through the turbulence to get to *Grande Allée,* where they could fly with more visibility. Marthe and Émile needed to get the hell under *Grande Allée* before they were seen.

They hooked another section of the improvised radar curtain to the roof and heaved the ends over the edge. While she distracted herself with this, the ceiling of *Grande Allée* got farther and farther from their heads.

And finally, the mist of the middle deck swallowed them. They pulled out the next curtain. She was getting tired. This was harder lifting than she was used to. Even Émile, outmassing her by thirty kilos, sounded winded. They tied down the third curtain of rope, cabling, trawler and blastula scraps, everything they could afford to lose that would absorb radar.

"*Causapscal-des-Vents,* can you report?" control asked.

"We're still sinking. Trying to find something that hasn't been damaged to tie an emergency balloon to. I don't think we can use anywhere on the envelope. Émile is in the envelope trying to feed a cable straight through to the gondola so the struts don't bear most of the weight."

"Good thinking, *Causapscal-des-Vents.*"

"Could use some extra hands," she said. "Crew almost here?"

"It took them time to safely get through the transition layer. They're listening and are on their way. Maybe eight minutes."

"You've got my transceiver fix?"

"*Oui.*"

"*D'accord.*"

"Have you got personal emergency balloons?" control asked.

"We won't need them."

Marthe switched to their private channel. A light brightened in her helmet. Radar. "You ready, Émile?" The fine mist was turning into the lightest of rains of sulfuric acid. She wiped her faceplate.

"You?"

"*Oui.*" She slapped his arm. "Hustle," she said. "And get back up as soon as you can leave the habitat with Pa."

"Worry about yourself," he said.

She grabbed their netting and scampered down the side of the envelope, until she had to swing inward to reach the big silver parachute hanging underneath. She clung to that and climbed down. She found the foot rings at the bottom, just above a hanging tank of pressurized gas. Standing in the ropes, she clipped D-rings to her shoulder harness. Brisk tugging assured her that they would hold.

Then she gave a verbal command on the private channel. The hook under the gondola opened and she fell. The weirdly-shaped parachute expanded, catching her. She turned north. Émile had already started small inner thrusters, which dragged the *Causapscal-des-Vents* south.

Marthe reached down, hooked a hose from the parachute above her to the tank of pressurized gas below, and then turned the handle. The second layer of the parachute revealed itself as carbon dioxide inflated it into a firm lozenge shape, almost as long as the *Causapscal-des-Vents*. Below, it was concave, working like a parachute, but from above, its painted surface would be almost as radar-reflective as a habitat. Clumsy as hell to maneuver with, though. Inflated as it was, it caught the wind and handled like a balloon rather than a parachute.

"Control, we're still descending, but the temperature is within tolerances. In another few minutes, Émile and I are going to try to stop our descent with an emergency balloon attached to the gondola roof. We're drifting straight north on a cross-current. Can you use my transceiver to follow?"

"*Causapscal-des-Vents*, we're following your transceiver. Radar is a mess down there. We have a search plane with radar at sixty-fifth *rang*. He can make you out. What's your altitude?"

"It's looking like fifty-sixth *rang*," she said. "Half an atmosphere. Twenty-four degrees."

"You're getting low."

She was. But by turning north-east, she would keep herself farther away from the repair crew coming from the west, and the deeper she sank, the more they'd have to fight a headwind to get to her.

"*Tabarnak*," she said. "It's not working."

"What?"

"We've inflated the emergency balloon and we're not slowing."

"*Tabarnak*," control agreed. Although her radio would only carry so far in the clouds, no doubt everyone who could hear her transmissions was glued to their radios. *La colonie* hadn't lost a habitat to the clouds in a decade. She had to give them a show.

"I'm going to use my personal emergency balloon on the *Causapscal-des-Vents*."

"No!" control said. "You have to have one at all times! You can't put it on anything else!"

"I have a wing-pack. So does Émile."

"And if they don't work? If they break? It's the law. You can't throw away your safety device."

"I'm not losing my home, either," she said.

Lying to the government didn't bother her so much. But she was lying to her neighbors. Her friends. Her enemies. Up until now, she'd been honest with *l'Assemblée*. Cunning, yes, but honest. Émile had accused her of trying to take *maman's* place in the family, but *maman* never would have done this. Pa would.

"Marthe, you are not authorized to use your emergency balloon on the *Causapscal-des-Vents*. It won't have enough buoyancy to make a difference."

"Roger, control, but it will as I get deeper."

"Not authorized. We're keeping our fix on you. Crews will be there soon."

She turned the unwieldly wing-chute above her to east-north-east, dropping a few hundred meters into a cloud bank, into gradually slower winds, and then into a wash of pelting acid. The rain would confuse the radar, possibly enough for the rescue team or the radar plane to pick up Émile.

"I've entered a small rain cloud, control," she said.

"Can you still see me?"

"Do you have any control over your drift, *Causapscal?*"

"That isn't an answer," she said.

"We can still see you. Radar is circling and sees you. But you're drifting north-east now, into a storm. Single-cell."

"What's the altitude of the storm?"

She'd looked at the met reports every hour for the last day. There wasn't supposed to be a storm. But weather on Venus was capricious. The atmosphere was just a big engine to redistribute heat. With a baking hot atmosphere seventy kilometers thick, weather conditions turned on Venus's whim. If the *Causapscal-des-Vents* hit a storm, it might not survive. And storms weren't any good for lying father's daughters, either.

"Looks like fifty-third *rang* up to fifty-eighth, directly east of you."

So a tower of a storm, no matter that it was just a single storm cell. She dialed one of the channels on her helmet to the radio frequency that would let her hear the lightning. That band was crackling. A tower, all right. And the more she sank and slowed, the more it would bear down on her.

"Roger, control. My signal's still clear?" She hoped Émile was making good time, or this would all be for nothing and they'd get arrested.

"We know where you are, *Causapscal-des-Vents.*"

La colonie only built the things they needed, so the flotillas only had two kinds of radar. One frequency bounced off clouds, which allowed the flotillas to avoid bad weather, or at least get ready for it. The other frequency of radar, mostly used by the *coureurs*, penetrated the clouds and could find objects suspended in the atmosphere, but its resolution was low. At a distance, it was hard to tell a trawler from a habitat from the inflated wing she was riding into the depths. She hoped.

The wind buffeted her and the pressurized tank. The stitching she and Émile had done with woody trawler fiber wasn't bad, but she was suddenly questioning how long the inflated wing would last in a storm. The wind stilled and darkened. Tiny pattering droplets of sulfuric acid slowed and quieted before a plunging wall of fat drops roared on the surface above her like drum strikes. As the wing lurched in arguing winds, she swung wildly.

Between fortieth and forty-fifth *rangs*, from the age of thirteen, she'd only been outside in calm weather. During storms she might be outside, but on the gantry, or flying on short, sturdy wings, away from angry winds. Now she was strapped to a big disguise whose only aerodynamic property was that it caught the wind. The whole wing plummeted on a downdraft, then lurched back, yanking her in the cables, wrenching her shoulders. She nearly blacked out, and the sudden, sucking updraft was a blur.

"*Causapscal-des-Vents,*" Control said, "we've still got your position. What's your status?"

The wing and cables found an awkward resonance in the tearing winds, shuddering around her.

"We're holding on," she said, even her voice vibrating in her chest.

Lightning lit the clouds blinding yellow, before the

wind punched the wing sideways and she swung all the way up and slammed into it, bouncing off the inflated surface, right into the empty pressure tank. The crack of impact was so loud that she couldn't tell if it was in her head or her helmet. She fell back under the wing, but one of the cables circled her arm, slipping closed like a noose. All her weight, and the tank's, was suspended from the cutting cable, and she cried out.

"*Causapscal!*" Control called.

A light blinked in her helmet. Émile calling on another channel.

She swung wildly again, pulling at her shoulder. Her arm was getting crushed. Images crashed through her mind. Her sister Chloé, taken with her husband by a storm. No one knew how they'd died. Maybe a blow to the head? Cooking as they fell into the depths? Punctured and bled out? Venus rarely left clues when she struck. Her victims just dissolved, one way or another. However it was that Venus had taken her sister, Chloé had likely had at least a moment of realization, a terrible instant of fear and clarity. Like this. She didn't want to follow Chloé.

Marthe's right hand found the hilt and release for a carbon-bladed knife. She reached up, not thinking, vision entirely focused on the cable and the blade. She sawed and sawed, twisting helplessly around the agony in her trapped arm. The blinking light and the sounds of Control yelling to her were static against the pain.

The cable frayed, but wouldn't cut. Too tough.

The churning lifted her again, flung her upwards, and the cable loosened off her numb arm. The wing came down, about to slam her from above, and she had enough presence of mind to fling the knife away before it got pushed into her suit. Her face slammed into the faceplate, leaving blood, then she was falling again, jerking against the cables.

Dazed, she swung as lightning blasted behind her. Cables whipped against her in the wind, torn loose from the wing. Through the smear of her own blood, she saw the wing losing its shape, bending, getting ready to fold. The cables had yanked out chunks of fabric.

Ostie.

Sulfuric acid poured around her. A torrent of storm-tossed drops. She wiped her faceplate. The rain and clouds darkened the world. Marthe was just a flake of alien life in a sea of acid wind. And she had to get away from this improvised wing before it dragged her into the depths.

Her left arm barely lifted on its own. She had to stand in the foot straps to unclip herself with just her right hand. She'd wanted to step off properly, but a gust flung her away and then she was tumbling in the wind. The wing was there for a moment, and then rain erased it. Marthe spread her legs, dropping head first in the ocher mists. But something ground in the wing-pack machinery, over and over. Her wings wouldn't unfurl. *Tabarnak.*

She blew her personal emergency balloon. It took about half the oxygen in her breathing tanks to fill, and the fabric wasn't made to survive a storm. She'd intended to fly out under her own power.

Her descent slowed and stopped. She dangled in the

pouring rain, swaying in the wind. With her good arm she drew the acid-proof sheet out of her survival pouch and pulled it over herself. Her left shoulder and arm hurt badly and her head ached. She smelled chlorine inside her helmet. That wasn't supposed to happen.

The clouds of Venus had very little chlorine, and what there was of it was bound into the rain as hydrochloric acid. Something was hissing in her helmet. At the edge of her faceplate, hot little bubbles grew and popped inside the seal. Where her face had hit, there was a tiny web of cracks in the glass, bleeding in atmosphere. The wind swept her deeper into the storm.

SIXTY

TÉTREAU FLINCHED AS *Présidente* Gaschel threw a book across the office. It wasn't at him, but he'd never seen her so angry. He shouldn't have been here. Labourière should have been here. But the chief of staff was in meetings in a flotilla six thousand kilometers west of the *Baie-Comeau*. It would be hours before he made it back. Cécile Dauzat was standing, taking the brunt of Gaschel's frustration.

"This is not going to be my goddamn *Matapédia!*" Gaschel yelled.

Fifty years ago, a big habitat, shipped from Montréal, had sunk into the clouds, taking with it *colonie*-crippling resources and twenty-two souls. The rest had escaped, but the economic and psychological blow to *la colonie* had been devastating. Dauzat murmured platitudes.

"This is no one's *Matapédia, Madame la Présidente,*" Tétreau finally said. "The *Causapscal-des-Vents* was a crumbling habitat owned by political enemies."

Gaschel's warning finger came up, silencing him.

"Habitats don't just sink anymore. There are too many redundancies. Something massive would have to go wrong to sink a habitat now. What if this was sabotage?"

Tétreau wasn't sure if he should answer. His boss wasn't answering. But Dauzat was too cautious. Tétreau could already see that. She was just an administrator.

"If the D'Aquillons have a good motive, maybe," Tétreau said. "If we find a motive, we can deal with saboteurs as criminals. What's more likely, though, is that something big really did break on the *Causapscal-des-Vents*. If the brother and sister don't survive, that's tragic, but it's also an irritation off the table. Even if they do survive, the story can turn positively for you. If the D'Aquillons had been more cooperative, the habitat might have been recycled for the good of all."

Gaschel breathed heavily, her face flushed.

"You don't understand anything," she said. "It doesn't matter how much political irritation they can cause! It's not worth the forty-one tons of metal and electronics that are dropping into the clouds." Her voice was low. "How the hell are we going to stop it? We can't afford to replace the materials."

"Air Traffic Control is coordinating the rescue mission, *Madame la Présidente*," Dauzat said.

"They haven't rescued it yet, have they?" she demanded. "They fell too far behind! Where the hell was Air Traffic?"

A tone rang on the pad on Gaschel's desk. Tétreau didn't recognize it, but Gaschel and Dauzat obviously did, and they didn't look happy. That could only mean one thing. Gaschel stalked back behind her desk, took a deep breath and schooled her features. When she touched the screen, Leah Woodward's face appeared.

"Leah. It's good to see you, but your call has come at a bad time," Gaschel said in rough English.

"I saw," the branch manager said in her correct but awkwardly-accented Parisien French. "I realize your teams are busy. Our mapping satellites use cloud-penetrating radar. Can I offer you extra sets of eyes?"

Gaschel's face was stiff, but polite. Tétreau had heard from Dauzat that Gaschel had never liked the idea of Bank owned and run satellites. She had little confidence in the Bank of Pallas's charity or interest in scientific mapping. But *la colonie* hadn't paid for the satellites, and they provided global positioning for the entire planet.

"That would be very helpful," Gaschel responded, still in English. "Perhaps I could send over Laurent Tétreau to liaise with you? He's an aide to *l'Assemblée*."

"I'll wait for him in the branch office," Woodward said, finally switching back to English.

"Thank you, Leah."

"We'll save the *Causapscal-des-Vents*."

Gaschel nodded to the screen and terminated the call. Her face hardened.

"She's probably counting our losses now," she said. "If we lose the *Causapscal-des-Vents* on top of everything, Woodward will have us in a corner."

SIXTY-ONE

ÉMILE STOOD ON the envelope of the *Causapscal-des-Vents*. He bent his knees, rolling with the uneven descent. He hadn't been this deep in years, since he'd left home. The heat pressing against him made him feel young again, excited, uncertain, strong, and fearful. The world had been hitting him in the heart for so long that the prospect of hiding in the depths had its charms. He wanted to see Jean-Eudes and Alexis. And Pascal.

And he wanted to see this project. This bridge to the stars they'd found. What was it? Some truth that might finally make them whole? The word to bring Venus to life? Those were not exactly his goals. Or were they? Had he, despite being dumped by Thérèse, learned something important from her, that still stuck in his heart?

He struggled with the feelings, tried to sort them into different piles. Words needed walls to distinguish one experience from another. That was fine for cups and plates but wasn't the way feelings worked. Feelings

511

throbbed like clouds, powerful, shapeless, resenting control or even definition. Clouds could be described by temperature, droplet size, pressure, and acidity, but those numbers got no closer to their essence than words did to emotion.

A rage didn't tower. A loss cast no shadow. A heart couldn't ache.

And yet they did. Words were all he had to touch another heart. Poetry was imprecise imagery, stilted form, artificial resonances, constantly overshooting the essence. It demonstrated, more than anything else, the depths of solitude separating one person from another. He was a brother, a son, and yet he was all alone, riding a piece of metal and plastic into the deeps of a world that didn't want them, chasing his own grail. This was both true image and truth, and yet there was no way to give this to anyone else, no way to share.

The habitat bucked in a cell of warm air. He adjusted the rudder and prop speed. Marthe's radio chatter with Air Traffic Control was good. She was leading them away. He'd shut off everything else that could have given an EM signal. He accessed the habitat's network and activated a small directional dish below the habitat's gondola. He pointed the maser in the general direction of the rendezvous point and pinged with low wattage. He did this in a pattern they'd established beforehand. Four second gap. Six second gap. Two second gap. Moments later a maser touched the dish from below.

Émile? appeared in his helmet.

Oui, he wrote back.

C'est Pascal.

A weird excitement filled him. He wanted to say something to bridge the gulf left over from their last meeting, but he couldn't. If the maser missed and was intercepted by a satellite, the game was over.

The *Causapscal-des-Vents* kept its steady sinking rhythm. The carbon dioxide in its envelope gave it no buoyancy, but its bulk made its terminal velocity in the atmosphere of Venus slow.

Five kilometers vertical, the maser signalled. *Make for heading one-nine-zero and increase speed to four kph.*

D'accord, he answered.

The adjustments were so precise, they had to be coming from Pascal. He wasn't sure what he'd say to Pa when they finally saw each other. Pa wasn't the forgive and forget kind, and neither was Émile. But he was going home. He was going to see his brothers again. Laugh with them.

They really did need an engineer for this. Catching this thing would be a bitch. It didn't matter how much Pascal, Pa, and their partners had planned this out. Catching a habitat in mid-drop in the deep clouds was dangerous. Some of them might get injured or killed. The thought didn't bother him for himself, or even for Pa or Marthe. They were grown adults who'd made their choices and bore their scars.

His suit's water recirc system switched to medium, taking the heat that had penetrated the insulation and running it through a small radiator on his wing-pack. The air outside was sixty degrees and the pressure had risen to almost one atmosphere. It almost felt normal, but not home. At home, he felt the heat and pressure in his bones.

The *Causapscal-des-Vents* was assuming a new aspect. Gone was the shiny, transparent envelope over a metal gondola, filled with green plants, reflecting bright sunlight as it sailed above an endless sea of clouds with a fleet of ships that never touched Venus. Acid droplets etched the envelope, clouding it like cataracts. To approach Venus, even just her cloudy skirts, one left beauty behind, rendered it to Venus like a sacrifice. Some sacrifices were just scars, Venus marking her territory. Other communions with Venus cost everything, as they had with Chloé, Mathurin, and *maman*.

The *Causapscal-des-Vents* was no longer of the high winds. She would never be shiny again, nor even elegant, and she'd never been beautiful. Veiling the *Causapscal-des-Vents* in the ghoulish detritus of Venusian life prepared her for a primal sacrifice. Sacrifices were all bargains with gods. Shaman-like, Thérèse had sought the way to Venus's soul, failing over and over. She'd marked her body, breathed Venus's air, looked upon her directly. Émile was no ancient priest or shaman, but here he was, a supplicant offering in Venus's name, giving away one of their homes like a fatted bull, festooned in the fetishes of the goddess whose favor they sought. He was returning to the underworld he'd escaped in an effort to lift his family to the stars.

The habitat shifted under him. Clouds rose all around, a counter-intuitive, magical image like gravity in reverse or entropy in retreat, something that couldn't be felt in a quick parachute or on a speeding wing-pack. In this pilgrimage, the rules of the world were reversed.

He found his cheeks were wet. He'd offered to take Thérèse to the depths. They could have made a home in the depths. They could have borrowed a habitat, and lived like Pa, Émile teaching Thérèse how to live like a *coureur* until they could trade enough to buy their own habitat. Or they could have learned how to grow their own habitats to trade to others. They could have kissed the real, savage scars they would have collected. The tears tickled, but he couldn't wipe them away. This was his offering to Venus: the hopes he'd had with Thérèse, his dreaming futures.

The pelting sulfuric acid relented. The clouds flexed with the pressure changes, then thinned and released him into the somber cavern of *Les Plaines*. The impression of vastness was overpowering, even more than when there was nothing above him but stars. He clung to a rope, peering over the fat, round edge of the envelope. Sulfuric acid dripped from the curtain of debris the *Causapscal-des-Vents* wore. The habitat was sinking fast. The tops of the browned clouds rose, swallowing him in a hotter rain.

Three kilometers vertical, Pascal signalled again by maser. *Make for two-zero-zero and increase speed to six kph.*

How far off course were they? After all this, were they going to miss? Winds were fickle, changing at different levels, rolling and twisting, following an aerial topography of pressure and temperature. Pa said you never knew what the winds above and below you were doing, only the winds you were in. Émile revved the props and adjusted the heading. Then he opened the top hatches and tied the emergency balloons to the cleats along the middle of the envelope's back. The plan was to blow them all to slow the descent as soon as they got close, but it was going to be touchy. It would take all of them to catch the *Causapscal-des-Vents*.

Marthe's chatter with *Baie-Comeau* was sounding real. A little too real. How good an actress was she? He switched to the encrypted private channel the two of them used for *Causapscal-des-Vents*.

"*C'est beau,* Marthe?"

She didn't answer for many seconds. Then *Baie-Comeau* warned about the storm. He was Venusian enough to know that a tower from fifty-third to fifty-eighth was no joke.

Ostie! He knew he should have been the one to lead the wild goose chase with the clumsy wing. Then Marthe would have been the one to work closely with Pa and Pascal to catch the habitat. It wouldn't have mattered if he'd been the one in danger.

But he couldn't have. Marthe was right. Too many people thought he was a fuck-up. They'd blame the loss of the *Causapscal-des-Vents* on him, rather than chalking it up to an accident brought on by too little maintenance support. Marthe was a thorn in the side of the government, but no one thought she was lazy. She was out there now because of him. And she still hadn't answered.

"Marthe! *Ça va?*" he said.

"I'm here," her voice crackled.

"*Correcte?*"

"No," she answered weakly, sounding far away. "Wings busted. I think I broke a shoulder. I'm on an emergency balloon. I patched a crack in my faceplate, though, so I'm okay."

She wasn't okay. That was the opposite of okay. An emergency balloon would carry her up to fifty-eighth or fifty-ninth, but it was less than even odds whether it would carry her safely through the turbulence of the *Les Rapides Plats*. Which meant that the flotilla would have to work hard not to be carried farther and farther from her in the high, fast winds. And personal balloons weren't storm-worthy.

"I'm on my way," he said.

"*Non!* Mind the *Causapscal-des-Vents!*"

Émile had a fair sense of where Pa and Pascal were waiting, from the course they'd laid out for him. He switched channels and sent a message down on low wattage.

Pascal. Take over for me. I'm going to help Marthe.

Émile checked the straps on his wing-pack. He was wearing his stubby-winged, low-atmosphere pack because the force of hot, high-pressure winds would have bent or ripped the wings used at sixty-fifth. The stubby wings would get him to Marthe but would be useless for high-atmosphere flying.

We're not ready, Pascal wrote back.

Émile pulled out a spare personal balloon and checked

his pockets for his patch kit. He had a worn kit made for fabric. The time it would take to dig something out for the glass of the faceplate wasn't something he wanted to risk. And glass could only take so much patching. He wasn't so worried about her faceplate in the depths. Leaks would bring in a bit of acid, but she'd still be able to breathe. When they got higher, though, her air would leak out into the low pressure of the upper atmosphere and she'd asphyxiate.

Deal with it, he sent back to Pascal. *Leaving now.*

He abandoned his sacrifice to Venus and throttled the engine of his wing-pack to a high whine.

SIXTY-TWO

TÉTREAU HAD BEEN aboard the Venusian Branch of the Bank of Pallas before, but never past the glass doors into Woodward's offices. Woodward's title, Branch Manager, was deceptive. The laws of the Earth didn't work in the solar system; the distances were too great. A person could be charged with a crime, but if he was on the other side of the solar system from Earth and couldn't be investigated—much less apprehended—for two or three years, in what sense were laws enforceable?

Banks like the Lunar Bank, the Bank of Ceres, the Bank of Enceladus, and the Bank of Pallas, already major financial and industrial powers, had emerged in that legal vacuum. They'd incorporated in space, under the jurisdiction of no country, creating their own laws even as they financed the growth of nations into space. They engaged in transport and trade, and even made and enforced law, much like the Hudson's Bay Company founded to service early Canadian *coureurs de bois*.

As Branch Manager, Woodward exercised the Bank's authority on Venus, backed by the financial, trading, and even police powers of a solar-system-spanning company.

The glass doors slid open. A financial secretary, Amélie d'Argenson, escorted him past Woodward's office to a room neatly labelled Mapping Survey Office in English. Miss Woodward was already there, with a meteorologist Tétreau recognized as Mark Nasmith, one of the imported Bank staff.

The wall screens projected a dizzying array of data. Several side screens, each a meter square, showed polar maps in false color at exquisite resolution. Mineral maps. The central screens had parallel views of low-wavelength radar images of clouds, along with fuzzy, largely empty images of the cloud columns.

"Good afternoon, *Monsieur* Tétreau," Woodward said in English, offering a hand.

He felt a bit baffled by all he saw as he shook her hand. What were they doing with such detailed mineral maps? Most of Venus's surface was basaltic, old magma, with the metals buried far below. Did the Bank have tech to exploit the surface?

"Do you know a lot about mapping technology, *Monsieur* Tétreau?"

He shook his head.

Nasmith pointed at the topology of the cloud surface in one image.

"Here we shoot high-frequency radar at the clouds," he said. "Great for watching cloud formations and trying to figure out how weather works on Venus. Most of your habitats have something like this, but this is a bird's eye view."

Tétreau had never seen a bird, and found this English expression odd.

Nasmith's finger pointed to the surface maps.

"If we go with longer radar waves, we can see through the clouds to map the radar reflectivity and smoothness of the surface, but our resolution goes down," he said.

Tétreau had never made the intuitive leap that would allow him to interpret radar maps without effort. Smooth flat things reflected radar and so they were bright. Rough things and slopes reflected radar poorly and so were darker. A contour map could be built of radar maps, but not by him; too abstract.

Nasmith was shifting the view, neither fully long-wave nor short-wave. Fuzzy blobs formed in the projection. They looked like out-of-focus cells seen through a microscope. Tétreau squinted.

"Focusing the radar emissions differently, we can resolve things in the clouds," Nasmith said. "These are probably trawlers. Their surfaces are partly smooth and partly rough depending on how much they've been colonized by epiphytes. Here you've got some small wildtype ones and some bigger engineered ones, or several in a column, but at different altitudes. But here," he said, pointing at the bright spot, "is the *Causapscal-des-Vents.*"

The hard white blob was falling further and further behind the flotilla, and it was already deep, at the edge of a storm.

"The transceiver from the habitat doesn't look like it's working, so we've confirmed this is the *Causapscal-des-Vents* with D'Aquillon's transceiver."

"Missing parts," Tétreau said absently. "What are these?" He indicated small bright shapes.

"Your crew planes. The fainter ones are rescue drones," Woodward said. "They're following the transceiver signal and using their own cloud-penetrating radar, but the resolution might be lower."

"We can triangulate with this signal," Tétreau said.

"Please do," Woodward said.

Tétreau called Air Traffic Control from the Bank and began reading them coordinates for the *Causapscal-des-Vents*.

"Thank you for letting us access this," he said. "We're very concerned with the safety and property of those living on the *Causapscal-des-Vents*. Additionally, the habitat was... is," Woodward corrected herself, "collateral for a loan. Should it not be rescued, some other material goods will have to become collateral, or the *colonie* will be in breach of the terms of its debt."

She said it evenly, neither harshly nor softly, but Tétreau didn't mistake the intent of her words. Nasmith gave Tétreau comms access at the next work station. He had access to the common band and the encrypted channel the searchers were using for the radiation search. He hadn't realized that Gaschel had shared that with the Bank.

"Control, *Les Plaines* is collapsing," one of the pilots declared on the radio. "We can't get around the storm, or under it. Do you want us to come back?"

"Negative, rescue team," control replied amid the static. "Keep going."

"Roger, control," came the resigned reply.

"Control, this is one-five-six. I've got a signal!" a pilot said in the encrypted channel. "Straight under my position. It's faint."

Woodward lifted one questioning eyebrow, observing him.

"Start pinging, one-five-six, and start diving," control said. "One-hundred-level units, converge on one-five-six and start triangulating. Two-hundred-level units, stay on search and rescue."

"One-five-six is a good constable," Tétreau said.

"*Câlisse*," one-five-six said. "Okay."

SIXTY-THREE

MARTHE'S MOUTH WAS dry. She'd blacked out. The world seemed to happen fast, and yet time also stood still. The storm played with her, and the world moved, yet nothing changed. Clouds surrounded her. Hot rain pelted. Heat pressed suit to skin. They all blended into a confusing set of feelings and images without order.

Bright red smeared the inside of her faceplate. Her own blood. Acid bubbled at the cracks. That meant she was sinking. She was so hot. The worn plastic straw gave only air when she sucked. No water. Her head ached. And her shoulder. With her good hand, she slowly pulled the acid-resistant tarp out of a pocket and gingerly unfolded it, using her injured shoulder as little as possible. One-handed, she clipped it above her on the balloon cable and tried to extend it over herself. By this time her head was pounding so hard that blotches of black floated in her vision, the rain pattered onto the tarp and not her helmet, torso and arms. The rain washed over her dangling legs, but nothing was to be done for it. She couldn't make her shoulder do more.

She woke again. The rain had stopped. She didn't know when she'd passed out, or for how long. The readings in her helmet were weird: temperature way up, close to a hundred, but pressure way down. Her barometer was broken.

Thunder rolled in the formless world outside, strong enough to rattle her bones and set her head to aching harder.

Edging close to a hundred degrees; that put her almost at the bottom of the lower cloud deck, just above the sub-cloud haze. Her safety balloon must be leaking. She moved the tarp out of the way and looked up, making her head throb so hard that she nearly passed out again. She couldn't reach the balloon to patch or refill it. And the gauge on her oxygen tank wasn't healthy. She had a couple of hours. Maybe less. At least Venus was leaking *into* her helmet rather than the reverse.

The clouds still had shape, were still made of tiny droplets of sulfuric acid floating in the air, so she floated above the virga zone, but this wasn't good. She tried activating her radio. She couldn't tell if it was on. The HUD was buggy.

"This is Marthe D'Aquillon," she said, "calling anyone. SOS. Severe distress. Equipment failing. I think I'm at about forty-ninth *rang*, maybe deeper. Can't fly. Safety balloon failing. Injured. Please respond."

She said this four more times before her HUD gave out. She couldn't tell if the helmet's CPU was working, but just not displaying. Acid might have gotten into the projector, or, more dangerously, beneath the seals and into the CPU, wiring or battery.

She couldn't talk anymore anyway. Breathing was hard, raspy, and for a time, her forehead pressed against the faceplate of her helmet. She only came to properly when it felt like her forehead was burning.

Marthe couldn't see any way out. She couldn't use political cleverness here, no cunning survival maneuvers from the sunlit world or from the *coureurs* to get her out of this. Sometimes Venus just caught up to the slowest gazelle and pounced. Despite all the respect with which they treated their new world, her jaws sometimes snapped shut.

Maman hadn't died like this. She'd died at home, surrounded by crying children, a loving husband. No one knew how Chloé had died. Marthe hoped she'd at least been with Mathurin.

Marthe didn't want to die, but maybe it was easier like this. She was probably concussed, passing in and out of consciousness, unable to raise the panic that came before death. Her head hurt so badly she felt like she was going to throw up. She breathed the stifling air with eyes closed until the feeling retreated. She would hold on, until she passed out for the last time. She hoped it was painless.

She hoped her new family was happy. Marie-Pier and Gabriel-Antoine deserved it. She hoped Alexis grew up smart and strong and happy. She'd hugged him hard on her last visit. She hoped he never forgot how much she loved him. She'd made peace with Émile, as much peace as they could make. *Peace, brother.* And she wished Pa some kind of peace. He'd tried so hard to give them what they needed. He'd succeeded and they'd grown up all right, but losing her would kill him. *Let me go, Pa.* And she wished Pascale all that she wanted and needed. Pascale had the hardest path in front of her. *Goodbye, little sister.*

Blotches of black swam in front of the vision of plastic and cloud beneath her. She rested her head against the padded sides of the helmet. She needed water. So hot. She needed rest. For a little while.

SIXTY-FOUR

"ÉMILE WENT WHERE?" George-Étienne demanded.

Pascale stood on one of Marie-Pier's trawlers. It was bigger than their habitat, with two layers, the inner of which would be capable of maintaining a pressure of just one atmosphere and a livable temperature of about twenty-five, even at the bottom of the sub-cloud haze. Pa, Marie-Pier and Gabriel-Antoine were with her.

"I don't know, Pa," Pascale said.

"*Crisse*," George-Étienne said.

The clouds of forty-eighth *rang* drifted around them and Marie-Pier's deep habitats arrayed under them.

"We've got no one on the *Causapscal-des-Vents*," Pascale said.

Why was Émile going to Marthe? Pascale wanted to go too. But if Marthe had followed the plan, she might be as much as thirty kilometers northwest and ten kilometers higher. Whatever was wrong, Émile was closer. Who would go to the habitat?

"I'll go," Pascale said.

"I'll go with you," Gabriel-Antoine said, smiling behind his faceplate.

"I will," George-Étienne insisted.

"You're a better flyer down here," Gabriel-Antoine said, "better than me or Marie-Pier. And I know habitats."

Pa looked like he wanted to object, but finally pressed his lips tight. "We'll get ready here to catch the damn thing," he said finally.

Pascale scanned the area quickly, trying to think of what she'd need. They'd accomplished a lot in the days of sweating and dehydration and sleep deprivation. The hard part had been building a square frame with a hollow ring at each corner big enough to fit a trawler, and then to put the four trawlers into place. Pa had broken a finger, Gabriel-Antoine had ripped his suit and gotten a nasty chemical burn on one arm, and Marie-Pier had been knocked off a trawler and caught by her harness. Pascale had avoided injury, even though she was distracted by the world opening up for her. Now the trawlers creaked in the harnesses against cross-winds, like them, waiting to start.

It wasn't just the possibility of going to the surface and reaching the stars that gave Pascale hope. Marie-Pier had brought down two small packets of pills in a thermos case. She'd pulled Pascale aside and switched to a private channel and told her what they were. Elation and terror swelled in her chest.

Yet there was nothing hopeful or safe about what would come next. Causing two floating objects to intercept in the immensity of the clouds was phenomenally difficult, and usually wasn't attempted because of the danger of collisions. Most of the time, a wing-pack, airplane or drone did all the moving, treating both habitats as stationary objects. When the *coureur* habitats wanted to approach each other, they would match altitude first, which meant neutralizing wind speed and direction, before using propellers to approach. The problem here was that the *Causapscal-des-Vents* wasn't meant to be at this altitude at all, and once the descent had begun, it sank unstoppably. Its steep descent angle helped evade detection, but if they missed the catch, the *Causapscal-des-Vents* would just keep falling.

Gabriel-Antoine touched Pascale's arm. The touch was hot. Everything was hot. Her suit's refrigeration system was working hard, but spots of forty or fifty degrees just had to be taken in stride. "Everything we need will be on the habitat," Gabriel-Antoine said.

"*Oui,*" Pascale said.

"*Bonne chance, mon cher,*" George-Étienne said.

The *mon cher* gave her a twinge. Pa called Marthe *ma chère*. Pascale hadn't told Pa anything yet. Or Gabriel-Antoine. She wasn't sure of anything. No, that wasn't true. Some inner realization had clicked, like something that had been missing all her life, the puzzle piece that would make everything make sense. She didn't know how to tell anyone. She felt brittle, like the least anger or rejection would crush the fragile understanding she had of herself.

"*Merci,* Pa," she said.

She stepped away from them, unfurled her wings, spun up her engine and leapt from the top of the trawler. She accelerated and climbed. She didn't throttle up all the way yet. She looked back for Gabriel-Antoine. He flew well in the lower decks, cute in his occasional struggling. He climbed behind her. They were close enough that low-watt radio bursts, squawks not strong enough to leave the clouds, would start to trigger a low-energy homing beacon in the *Causapscal-des-Vents*, two kilometers higher. If not for smothering clouds, they would already see it. Pascale had a brief urge to tease Gabriel-Antoine, but she was too nervous about everything else going on. She revved her droning engine louder and rose.

The *Causapscal-des-Vents* emerged from a dark cloud bank pregnant with rain, descending like a bloated caricature of a habitat, covered with stringy black cables and bits of old trawler husk, dripping fat drops that refracted dull light. It was ugly. It had never been beautiful, but it was particularly ugly now, masked, almost like a spiny cocoon to protect its transformation from one form to another. Pascale climbed, banked, and flared just as she crested the roof of the habitat, landing with a little hop. She turned immediately, stepping back to help Gabriel-Antoine land. In seconds, he looped in slower; unpracticed at making a pinpoint landing with these wing-packs at this pressure. He stumbled, but didn't fall. Pascale steadied him and he smiled at her behind his faceplate. Émile had already tied three of six emergency balloons to the roof cleats. Two others were wound with their cables in the storage bin that he'd left open.

"We can already blow the first and last," Gabriel-Antoine said, pointing at the balloon lying flaccid at the sternmost cleat. He headed to the bow cleat. Pascale connected an oxygen hose to the balloon.

"Ready?" she said.

"*Vas-y!*" Gabriel-Antoine crackled in the radio.

They both turned the valves. Oxygen rushed into the balloons, immediately lifting them from the deck. The cabling was only about two meters long, so Pascale could stand under the distending balloon, and extricate the hose when it was full. The next sternmost cleat was tied to a balloon, but Gabriel-Antoine's corresponding one wasn't. His fingers moved quickly in thick gloves. Pascale accessed the habitat's systems, initiating the sequences to close all the openings in the envelope and start draining carbon dioxide from the cells, replacing it with oxygen.

"*Prêt!*" Gabriel-Antoine called.

Pascale cast a quick verifying glance back. Gabriel-Antoine had done so as well. They didn't trust each other enough yet not to double-check. Pascale cranked the oxygen feed and her balloon inflated, joining the first, bouncing lightly. The roof of the *Causapscal-des-Vents* groaned. The big emergency balloons weren't made to do more than slow a habitat's descent, to get families and equipment out, or maybe hold it up enough for a better rescue operation.

The balloons strained the frame. They could still lose the *Causapscal-des-Vents*, and the ugly home would tumble all the way to the surface, leaving its transformation stillborn.

They repeated the process for the next two emergency balloons. It didn't feel like the *Causapscal-des-Vents* had slowed, and it would be ten to fifteen minutes of pumping until enough of the envelope was filled with oxygen to make a difference. But it was doing something. Math said it had to. The single middle cleat, with three balloons on each side of it, was empty, ready to be attached to the cable connecting to the floating harness.

Are we close, Pa? Pascale sent.

We're driving towards you, Pa wrote back. *About six hundred meters vertical to go, but you're coming down fast.*

What's the horizontal? Pascale asked.

"*Calvaire!*" came through the helmet speakers. They were close enough for their low-wattage voice transmissions to make it. "You're too low!"

Pascale spun up her wing-pack and leapt from the roof of the *Causapscal-des-Vents*. Hazy below them, the four trawlers floated in their harness. They were too far. The cable wouldn't reach. She banked. The props beneath the *Causapscal-des-Vents* churned at full speed. There was no more throttle to give.

They would miss by just a bit. A hundred meters. But they would miss. It was the winds, the stupid, always-shifting winds.

"Pa! Get ready with the cable!"

She wasn't going to let them miss it. They weren't going to lose the stars, the true Venus.

"I'm ready!" he said. "Can you get her closer?"

Pascale revved her engine hard, swooped up, and then

cut it. Her momentum carried her to an apex just over the roof and she landed between the taut cables holding two balloons.

"What are we doing?" Gabriel-Antoine said.

Pascale looked through one of the lockers and heaved a coil of cabling so hard she fell back. Both ends had tough carbon nanofiber hooks. She shoved one end at Gabriel-Antoine.

"Hook this into the main cleat and make sure it doesn't come out."

"What are you doing?" he demanded again, even as he helped her make sure the cable wasn't tangled.

"We need more line."

"You can't reach the frame from here with that."

"I can reach Pa with it," she said, dragging the coils to where the envelope began to curve steeply.

"What are you talking about?" he said. "You can't meet someone in mid-air."

"Fly with the cable, Pa!" Pascale said. "We have to meet in the middle."

"*Ostie,*" was the only thing that Pa grunted back.

"But..." Gabriel-Antoine said.

"Don't let that hook loose!" Pascale said.

She leapt into space, holding the other hook with two hands. The cable was heavy and even as she throttled up, the weight dragged her Venus-ward. Her wing-pack engine howled, a long high alarmed note, and her suit began to feel hotter. When the engine ran hot, it did a worse job at transferring heat to the radiators. This was going to be tough. Pa was already in the air, about a hundred meters below her. His cable bowed downward, his own wing-pack barely holding him and the cable up.

But Pa had read her mind, her crazy plan. He flew with his hook before him too. Now that they were within sight of the stationary harness and four trawlers, it was clear that the *Causapscal-des-Vents* was sinking faster than they'd planned, even with everything inflated.

Pascale banked left and right, snaking as she approached him, the weight of the cable pulling her back more and more. She flew at the edge of stalling even at full throttle.

"This is crazy, Pascal!" Gabriel-Antoine called. "Even if you're close, you'll collide!"

She ignored him.

"Pa!" she said. "Fly straight at me, full thrust. We have to stall right at the same time, right in front of each other!"

She didn't know what Pa was thinking. Whether it was right or wrong. But he trusted her. Or he was just as crazy. Or maybe he needed this. Maybe the Axis Mundi to the stars would give some meaning to all he'd lost. Venus owed him. He just needed to collect.

The shriek of her engine felt like it was burning behind her. The *Causapscal-des-Vents* was nearly level with the floating frame. Pa was coming at her just as hard, dragging his heavy cable. Twenty meters. Ten. Five.

They both pulled up at the same time, but they were so heavy, they stalled early, and they were falling, together. Pascale dipped forward, revving to recover from the stall. She grabbed Pa's hook and yanked it closer to hers.

Falling as he was, Pa nonetheless also got a grip on both

and pulled them closer. Almost there. Muscles strained as the pull of each cable became irresistible.

The tip of one hook was against the concave top of the other. And they still fell, engines screaming, bodies straining.

Then suddenly, the hooks found each other, just as Pa snapped his fingers out of the way. The immediate tension on the cable whipped it out of their hands, flinging them spinning into the air. Cables and metal and carbon struts creaked warningly, an alien sound in the clouds.

She spread her legs, head down, pointing her hands to get control again. With unnatural speed for its size, the *Causapscal-des-Vents* swung beneath her, right into her dive path. If she hadn't been so terrified, the image of Gabriel-Antoine bracing himself on the envelope, looking up at her in astonishment, would have been comical.

Pascale's engine bit at the clouds. She pulled up and swooped out of the way. Pa flew counter-clockwise as well, rising on the winds, on the opposite side of the float frame.

No. He wasn't rising. The float frame was sinking.

Marie-Pier was scrambling across the shaking frame, quickly turning valves to pump oxygen out of the woody bulbs of the trawlers. They were filled with oxygen, which gave them enough buoyancy, but in extremis in the depths, they could lower the pressure inside their buoyancy chambers, giving them additional lift. Marie-Pier sped the process along with mechanical pumps.

The *Causapscal-des-Vents* swung pendulum-like, dragging the float frame down into a bank of clouds which rained on them and cut their visibility. They were at forty-ninth now, almost home for Pascale and Pa.

"Gabriel-Antoine, check all the cleats and the structural stability on the envelope," she said. "And get ready to get out of there in a hurry if something goes wrong. Pa, check on the cable mounting on the frame. I'm going to check along the cable."

She swept upward, around the sinking frame. She couldn't get too close because the four bobs from the four trawlers hung there. A collision would smash her helmet and cook her instantly. She banked tightly, circling the cable over and over, shining her light down its length, looking for fraying. She turned more tightly where the two hooks held tight to one another. They looked ok.

She followed the cable down and landed on the roof of the habitat. The *Causapscal-des-Vents* creaked ominously. It didn't like this depth. Too hot for it. Too crushing. She checked all the cleats that Gabriel-Antoine had already checked. He was below decks, just coming up the envelope stairway.

"It's holding," he said.

He was sweating in his helmet. So was she. He came close and pressed his faceplate against hers.

"I can't believe what you did!" he yelled, not transmitting by radio. His voice was both distant, muffled by two helmets, and amplified by the high temperature down here. It existed in multiple places, like her emotions. His face was admiring and stormy with anger. "You were so brave! But you could have been killed!"

Pascale didn't know if she was blushing. Her suit's

cooling system was working on a deficit. Sulfuric acid rained on them, like a spring shower. She wiped his faceplate clear with her glove. It seemed a very intimate gesture, like preening, and he did the same to hers.

"If we weren't trapped in these things, I would kiss you!" he yelled.

"I would let you," she laughed.

"You're not like anybody I've ever met."

She felt like crumpling at the heart-squeezing happiness and the heart-stabbing irony.

The *Causapscal-des-Vents* sank more slowly now, the cable groaning with geriatric protest. Hot clouds rose magically around them.

"This cable will only hold so long," Pascale said, looking up.

The frame they'd built to harness the four trawlers was holding. The habitat hung from the x-shaped cross-struts a hundred and fifty meters above. The weighted ends of the trawler plumb lines swung pendulously in the wind. They weren't in resonance, which they'd worried might be dangerous enough to rip the frame apart.

"We're going to need a lot more cable to bridge this," Gabriel-Antoine said, "or we're going to have to winch the *Causapscal-des-Vents* higher."

"I'll get the winch ready with Pa and bring down a second cable. You get the balloons deflated before stray radar recognizes us!" she said.

She leapt from the roof of the habitat, flying up, her wing-pack engine whirring. Gabriel-Antoine followed. The plumb lines under the trawlers were acting funny.

They bowed gently outward, all of them. There was no resonance with the wind to do that. She circled, climbing. Her suit had a crude voltmeter that normally showed electrical fields when they flew around trawler plumb lines. The cables bridged slightly different levels of the clouds, turning static into current, but they were variably conductive. If not, a lightning strike would blow out the biological capacitors in the trawlers. And Marie-Pier had already turned the conductance of these cables off.

"I think the plumb lines are live!" Pascale said. If they were conducting, that was trouble.

Everyone was on a different trawler head, checking the ties on different equipment. Marie-Pier pulled out a better voltmeter and began checking as Pascale flew close over the frame.

Above the x-cross where the habitat was attached, a bright blue arc of electricity leapt four meters to shock her. Pascale's body seized, and she dipped and glided down between the struts before the arc let her go. Black crawled inwards from edges of her vision and her muscles continued to tremble, but she managed to pull up and crash on top of the nearest trawler head, where Marie-Pier kept her from falling over the edge. Then dizzy black loomed over her vision like a storm cloud.

SIXTY-FIVE

GEORGE-ÉTIENNE LANDED BESIDE Pascale just as Gabriel-Antoine did. A stripe of black lined the front of Pascale's suit from shoulder to knee. Pascale was moving sluggishly as George-Étienne prodded at the burn mark.

"What are you doing?" Gabriel-Antoine demanded stridently beside him.

"Quiet!" George-Étienne said. He continued probing with his fingers, feeling for crackling, listening for crunching over the patter of raining sulfuric acid.

"We need to get him inside somewhere," Gabriel-Antoine said.

"Make a shelter here," George-Étienne said. Without stopping his probing of the suit, he opened a pocket of Pascale's suit and pulled out a silvery acid-proof sheet.

"We have to take him somewhere!"

"*Non,*" George-Étienne said. "We have to finish checking to see if his suit is breached. If it is, at this depth, acid and heat will get in and cook him."

Gabriel-Antoine looked stupid for a moment, processing everything. He was pretty dumb for a smart guy. Marie-Pier took the sheet out of Gabriel-Antoine's hands and laid it over Pascal's legs where George-Étienne had already checked.

"To be sure, apply some base," George-Étienne said.

This time, Gabriel-Antoine reacted with more self-possession. He pulled out his own neutralizing paste and dabbed it along the burn mark on the suit. George-Étienne got to Pascal's shoulder.

"*Pas mal, mon p'tit gars,*" he said. "You were lucky."

Pascale weakly held up a thumb.

"*Reste içi,*" George-Étienne said.

He stood. He and Marie-Pier looked down on the *Causapscal-des-Vents,* swaying gently in the breeze at the bottom of the cable. The plumb lines from the four trawlers holding it up bowed outward noticeably.

"What's going wrong?" he said.

"The plumb lines are conducting," Marie-Pier said. "They shouldn't be. They should be in their non-conductive state right now. They're not; they're conducting enough to make magnetic fields to repel each other."

The inside of her helmet was so bright with heads-up displays that her frown was apparent.

"My diagnostics say the plumb lines should be off," she said. "I don't know what's causing this."

Gabriel-Antoine was behind them.

"It's the middle cable, the one holding up the *Causapscal-des-Vents,*" he said. "It's longer than we intended, so it's connecting clouds across a greater distance. It's conducting, either inside, or along the rain on the outside, and it's probably inducing a current along the plumb lines."

George-Étienne nearly whistled appreciatively. "Is that right?"

"*Ciboire,*" Marie-Pier said. "Maybe."

They'd done it. Against all odds, they'd sunk it and caught it in mid-fall. But if the cable holding up the *Causapscal-des-Vents* had started building a charge, they were in a lot of danger unless they could put that charge somewhere. Healthy trawlers stored excess charge in electroplaques, and then shut off their conductance. Now, they could build up enough charge to induce lightning from the clouds. Or burn themselves out.

SIXTY-SIX

ÉMILE WINGED NORTHEAST at full throttle. He was probably still twelve kilometers from Marthe, and even once he got close, he'd still need to find her in the air column. He didn't hear anything from Pascal behind him. The radio crackled ominously ahead, synchronized with brilliant flashes smothered behind layers of ocher cloud.

He was already at forty-sixth *rang*, but picked up airspeed by angling into a long descent. Gravity sped him, moving him to a slower layer of winds. Fat drops pelted him, knocking loudly on the crown of his helmet and shrinking visibility to a few hundred meters. Chaotic gusts became violent and a crack of lightning lit the world bright yellow. Deep, bone-vibrating sound reached him nearly at the same time as the blinding light. He was wrenched a hundred meters higher and then plunged down two hundred meters, as if the storm wanted to shake him to death. His upper-deck wings would have snapped long ago. Even the stubby *coureur* wings strained. The

545

coureurs avoided storms.

Smart *coureurs,* anyway. No one had ever called him smart.

"Marthe!" he called. "Marthe!"

The static in his helmet was dialed painfully loud, but he didn't hear an answer.

An updraft hit him like a fist, stalling his lift, flipping him onto his back and into a tumble. He fell half a kilometer before he could level out in the punishing turbulence. He couldn't remember the last time he'd been in a storm like this. He was a bit scared. This really might be it.

Something clenched his heart too. Not his own end. He was thinking about Chloé. She and Mathurin had vanished in a storm. He'd loved his little sister. She'd been romantic, dreamy, a good mother, a forgiving sister, and too young to die. And she'd only died because Venus had been in a mood that day. Venus didn't care who her victims were. She *couldn't* care who they were.

Les colonistes made of Venus a hungry and capricious goddess, because their minds were wired to find intent in the world. They looked for meaning because they had none. Thérèse dug for meaning with all her heart. And what did he do? Did he really sacrifice at Venus's altar? He hadn't sacrificed anything that was his own. He'd lost his sister, his mother and in some ways his girlfriend, but those weren't his sacrifices. He'd helped drop the *Causapscal-des-Vents* into the clouds, but he'd not yet given anything that was his.

An updraft grabbed him, throwing him upward so fast that breath left him, and the vibration of his wings straining in their mountings went straight into his bones. Venus threw him high, so high that he met another wind going in another direction that plowed him downward. He climbed into a slower-moving pocket of air and turned east again. After the pounding, the moderate rain gentled. This might be it. Really it. He might go not as a willing sacrifice to Venus, but as just another of her murder victims.

"Marthe! Marthe!" he called.

In the distance of static, he heard a voice talking. *Baie-Comeau* control on the common channel, so swamped that he couldn't make out the words.

"Marthe!" he called.

His battery level was starting to worry him, but he kept climbing. He was getting close to her last coordinates. From here, the storm could have thrown her in any direction at any speed, with her emergency balloon and cracked helmet.

Every suit had an emergency beacon, and a weaker one on the balloon, but he couldn't hear hers. If her balloon had endured so far, she'd be somewhere between fifty-third and fifty-eighth *rangs*. Big range. And if her balloon had burst, or even just been leaking, she'd be below fiftieth *rang*. Ambient pressure told him he was at forty-eighth *rang*, but GPS put him at fifty-second.

Up or down?

"Marthe!"

A very faint ping sounded in the static. His suit had heard it, at the edge of detection. Down.

Émile jack-knifed and dove. The wind rushed past, the rain flying upwards, receding above him, nature running in reverse, time flowing backwards. He was descending into Venus, becoming more primitive. In his heart, he offered himself for Marthe. All of them—Pascal, Jean-Eudes, Alexis and Pa—needed her. He did too. And he was willing to bargain with a goddess for Marthe, no different from any hunter burning animal remains to the gods fifty thousand years ago.

The ping became louder, enough that his helmet began to resolve its location. Forty-seventh *rang*, about five kilometers east. Below the storm, and twenty kilometers below safety. She'd somehow dropped so low that she'd gone beneath him. She was at the limit of the zone where her emergency balloon could function. And to have gotten there at all, the storm must not have treated her well.

Droplets of hot sulfuric acid spattered the glass of his faceplate, beading off in the wind. The heat sweltered, pressing his suit hard against his skin, not burning yet, but uncomfortable. He hadn't been this deep in a long time. Then he broke into clearer clouds of smoky brown. There was no more rain, but the light was reddened and scattered, shadowless and coming from all directions. The occasional crash of lightning far above painted lumpy textured shadows onto the clouds.

He passed forty-eighth *rang* before pulling up, circling to home in on her signal.

"Marthe!"

Her signal was stronger. East four hundred meters. Down eight hundred. The clouds finally broke into the trackless uniformity of the sub-cloud haze. This virga zone was the world without definition, the chaos that existed before clouds, before ground, before stars or even storms.

A shape came into blurry view in the distance. A silver-white balloon, half-inflated. Beneath it, on a short cable, hung a body. The nature of the attachment point of the balloon to the wing-pack made it look like someone had been hanged. The silvery sheet hanging over didn't help.

"Marthe!"

He circled, bleeding off airspeed before climbing into a stall with almost no forward speed, right beside her. He grabbed the balloon string with both hands and wrapped his legs around her body. His weight caused them to plunge. But she didn't move.

He furled his wings and activated his emergency balloon. It inflated off the top of his wing-pack, jerking sullenly at him until they stopped descending. Then they hung together in the featureless haze at forty-sixth *rang*.

He pulled another emergency balloon and hooked it onto Marthe's wing-pack. He twisted in the end of a hose, and attached the other end to his oxygen tank, and then blew it. After moments, they began rising, slowly and calmly. He opened a strap on his suit and attached himself to Marthe's wing-pack so they couldn't be separated. Then, hanging there from his own balloon, he pulled up the protective tarp that had been hiding his sister.

Her sweaty forehead was pressed against a bloody spot on the inside of her cracked helmet. Shallow breaths fogged a tiny patch of the glass and her cheeks were pink. He tried patching into her suit to read some of her vitals, but her processor was offline. The radiator on her wing-pack was blistering hot.

If he thought she could go deeper and that they were close enough, he would have brought her to the *Causapscal-des-Profondeurs,* but he didn't trust her suit.

"*Baie-Comeau,* can you read me?" he said.

No response.

Ostie.

With two and a half emergency balloons, they would rise, slowly, over four or five hours. He didn't trust either of their suits for that, nor their oxygen supply. They'd gone too deep to depend too much on balloons. They were below the storm, and it might be moving past them if it was contained enough. Towering storms could be quick hits. Or they could become monsters.

He unfolded his wings and checked the engine readings. He had a third of a charge left on his battery and his coolant system was still okay. And what he was about to do went against every piece of advice any smart person would ever give.

He clung tightly to Marthe and looped the cable he was dangling from round a tie-loop on her wing-pack. Then he carefully popped the attachment on his own wing-pack and brought the end to her pack and tied it firmly. His emergency balloon was now her third balloon. He had no more safety margin. If for any reason his wing-pack failed, he was going to meet Venus up close.

Then he let go and throttled up his engine. Without his weight, Marthe rose fast. He circled her, following her up. Every so often, he flew beneath her, grabbing a trailing cable, yanking her eastward. He needed to get them east of the storm, and higher.

SIXTY-SEVEN

"WE NEED TO stop collecting the charge, or we have to put it somewhere," Marie-Pier repeated to him.

George-Étienne stood with Marie-Pier and Gabriel-Antoine on one of the four trawlers forming the buoyancy frame. The trawler cables bowed out more and more. The charge on the cable holding the *Causapscal-des-Vents* was building.

"The cables aren't designed for that much weight," Marie-Pier said, "and the strength of the cables is weakest in their conducting state."

George-Étienne chewed at the inside of his cheek. Sweat rolled through the stubble on his chin.

"What if we power the *Causapscal-des-Vents* off the charge?" he asked.

"*Oui,*" Gabriel-Antoine said, "but if we run too many things, someone might see it."

"Oxygen," Marie-Pier said. "Use the electricity to crack carbon dioxide to produce oxygen. It takes a lot of power but doesn't have any moving parts. Nothing to make noise or create electrical static."

"The trick will be wiring it up," George-Étienne said. "If we land on the *Causapscal-des-Vents* now, we'll likely get a shock strong enough to knock us out. Any ideas?"

"There's no place for the charge to go right now," Gabriel-Antoine said, "even if we could ground it."

"The other bobs," Marie-Pier said.

"What?"

"The four surrounding trawlers are conducting properly," she said. "Their electroplaques will soak up additional charge."

"To a point," George-Étienne said.

"To a point."

"But by then, one of us could get to the *Causapscal-des-Vents* and run a line from the cable to the electrical system," Gabriel-Antoine said.

"The dangerous part is all of it," Marie-Pier said.

"Are you joking?" George-Étienne asked.

She shook her head. He wasn't sure what to think of her right now. She handed him a coil of cabling and clipped a different one to his chest harness.

"Lower yourself down to the cable on this trawler and tie that around," she said. "Then come back up. I'll do the same on the other three."

"This'll carry a charge?" George-Étienne said dubiously, hefting the coil of cable.

"Enough for now."

"How do we connect it to the central cable holding up the *Causapscal-des-Vents* without electrocuting ourselves?" he asked.

Gabriel-Antoine judged the cable for a few moments and pulled a small steel hammer from his tool pockets. Then he explained. It wasn't the best plan George-Étienne had ever heard, but they were close to losing everything, and he had none of his children around him to help. George-Étienne clambered down the rope and swung on the line until he could grab the trunk of the central cable under this trawler. It was thicker than he was and tingled as he wrapped his legs around it. He moved quickly, tying a loop around it and let go, swinging back out into space before the uncertain currents started seizing up his leg muscles.

Marie-Pier flitted over to the next trawler head like she was born for the depths and George-Étienne felt a weird pride, not through the artificial marriage that they'd made, but from the simple fact that such a competent woman had agreed to partner with him in any sense. He'd spent a lot of his life second-guessing himself. That this dream of his was worth others risking their livelihoods and lives gave him an inner solidity he hadn't felt for a long time.

"And you?" he said, turning to Gabriel-Antoine.

The young engineer was shifting nervously. And he was still just looking down at George-Étienne's youngest child. Gabriel-Antoine faced him, a bit distracted, but after a few moments, he looked up at the clouds that pressed down on them, like he'd just realized he was twenty kilometers from open sky. It took time to adjust to the depths. The sky and stars were far away, but radar and radio made *la colonie* feel far too close sometimes.

"I'm here," Gabriel-Antoine said.

George-Étienne handed him the coil of cabling and then the small hammer which he'd left on top of the trawler head. The younger man tied the cabling around the T of the hammer and tested its weight.

"How are you going to make it hold?" George-Étienne asked.

"It should hold itself," Gabriel-Antoine said, positioning himself for a throw.

Gabriel-Antoine heaved with a loud grunt that sounded through their helmets and through the hot, thick atmosphere. The hammer carried the cabling on a wide arc that swung short of the cable holding up the *Causapscal-des-Vents*. Gabriel-Antoine cursed as he pulled it up. Little arcs of blue electricity licked between it, the side of the trawler, and Gabriel-Antoine's gloves.

Their suits were rubberized as much as Venusian acid and heat chemistry allowed and laced with grounding wires, but they couldn't block more than small charges. If they'd designed the suits to handle the big charges, the suits would be so bulky as to be dangerous or the conduction of electricity would melt parts of the suits, creating new problems. They had to take some small shocks at times to live down here. But the more Gabriel-Antoine pulled up the cabling, the less charge it had left.

The engineer steadied himself as the wind came up and the trawlers lurched unnaturally. A single trawler could ride the wind like a boat on slow ocean waves. But the buoyancy frame they'd made caught the wind in counter-intuitive ways, and the *Causapscal-des-Vents* was a big awkward windbreak right now. George-Étienne's wind legs were not much steadier.

Gabriel-Antoine swung the hammer on the end of the cabling faster and faster and then finally released it with a loud heave. It fell through the air, long and wide. As it came to the end of its length, it swung around, describing an arc that crossed the cable holding up the habitat. A loud snap and a burst of electricity sounded as the cables touched. The hammer orbited the cable in a tightening spiral that ended abruptly when the hammer touched the cable and stuck.

"Woo!" Gabriel-Antoine shouted, pumping the air with his fist. The cable and bob beneath their trawler stopped bowing outward and hung straight, now swinging gently in the wind like a pendulum as it came to a new rest.

"The hammer stuck," George-Étienne said.

"The cable is magnetized for now," Gabriel-Antoine explained.

Marie-Pier had finished tying an extra loop of cabling to the adjacent trawler and was moving to the third. Gabriel-Antoine flew to that trawler while George-Étienne flitted quickly to the last one and did the same. As the grounding cables were tied, he and Gabriel-Antoine heaved them with ferro-magnetic weights, trying to catch the middle cable. It was harder than it looked, and it took them a few tries to loop around the new connections.

"It's not real grounding," Gabriel-Antoine said. "The whole structure of the four trawlers and the habitat is collecting a big static charge as they move through the clouds. But at least everything has the same charge now. We'll still need to discharge it soon, or drain it off."

"Let's drain quick," George-Étienne urged. The dangerous part.

"If I get shocked senseless, you'll catch me," Gabriel-Antoine said to him.

His voice had a tremble of nervousness. No one had ever done this.

"*Bien sûr,*" George-Étienne said.

Gabriel-Antoine flexed his knees a few times, as if working up the courage to jump. Seeing his youngest son laid low, watched over by a young man with tender feelings, made George-Étienne feel his age. Until a few months ago, he would have guessed that his best years were behind him. Not so much now, on the edge of a dream he could give to his children. He put his hand on Gabriel-Antoine's shoulder.

"Go," George-Étienne said, "for the whole family."

Gabriel-Antoine stepped to the edge of the slope. George-Étienne followed, banking wide and staying high so that he could dive after Gabriel-Antoine quickly if he fell.

He watched Gabriel-Antoine swoop down over the roof of the *Causapscal-des-Vents,* stalled a little too high, and dropped awkwardly to the flat surface between the emergency balloons. The crack of an electrical discharge shone between boot and habitat. Static swamped the radio band in George-Étienne's helmet and Gabriel-Antoine flopped to the roof like a marionette.

"Is he okay?" Pascal asked.

Gabriel-Antoine silently lifted his fists in the air. George-Étienne felt himself laughing.

"*C'est bon*," George-Étienne said. "He took a good shock, but he's okay."

Suddenly his earpiece sounded with radar pings and his blood went cold. The *colonie* had not fallen for Marthe's distraction. George-Étienne landed on the *Causapscal-des-Vents* and started deflating emergency bags. Gabriel-Antoine rose beside him and began to do the same. The radar reflections of the emergency oxygen bags would be easy to spot. Up above, Marie-Pierre was pulling out the extra covering of nets over the four trawlers in the float harness to reduce their radar reflectivity. Radar pings sounded again, but his suit wasn't equipped to tell him how close the searchers were.

SIXTY-EIGHT

TÉTREAU PATCHED A private message through control comms down to one-five-six. Woodward was watching the display, as if not listening. He knew some of the other pilots but not as well, and didn't know anyone in the Bank plane helping in the search for the radiation signature.

"Réjean, this is Tétreau. How's it going?"

"I'm a kilometer above the bottom of the lower cloud deck," Réjean's voice crackled back. "I'm ready to piss my pants."

Woodward crossed her arms.

"I'm in sight of one of the deep *coureur* habitats. It's ugly as fuck."

"Control, give me helmet cam on one-five-six," Tétreau said.

After a moment, the screen on Tétreau's station showed a gloomy yellow haze through a cockpit window. A living habitat floated in the foreground.

He'd seen pictures before. This seemed smaller than the ones they made now, green-brown with stringy black plants growing off it like dirty hair. Beneath the main head hung a gantry that looked too flimsy to stand on. It didn't give off any light.

"Whose is it?" Woodward said. In the screen, the plane jerked to a stop. "What's happening?"

"They can't land a plane down there, so they blow float balloons to stop," Tétreau said. "I don't know who lives there."

The screen showed Réjean's plane coming to within forty meters of the habitat. Other planes had as well. The cockpit window opened and Réjean's helmet cam moved wildly as he inflated a personal balloon and a propellered drone ferried him to the habitat.

Other pilots were ahead of him, holding tasers and even guns awkwardly as they crossed the distance. Two drones with Bank of Pallas insignia painted on their sides were in the picture too on little one-person dirigibles that looked more maneuverable. He hadn't known the Bank had that tech. One of the Bank guys held back, holding a tall whip antenna. The other approached the habitat with Réjean and the other pilots.

Woodward was probably looking at the crappy equipment on the constables as much as Tétreau was evaluating the shiny armored survival suit and sidearm of the Bank guard waiting on the gantry. He had no authority here and couldn't go first. He was an observer and backup. Arsenault was first and Réjean second. Then, a clearer image showed on Nasmith's screen, from the helmet cam of the Bank guard.

"Let's go," Arsenault said to Réjean and another constable. "You two follow after we're in."

"*Crisse. Crisse. Crisse,*" Réjean was saying in his helmet microphone. Arsenault handed Réjean the clicking Geiger wand and unholstered his taser. Then he started opening the airlock. The Bank cam watched the door close, while the static on Réjean's feed became worse. Arsenault worked the controls.

"You nervous?" Arsenault asked.

"No," Réjean said, an octave higher.

"Going in," Arsenault said. "Follow as soon as the airlock has greened."

Arsenault spun the other wheel and pushed the door open. The two of them spilled onto a darkened room with a curving wooden floor. Arsenault slammed the door behind them, spinning the wheel closed so that backup could get here quick. Réjean's helmet cam darted nervously left and right, making it hard for Tétreau to make much out. His taser trembled as he swept the dark. Arsenault shone a shaky hand lamp and advanced.

"This is *Sûreté de la Colonie,*" Arsenault called on a speaker on his suit. "Come out. We have a warrant." The Bank guard's helmet cam showed them coming into the dark habitat. "And backup," he added.

No one came out. Réjean was waving the pinging Geiger wand, towards what looked like a back room.

"I don't recognize the layout," Woodward said in her clumsy English accent. "Is that normal?"

Tétreau shrugged. "The *coureurs* can grow as many

internal walls as they want and then cut out the ones they don't. I've only ever been in a couple. They were newer."

Réjean screamed. The Geiger wand dropped and his light shine wobbled with jerky movements. Someone was tackling him. Réjean's helmet cam watched his taser needles spike the ceiling. Through the Bank guard's helmet cam, they saw Arsenault slamming his fists into the man in the half-dark, failing to dislodge him. Réjean kicked and kicked.

"*Ostie d'tabarnak de gouvernement!*" the attacker said, getting enough of the upper hand to knock down Arsenault too.

Thunder sounded in both helmet cams, with bright flashes of light. The man stilled and rolled off Réjean, collapsing on the floor. Réjean scrambled away on his back. He had blood all over his suit. He patted himself all over, looking for the leak or the stab entry wound. There was nothing. Arsenault helped him stand. A bearded man lay on the floor, gasping as he bled away. Réjean kicked him. The Bank guard held a smoking gun in his hand and he was looking at Réjean.

"Find the radiation," he said in English.

Tétreau held himself still and Woodward didn't say anything either. Réjean's helmet cam showed the trembling Geiger wand, leading them to a dark bedroom. Arsenault's light showed a small workshop. A lead box in one of the sloping corners pinged louder. Arsenault carefully lifted the lid and the wand went crazy. He shut it.

"Grégoire Tremblay," the other constable said of the dead man on the floor.

"Who'd he get this from?" Arsenault asked.

Réjean's helmet cam pointedly didn't swivel back to give Tétreau a view of the idiot Bank guard who'd killed the only one who could answer.

SIXTY-NINE

THIS WAS THE hardest flying Émile had ever done: swooping forward, jerking on a cable attached to his floating sister, stalling, recovering from the stall, and climbing until he was yanked back again. Every few pulls, he tried the radio, but hadn't been able to raise anyone. The clouds of Venus were an ocean too big and he was a speck, pulling over and over in a shapeless world of hot, melting colors. Through it all, they'd gained a few kilometers. They had risen from the haze into the clouds at forty-eighth *rang*. The storm still batted them around with inscrutable updrafts and cross-winds, but the temperature had dropped to eighty degrees and the pressure to one and a half atmospheres. A drizzle of sulfuric acid began to fall just as the engine of his wing-pack began to sputter.

With a panicked twist, he turned in the air, circling Marthe tightly as he tried to grab a hold of the cable holding them together. His engine gave out before he got a good grip. He fell to the end of his line and his weight briefly pulled down Marthe's motionless form and the balloons.

He swore, folding back his wings and at least righting himself on the end of the line. He was hanging about twenty meters below her. They weren't sinking anymore, although the speed of their rise was hard to measure against the sputtering winds mixing the clouds.

He forced himself to be calm and let himself dangle as he ran a check of the engine. All the telltales were red. It wouldn't start. A few things could chew up an engine that fast, and all of them were different ways in which concentrated sulfuric acid could get past the carbon casing and into the working parts. Acid would melt the smart circuitry, the electrical connections, and even wreck the battery chambers. It might be repairable, but not hanging under his sister at the edge of a storm forty-nine kilometers above the surface of Venus.

Calvaire!

He took a deep breath, checked the attachment of the cable. Falling and cooking wasn't a quick death.

He opened the latches over the straps of his wing-pack and tugged the release loops. The straps made a zipping sound as they slid off his shoulders and his wing-pack fell behind him. He twisted his neck and then body and caught sight of the wing-pack shrinking beneath him. It became fuzzier, blurring, becoming one with the clouds. There was never closure, no instant of "was" turning into "was not". Not with his wing-pack, not with Chloé, and not with Thérèse. Not even with the *Causapscal-des-Vents*. Things just drifted out of sight.

He didn't have the spare D-rings and straps to set up a climbing harness. He heaved himself up twenty centimeters with just his arms. Then twenty more. The cable was slippery with acid, but he heaved twenty centimeters again. After a meter, he could wrap his legs around the cable too and give himself a bit more leverage.

Nineteen meters to go.

The wind picked up, howling outside his helmet in the sonorous closeness he'd not heard in five years. Sound was a washed-out, slow thing up in the flotilla. Supposedly fifty-fifth *rang* was the same pressure that humans had evolved in. He'd listened to sounds at fifty-fifth. It didn't feel natural to him, no matter what evolution said. He'd grown up at two-and-a-half atmospheres of pressure and close to a hundred degrees Celsius, where noise felt close and rich. He'd tried describing this to Thérèse and she'd just thought it incomprehensible and perhaps charming.

He kept climbing. Arm over arm, a hundred kilos of bone and muscle, and another twenty of suit and air tank. Climbing out of Venus.

When putting them into their swinging hammocks for bed when they were young, his father had told them that the wind carried the voice of Venus. The wind had been howling outside their first trawler habitat that evening, the voice of Venus angry and edged with storm. Pa had been trying to be comforting but hadn't done a good job. Jean-Eudes and Chloé had slept quick enough, but even then Émile had understood the anger of Venus. After a while, he'd carefully crept from his swaying hammock and climbed into Jean-Eudes's, where he'd wrapped his older brother's arm over himself.

Venus howled at him now. He didn't know how to satisfy her any more than he'd understood Thérèse. His arms trembled as he reached the last few centimeters and wrapped his legs around Marthe's. Hugging her with an arm, he clipped his main strap to the balloons beside her. Only when he was sure everything was solid did he let his shaking arms lower.

His shoulders burned. Their four booted feet dangled nervelessly beneath them, framing dark ocher clouds dumping torrents of rain only a kilometer below. Marthe's breath continued to softly fog the front of her faceplate and her bloody forehead still rested against a web of cracks. Tiny bubbles of blood formed and popped on the outside of the cracks as her suit shed air to equilibrate with the lowering pressure of the clouds. He shook her gently. Said her name. But she didn't respond.

His weight hadn't helped but dropping the wing-pack had. His suit said they'd risen to fifty-first *rang*. The balloons blocked his direct view, but the clouds brightened to a light brown, looking wispy. Then the clouds opened up to show him *Les Plaines*.

It wasn't the full view of the clear air going on forever with a floor and ceiling of clouds. The storm to the west had bulged up the floor of clouds like a distended mountain, so that it almost touched the ceiling a kilometer higher. The distortion had also dropped the floor of *Les Plaines* around him, so that nearly two kilometers of clear air separated him from the middle cloud deck. Wild trawlers floated, so distant that they looked like bits of dander.

"Control. Can you hear me?" he said. "This is Émile D'Aquillon. In distress. At *Les Plaines*. I have my sister with me. She's unconscious. We're both on emergency balloons. Control?"

Static filled the response. A storm could swamp weak radio signals.

Their rise rate was clearer now that he had something to landmark against, but not fast enough. He unstrapped Marthe's wing-pack and wrapped his legs around it. He didn't need to look at the external diagnostics. Something hard had hit one of the wings and the mounting assembly. It would take a machine shop and replacement parts to bring it back to life.

He pulled out the spare oxygen tank and hung it on his harness. Then he did the same to the main battery. It was good, but the cracked mounting had let sulfuric acid into the case of the emergency battery. Unsalvageable. He took a deep breath. He let the wing-pack go. It tumbled in the clear air, then vanished into the dark ocher clouds of the lower deck.

"Another offering," he said to Venus.

He felt them rising faster now, as he and his sister rose into the orange-yellow of the middle deck and it began to rain. Clouds visibly dropped around them, inexorably. The balloons expanded as the pressure dropped. It was still one and a quarter atmospheres. When they got into the very low pressures the balloons would distend, sometimes dangerously. And when the pressure dropped still more, the cracks in Marthe's faceplate would let her air hiss away until she didn't have enough oxygen. She would pass out, maybe forever.

They reached fifty-fourth *rang*. The sulfuric acid rain steadied now, like a summer shower. Very soon, they'd be at the magical fifty-fifth *rang,* where the temperature hovered around twenty-five centigrade and the pressure was not far under one atmosphere. He looked at his sister's unconscious face. The skin was smooth, with a few marks where droplets of acid had touched her, as Venus caressed all of them at some point. In this false sleep, she was peaceful, vulnerable, not the ball-busting bitch she could be with him. But even when she was that bitch who was never pleased with anything he did, when she was their father given new shape, she was still his sister and he loved her. And truth be told, someday Pa wasn't going to be there, and somebody needed to take care of Jean-Eudes and Alexis, and even Pascal a little bit, and Émile could see what everyone else saw: he was the last choice for that job and she was the first. She already took care of him in a strange way. This was his turn to take care of her.

He pulled out a survival sheet and unrolled it. It was a light weave of silk-fine carbon fiber, waterproof and capable of surviving for hours outside in the fiftieth *rang* before the acid could gnaw holes in it. He put it over their heads so that the rain pattered off it. Inside this meager shelter, he pulled a bicarbonate pad out of one of his sealed pockets and began wiping her helmet and then the inside of the survival sheet where the acid from her helmet had touched. Then he neutralized her shoulders and the sheet around her. Then him. It was awkward work and he knew he wasn't going to get everything. Her blood continued to make little bubbles over the cracks in her faceplate. They hissed when they touched the bicarbonate residue his wiping had left.

His display showed the temperature was thirty degrees and the pressure about one atmosphere.

He took a deep breath.

Then he cracked the seal on his helmet and quickly took it off and hung it on his harness. He felt the tiny sting of acid burning on his scalp as the survival sheet touched it. He hadn't gotten everything.

He didn't breathe. That wouldn't help. It was all carbon dioxide, but the faint smell of chlorine tickled his nostrils. Then he cracked the seal on Marthe's helmet and took it off.

He hung it quickly from her harness as her head lolled. He tried to keep the sheet from touching her head and he gave a quick wipe of bicarbonate paste before putting his helmet on her head. He locked it into place and tightened the seal. Then he gave his scalp a quick wipe with the pad, wiped some of her blood off the inside and put on her helmet.

He breathed big gulps of air, and the smell of sulfur and chlorine was bad, and he didn't get any oxygen. It was still the atmospheric air. He dialed up the oxygen feed in his suit to full and panted as black encroached on the edges of his vision. He held tight to Marthe's shoulders as he kept breathing, and the feeling of suffocation started to pass.

He'd smelled Venus, directly again—but not like the

amateurs had done, high up in the sunlight under the black sky full of stars, out of her reach. He'd revealed himself to Venus in her own domains. He didn't know if he felt defiant before a spurning lover, or supplicating before a powerful liege. He ached inside. Not from his brief and impending suffocation, but in his heart.

He was still a dispossessed man among a dispossessed people. He was beside Marthe, who could not answer, could not hear him. He had two brothers who no longer knew him. He had a father who rejected him. And he'd reached for Thérèse without ever making contact. All of them lived like the souls in Dante's *Inferno,* beyond the touch of a god; incapable of touching each other.

"Mayday. Mayday. Control, this is Émile D'Aquillon," he said as the view from under their sheet turned from cloud to the brighter open sky of the second world-spanning layer of clear air. Above, he heard the boom of thunder, not so far off. "We're at *Grande Allée* and rising. Marthe is still unconscious. One of our helmets is cracked. We're on balloons and have no wing-packs. We need help."

Again, nothing but painful static came as reply as lightning hammered the clouds above and to the west. Of course. As they rose, the east wind accelerated. The storm was higher than he'd thought, and they were going back in.

Câlisse.

And he blinked at black spots in his vision.

The pressure outside had dropped to a third of an atmosphere and the inside of his suit was down to half an atmosphere. His chest felt heavy, empty. The damage to Marthe's helmet was more than he could fix with the little kit he'd brought. He dialed up the oxygen feed. He could operate on low pressure, high oxygen for a while. But the time to empty on his tank had just gone from eighty minutes to thirty. He took deep breaths, calming his thumping heart. As they rose, the pressure would drop more, but if he stayed here, the chance of being rescued went down.

The storm wind grabbed them both, the balloons catching the wind like a rope on a winch. Their harnesses yanked them into the heights of the storm. Lightning boomed and flashed around them, great bone-rattling cracks in the sky only a kilometer away. Warm, acid-laden clouds emptied torrents of spite over them. The wind whipped away their survival sheet.

The sky above them, which before had seemed so close and bright, darkened. The pressure readings on the suit jumped around with the gusting, and the GPS signals became unreliable. He didn't know if they were going up or down anymore. He wrapped his legs and arms around Marthe before the wind threw them together hard enough to knock them out or rip their suits.

He yelled at Venus, maybe transmitting. Maybe not. It didn't matter. She always ignored them.

"Go back to hell, you bitch!"

His throat was tight and his voice cracked.

"You can't have Marthe, and you can't have me!"

A sudden cross-current caught the balloons and swung them wildly, so hard that centrifugal force held them horizontal, staring up at curtains of dark falling acid. He held Marthe tight, like they were little children again.

It wasn't just that they'd been children. The D'Aquillon family had been childlike in its optimism. They thought they could keep Jean-Eudes and make their own way in the clouds, scrape by on hard work and trading and family. Pa and *maman* couldn't know then what it would cost them. Émile's bitterness was blacker because he'd been that innocent too once. It had once seemed okay to believe that things could turn out right.

He didn't know where things had gone wrong, didn't know if Venus really was stalking them, or if it was their own fault. How could the world turn out like this? It wasn't fair. And part of the anger he felt as he swung wildly on the end of a harness in the storm, perhaps most of it, was that, for all that he'd hardened, and all that he'd made mistakes, he still carried a flicker of optimism in his heart, still carried a terrible place where he could be hurt. He'd given the key to that place to Thérèse, and by extension, to Venus herself. He hurt now and he couldn't make it stop. He was lonely, holding an unconscious little sister who had optimistically bought into Pa's crazy new dream. He held her tighter.

And in that moment, Venus pounced. The strap holding Marthe to the balloons had twisted over and over, and rubbed against the other cables, and frayed with the acid and heat. It snapped. All her weight was in his tired arms and legs. He was the only thing holding her from a sixty kilometer fall.

The balloons readjusted their weight with a jerk.

She slipped in his acid-wet arms. He tightened his legs around her and squeezed her so tight he worried that he might hurt her. Her face rolled against the inside of the faceplate, leaving little blood marks as the wind dropped them, trying to shake his grip. All the weight was on his harness now. And his vision started to blur again. His depleting oxygen was slowly suffocating him.

He hyperventilated, trying to keep himself oxygenated and conscious as, one-handed, he tried to find the side-straps of his harness to clip her to himself. He didn't have time to check the oxygen or dial it up or even use voice commands. He had to get the straps attached.

The blackening of his vision started in sparks and bursts, expanding into clouds—the same way Venus swallowed objects and people, blurring the sharpness of things, infecting them with her chaos. Life couldn't survive raw chaos.

His chest worked and worked as his hand fumbled through gloves for a strap and a clip, but it felt like an anvil lay on his sternum. He tasted blood from his nose and in his mouth. He didn't know what the pressure was now. He held tight as the blackness swallowed him, but he heard a clip snap closed.

SEVENTY

PASCALE HAD BEEN electrically shocked before. Everything in the clouds collected a static charge. Most of the time, the shocks were small. This time her muscles ached. They'd waited for the radar pings to get closer, but they'd gone west and south. She got up and descended to the habitat. And like a weight had been lifted, she scrambled over the *Causapscal-des Vents* like a child with a new toy. She'd never explored a habitat like this. The lines of the *Causapscal-des-Vents* were strange, inorganic, something wholly made by people. She'd spent her life inside another living thing, a bioengineered Venusian trawler, a creature of wood, electrical arteries and curving lines. This was so different, lifelessly elegant and cleverly creative.

The *Causapscal-des-Vents* had been damaged on its way down, though. It wasn't made for these pressures or acidities. Corrosion burns ran over its sides like rain tracks, rendering the plastic of the envelope greenhouses opaque. It had been a big job to move the radar-obscuring curtains of old trawler cabling out of the way, then to hang big acid-resistant sheets over the whole habitat before replacing the curtains. It would take weeks, months to remove the metal and retool it into the pieces they could use to cap the cave.

In wonder, Pascale came down the inner walkway in the envelope, to the airlock to the gondola. Pa, Gabriel-Antoine and Marie-Pier inspected the condition of the gondola, pulling up the wall panels to see the wiring and support ribs. They measured and inventoried and planned.

Gabriel-Antoine's voice sounded as giddy as Pascale felt. They were going to try to see the true soul of Venus, questing like the knights of old French romances. A thousand things could go wrong. But if they succeeded, they might reach the stars.

Impulsively, Pascale patted her father's arm, then turned it into a one-armed hug that he returned. It was an awkward gesture in survival suits, but she felt her father through the layers, solid, real, seasoned by Venus. Yet Pascale was different from him, conceived here, raised here, still seeking her roots, her true self. She was closer now. She saw in herself what was hidden from the world.

"*Pi'?*" Gabriel-Antoine said to her.

She felt herself grinning. Gabriel-Antoine gave an awkward hand-signal to switch channels, trying to give the *coureur* one. It was adorably inept.

"I'll teach you how to signal properly," Pascale teased, "when your hands aren't in gloves."

"I can think of better things to do with my hands when

they're not in gloves," he said.

The gnawing dread—how to tell Gabriel-Antoine about the self emerging in her—was still distant enough that the euphoria of the moment could hold it away. She was happy. They were happy. She couldn't wait for Marthe and Émile to get back here. They had all they needed to reach the stars.

SEVENTY-ONE

LIGHT CREAKED INTO Émile's head through itchy, irritated eyes. His groan sounded hollow. He shifted an arm. He wasn't wearing a suit. Sheets rubbed flesh. His eyes stung. LEDs shone too brightly on the ceiling over him. A big face mask covered his mouth and nose, hissing cold air. He reached and pulled it away on elastic straps.

"Leave that on," someone said. "You need the oxygen."

He raised himself up on his elbows and sharp pains shot through all his muscles, like every part of his body had run its own marathon. A nurse crossed the small bay between a dozen other sick beds. He was in the hospital on *Baie-Comeau*. She put a small hand on his chest and tried to push him back and replace the oxygen mask. She succeeded at neither.

"What happened?" he said.

"You're really lucky, *monsieur* D'Aquillon," she said. She was in her mid-forties, black-haired and dark-eyed. She indicated a hard-faced woman in a pilot's suit leaning against one of the ward's doorframes. "A rescue team found you around sixtieth *rang*. You almost suffocated. Your oxygen supply had run out. You also suffered from decompression."

"How's Marthe?"

"Who?"

"My sister."

The woman in the pilot's suit frowned and stepped closer.

"I found you, *monsieur* D'Aquillon," she said. "There was no one with you."

Cold terror leapt into his stomach. "She was with me!" he said, sitting up fully despite the nurse's pushing hand. Pain lanced every muscle but the horror in his chest was worse. "I strapped her to me!"

A growing sort of horror and loss crept into the pilot's expression.

"I'm sorry, *monsieur* D'Aquillon," the pilot said. "You were alone. Unconscious. It was lucky that we found you at all. The transceiver in your suit was almost out of power. I didn't see anyone else."

"She was with me!" he said.

The pilot's shoulders slumped slightly. "I'm very sorry, *monsieur* D'Aquillon." Then she backed out of the room altogether.

The nurse was teary eyed and her small hand pressed again on his chest.

"You need oxygen, *monsieur* D'Aquillon," she said in a quiet voice.

She stopped trying to push him back and just put the

mask over him again. He breathed, numbly. The nurse backed away too. He stared at his sheet-covered toes, rubbing every so often at watering eyes. But soon, rubbing didn't help anymore. Tears spilled down his cheeks, around the mask.

He'd been holding Marthe. They'd been strapped together. He'd found her in time. He'd traded helmets with her so that she could breathe. She'd been breathing. He'd been holding her.

His throat tightened painfully over silent weeping.

Marthe had been with him. He'd had her! They'd side-stepped most of the storm.

He slumped onto his side. Every part of his body ached in resonance with the throbbing in his heart. This wasn't a death like Thérèse had nearly had. Marthe hadn't been looking for it. She'd been doing her job, living. A storm had taken her, with the predatory zeal of a shark. Venus had consumed her.

His body shook. Tears ran faster.

His little sister was gone, the chop-haired little girl who'd wanted to keep up with him and Jean-Eudes around the habitat. The one who'd gotten spanked for hitting him with a piece of cable, and who had come to him for comfort. The girl who'd become a hard-ass and had started to run the family. Marthe was gone, blown away like a leaf. He'd loved her. His tears were volcanic, drops of acid from the depths he'd been raised in, radiating stinging pain.

SEVENTY-TWO

THE AUTHORITIES DIDN'T show up to bother Émile. The *Causapscal-des-Vents* was lost. Investigators could draw their own conclusions from the initial information. They would interview him soon enough. His suit was beat up but had no leaks. He traded in Marthe's old cracked helmet for a used one and signed out an upper-atmosphere wing-pack until Ressources could get him a new one.

He flew from the busy landing deck of the *Baie-Comeau* at night. His arms and legs ached as he stretched them out. Everything felt unreal. The air was too thin, the stars too bright. The clouds felt like they ought to be surrounding him with menace, but instead lay somber beneath him, partly lit by sunshine scattered through the atmosphere from the other side of the planet.

He had no place to go—really no place—so he went to the Phocas habitat. The old lady and the old man had lots of questions about the loss of the *Causapscal-des-*

Vents. He got away quick enough on the excuse of getting the *Marais-des-Nuages* back to top shape. It seemed remarkable that he'd only been gone eighty hours. The two kids, especially Louise, had been doing the routine work. And he needed a drink. Or better yet, two. He had left some of his own stuff but found Gabriel-Antoine's too. It felt good, but after a time, he ended up crying instead.

He was waiting not just for the Phocas family to go to bed, but for the *Causapscal-des-Profondeurs* to come into maser range. The flotilla and the *Marais-des-Nuages* had nearly circled the planet in eighty hours, while down at forty-fifth, the family's two habitats plodded along on their two-week cycle. When the Phocas family was all asleep, he went out the airlock on the roof of the envelope and patched himself into the maser comms system.

"*Marais-des-Nuages* to *Causapscal-des-Profondeurs*," he said.

After a few moments, Pascal's voice came on.

"*Causapscal-des-Profondeurs* here."

"Are you all okay?" Émile asked.

"Yes."

"Put Pa on."

Silence. Long. Maybe awkward. He hadn't spoken to his father in five years. Amid the crackling, Pa's voice finally came on.

"You sober?" Pa grunted.

"Marthe is dead, you bastard."

Crackling was all he heard on the radio. The tears spilled again.

"*Quoi?*" Pa said. The single syllable was pinched, like he'd sprung a leak and was deflating.

"You killed her. You got greedy. You were only thinking about you again, and someone else we loved paid for it."

Émile blinked at the stinging tears. He couldn't wipe them away in his helmet. The crackling continued for so long that he wondered if Pa was going to answer.

"What happened?" Pa said. His voice cracked.

Out of spite, Émile briefly considered not telling him. But it would probably hurt more if he knew.

"A storm caught her, shook her up bad," he said. "Cracked her faceplate and her wing-pack. I got to her. We were rising on emergency balloons. I traded helmets with her so she'd have enough oxygen. She never woke up and the storm caught us again. Snapped her harness."

The maser line was all crackle now.

"*Marais-des-Nuages* out," he said after a minute.

He shut off the comms and stood on the gently swaying roof of the habitat, above the entire world, out of reach of Venus, under naked stars he could not reach either. His little sister was gone. Her goddamn, pain-in-the-ass, nagging voice was gone. Her judging, no-bullshit stare was gone. And her tough caring for every stupid person around her was gone. He had no more family, not really. Pascal was in Pa's pocket. Jean-Eudes would be too. Émile's knees folded and he was kneeling, and then crying like he'd never cried before.

SEVENTY-THREE

TÉTREAU CAME WITH the bad news, but Gaschel had already heard it. Dauzat was with her, sitting on the other side of the big desk. At first Tétreau almost retreated. They were sitting so still, he thought he'd interrupted an argument. No one signalled him in, but finally, he entered, closed the door, and sat beside Dauzat.

"*Monsieur* Labourière isn't here, so I drafted a statement for you, *Madame la Présidente,*" he said.

Gaschel's eyes locked on him from the first word. She checked her pad, where the draft was already in her files. As she read it, Dauzat looked at him inscrutably. The statement lamented the loss of life and the valued advice of Marthe D'Aquillon in *l'Assemblée*. It also minimized the loss of the *Causapscal-des-Vents,* an old habitat that had already been slated for recycling.

"It's fine," Gaschel said. She put down her pad. "Not true, but it's fine."

"The *Causapscal-des-Vents?*" he said.

589

"More than forty tons of materials," she said. "And Marthe gave no valued advice. Ever. She never understood the decisions that needed to be made for four thousand people."

"At least it wasn't sabotage," he said after screwing up his courage.

"You know something we don't?" Gaschel said in irritation.

"Marthe D'Aquillon wasn't stupid. She was trying to save it until the end, long after she should have given up. And she died for her trying. That's not the sign of someone committing sabotage."

Gaschel regarded him for a few moments, and he thought he'd overstepped. Then she waved her hand.

"And the radioisotopes," she said. "Woodward probably already reported the radiation to her superiors. They'll be pressuring her for answers and closure."

"The radioisotopes *are* really strange," he said. "Uranium and thorium, along with decay products like polonium and radium, but all of them as salts and oxides. They haven't been refined at all, or even purified. The different radioisotopes have been pressed together in a jumble."

Gaschel frowned. "That doesn't sound like anything a Bank would provide."

"It sounds like what someone might have found on the surface or in a mine," Tétreau said.

"Against the odds, someone found a vein of radioactives in the crust and has been mining it," Gaschel said. She looked into the distance, at the cloudtops. "That's good news for our credit rating with the Bank. Now we have to find our busy little miners. Get to it, Tétreau."

His chair scraped on the floor. "*Oui, madame.*"

SEVENTY-FOUR

SOMETHING WAS WRONG. Pa wasn't talking anymore. Just staring. Was Émile still talking? Pascale had a bad feeling. She stopped shifting the camouflage netting with Gabriel-Antoine on top of the *Causapscal-des-Vents*. The roof was treacherous now with uneven and slippery knotted cable fragments and she stumbled twice reaching Pa.

"Pa?" she said, touching his shoulder.

He turned his face her way. The dim light of the HUD reflected in tear lines. He was speaking but she couldn't hear anything. She made the hand sign for channel switch. Pa came onto their common channel. His breathing was uneven.

"What is it, Pa?"

George-Étienne took her shoulders and hugged her tight.

"I'm sorry, Pascal. I'm so sorry."

"What?" Pascale said desperately. "What is it?"

The habitat beneath them shifted, up, then down, as it rode over the turbulence of a pressure cell.

"Marthe is gone," he said in a cracking voice. "Venus took her."

The words stabbed deep in her chest, injecting a profound, spreading ache. Someone gasped on their family channel. Pascale wanted to move, to look to see the truth in Pa's face, but he held her too tight.

"What?"

"A storm took her."

The light around them became more polarized, colors shifting out of perception. The sound of the wind vibrating the cables around them hollowed, becoming watery and distant, not matching the sight of them before her eyes.

"When?" she said. He still wouldn't let her go. Pa was shaking. Pascale's eyes stung.

"I don't know." His voice shook like his body.

An hour? Less? More? Her body might still be falling. Terminal velocity got slower and slower near the surface. But that didn't matter. If she was deep enough for terminal velocity to slow, she'd be cooked through already. It was a stupid thing to think about now.

Marthe had helped find the real Pascale. Marthe had been going to rescue her. And now she was gone, tumbling through the clouds, the haze, and the terrible open space over jagged basalt. Marthe was carbonizing now, blackening and boiling in a suit flaking away with heat, incinerating. Marthe would never touch the ground. Only some of the metal weave of her suit and the faceplate and her bones would arrive, blackened beyond recognition, added to the blasted ugliness of Venus's surface.

Pascale's eyes were wet. She stood straight. Pa let her go. Behind his faceplate, his beard was wet and steaming where its wiry volume pressed against the faceplate. Marie-Pier was behind him.

"I'm sorry, Pa."

He nodded and sat abruptly. Marie-Pier sat beside him and put her arm around his shoulders as a speckling of sulfuric acid rain began falling around them.

"How do I tell Jean-Eudes and Alexis?" Pa whispered hoarsely.

"I'll help you," Marie-Pier said.

Marie-Pier's children had no father. Had she told them their father was gone? The way Pa had told her and Jean-Eudes that Chloé and Mathurin were gone? Pascale turned. She couldn't look anymore. She stumbled on the netting and Gabriel-Antoine caught her.

She must look like a mess. It didn't matter. They couldn't really be together, could they? Gabriel-Antoine wanted a boy. Pascale was a girl, just in disguise. Her eyes were wet, but the world prickled, pregnant with a rain much harder than what fell around them now. Her thoughts flitted everywhere. To the habitat they would disassemble. To the nervous kisses she'd given Gabriel-Antoine. To seeing the sun above the clouds, hostile and overbright. To seeing the stars within Venus. Thinking of everything but Marthe.

Gabriel-Antoine signed to change channels. She did. He took her hands.

"I'm so sorry, Pascal. I don't know what to say."

"There's nothing to say."

The wind swayed them.

"She told me to be gentle with you," he said.

The stabbing in Pascale's chest deepened and her eyes burned. "She did?"

"She threatened me if I ever hurt you."

A lonely sob slipped out of her like a hiccup. Pascale tried to pull one hand away.

"She made me promise to take care of your heart."

"Why?" Pascale said. The question sounded like a whine in her ears. Tears spilled fast.

"She loved you."

Another sob emerged. She yanked her hands free. "I don't want this now! This isn't what I want to hear."

She stumbled around him, stepping high over the debris and the cables and wires. Pumps emptied the carbon dioxide from the habitat, giving it buoyancy again to take the strain off the support cables and the trawlers above. How long? She and Gabriel-Antoine had rough ideas of how to cut apart the *Causapscal-des-Vents,* Marthe's home, but they would need to crawl around its inside and measure and weigh and take everything out. It was stupid. It was all stupid and useless.

Pascale took a wrench out of her tool belt, to check the torque on the nuts holding in the cleats along the roof of the *Causapscal-des-Vents,* but the wrench was too small. The metal of the cleats and the plates around them were already beginning to corrode. The acid down here was harsher, more concentrated and hotter than anything the *Causapscal-des-Vents* ever saw under the bright sun. Pascale knelt, not sure what to do with the corrosion.

Gabriel-Antoine knelt beside her. His hand was on her shoulder. Her shoulder. Marthe had helped find her as if Pascale had been trapped like a fairy-tale princess under a spell. And now Marthe the questing knight was gone. Burnt up. Pascale was crying now, so much she couldn't see the corrosion, couldn't figure out how to fix it. Gabriel-Antoine's arms were around her, pulling her to sit on his lap.

"Come on, *cher*," he said.

She clung to his arms through glove and suit as she shook and sniffled and cried. Gabriel rocked her.

"She brought you and me together," he said quietly. "She brought all of us together. She invented the House of Styx. She made us a family so we could live your dream of the stars. What she gave us will change Venus."

Spongy orange clouds were slowly darkening to red around them as the wind carried them away from the sun.

"She won't get any of what she made."

"She would want us to enjoy it though," he said. "She would want us to reach the stars on the other side."

Pascale slumped against Gabriel-Antoine's chest. When Pascale was little, Marthe and she had talked favorite colors. Pascale had been choosing between green and blue. Marthe had described a particular purple that existed nowhere except in the vaporous haze at forty-sixth *rang*, a product of the low angle of sunset light scattered through two atmospheres of sulfuric acid and carbon dioxide. Marthe's favorite had struck Pascale as a kind of proof of magic all around them, on the edges, hidden in common things. Pascale had found the color, after looking for it. She couldn't remember it anymore, and in the reddening vapors around them, it was like the memory of that happy wonder had dissolved.

"I don't feel like enjoying anything right now."

"Me neither, *cher*."

EPILOGUE

PA WAS GOOD with a welder. Pascale had never seen him welding like this before, but in Québec he'd been a tradesman and his trade ticket had gotten him to Venus all those year ago. Beside him, harnessed to the structure of the half-disassembled habitat was Alexis in a cut-down survival suit. He didn't have a wing pack. He was too young to fly, but wore an emergency balloon on his back in case.

Even though Marie-Pier was scandalized that they'd brought a ten year old onto a dangerous work site, she'd probably learned to navigate the clouds young, even if not this young. But Alexis needed to learn and Pa needed to teach him. It made both of them feel good.

Pascale tied off two more balloons to the steel struts she'd cut free and inflated them until the beam floated. A small set of propellers started driving it towards the forge Gabriel-Antoine had built beneath the tool gantry of the old habitat. She paused to watch it and drink from the helmet straw. They were six to eight weeks of hard work before they could even begin transporting down any of the materials, but already the forge was making frames and sheets to hold back the hot fury of Venus, to dam the river of self-hate that led down to the goddess' heart.

Gabriel-Antoine flitted from the old habitat to the Causapscal-des-Vents, about a kilometer off in the mist. Even on little jumps he pirouetted and looped in the haze, like a fish reveling at its strength in a river. Despite the heat, they'd slept in the same hammock each night this week.

Gabriel-Antoine's landings on the Causapscal-des-Vents still made noise enough that Jean-Eudes would hear, but despite her brother's excitement, he would respect their new radio quiet. This was Jean-Eudes' first time utterly alone in the habitat and Pa was teaching him about station-keeping in the wind. Jean-Eudes didn't have to do much, but her brother had nervously embraced the chance to prove himself, to be more useful.

They all tested themselves against Venus, each according to their gifts, all in the process of becoming something else, something better. They might die. They each had lost loved ones to the clouds. And although Venus would resist them, although Venus herself did not know she was beautiful, they would show her.

The End

ACKNOWLEDGEMENTS

THANK YOU TO Greg Kumpula, Nick Carter, Bill Dicke and Mark Nasmith for aeronautical advice and storm-chaser Mark Robinson for meteorological advice, and for taking an early draft of this novel into a volcano.

Thank you to Emmanuelle Arsenault, Marie Bilodeau, Stephanie Arsenault for help with French grammar and filling in my gaps in Quebecois swearing. I owe an additional thank you to Marie for an early critique of this novel.

Thank you to editors Michael Rowley, Trevor Quachri, Kate Coe and Emily Hockaday at Solaris Books and Analog Science Fiction and Fact.

I also greatly appreciated Talia C. Johnson's sensitivity editing advice. If you feel you need someone to advise you on portraying autistic, queer or trans characters, I highly recommend her and you can find her at taliacjohnson.ca.

And as always, thank you to my agent Kim-Mei Kirtland. She not only identified many early draft improvements to

The House of Styx, but negotiated contracts, shepherded the novel through the interacting publishing schedules, chased editing notes and led me through tax treaty fun. Because Kim-Mei is looking out for me, I can sleep soundly at night, focus on writing, and take my son for celebratory feasts.

GLOSSARY

Bébittes—literally "bugs." I have been bitten by many.
Ça va—literally "it goes," figuratively "I'm okay"
Câlisse!—literally "chalice," the cup in which the Catholic priest pours the communion wine, figuratively "fuck"
Champion des épais!—épais means "thick" which is like "idiot" in this context, so "champion of idiots"
Con/Conne—masculine and feminine variants of a word I don't say literally. Figuratively, I don't say it either.
Crisse!—literally a variant of "Christ", but figuratively equivalent to "fuck"
Gang de caves—like "champion des épais"; gang means gang and "un cave" is a kind of idiot.
Mange d'la marde—"eat shit"
Minute!—literally "minute", figuratively "hang on a minute"
n'est-ce pas?—"right?"
Ostie—literally the "host" wafer that becomes the body

of Christ during communion, figuratively "fuck"

Pas mal, mon p'tit gars—"not bad, my boy"

Prêt—"ready"

qui s'est emmerdé—figuratively "the one who got mad"

Reste ici—"stay here"

Sapristi!—I don't know the literal meaning, but sapristi is a light curse that my aunts will say in good company

Tabarnak—literally "tabernacle," a liturgical furnishing used to house the Eucharist, figuratively, "fuck"

Vas-y—"go ahead"

Viarge—a misspelling variant of "virgin" literally referring to the Virgin Mary, figuratively expresses anger, but this is not one of the big Québécois swears

Voyons—literally "look", figuratively "come on"

IN QUÉBÉCOIS SWEARING, the meaning is made harsher and stronger by concatenating swear words. It's like building a train. The longer the train, the harder the swear. So "ostie d'tabarnak" is worse than either "ostie" or "tabarnak" on their own. Another example of concatenation is "ostie d'con" and "Maudit câlisse de tabarnak de gros problème" which is worse with three. The internet has lots of resources on Québécois swearing, so you can learn to build your own train!

Read more from the world of
The House of Styx...

THE QUANTUM
MAGICIAN

CHAPTER ONE

BELISARIUS ARJONA WAS perhaps the only con man who drew parallels between his confidence schemes and the quantum world. Ask a question about frequency, and the electron appeared to be a wave. Ask a question about momentum, and the electron appeared to be a particle. A gangster looking to muscle in on a real estate scam would find sellers in distress. A mark looking to cash in on a crooked fight would find a fighter ready to take a fall. Nature fed an observer the clues needed to turn the quantum world into something real. Belisarius fed his marks the clues they needed to turn their greed into expensive mistakes. And sometimes he did so at gunpoint. To be precise, the muzzle of Evelyn Powell's pistol rested on her knees as she talked to him.

"Why the long face, Arjona?" she asked.

"No long face," he said sullenly.

"I'm going to make you really rich. You won't need to scrape by with this freak show," she said, waving her hand expansively.

They sat in the gloom at the bottom of the cylinder of glazed brick that was his gallery of Puppet art. A column supporting spiral stairs and landings speared the gallery. The paintings, sculptures and silent films set in bricked alcoves had to be appreciated across a three-meter gap between the edges of the stairs and the wall. Belisarius was curating the first exposition of Puppet art ever permitted by the Federation of Puppet Theocracies. Smell, lighting and sound invoked the aesthetic of the Puppet religious experience. Far above, near the entrance to the gallery, a whip snapped arhythmically.

"I like Puppet art," he said.

"So when you're rich, buy more."

"You don't get to buy art from prison."

"We're not going to get caught," she said. "Don't lose your nerve. If it works here, it will work in my casinos."

Powell was a beefy casino boss from Port Barcelona. She'd crossed the embargo around the dwarf planet Oler to see if the news of Belisarius's miracle making the rounds in criminal circles was true. She tapped the nose of the pistol against her knee, drawing his eyes with the movement.

"But you haven't been totally honest with me yet, Arjona. I'm still not convinced you really hacked a Fortuna AI. I've seen people try. I'm paying people to try. What are the odds that you, by yourself, surrounded by Puppets all the way out here, got it?"

He let her stew in the conviction of what she'd just said for two breaths—eight point one seconds. Then, he lowered his eyes, matching her expectations, buying him another second of her patience.

"No one can hack a Fortuna AI," he admitted. "And I didn't either. I broke into a security graft and snuck in a tiny bit of code. I couldn't make it big, or the rest of the AI would notice, but this tiny change added a factor into its statistical expectations."

Powell was calculating behind her stare: the odds of this being the secret to beating the Fortuna AI, the number of casinos vulnerable to this modified graft, and what Belisarius had changed to crack the graft.

Statistical expectations were the core of the Fortuna AI. Technology had leapt so far past games of chance that any casino could rip off its patrons pretty easily. For that matter, any patron could cheat an unprotected casino. The presence of a Fortuna AI was the seal of approval on any casino. In conjunction with an advanced surveillance system, the AI monitored ultrasonic, light, radio, IR, UV and X-ray emissions. It also calculated odds and winning streaks in real time. For the clients, it was proof the games were fair. For the casinos, it was protection against cheaters.

"The security grafts are unhackable too," Powell said. "I've got people working on them."

"Not if the code-breaker is fast enough to intercept the patch during transmission, and the change is small enough," Belisarius said.

The Fortuna AI *was* 'unhackable,' in the sense that Powell meant. All AIs were, because they were grown. They could only be evolved, or patched with small grafts.

Powell considered him for a while.

"My people are close, but we don't have a system to go with it yet," she said. "Using body temperature is ingenious."

A whip sounded far up the gallery again. A recorded Puppet moan of religious ecstasy echoed softly.

"My people say you're pretty smart," she said, "that you're one of those *Homo quantus*. Is that right?"

"You've got good sources," he said.

"So what's a super-smart *Homo quantus* doing in the ass-end of civilization?"

"I reacted badly to the medications that let the *Homo quantus* see quantum things," he said. "They kicked me out. The Banks didn't want to pay for a dud."

"Ha!" she said. "Duds. I hear you. Fucking Banks."

Belisarius was good at lying. He had a perfect memory, and every *Homo quantus* had to be able to run multiple lines of thought at once. Most of the time it didn't matter which one was true, as long as they didn't get mixed up.

"Let's get this done," he said finally, pointing at the pills in her palm.

"You wouldn't be trying to poison your new partner, would you?" she said, grinning. Behind the grin was something very hard.

"Get interferon from your own sources if you want," he said.

She shook her head and popped the two pills. "My augments wouldn't let me die of a fever."

That was probably true. His brain began running dosage and toxicity calculations, accounting for the abilities of black-market augments like the ones she was probably carrying. He let one part of his brain keep itself busy with those calculations. He wasn't jealous of her ability to fight a fever, but those kinds of augments wouldn't work in him anyway.

Powell's fever would start very quickly. He'd explained the scam to her three times, so she should understand it by now. Powell running two degrees of fever wouldn't trigger casino security, but that difference would activate the statistical algorithms in the security patch. The Fortuna AI would expect her to win more, and so when she did, no alarms would go off. That was what had brought her all the way to the Puppet Free City.

"Come on," she said, her breath fogging the air. "Your gallery is creeping me out."

They walked up the helical stairs, past all the eerie displays that were so good at attracting the pattern-seeking portions of Belisarius's engineered brain without triggering deeper mathematical reactions. Complicated confidence schemes did the same thing.

The street was colder. They had a nine point six minute walk, long enough for Powell's fever to rise. The decor became slightly cheerier as they went. The Puppet Free City was a warren of sub-surface caves dug into the icy crust of Oler. Some were bricked. Some were bare ice, stained with the remains of food or drink. Many of the tunnels were poorly lit, with lumpy garbage frozen to the streets.

The Free City liked its gambling, from holes in the wall and street craps to places that actually called themselves casinos. Blackmore's was the only one with a Fortuna AI, so it attracted the well-heeled gamblers and kept its icy streets relatively clean and garishly lit. Belisarius liked the way the lurid greens and soft blues mixed and reflected off every smooth patch of ice.

Along the sides of abandoned apartments and shops, rows of mendicant Puppets stood in rudely constructed Toy Boxes and fake Cages, with their hands out. They looked like humans descended from pale Old European families, shrunken to half-size. One emaciated Puppet woman had even set herself up at a folding table with a real Cream Puff pastry, long since dried to wrinkles. Belisarius threw her a few steel coins. Powell made a face at him and kicked the folding table onto the Puppet woman, who yelled a stream of filth at them.

"Shouldn't she be thanking me?" Powell guffawed.

"That's not how Puppets work."

"You got no sense of humor, Arjona," she said as they approached the entrance to Blackmore's. Human security were scanning patrons with wands, giving the casino a grasping touch of class over automated scanning. "Loosen up."

The scan took nine point nine seconds, an eternity for his brain. He played with parallels and patterns. Money flowed through casinos in gradients, the same way energy flowed down gradients from high-energy molecules to low-energy ones. Life colonized the energy gradients: plants put themselves between sun and stone; animals put themselves between plants and decay. Criminals infiltrated casinos like vines on a tree.

Anywhere money flowed, someone would try to siphon off some of it. Even in clean casinos, convergent evolution created new people ready to try to scam either the casino or its customers. Dealers could be bought off. Gamblers could collude with casino owners. Cheaters invented new cheats. That made the Fortuna AI critical. Without the trust created by Fortuna's inviolability, the honest money didn't flow.

Powell shouldered past him. He followed her to the craps table. The boxman was one of their plants, as was the stickman. Powell and he had secretly met them yesterday in the gallery. Powell waited her turn to make her pass line bet and held out the dice to him. He rolled his eyes and blew. She smiled with her big, flushed cheeks, and rolled a seven for her come out roll. That was the easy part.

Three other players made their pass lines and picked their service bets. The stickman put Powell's service bet of a hundred Congregate francs on cornrows and moved a new set of dice to her. The dice were of Belisarius's design. They contained embedded liquid-phase nano components. The transparent liquid inside the dice underwent a conformational change with small changes in heat, weighing down the single-pip side. The dice had been under the hot white light near the boxman, and were now in Powell's fever-hot hands.

Powell rolled a pair of sixes and the watchers cheered.

The next player took the dice with cold fingers and fogged the air with her breath for luck. Sevens. She was out. The next rolled craps with a three and the watchers cheered. The last rolled a hard ten and was out.

Powell flexed her fingers, then held them under her armpits. She jerked her chin to the stickman to keep her bet on cornrows, and twitched her fingers for the dice. The stickman slid them back. She held them between her hot hands for long seconds, closing her eyes as if praying, and then rolled.

The onlookers cheered at another pair of sixes.

Powell grinned at him. The boxman seemed to be expecting the Fortuna AI to go off, but he turned back to the table and nodded to the stickman. Belisarius made himself look happy. The dice cooled on the table, one of the advantages of a casino in a city buried in ice. The only remaining player rode out his combined bet, but rolled a nine. Out. All the attention was on Powell.

"Cornrows," she said, and passed the boxman a money wafer. The boxman's eyebrows rose in surprise. Ten thousand Congregate francs, a small fortune added to the smaller fortune she'd just made.

"Take it easy," Belisarius whispered. "You sure you don't want to wait?"

She took the dice, held them tightly for ten seconds and then rolled them against backstop. Two sixes came up. People threw their hands up in the general cheer and Powell was laughing and looking around. Then, her face froze and her hands lowered slowly.

A young Puppet priest had come up behind them. Her skin was old European pale, like her hair. She stood at eighty-five centimeters, proportioned like a human adult in miniature, but she wore armor over her robes.

Forming a quarter circle on each side of her were a dozen episcopal troopers, their sealed armor giving them an extra ten centimeters of height. They levelled their rifles at Powell and Belisarius. The casino-goers slowly backed away. Some screamed and moved for the door. Belisarius and Powell were trapped.

Belisarius bolted for the back of the casino. The priest pulled a pistol and flashing, loud bangs echoed. People screamed. Along Belisarius's side, microexplosions of blood and smoke burst through his coat. He fell to the ice floor, where blood froze in an expanding pool. He looked beseechingly at Powell, but she was horror-struck as the other patrons ducked and ran for the exits. The priest and the episcopal troops ignored them.

"Evelyn Powell, you're under arrest for blasphemy," the Puppet priest said.

Powell's jaw ground and her forehead wrinkled. "What?" she said.

"Cheating in Blackmore's is blasphemy," the Puppet said.

Powell looked helplessly at the ceiling, where the Fortuna AI would have made some noise if it had detected anything underhanded in a game. She gestured upward. "I was lucky!"

Then the alarms went off, and a spotlight fell on Powell. She made soundless mouthings as one of the episcopal troopers put her hands behind her back and disarmed her. She was marched out at the end of batons and firearms. It took ninety-six seconds more for the other troopers to shoo the terrified casino-goers out and close the casino.

"Enrique," Belisarius said, rising and rubbing his hands together, "your floor is freezing."

The olive-skinned boxman hopped down from his perch behind the craps table. "Don't lie down."

Misfortunes and bad debts in the Anglo-Spanish Plutocracy had blown Enrique all the way to this armpit of civilization, where he'd gotten a job at Blackmore's. He helped Belisarius sometimes. Belisarius opened his coat to remove the device that had blown holes in it in response to the blanks. Fake blood still leaked.

"Nice work, Rosalie," Belisarius said.

Rosalie Johns-10 wasn't a priest yet. She had a year or two left in her studies as an initiate, but in a world of listless, work-avoiding Puppets, no one cared if she dressed as a priest sometimes and hired some off-duty troopers as muscle. She punched Belisarius in the arm. She couldn't reach very high, but it was the spirit that counted.

From the office, a man and a Puppet emerged. The Puppet was the custodian of the national treasure that was the holy site where Peter Blackmore had gambled. The Puppets had named a lot of things after Blackmore, but this one actually made sense. The man was an Anglo-Spanish investigator with the Fortuna Corporation. He shook Belisarius's hand.

"We never would have gotten Powell under Anglo-Spanish law," the investigator said.

"Thank Initiate Johns-10 and the Puppet blasphemy laws," Belisarius said, indicating her.

"Better yet," Enrique said, pushing past the investigator

to hand Belisarius the money chip, "just thank us by getting out of the way while we split Powell's stake."

Enrique handed him his pad. Belisarius transferred two thousand francs to him. Enrique grinned. Rosalie handed him hers, and Belisarius transferred her three thousand. She had to pay the troopers, the fake businesspeople who'd helped them, the episcopate's tithe, and the officials in the Puppet Constabulary.

"You got any other jobs coming down the line, boss?" she asked.

Belisarius shook his head. He really didn't. This con had been good, distracting, but the rest of his leads were meat and potato cons on small-time targets. Nothing that would keep his brain busy. "It's slow, but I'll call you if I get another one."

The custodian of the gambling shrine gave them all a drink, delighted that the casino's reputation was going to go up for once. It wasn't the best stuff, but the Puppets were under an embargo.

Enrique drifted away. So did the investigator. The owner went to setting up the casino again. Belisarius and Rosalie grabbed a booth and used his new money to crank up the heater and buy something better to drink. They were cousins in a way, she a Puppet, more properly a *Homo pupa*, and he one of the *Homo quantus*. Rosalie was young, insightful and curious.

"Was that guy really from the Fortuna Corporation?" she asked in wonder.

"In the flesh," he said. "How did you think I got the alarms not to go off with the weighted dice?"

"I thought maybe you really did hack the AI," she said sheepishly.

"Nobody can do that." He swirled his drink. He didn't enjoy lying to her. She was too innocent, too trusting. "Fortuna knew that Powell's people were getting close to hacking their security patches, and they don't have a solution yet. They were eager to take her off the board, eager enough to temporarily install a bad AI in Blackmore's. It'll take them days to install a new one, but to them, it's worth it."

Rosalie had a few more questions about confidence schemes. It still seemed like such an alien world to her, even though she'd helped him on four cons already, not including the sting on Powell. The conversation drifted, and finally fell to theology again. In this, Rosalie was a stronger conversationalist.

Her thinking drew lines of defensible logic over the surface of Puppet madness, and she had no natural pauses when discussing theology. This forced Belisarius to sharpen his own questions about the natures of humanity, and his logical constructions usually inspired Rosalie's thinking. By midnight, though, they'd finished drinking two bottles and discussing three of Bishop Creston's early ethical models. That was enough of both for Belisarius, and he headed home, vaguely dissatisfied.

His restless brain counted the stones of the arcade, measured the angular errors in the joints of walls and buildings and roofs, and tracked the gradual deteriorations that no one fixed. The magnetic organelles in his cells felt the unevenness of the electrical currents in the neighborhood, and his brain assigned notional probabilities to different service failures. His brain wouldn't have done all this if small scams on off-worlders were enough to hold its bioengineered curiosity. The jobs were lucrative, but they were getting too easy, too small to hide behind.

His gallery AI spoke in his implant as he neared. "Someone is looking for you."

CHAPTER TWO

BELISARIUS STOPPED. HE hadn't done enough jobs to warrant an assassin, but he'd started fleecing higher-level crime figures lately. And even with assassination off the table, a few people would probably pay to have him beat up.

"Show me," he sub-vocalized.

The gallery AI projected a picture into his ocular implants. His art gallery appeared as a cylindrical schematic of glazed brick with a winding staircase spearing the hollow in the middle. Late night patrons moved up and down the staircase, whispering, pausing in pools of light at the landings to examine paintings, sculptures and even silent films set into alcoves. The image zoomed onto a figure just inside the lobby on the top floor.

Her skin was darker than his by many shades, and an uncomfortable-looking knot held her black hair tight. She didn't seem to know what to do with her body. Her hands rested awkwardly behind her. She stood with feet apart, poised, suggesting a readiness to move. She wore an off-the-rack tunic and loose pants, neither daringly nor conservatively cut.

"Sub-Saharan Union?" he asked.

"I don't know," the gallery AI said. "Checking her financial links. Would you like a genetic analysis?"

"Armed?" Belisarius asked. He resumed his stroll.

"No. She has some quiescent augments, though," the AI responded. "I can't tell what they are."

Belisarius magnified the image, considering the woman's expression. "How much is she worth?"

He reached a squat brick building of sintered regolith growing into the ice-enclosed tunnels of Bob Town, a suburban lobe of the Puppet Free City. Within that building, plunging deep into the ice, was his art gallery.

"No credit limit I can find," the gallery reported, "but she has one link to an account held by the Consulate of the Sub-Saharan Union."

The Sub-Saharan Union was a small client nation with two worlds and some industrial habitats on the other side of the Freyja wormhole. Their patron nation gave them second-hand weapons and warships. In return, the Union undertook military expeditions or stood garrison duty. Not wealthy. They'd never been his clients or his marks, and they didn't have a reputation as the kind of muscle he might worry about.

He opened the door and stepped into the lobby at the top of the helical stairs. Belisarius sold legal and illegal Puppet art and was curating the first exposition permitted by the Theocracy. Smell, lighting and sound influenced the aesthetic of Puppet religious experience, and for the exposition, Belisarius had laced the lobby with the faint citrus odor of Puppet sweat. From the gloom below, a whip snap echoed. The woman seemed aware of all this, but untouched by her environment.

She stood taller than Belisarius by a good ten centimeters and had intense eyes. Her waiting stance shifted, shoulders back, hands at her side, but nothing close to the body language of resting. She was an unfired bow.

"*Monsieur* Arjona?" she asked.

"I'm Belisarius," he said in *français* 8.1.

"I'm Ayen," she said. "Can we speak somewhere more private?" An odd accent laced her French.

"I built an apartment into the gallery," he said, leading her down a hallway.

Brick made of cooked asteroidal dust surfaced the ice of the walls, giving the illusion of warmth. His apartment was opulent by the standards of Oler, with several bedrooms, a wide dining area and a sunken living room. The walls and ceilings were white and devoid of decorations. The dining room was spotless, and the living room barely furnished. All low stimulus.

The gallery AI had soft colored lights glowing in sconces and the heaters running. A bottle of rice soju stood on the table between two small glasses. Belisarius stepped down into the living room, slumped onto the couch, and motioned for Ayen to select a seat. She sat.

"How private is this conversation?" she asked in a low voice.

"The apartment is secure. The Puppets aren't very nosy outside the Forbidden City anyway," he said. Her face remained taut. "Did you want to secure this conversation by your own means?"

Her eyes narrowed, and she produced a small device. It looked newly made, but its design was antique, maybe thirty years old.

"Multispectrum white noise generator?" Belisarius asked.

She nodded. He regarded the device with some doubt. Last decade's surveillance systems could probably have cracked the little generator, but she must have known that. She switched it on and the carrier signal from his house AI became faint in his ear, transmitting small alarms that its surveillance of the room was deeply compromised. Interesting. More questions congealed in his brain.

"I need a con man," she said.

Belisarius poured two shots of soju.

"You're five years too late," he said. "I'm on a spiritual journey."

"The right people say that you get impossible things done."

She leaned for her glass with wiry, contained power. She sniffed warily, then drank it down.

He memorized her pronunciation as she spoke. Like her white noise generator, her dialect was antique, an early variant of *français* 8, but where had it come from? His augments carried all the accents, dialects and versions of French, but her accent didn't match any of them.

"That's as flattering as it is inaccurate," he said. "I don't know who does cons anymore. They're all in prison, I suppose."

"People call you the magician."

"Not to my face."

"My employer needs a magician."

She stared at him with unnerving intensity. His brain began constructing patterns, theories, abstractions of the identities of Ayen and her unknown employer. Why couldn't he place her accent? Who was she working for? What did she think he was?

"What kind of magic does she need?" Belisarius asked.

"She needs something moved through the Puppet wormhole. Distal side to here."

"Puppet freighters ship through the Axis all the time," he said. "They don't care what you move, as long as you pay."

"We can't afford their price."

"If you can't afford them, you certainly can't afford me."

Her stare hardened, the bowstring drawn tight. "We aren't short of money," she said, "but they don't want money."

"The Puppets do like to be paid in weapons."

"They want half," she said.

"Half of what?"

"Half of a dozen warships."

The story continues in
The Quantum Magician...